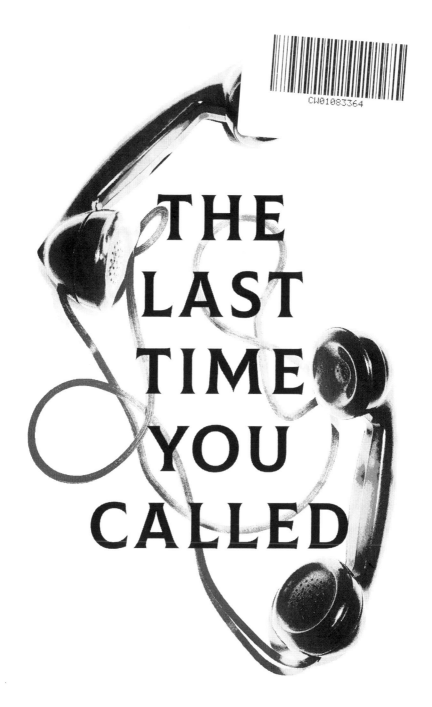

THE
LAST
TIME
YOU
CALLED

CARMI HEYMAN

This novel is a work of fiction. The names, characters, locations and incidents portrayed are the work of the author's imagination. Any resemblance to actual persons, living or dead, events or locations is entirely coincidental.

ISBN: 9789083360409

Contact information: carmi@chfiction.com

Cover art by Luísa Dias

First edition: September 2023

To my dearest *Ouma*, Naomi Maree.
If I get to write half as many books as you, I'll be a happy girl.

CHAPTER 1:

CAT

Present Day

"This shower is going to kill me."

Fred's voice echoes through the tiled bathroom. Despite keeping my hand over the phone speaker, his voice vibrates through the tiny stall I'm hunched in.

"Keep your laptop on the counter and put Netflix on," I say. My voice doesn't sound calm and collected like it's supposed to. Like a counsellor is supposed to. Instead, it's croaky, my hesitation palpable.

I'm sitting on the toilet seat, my feet pressed against the stall door to keep it closed. The lock's broken, and there are words scribbled across the door. The usual mix of epithets and love declarations. If anyone comes into the bathroom now, they'll hear me.

"Remember what we talked about," I whisper into the phone. "Breathe first, act second."

Fred's response comes fast, accusing. "This is ridiculous."

I lean back against the icy wall. *You're telling me,* I want to say. I'm supposed to be teaching my first class of the day. Instead I'm hiding in a restroom, talking a man into a shower.

"You know, people do weird things to get by," I say, feeling the cold air seep through the window. I can hear the drone of the morning traffic outside. Angry car horns. Squawking sirens.

Fred sighs. "Yeah, but who's afraid of a shower?"

I picture him in his bathroom—somewhere, anywhere—stark naked and pacing. I imagine him placing his laptop on the counter like I've told him to, the *Friends* theme song playing in the background. In my mind, he trudges towards the shower, fear bubbling under the surface as he turns on the shower head and seeks the warmth of the water. The same warmth that reminds him it's just that. Water.

I close my eyes and repeat our mantra. *"Nothing is going to hurt me here."*

Fred's distress reminds me of my own, months ago. A distress that still lurks. Only it's not a shower that scares me, but a ghost.

"Anxiety makes us afraid of anything," I tell Fred. "It can feel almost—"

I hear the door opening, the hinges creaking. Like a kid in a horror film, I curl up, trying to make myself as small as possible.

"What?" Fred calls. "You there?"

But I'm holding my breath, watching for shoes beneath the door.

Please don't be grey heels. Please don't be grey heels.

"Whatever, I'll give it a try," Fred says. I see a pair of platform heels under the door. They're grey. I want to end this call right now and step outside like nothing's wrong. But I can't. Fred still needs to hear my voice and know that he's safe.

It's my job to keep him safe.

I straighten up. "You can do this. You've done this so many times."

As soon as I've said the words, I feel the presence on the other side of the door turn towards my stall. They know I'm there.

"I will. I'm going now," Fred says.

It's amazing how quiet it is in this stall.

"Okay," I reply, "I believe in you."

He hangs up just as the voice on the other side speaks. "Cat? Is that you?"

Busted.

I want to stay quiet, but it won't help. "Just a second," I call, stuffing my phone into my back pocket. As though I've got nothing to explain, I get up and open the door to find Sam facing me. She blinks. Three times. Rapidly.

"What are you doing?" she says.

From this vantage point, she looks harmless. She's almost a head shorter

2

than me—even in those grey heels—with straight honey blonde hair grazing her shoulders, a contrast to my auburn curls. Her green eyes are large, searching.

I laugh nervously. "What do you mean? I'm using the bathroom."

She cocks her head to the side, like she's trying to look behind me. *Around* me.

"Where's your phone?" she says.

Instinctively, my hand reaches for it, but it's too late. She's already seen the bulge in my pocket. When my eyes meet hers again, she's frowning.

"You know how I feel about taking phone calls during work hours."

I can tell her it was an emergency. A family member that needed me. But Sam already knows everything there is to know about me. It's what I get for working with a friend.

"Sorry," I mutter. "It was only for a second."

She shakes her head. "You're supposed to be teaching a class right now."

Sam and I play this game often, where we pretend we're just work colleagues having fun together. But in reality, Sam's my boss and I'm her employee, working for her at the language academy she inherited.

It's not fun. But money's the hardest thing to make these days.

I try to smile. "It won't happen again."

"Who was it?"

Her question brings heat to my cheeks. "Who?"

She's looking at me expectantly. "On the phone. Just now."

"Oh," I say, trying to sound as nonchalant as possible. "My mom. You know how she is. She doesn't know my work schedule."

I was never good at lying. And it's a cheap shot, going after my mother's forgetfulness like that. The way Sam's looking at me confirms this. Like I've said something in bad taste. She gives a sigh and in a split second opens her palm towards me. In the time it takes my eyes to look down at it, she removes her hand and places it behind her back.

Was she going to ask for my phone?

We stare at each other. Me, blinking. Sam, fighting an internal battle. She wants to be in control, but she doesn't want to make things uncomfortable

3

between us. She's struggling for the right thing to do here.

I decide to help her. "How about I keep my phone in the common room?" I offer. "You keep yours there too, right?"

Instantly, Sam looks relieved. "Yes," she says, a tired smile on her face. "I do. We could do that."

I nod and head for the bathroom exit, walking around her, hearing the click-click of her heels as she follows me.

"We only have to keep them there when we have class," she says with newfound conviction. "We can use them anytime we have breaks."

Sam's excited by my conformity. I, on the other hand, am surprised by my words. Why did I just willingly give up my phone?

We're in the corridor, and I take a moment to breathe. The smell of stale popcorn fills my nostrils—a smell passed down with the royal blue carpet of the place—mixed with the scented candles lit down in reception. They're part of Sam's efforts to make this rundown building seem more complete.

Around us are glass-walled meeting rooms with whiteboards. Some empty, some filled with faces turned towards standing figures.

Teachers.

I'm supposed to be one of those right now.

We walk into the common room, where I put my phone next to Sam's in a drawer. I turn to look at her, and her face has softened. Moments ago, she was the boss. Now she's just Sam. My best friend from high school.

"You like it here, don't you?" she asks in a smaller voice, and immediately I want the earth to swallow me whole. I'm lucky to have this job. Not many people have jobs right now. Sam's only ever been nice to me, throwing me a lifeline when I needed it most. And this is her business. One she's proud of. The least I can do is be proud with her.

"Of course I am," I say. "I'm sorry. I've been distracted lately, but it won't happen again. I promise."

Sam opens her mouth, then closes it abruptly. I'm thankful, because I know she wanted to ask about my other job. The one I'm actually passionate about. It's moments like these that make me regret telling her about it.

We part ways and I rush towards my classroom. It's called the Manchester room, which I associate with red brick buildings, even though I've never been to England. It's fitting, because as I enter the room, I feel my face turn red. Seated students all staring at me.

"Sorry about that," I say. When I look up, I see six students with notepads out. Waiting for me. I turn to face the writing board, the word *Welcome* written on it.

I study their faces, these people I'm teaching. They come from afar. Zimbabwe, Botswana, Swaziland. Some from Cape Town. They have all come to Johannesburg—the financial capital of South Africa—for a better life.

Where they'll need to speak English.

The class passes quickly, with almost no questions. As I take the students through the curriculum, I think of Fred and wonder how he's doing. If he could get into his shower.

I know I should care just as much about these people; the ones learning a new language to get better jobs. To put dinner on the table for their families.

But all I can think about is Fred and his shower.

Juggling two jobs is tough. An English teacher and a counsellor don't have lots in common, and their work schedules don't line up. This morning was evidence of that. But I need both jobs; one to feed my body, one to feed my soul.

When class is over, I take my worn army jacket and collect my phone from the common room. I head outside for a smoke, and the cold burns my eyes and my fingers shake as I light a cigarette. Sam's language school is in a boxy old building, surrounded by similarly boxy buildings. The area isn't bad; twenty minutes from the outskirts of Pretoria, technically still Johannesburg. But far away enough from the nightmare traffic of the CBD.

It's the type of place people work day in and day out.

People like me.

But recently, I've been slacking off at work. Re-evaluating. My mind keeps bringing me back to counselling. Urging me to take what I love seriously and leave behind the conventional. Take a leap of faith. But at the same time, I'm cautious, scared I'll mess it up.

My phone vibrates in my back pocket. There's a text from Fred.

Showered. Didn't even need to watch Friends. Thanks!

There's no question. If I could do anything permanently, it would be counselling. And as I walk back into the academy, I remind myself that I'm not that bad at it. I'm pretty good at it, actually. But then there's another reminder that crawls into my psyche, one that sends a sickly feeling through me.

Pretty good at it, except for that one time.

CHAPTER 2:

LISA

Six Months Ago

My mother loves day drinking. But not with me, so we're meeting in a coffee shop.

The train from Oxford whizzes past the low-lying greenery of the British countryside. We make our way through Reading and Slough, and as we approach the outskirts of London, I have the urge to scratch at my inner thighs. Feel the lines of scarred skin I've created there. For a moment, I contemplate going to the bathroom, but it's occupied.

Instead, I lean my head against the window, eyeing the grittier part of the city, trying to forget that taking the train to see my mother is another ploy of hers to maintain control. *I just don't think you should be driving*, I can hear her say.

Ruth was still sleeping when I left, remnants of last night sprawled across our tiny flat. Empty wine bottles, discarded pizza boxes, cigarette butts lining the balcony. I think of leaving my best friend behind and my heart aches.

I'll be alone for the first time in three years.

I let the memories of our uni days warm me in the metro, distracting me from the busyness of the underground. As I step out onto Mayfair, I'm greeted by the Georgian townhouses with their rigid symmetry and multipane windows. I breathe in the chilly air that feels ripe with opportunities.

Opportunities like the one I'm about to embark on.

My mother has chosen a coffee shop a few streets from leafy Hyde Park. As I enter, the interior is sleek, with upholstered chairs in teal and wooden tables with golden place settings. The space is loud with the upper-class crowd, and I ruffle a hand through my hair, attempting to salvage it, the raindrops still fresh on my scalp.

I spot my mother sitting in the corner with an untouched latte, eyes on her phone. A Hermes bag beside her. From here, the differences between us are clear. Her, tall and lithe with milk skin and dark curls. Me, short and a stone too heavy, with freckles across the bridge of my nose and my long hair dyed dark blonde to compensate for my forgettable facial features.

You wouldn't think we're related.

My mother barely looks up as I sit down and fiddle with my jacket, cursing myself for not picking something she bought for me, anything to convey a sense of camaraderie.

"Hi, mum."

Her head shoots up, and she opens her perfectly lined lips. "Hi, darling."

"Sorry I'm late."

Her eyes inspect me, moving from my wet hair to my unpainted lips, her smile fading with every moment. When she lands on my jacket, she raises an eyebrow before picking up her mug. "How's Ruth?"

She doesn't care how she is. She's just prying.

Ruth was my choice, you see. My parents chose my core courses and electives, my extracurricular activities, the elements that would determine my future.

But I chose my best friend.

I could have rented my own flat. That was the preferred option. Instead, I showed up at Ruth's apartment viewing with a colourful shawl that matched her living room furniture.

"You planned this," Ruth had said to me then, a smile playing on her lips. "We have to be roommates now."

Since then, she's been like a candle that's always burning. A bold, unapologetic force that makes my life feel less orchestrated.

But all that is about to change.

"She's fine," I say.

"Good. And how are you?"

"Packing's been rough. There's so much to do."

My mother's face is frozen, her unlined forehead and halted creases around the eyes both beautiful and scary. Sometimes when I look at her, it's hard to imagine she's my mother. My *mum*. It's easier to believe she's just Eleanor, the beautiful woman I can never quite figure out.

She studies me from beneath thick lashes. "Right. Well, I don't need to tell you how I feel about this trip of yours."

"It's not a trip. It's a move."

"Is that what Seb is calling it?"

I sigh. "It's what *I'm* calling it. Why can't you trust that?"

She sits back, her eyes giving nothing away. A waiter approaches and takes my coffee order. When he's gone, I purse my lips as I look at my mother, unwavering. "Seb says he needs to be home for a while. Visit his mum and check on the winery."

"It's hardly a move, then."

"It's still up for discussion," I say, raising my voice.

She entwines her hands, perches them on her lap. Just like a proper lady. "Lisa."

"Mum."

Her eyes narrow. I think she doesn't like being called *mum*, either. "Can we please stop playing games?"

"I'm not playing games. Seb and I are moving to Spain together. What's the problem?"

She speaks as if she's explaining dress alterations. "The problem is, your support system is here, in the UK. Your father and I have no visibility in Spain."

Visibility. More like control.

It's the way of our family. Being born into a good name has its perks. Access to top schools and universities, despite the lack of grades to support it, and free-flowing cash trees. But on the flip side, there's a disregard for the things I long for. Passion. Friendship. Love.

A law degree is required, but a career is not. Aloofness is advised, but not enough to scare off a prospective husband. It's like living in medieval times, the only consolation being the heaps of cash available at the snap of a finger.

It's not that I don't love my family. I do. I just struggle to be like them. And I've tried. Whether it was following my mother around the house with florists, to listening in on my father's business calls in the study, I've loved being in their vicinity. Seeing how they did things.

But I was always out of sync.

I owe my law degree from Oxford to my father's connections. A safety net, a topic I avoid. And as for my looks, I've barely inherited anything from Eleanor. My body's plumper and my face is wider. Every decision I've had the ability to make has either been met with discern or indifference. Disappointment has been a constant, a given.

Until Sebastian—Seb—came along.

Of all the things that could have happened to me—*had* happened to me—I doubt my parents ever thought I'd find a man like Seb. Someone so put together. What started out as a fling only months ago soon turned serious. And here I am, about to embark on a new adventure with him.

"I'll be with Seb," I reassure her as the waiter brings my coffee. "I thought you trusted him?"

When I first brought Seb to meet my parents, I was met with awe. My mother was drawn to him, keen to understand what attracted him to me, wondering how I had tricked my way into bagging a wine estate heir.

She was rarely proud of me, but that night she was.

"What an impressive young man," my father had beamed. It stayed that way for months. As our relationship blossomed, the more interested my parents became. In their eyes, I had a future. Seb was good enough. And he wanted to marry me.

He was my golden ticket to a trouble-free life.

On the night of our engagement, my parents were over the moon. Excited to introduce Seb to their social circle, proving how their bad egg had become good. So when I broke the news that we would move to Spain, their tonality changed. My shiny new prince wouldn't be around to parade to the masses.

"I do trust him," my mother says. "But that changes nothing. You've never been on your own before."

"I've lived in Oxford for years now. And besides, I won't be alone. I'll be with him."

She sighs, looking annoyed. I could be a mess, but it's not like Eleanor to have a hair out of place.

"And what will you be doing?" she says.

"Getting to know the area. It's Spain, so there will probably be a lot to see. Maybe I'll even try to write something."

She shrugs and I know what she's thinking. *Writing is nothing more than a hobby.*

"And spend time with his mother. Get in her good books," I add.

"I hope so," she says and looks toward the ceiling, eyes searching for a solution. One that can keep me close without alerting Seb that something is wrong. That he's about to purchase a broken item.

The guilt builds, a throbbing in my throat. Seeing her like this, searching for solutions to my life, like she's always done, makes me want to reach over and touch her hands. Reassure her that everything's going to be okay this time.

Instead, I take my lipstick from my bag and apply it. When I'm done, I meet her eyes. "It'll be fine. I promise."

And I believe it will be. Spain will be a new chapter. One where I'll find out more about my fiancé and get to see where he came from.

My mother speaks, but her voice is low. "We've spent a lot of time recovering. And forgive me, but I worry things will go wrong again."

My face flushes. "I'm not the same person I was."

"Well, now we have no choice *but* to trust you," she says, and her words are like a slap to the wrist. "We can't keep tabs on you forever. Seb is a good man. A man you *need*. I hope you see that."

"I do. And I won't let you down."

A smile hovers on the corners of her mouth, but it looks forced, her forehead working overtime. She nods, turning her focus to the menu. A raise of her hand to call the waiter. "Do you know what you want?"

The carbonara, I think. I studied the menu on the train, picturing the portion, imagining the swirl of pasta, the silkiness of the egg, the crunch of the guanciale. My mother smiles and her eyes are warm again, like I'm a friend she's conspiring with. "The Cobb salad looks lovely. Shall we have that?"

My fingernails find the inside of my thigh, scratching against jeans that feel unbearably tight. But I smile back and raise my eyebrows. "I was thinking the same."

We order and there's a moment of silence as we both look out at the busy street. The rain has picked up again, the sound distinct above the clattering of plates and utensils. I find myself thinking of sunny Spain; a new beginning that's waiting for me with Seb; a man who loves me for who I am.

What could possibly go wrong?

CHAPTER 3:

CAT

Present Day

The apartment is dark, and I can smell stale takeaways.

Turning on the overhead light, I spot the culprits on the counter. Empty brown bags. Not a lone French fry in sight. Pulling off my sneakers, I look at our living room, the last bit of sun piercing through the window. No one's home yet.

Living in other people's homes isn't that bad. You leave with the same things you came with. When I look around, there are traces of their lives everywhere; Ben's Xbox, Sarah's marketing textbooks, the stained suede couch they bought together at a flea market.

I sink into it, legs underneath me. They're probably at the movies. Cinema Saturdays. I look towards the empty takeout bags again. The perfect hangover cure. This morning, Sarah was draped over Ben like a blanket as I waved goodbye to them. It can't be easy, living with a stranger who pays rent, but isn't really part of your inner circle.

But rent is expensive and I'm happy to be here.

Ben and Sarah live in a gated community, enclosed by walls and equipped with access gates and security guards. The safety is an upside.

The downside is the location. There's a general rule in Johannesburg; the closer to the airport, the worse the neighbourhood. And so you have Greenpark, our treeless suburb frequented by the young working class. There are no metro stops, no upscale clubs, no vegan bars. Instead, there are farmers' markets, DIY stores and gated communities, with room rental prices that make it barely affordable for someone like me to live here.

I was lucky to find Ben and Sarah. But they were lucky to find me too. I fade into the background, like I want to.

My phone vibrates in my pocket. There's a message from the counselling app, InCheck. I dab my thumb on the screen and the message lights up. It's from Susana. Another client.

Are you free?

I tell her yes, and schedule a call in five minutes. After closing my bedroom door, I sit on the floor, resting my head against the bed. Susana picks up after three rings.

"Hi Susana," I say in a deeper, older voice. Acting the part.

"I'm so sorry," she says. "I know this is a bad time. It's the weekend and all, but everything just feels… *overwhelming* today."

"You don't have to apologise," I tell her. "Take me through your day."

I sit cross-legged, ready for business. Susana does what I ask. She explains how her day was centred around taking care of her newborn, staring at her morphed figure in the mirror. I voice sounds of encouragement as she continues.

"Sometimes, I look at my life and wonder if I chose to be here," she says. "Every weekend reminds me of how I'm living the same story over and over again. And I don't even know if I like it."

"It's normal to feel stuck in your life," I say, keeping my voice even. "Even if you choose it every day. It happens to everyone, even if they say they're happy. I know that's hard to believe, but it does. And there's some comfort in knowing that."

"How do I fix it? Some days I feel like I'm going mad."

I mull this over. "Start small. What made you smile today?"

She's quiet for a second. "When Zaika giggled."

I swear I can feel her smile through the phone.

"Then more of that," I say. "Start by adding more positive reinforcers in your life. Start with the giggles."

"Baby steps, I guess."

14

"Be open to them when they happen," I say, the energy building in my chest. "It's important to notice those moments and register them. Literally stop and tell yourself that this is a moment that makes you happy."

"A confirmation for myself," she says.

"Exactly. It's retraining your brain to notice these things."

She's silent for a moment, but then she speaks again, her voice softer. "You know, I can't remember when last someone said something like that to me. I'm around Zaika all day. Dave's here, of course, but I don't talk to anyone. I mean, I have conversations, sure. But like this? Not really."

I'm nodding. Because she's got it. She knows that sometimes all it takes is a talk. A real conversation. To make you feel like you're human again. It's these talks that make my day.

"Be gentle with yourself," I say.

A few minutes later, we end the call, Susana sounding more optimistic. I hover over our chat, InCheck's logo displayed on the top of the screen. I sigh.

Psychology isn't that hard to grasp. It's like riding a bike. You fumble at first, but then the pedals become a constant, your moving legs second nature. And so the psychological jargon—the soft, encouraging words (*you're allowed to make mistakes, let's go through that one more time*) and questions (*how does that make you feel?*)—form part of your vocabulary, your frequently used phrases. Playing the role of listener and analyser becomes easy to do.

And it's been even easier online.

I tap the *Info* icon, a warm colour gradient of orange and green orchestrated to reflect just that. A place of warmth. Somewhere to rest your head, to check in. I stare at the logo, wondering how different things would have been if I had found this app sooner. If I knew counselling was something you could do for a living, with the right education. Maybe I would have studied psychology instead of law. I might even have finished my degree.

But then the memory of the last year returns, and there's that sickening feeling in my stomach again.

I walk to the kitchen, take out a pot, and start boiling water on the stove.

As I cut onions and tomatoes, I add the spaghetti to the bubbling water and watch the starch separate from the pasta. I fry the onions and tomatoes, adding chilli flakes and curry powder to the simmering sauce.

It doesn't matter what I have going on, cooking remains a constant.

When the pasta is ready, I mix in the tomato sauce and head to the fridge. I look at the beers in the door. *Just one*, a thought comes. But I shake it loose and reach for the cheese. I grate too much of it and sprinkle it all over the pasta bowl. Feeding my hunger cures my thirst for alcohol. I can't go back there. I won't. Not after what happened.

I walk back to my room with the steaming pasta and plop down on my bed, opening my laptop to Netflix. I eat, occasionally eyeing my phone on the bedside table. When I'm done, I pick it up and log into InCheck again. I navigate to *Your Counsellor Profile*, looking at the picture staring back at me. The woman in the picture looks about forty, with blue eyes and short blonde hair. Her name is Alice Morrison. The profile states she's British, but her name sounds American. Either way, I wouldn't know.

But she's me. The woman I pretend to be.

"Goodnight, Alice," I mutter into my dark room, the air with tomato and onion sauce. I try to fall asleep, but thoughts keep niggling at me. *Wasn't tonight great? Talking to Susana like that? Don't you want to do that all the time?*

Of course I would. I wrap the duvet around me, covering my head in the sheets. I'd love nothing more than to quit the teaching job at the academy and throw myself into the work I'm doing at InCheck. Double my minimal hours and take on more clients.

If only it were legal. If only I could be me, and not Alice, both online and offline.

Then maybe I could stop lying to everyone. Including myself.

CHAPTER 4:

LISA

Six Months Ago

I love the bicycles in Amsterdam.

As the taxi swerves through the cobbled streets, I see them all. Some black, some brown, some with baskets. I once read there are more bicycles than people here.

When we arrive at our hotel room it's small, but the view is fantastic. From our window, the canal glistens in the sunshine breaking through the thick white clouds. It'll rain soon, just like it does back home. But I bet it'll feel different here when it does.

I open the window, the chimes from the tram singing, announcing the whimsical potential of the day. Behind me, my suitcase lies unopened on the bed. I've brought my nicest clothes, the ones Eleanor—Mum—would approve of. Along with lipsticks in shades of plum, velvet and crimson. The best tools to construct my best self.

I hear the shower cut off. Walking to the bathroom door, I hesitate and stand in the tiny hallway. The light from inside peeks through and stains the wooden floor. There's the movement of a shadow on the other side.

I feel like a child, sneaking up on my fiancé. Another footstep. A twist of the door handle. Light flooding through the opening.

And there he is.

Seb is tall and broad-shouldered, his eyes the colour of milk chocolate with green specks that sparkle even when it's dark.

"Hi," he says, locks of his chestnut hair wet. There's a towel wrapped around him, the fabric damp against his thighs.

My face cracks open in a grin. "Hi."

"Someone's excited to go explore," he says.

"Is it that obvious?"

"A little," he says as he walks toward me, one hand clenching his towel and the other wrapping around my lower waist as he pulls me close. "I like it when you're excited."

I smell the hotel soap still fresh on his skin as his lips find my earlobe. But my mind wanders outside again, to the tram and the tourists.

"We should get going," I say.

"We should do a lot of things," Seb whispers, and inside, a part of me lights up like a bulb. But when Seb's eyes meet mine, he must see my eagerness to leave, because he pulls away.

"Okay, okay," he says with a grin. "I'll get ready."

I watch him walk to his suitcase, drop the towel and find his underwear. As he changes, my eyes find the intricate finishings on the ceiling, the copper lamp next to the bed. The mint green armchair in the corner.

I hate changing in front of Seb. Sometimes I can avoid it, sometimes not. Even when we have sex, I never fully relax. I suck everything in and hide what I can.

Some nights when we're high on the evening air—coming back from some or other dinner—I allow myself a moment to imagine letting my guard down with him. He would discard his clothes like they were made of silk, urging me to do the same. He'd pull me in and I'd be so close to showing him everything about me. My body, my heart.

And then I'd think of *you*—of when we were together. And I'd close up again.

"Anywhere you want to go first?" Seb says, smiling in his Levi jeans and polo shirt. We have two days in Amsterdam before we leave for Spain—for our new life.

"We could just walk around," I offer. "Find somewhere to eat?"

In a few minutes, we're out the door and on the street.

Seb takes my hand and we cross the road to the waterfront. We walk down a narrow street, merging with the crowds as we walk within a bigger ring of the city. We walk towards De Pijp and cyclists pass us by, some in a hurry, some not.

Ahead of us, a woman dismounts from a bright blue bike, her blonde braid flicking against her back as she adjusts her shirt. I look at her slender arms and legs, feel my hand edge towards my thighs. But I remind myself that I'm wearing my nice jacket today. The one Mum said was deceiving to the eye.

We sit in a small bar. I lean back in my chair, eating a fried meatball—the Dutch *kroketten*—whilst Seb sips his beer.

"We needed this," he says.

I breathe in. "We did."

Our trip to Heathrow felt awkward—forced—like being dropped off at a sleepover where you know no one. It was our first international trip as a couple. As we strolled towards the check-in counter, we smiled at each other hopefully, holding our breath.

This would be a new chapter for us. Our new relationship thrust into deep, challenging waters, the current deciding if it sinks or swims.

"It's fun," he says, eyes hidden behind sunglasses. "Holidaying with you."

I met Seb on campus a few days into my final year. He was attending a guest lecture on Real Estate Finance and Investment. I was interviewing anyone I could grab hold of for a piece I was writing, my notepad and pen glued to my hand.

"Excuse me," I called, trying to grab his attention when I saw him. "Can I ask you a question? It's for a piece in the student newspaper."

"Sure," he said, with a look of amusement.

I puffed out my chest. "Do you think alcohol needs to be limited at parties to protect men from being accused of rape?"

His eyebrows shot up. "Say that again?"

I repeated it, adding more context. "They say that male university students are twice as likely to be accused of rape at parties if they were drunk. By limiting the amount of alcohol at parties, do you think this will protect them against these accusations? And as a guy, would you feel offended or supported by this?"

"That's more than one question."

I flushed. I'd been so focused on gathering answers that I didn't register his face. And I liked what I saw.

"So, are we removing the girl from this theory?"

"That's debatable," I said.

A pause. "Tell you what," he said. "How about we meet at that coffee shop in two hours?" He pointed across the lawn. "And I'll give you my full opinion."

"Deal."

A few hours later, we were discussing rape culture over lattes and a sandwich.

"I think blaming the parents for a guy's actions is wrong," Seb told me. "There are so many things that indoctrinate a person. We're like clay, constantly being moulded. Everything is mixed. Desires, entitlement."

His voice was warm, kind. And his words lined up in perfect order. "The feeling of entitlement towards a body that rejected you."

We never concluded on the topic. I left the newspaper soon after, spending my evenings with Seb at the local pub, discussing everything from the fleshiness of olives to my desire of becoming a novelist.

On those nights, Seb's face came into focus like pieces of a puzzle. He told me his family owned a vineyard in the La Rioja region in Spain. Having grown up amongst people that knew everything about the craft, he had been a wine connoisseur since he was young. After his father died, he took over the business. Like me, Seb was used to a family with expectations of continued legacies.

"My father spent his life building this. It's up to me to continue it," he said one evening as we sipped wine in a pub.

"So why come here? To the UK?"

"I believe that to know something well, you need to do two things. First, you need to travel to places where winemaking is an art," he said. "France, Chile, South Africa, Italy. It's important to visit these places and understand how others master the technique."

Picking up his drink, he peered into it and grinned. "Second, you need to understand your market."

"So where do the Brits fit into this?"

"We have a lot of British that travel to Spain every year. It would be stupid to ignore the numbers. Why not understand them better?"

"Well, we're a cheap bunch," I said.

He laughed. "My father was traditional. He knew a lot about making wine. But with marketing, he needed some help."

And so Seb took over his father's legacy and prepared to build an empire. Travelling around the world, he sought insights about the art of winemaking, soaking up information wherever he went, ready to live his dream of taking the wines of La Rioja to the world.

I knew very little about wine, and he knew even less about literature. But we connected. Where our aspirations and ties to family legacies came together, that's where we were.

"What's wrong?" Seb asks me now, sliding his sunglasses up onto his head.

I stare at the red battery icon on my phone screen. "It's my battery again. It's already flat."

"You need to replace that phone, babe. I'm sure there's an Apple store here."

I sigh, willing the phone to recharge on its own.

"There's one ten minutes away," Seb says, showing me the map on his phone.

A smile forms. *I can get used to this*, I think. *Having someone look after me.*

It didn't take long for our relationship to take full flight. Seb flew between Spain and the UK for months, seeing me and exploring the British market.

"I want you to meet my mother," he announced one day. We'd been dating for ten months, my graduation approaching. The relationship felt big and daunting. Enough to swallow me whole. It scared me how dependent I felt.

"But I need to make things right first," he said. I didn't know what that meant, but a few days later he ushered me through the door of one of

London's top restaurants. As we sat down, I sensed there was something different. It wasn't a normal date night.

"Lisa," he started, air accumulating in his chest, "I've spent so much time looking for answers. But there was something I didn't even know was missing. It was you."

My heart raced as he continued. "Now, when I think of doing anything, nothing is as fun if you're not around."

He said the words as if he'd rehearsed them all day. And then it came.

He took the black box and placed it on the table, opening it. A ring sparkled. "Will you marry me?"

I said it before I could think. "Yes. Yes, yes, yes."

"Ready?" Seb asks me now, and I'm brought back to the present, the Dutch sunlight flooding down on us.

"Ready."

We empty our beers and walk toward the Apple store. As I take Seb's hand, there's a stir in my stomach. When the engagement was new, I was on a high. The prospect of living with him and meeting his family felt unreal. Like it was too far away for me to wrap my head around.

But now we're here, together. And I'm terrified that history will repeat itself. That I will make a mess of things again, like I've done before. I gulp the fear of it down and focus on the cyclists, the houses along the canals adorned with flower beds. *You're in it now, Lisa*, I can hear Mum say. *This is your first test.*

As we walk along a canal, I smell the earthy mix of the water and soil. We were never water people. Eleanor hated what the ocean did to her hair. My father hated the fear it brought up inside of him. He never explained why. And so we avoided oceans, lakes, rivers and places with pools, frequenting mountain chalets and hotels in cities instead. I never learnt how to swim.

But as we walk, I feel there's a whole other life I haven't lived.

"Is your house next to the ocean? The one in Basque?" I say.

Seb nods. "It is. We have water coming inland from the ocean. It's a beautiful view in the morning. You'll love it."

And I really think I will.

When the Apple Genius shows me my new phone, I beam. It's gorgeous, with no chipped corners and no drained battery. The Genius asks me if I want to trade in my old phone and I shake my head. "I still need to back it up."

The Genius moves my sim card to the new phone and we leave the store with both in my handbag, lying side by side.

"I'll just throw it away when I've backed it up. Not worth much now," I say to Seb. I'm trying to rationalise it. To act like it's not a big deal. Because throwing away my old phone means throwing away the memory of you. All our messages, our photos and videos. The only evidence I have that we existed together, once upon a time. I know I should do it, but I can't. At least not yet.

There's still time to pass the first test, I convince myself. There's still time to make this work with my soon-to-be husband.

"New phone, new adventure," Seb says, placing his arm around me.

We walk through the city, running into a shop to purchase an umbrella as thick droplets fall from the sky. Seb holds it over us as we walk, my hand curled around his arm. The droplets are surprisingly loud as they hit the water next to us.

"They say thousands of bikes are fished out of the canals every year," I say, willing the muggy water to reveal its secrets. It's a pandora's box of possibilities and mysteries, just like my future.

"If we ever need a bike, we can get one out," Seb says.

We laugh, our eyes marvelling at our surroundings. Seb's free arm finds my waist, and his voice is soft and flirtatious in my ear. "Are you still feeling excited?"

I grin. It might be the beer talking, but I *am* excited. Absolutely giddy, really. Giddy to be here with him, to make love to him. This time, hopefully, with no negative thoughts holding me back.

I turn to face Seb and whisper through a smile. "Very excited."

The hotel is a few blocks away, and we quicken our pace. We pass canal after canal, and I try to hold on to my feeling of freedom. Of knowing that I've found a partner I don't have to hide myself from. But the closer we get to the hotel, the more that feeling fades, and the old anxiety creeps back in.

When we're at the hotel entrance, I take one last look at the outside and think of those bicycles at the bottom of the canals. Their metal structures rusting in the deep unknown. Lost potential.

I say a little prayer for them, and for Seb and I. For the future that awaits us.

CHAPTER 5:

CAT

Present Day

As I pull into the parking lot, the engine groans and the brake pads screech. I kill the engine, trying to ignore yet another to-do on my imaginary checklist. I whizz past the entrance sign painted on the front window, the words *Pennyhill Academy* welcoming me in bright yellow and blue.

The sliding doors are still open when I hear Sam's voice. "Hey!"

When I turn, she's waving, her blonde locks bobbing. "Chilly today, right?"

She rubs her arms over her peach cardigan, the fabric so soft it puts my worn out black hoodie to shame. "It's the change of the season and I'm not ready," I say.

She laughs and holds her red binder close to her, the contents outlining the things she loves most; processes, rules. We pass reception, my hand reaching for the phone in my bag. Dutifully, I place mine next to Sam's in the drawer of the wooden desk. Sam gives me a thankful smile and I try to return it, but it's forced. I feel like a child at school, storing my phone away like this.

"How's the day looking?" I say, trying to take my mind off it.

"Busy," Sam says. "Today's my deadline for finding a video provider for our international courses."

"Can't you use Zoom for that?"

"The prices for groups are crazy high. I'd like to find another solution if I can."

One way Sam intends to up Pennyhill's game is by offering TEFL courses to international audiences. In the last few years, the academy has stuck to face-to-face classes. But the new age calls for new ways, and Sam's got it mapped out in her binder.

"Just one sec," she says, veering off towards her office. I pull my bag closer to me, fiddling with the pieces of fake leather coming off on my jeans.

Sam and I first met at uni. Her plan was to become a teacher, mine was to find my calling.

In Sam's final year of university, her aunt—the original owner of Pennyhill Academy—was diagnosed with a rare form of cancer. She had spent her life building the business from the ground up. But once she got sick, Sam managed the business for a small share of ownership.

"Sorry," Sam says, meeting me back in the hallway. "I dreamt there was a water stain in the office. But there's nothing."

"How's Bernadette doing?" I say, as we make our way to the kitchen area.

Apart from the flooring, the place is well kept. Vending machines line the corridors. Inspiring phrases decorate the walls. The kitchen is compact and does what it needs to, the counter equipped with a kettle and microwave.

"Good. The baby should arrive any day now."

Sam places a coffee cup on the counter, the words *"You're pawsome"* scribbled on it. "I know we spoke about it a few days ago, but could you let me know if you can help next week? There are new starters and with Bernadette off, it's going to be tough."

"Where's Adam?"

Sam shrugs. "China application. He'll be gone in two weeks."

Despite her focus on taking Pennyhill global, the academy remains small, and as the political and economic situation in South Africa worsens, lots of teachers are leaving the country to teach English in Asia or South America. Which means she needs all the help she can get.

I spoon instant coffee into my plain mug. "So, Adam's done teaching here?"

"Yep. Off to Shanghai."

26

I don't tell her I've thought about leaving too. For something better, something elsewhere.

"You know, if you stay longer, we could get a proper coffee machine," she says, eyebrows raised.

"It must be going well," I say. "If the academy can afford a Nespresso machine."

"More like a second-hand French press."

We laugh, and Sam pours hot water over her tea bag, bobbing the string up and down. I don't know why, but I ask her a question I'm sure I don't want to ask. "Could I teach online?"

Unlike Sam with her teaching, my calling never came. One moment I was contemplating a future. The next, I was barely surviving the present. My grades crashed, along with my relationships. Soon, I switched university modules, with each tick of a box dimming my future. I removed friends from my inner circles, replacing them with bottles of alcohol. By the time I was done setting fire to my life, I had graduated with no job prospects.

But I had money.

I still remember the day that lump sum landed in my bank account. It was like a punch to the stomach. I didn't touch it for days, my hands burning at the thought of spending it. But soon I was without a place to stay and a drink in my hand. So I sank even lower, spending money that had blood smeared all over it.

It was Sam who offered me a lifeline. I could take TEFL classes for half the price at Pennyhill. I could teach part-time, distract myself from the guilt. It was never meant to be a permanent position.

"All online teaching spots are filled," Sam says. "I need someone here at the academy."

Disappointment stirs. It's not like I wanted to work online, but still, I had to ask and keep my options open. But teaching face-to-face means keeping my phone in a drawer at reception, and that's no good.

"Can you give me until the end of the week?" I say.

I'm trying to buy time and Sam knows it.

"Okay. The next couple of months look busy," she says. "I think you'll like it."

I eye my mug, envious of its white exterior. No permanent markings. It could be any type of mug it wants to be. I cup the mug in my hands, turn to Sam and flash a smile, wondering how long I can keep this façade up.

"I'll let you know by Friday."

* * *

By the time I leave the academy, it's dark. With Sam short on teachers, my three classes have turned into five. I make a quick trip to the supermarket for essentials, and when I return home, my feet are dragging from all the standing and walking of the day.

And Sam wants you to do this full time, my mind mocks.

I sling the bag of groceries onto the kitchen counter. I'm so exhausted I almost don't see Ben and Sarah on the couch.

"Hey," they say in unison.

"Hey."

They've got beers in their hands, so I immediately grab a fruit juice from the fridge. I read somewhere that when others drink, you should too. Even if it's just juice. It takes your mind off the fact that what you're drinking is not alcohol.

I walk over to my roommates and I sense it—the tension in the air.

"How was work?" Sarah says.

"Pretty okay." I take a swig from the pink plastic bottle. "What's going on?"

Ben smiles and diverts his eyes. There's news. I can sense it. And Sarah's going to take the lead in telling me.

"Are you hungry? We were thinking of ordering pizza," she says.

Is it good or bad news?

"Pizza sounds great," I say. "But what's going on?"

They don't tell me anything, insisting that we order pizza first. As we do, their bodies are buzzing with energy, ready to divulge everything they've been keeping in. Finally, when we're done ordering, I ask them the question again.

I sit on the coffee table across from them. "So, what's going on?"

Sarah leans forward on the couch, Ben's hand on her back. "Well, we've been looking for a change. For a while now. We've been applying for jobs and we thought nothing would come of it."

She turns to Ben, a grin appearing. "But it happened. Ben first got a call and then I got one a week later."

I hold my breath.

"Anyway, we've both been offered jobs in Doha."

"Doha?"

"It's in Qatar. In the Middle East."

"Oh." I raise my eyebrows. "That's—wow, congratulations."

"Thanks," she says, flushed.

"We never thought about leaving South Africa. Maybe moving to Cape Town, but not this," Ben says, his voice feeling unfamiliar.

"Well, that's great," I say. "You both look happy." And really, they do. Through my clouded thoughts, I grab at a question. "When do you start?"

Sarah takes a breath. "They want Ben to start next month, and I'll follow in a few weeks."

My mouth feels dry and I sip more of the juice, staring at their happy faces. I have to remind myself that they might have felt like I do—stuck in their lives. And this is something exciting for them. Something I should be happy about, for them.

"That's soon," I say. "It sounds like an amazing opportunity."

Sarah is brimming with energy. "We're excited about it. We've never done something like this before."

I try to meet their enthusiasm. Even Ben's more relaxed now, sinking into the couch.

"It's brave," I say. "And like you said, exciting."

"Right," Sarah says, her hands fidgeting at her sides. The corners of her mouth sag and I feel that rumbling in my stomach. Here it comes.

"So, I guess—,"

"We have a month to get our stuff together," I say.

It catches her off guard. She looks at Ben, then back at me. "Yeah, I guess we need to figure that out."

"It's fine." I wave a hand. "I'll be okay."

Will you?

But their faces are drooped, and Sarah speaks again. "We thought about renting our room out and keeping this place, but it's tricky. If you know what I mean."

I nod. "The rental agreement."

My decision to freefall through my life produced some problems along the way. One of them being that I didn't hold a steady job; a job with an employment contract. This meant that wherever I lived, I was trail free. It also meant I couldn't take over rental contracts.

"Unless…" Ben raises an eyebrow.

"Unless what?" I say.

"Unless you also look for something abroad. You said you were considering it, right?"

I keep still as I watch Sarah light up. "Yes! Yes, you did. This could be the right moment."

I vaguely remember telling them this once in the first few months I knew them. Who knew they'd remember something I barely could?

"Yeah," I say. "Maybe."

"I'm sure there are a bunch of courses for teachers all around the world," Sarah says.

There are. I've looked. But they all have requirements I don't have.

"I'll come up with something," I say, eager to change the subject.

When the pizza arrives, they drink more beer—more juice for me—and we talk about the Middle East; the culture shock, the heat, the money. Between bites, I scan my phone to check for any messages. I have a two-hour window to respond to chats on InCheck. Company policy. But there are no new client requests and with my regulars, I still have time. Fred and Susana call over the weekends or late at night.

But my clients are the least of my worries now.

Sarah picks up a slice of pepperoni pizza, the oil glistening on her manicured fingers. Before she takes a bite, she meets my eyes again.

"Just have a look," she says. "I'm telling you, once someone opens a door, it's impossible to unsee what's inside."

CHAPTER 6:

LISA

Six Months Ago

"Just five more minutes", I say, snuggling up to Seb. I wish we could stay here in bed all day. Just the two of us. Forget anything else exists.

Spain isn't what I expected.

Bilbao's airport felt small, the scheduled flights not at all the international destinations I was used to seeing. I expected quaint, but it felt suffocating.

"Cold, isn't it?" Seb said, shivering as we arrived.

"Is it always like this?" I said, pulling my overcoat over my shoulders as we waited for our ride outside the airport terminal.

"Welcome to the North. It's Spain like you've never seen it before."

Maybe he meant it as a joke, but he had an unfamiliar look in his eye. It made me uneasy. I wished I was back on the plane.

A black Mercedes pulled up. A middle-aged man got out and put our luggage in the trunk as if he'd done it a million times before. Seb embraced him, greeting him warmly in Spanish. The man threw a smile my way, opened the backseat door, and closed it behind me as I got in.

Seb held my hand as I watched our surroundings change from industrial structures and grey fixtures to landscapes of green that stretched on and on. The houses nestled in the hills looked strange—too new to be romantic, too old to be modern.

I was also aware that something had changed between Seb and I. In Amsterdam, we'd been a proper couple, exploring the narrow streets together, sheltering from the rain. I felt at ease, like Seb was my best friend.

I thought less about *you*, too. So I had wrapped my old phone in a scarf and chucked it in my suitcase. I wanted it hidden from my next chapter. I didn't want you near my new life.

But in that Mercedes, on the way to the house, Seb got a call.

It's not *what* he said, but *how* he said it. It was his mother, calling to check when we'd arrive. But it was then, hearing him speak Spanish, that the unease grew. With me, he was Seb. My love. My travel buddy. But listening to him talk to his mother, he was someone else. He was Sebastian, a man with a whole other life who spoke a different language.

"Why Basque Country?" I said when Seb ended the call.

"My mother's from there, remember?"

"I know," I said. "But the winery is in La Rioja. And you told me you studied in Madrid."

Seb looked out of the window, my hand still in his. "The house belongs to my mother. After my father passed, she wanted to be closer to home. The house in La Rioja felt too big for her. She loves being back in her town again. I think she's just more comfortable there."

"Does she have family in Gexta?"

He shook his head. "Not anymore. But my mom keeps to herself. You'll see."

I gulped. I'd told my mother I'd make an ally of this woman, my soon-to-be mother-in-law. It was another test. And yet I knew nothing about her. She was the closest thing to family Seb had spoken of.

What will we talk about?

"Will your sister be visiting too?" I said, veering down another unfamiliar path. Seb talked about a lot of things, but not his family. I knew exactly three things about Seb's sister. Married with two kids. Lives in Barcelona. Works in consulting.

His face hardened momentarily. "No."

And then his face lit up again. "We're almost there," he said. "It's so light in the mornings. You'll love writing here."

But as we drove through the town, I felt the opposite. As in the countryside, the houses here followed the same architecture and style. Wooden roofs with green, blue, and red panels. The town seemed a bit worn, rough around the edges.

I wondered if there was something behind the small, closed-off windows. If the people who lived here knew something I didn't. Seb pointed out to the water that sparkled in the distance. There was an opening in the sky, and I felt thankful for some air.

"We're a few kilometres inland. This is actually a river," he said.

We drove past empty taverns, a few supermarkets and more houses perched on the hills. We finally pulled up next to the ocean, a worn and wooden dock visible in the distance. As I stepped out of the car, the salty air was fresh on my face.

Townhouses lined the street, with big bay windows peeking out at the ocean. Seb put his hand on the small of my back, guiding me forward gently. "A British couple lives there," he said, pointing up the road. "I'll introduce you later."

The house Seb's mother owned was pale orange with wood finishings. When the front door opened, I held my breath. The woman standing there was tiny, with long, grey hair. She was older than I had imagined. She kissed Seb's cheeks and spoke in words I couldn't understand. There was no glance in my direction.

Seb gestured for me to come closer. "This is my mother, Alma."

I greeted her in my basic Spanish. She smiled and moved forward, taking my hand in hers.

That night, I tried my best to communicate with her. She responded in broken English, but often just shook her head, looking at her son for clarity. Seb served as our translator, retelling our stories. When he laughed, his mother laughed with him.

But only a little.

The days went by slowly, one awkward moment after the next. Seb and I slept in his childhood room. By the looks of it, not much had changed. Everything looked 20 years old. The curtains were faded, the mahogany bed frame reminding me of my grandparents' bed.

I found the structure of the house odd. The kitchen was separate from the living and dining room. The tiles in the bathroom were showing their age. It felt trapped in time.

But the scenery was beautiful. I paused each time I passed the bay window in the dining room, the ocean calling me to stay a little longer, look a little closer.

In the mornings, I could hear Alma moving through the house, the floorboards creaking as she went. I didn't know what to call her. 'Mother' felt too strange. She stayed in the kitchen as Seb parked his laptop in the dining room, taking calls. We'd visit the winery soon, he'd said, but we would first stay here for a week or two. Alma seemed happy to have her son back in her house.

In between meals and walks to town with Seb, my mind was consumed with writing. He was right. The bay window was the perfect spot to write. I watched YouTube videos on plotting and character development, willing the water beyond the window to give way to a story.

But as the days turned to nights, I watched something else creep across the ocean. The fog would form without you noticing, and then, just when you turned your head, it would spread across the water like a white blanket. As the sun faded, it thickened, closing in on the house. On us.

It felt like a cycle. A coming and going. Each day thicker than the last.

"You'll get used to it," Seb said, his arms wrapped around me as I stared out into the fog. The thought of it made me surprisingly nervous.

In the few days we'd been there, Alma and I had established a routine. There wouldn't be a bond, a deeper understanding. Only polite words. We spent our days drinking wine, listening to Seb pivot from English to Spanish, and enjoying the fresh, salty air.

But something was happening.

Between his calls and talks with Alma, I had less of Seb to myself. She served him unfamiliar pork dishes, which he ate like he was starving, grinning as he did so. Half of everything he said was incomprehensible. Most of what he did felt foreign.

I didn't know what to do. I *still* don't know what to do.

"We need to get up," Seb whispers to me now, the sunlight peeping through the curtains.

"Just five more minutes", I say again, squeezing harder against him. I want to stay here, to feel the comfort of only him here. Because the more I get to see his world, the more alone I feel in it.

"I need to get up," he whispers.

I want to beg him to stay, in the places where he and I make sense, where we're not so different. But he's already up. I bite my lip, watch him walk to the shower, and close the door behind him.

A thought springs unbidden to my mind. *What if you don't know him at all?*

CHAPTER 7:

CAT

Present Day

Ben's on the phone at the dining table when I come out of my room. I grab the coffee pot in the kitchen and pour myself a cup.

"How do I know it'll get there undamaged?" he's saying, his pen scribbling furiously. The coffee jolts me awake, bringing back remnants of last night. The pizza, the beer I didn't drink, the thought that I have to leave this apartment soon.

Which means I have a month to find a new place.

And just like that, you're out on your ass.

The kitchen tiles are cold under my feet. I'd rather be back in bed, so I give Ben what I hope is a cheery wave as I walk back to my bedroom and close the door behind me. Coffee cup in hand, I sit down on the bed, pulling the covers over my legs.

Finding a new place is going to be a challenge. First, Ben and Sarah were generous enough to waive a deposit when I moved in. There's no way I'd get that lucky again. I think of touching the money in my savings account and my stomach turns. And the thought of another house search—another meet and greet—makes my heart sink. More boxes and garbage bags to gather my worldly belongings. The stress of learning someone else's timings, habits and life.

Or you could move back in with Mom.

I grab my laptop from the floor and type *"room share Johannesburg"* into

Google.

I browse through the listings, the filters demanding selections. *Area? Price? Dwelling type?* I think of Ben, on the phone with the moving company right now, full of energy to make things happen. To get stuff done. Instead, I close the laptop, sinking back onto the bed. I try to remember the last time everything didn't feel so exhausting. Was I always like this?

Maybe it's because I'm sober now. Or maybe it's because I'm living with a ghost.

Sarah's words from last night echo in my ears. *Once someone opens a door, it's impossible to unsee what's inside.* Isn't that the truth? We're raised in bubbles, protected from things with thorns that could hurt us. Things that threaten to expose us.

I decide there's only one thing to do. Do it all again. All of it. New home, new life. Because things are going to change, whether I like it or not.

But there's still some control left.

I sit up again, typing into Google's search box.

teach TEFL abroad

teach TEFL abroad south african teacher

I scan the pages of search results, all urging me to click through. Postings in China, Thailand, Taiwan.

TEFL certification. *Check.*

Previous experience. *Check.*

I imagine Sam hovering over my shoulder, questioning my loyalty. But I keep scrolling.

Police clearance certificate. *Uncheck.*

Income to cover expenses. *Uhm, uncheck.*

And suddenly I remember why I always stop.

This time, I keep going. I read testimonials from teachers around the world. My coffee turns cold as I dive into a rabbit hole of sites, forums and Instagram profiles.

There's no place like home, one Instagram caption reads. It's a South African woman living in Thailand. Her bio links to the website where I found her. *But there's also nothing like feeling safe in your own home.*

It's strange, really. The feeling of safety. It's at the top of a pyramid of needs I saw somewhere. It's a necessity, a right. But every time I double-check if my car door is locked at a traffic light, or pull my handbag closer to my body when I walk through the mall, I miss it.

I'm on a Facebook Group now: *I'm Staying Abroad*. One post catches my eye. *Living in South Africa is like being a frog in a pot. As the water slowly heats, you don't realise you're boiling until it's too late.*

I've seen enough. I close my eyes, my mind fatigued by the information overload. I think of the classes I have today, the calls with Fred and Susana. I'm about to close my laptop when I see it. A banner. Rolling green hills and a clear blue sky, the sun shining gloriously.

Teach English in Basque Country. Now hiring international teachers.
I click.

A video pans across mountains and dramatic coastlines. I see phrases like *Explore Northern Spain, A Different Teaching Experience.* I Google *Basque Country*, and I'm met with pictures of the same majestic views. Between the nature shots are wooden houses that look just like they belong on a postcard. Old, enchanting, different.

Interested in moving to a foreign country? Teach English in Gexta, a coastal town in the heart of Northern Spain. Enjoy living with a host family whilst exploring the landscape and socialising with locals.

There's a list of benefits, each more compelling than the last.
Teach and learn simultaneously.
Accommodation with a friendly host family.
Weekly allowance provided.

I read on, trying to find the catch. Anything that will crush the idea. But it doesn't come.

I scan the requirements, and my heart races.

Our ideal candidate is keen to explore a country and a culture different from their own. You're ideally under thirty years of age, fluent in English and holding a TEFL Level 5 qualification. Passport, CV and TEFL qualification required for application. All visa arrangements will be taken care of.

I read the testimonial, and I'm sold.

Gexta offered me the opportunity to see the world from a different perspective. It broadened my horizons and changed my life for the better.

I focus on that last sentence and hold my breath. How I wish I could change my life for the better.

The button at the bottom of the page encourages me to *Apply Now.* I don't hesitate. I attach my passport, CV, TEFL certificate and a recent picture for good measure. I click *Submit,* my body burning with renewed energy.

Thank you for your application! If you're successful, we will be in touch in the next 48 hours.

Shutting the laptop, I take deep breaths, imagining a different world. I'm a mole digging a new tunnel. One that's far, far away from here. When I go to take a shower, the water feels lighter on my skin. I realise it's me—I feel lighter. I dry off and walk back to my room, wondering when last I felt like this. Like there's something to look forward to.

Bing. A direct message on Instagram. *me_finds_you123 wants to send you a message.*

My finger hovers over the pictureless profile. I click through to the message, preparing for spam or a simple *hello.*

I know you're a fraud, Alice.

The phone drops from my hand, making a soft thud as it lands on the bed. My mind races. I want to pick the phone up again, but my hands are shaking. When the heat subsides from my face, I pick it up again, stare at the message. I read it until it stops making sense. I click on the profile name, but there's nothing there. Zero followers. No picture.

My brain works overtime to find an explanation. *Who did you tell? Who knows about InCheck? What about your clients?*

I look at my phone again, willing the message to disappear. *Who is this,* I want to type, but I'm stuck, my inner voice screaming for me to hide.

I open Gmail, looking to see if I have any response from the teaching job I applied for less than an hour ago. I need this more than I thought.

Because I can't change what I've done. Can't stop Sarah and Ben from leaving. Can't stop messages like these. Can't stop the world from coming apart at the seams.

CHAPTER 7 : CAT

But I can do something else.
I can run.

CHAPTER 8:

LISA

Six Months Ago

If Eleanor were here, she'd be so disappointed.

I messed up. And the worst part is Seb saw all of it.

The writing hasn't been going well. Every time I sit down to write I get lost, staring out at the ocean like I'm waiting for it to inspire me. And next thing I know, hours have passed without a word on a page.

I needed a change. So this morning at breakfast, I offered to cook dinner.

Seb thought it was a great idea. I think he was happy I was trying. Like my cooking skills, my relationship with Alma was almost non-existent. There were civil nods, polite laughs. But not much else. Food is a universal language. I wanted to show that I was worthy, not foreign as Alma thought I was.

Seb turned to Alma, translated my plan. She smiled as her eyes met mine, a faded version of Seb's. She felt more like a grandmother than a mother-in-law.

"Do you want me to go with you to the supermarket?" Seb said.

I shook my head. "No. I'll be okay."

I made my way outside, the chilly breeze grabbing at my hair. The street was on an incline, and as I climbed, I passed the house Seb pointed out on the day we arrived.

A British couple lives there.

I made a mental note to remind him to introduce me to them. Despite the cold, the walk was invigorating. With every step, my legs felt like they were shaking off dust. Seb would often take me for walks, pointing out the scenery and the history of the town, but this walk felt different.

It felt like I could breathe.

The supermarket was small, and smelled faintly of fish. I gathered the vegetables I needed, some meat that looked like beef. I used Google Translate to navigate the shelves full of spices. The selection wasn't great, but I figured what I couldn't find here, I'd hopefully find back at the house.

"Got everything you need?" Seb said when I got back, his head peeking out from behind his laptop. He always seemed to be working these days, or taking important calls about the vineyard.

I hung my coat, my heart still racing from the walk. *You carry so much water in your legs*, Eleanor would tell me.

"Most of it. But no tomato paste, and I'm missing a few spices."

"I'm sure we have some," Seb said. "I'll ask my mother."

As I unpacked the groceries, I could hear Seb talking to Alma. Moments later, she was standing in the doorway. *"Tomate?"*

I nodded and took out my phone, Googling tomato paste. But before I could show her, she was waving my screen away, moving towards a cupboard. Opening it, I saw jars of olives and canned beans. Her tiny frame stretched to reach a tin.

She put the tomato paste in front of me. I thanked her and started preparing the vegetables. As I cut the potatoes, I felt her eyes on me. But she didn't stay long, and I turned my attention to the meat. As it browned in the pot, the smell felt familiar and encouraging.

I knew little about cooking, but this recipe was a household favourite that Mary, our housekeeper, had often made on cold afternoons when I was growing up. I'd watch the bubbling stew like it was the most important event of the day. She'd always dish up a huge plateful for me. "Eat before mum gets home, okay?" she'd say.

I loved potatoes then, and I loved them now.

I added the vegetables, and searched the spice rack for paprika. Some of the bottles had labels as ancient as the floorboards of the house. I pulled out a bottle that looked like it could be paprika, the colour a deep and dry red. Seb was gone when I entered the dining room, and instead, I found Alma reading by the bay window.

I asked her in my broken Spanish if the spice was paprika, praying she would understand me. Walking over, she took the bottle from my hand, studying it. "*Si, si.*"

I shook a generous helping of paprika over the stew, the rich red powder merging with the liquid. Just like Mary used to do, I sat and watched it simmer.

I took my time setting the table, finding the right cutlery and utensils.

"It smells delicious," Seb said as I brought the pot out to the living room.

I carefully served them. When I had my plate in front of me, we clinked our wine glasses in an informal toast. Even Alma was smiling, joining in on the celebration that was my success. I could do something that brought us all together. No language required.

The room went quiet, save for the sound of cutlery against china as Alma and Seb dug into their stew. The meat had cooked for over five hours, and was succulent and tender.

Seb blew on a forkful of stew. I speared a chunk of potato and popped it into my mouth. And then I felt it. A distinct burning sensation, slowly spreading through my mouth.

I looked at Seb. "How is it?"

"It's great," he said, his voice oddly high pitched. "I didn't know you liked spicy food?"

"I don't," I said. "I'm not sure where the spice is coming from."

But I knew.

Alma put her fork and knife down. She dabbed a napkin on the corners of her mouth. Before I could make sense of what was happening, she spoke in a hushed voice, her Spanish rapid. Seb frowned, then turned to me.

"My mother," he started. "She cannot eat spicy food." He took a deep breath. "She can't eat it."

"It's the paprika," I blurted out. "She told me it was paprika."

Seb looked bewildered.

"I asked her if it was paprika and she said yes." I pointed at Alma, stopping myself midway. But Seb was already out of his chair. "Can you show me?"

We walked to the kitchen. I felt like a naughty child trailing the headmaster, waiting to see what the verdict would be. Seb took the spice container, sniffing at it. His nose crinkled. "This is chilli powder. Did you taste it?"

I stuttered. When the words came, they sounded immature. "She told me it was paprika."

Seb was silent, his eyes resigned. I should have said something else. Been a grown-up about it. But I felt exhausted.

There was a shuffling of feet and Alma was in the doorway, speaking rapidly in Spanish again.

"What is she saying?" I muttered.

Seb looked at me again. "Don't worry. She says she told you this was spicy, but I think it got lost in—"

"She did *not*."

"It's still delicious, my mother just can't—"

"I asked if it was paprika and she said *si*."

"Maybe it got lost in translation."

Seb looked defeated. I should have let it go. I should have sided with him. Been the bigger person. But Alma was talking again, the words babbling through the kitchen, and it felt like a personal attack.

"I can't be here," I said, moving to the dining room. I needed to breathe, but I also wanted to shove my stew down Alma's throat and tell her to learn some English. To be honest with her son.

"Lisa," Seb called, but I was already on the stairs.

"Babe, there's nothing wrong," he said. "My mother feels embarrassed, and she's sorry. It was all just a misunderstanding."

I turned to face him, my words cracking. "It's fine."

I didn't believe any of it. I didn't believe a word that woman said.

"Please come down."

"What will she eat?" I said.

"We can keep eating," Seb said, his arm outstretched to me. "She's going to make something else for herself."

Seb was pleading, and I searched in those eyes for something familiar. The longer I stood, the more it took me back to when it was just the two of us. But then I smelled the stew again and my stomach churned, my fingers itching at my sides. I needed a release.

"Just give me a minute," I blurted out, almost running up the stairs.

I closed the bedroom door behind me, flying across the room to my suitcase. I found my old phone wrapped in its scarf and fished it out, turning it on. The battery was almost dead, my thumb instinctively touching the golden circle in the centre. Back against the wall, I faced the door, watching for movement on the other side. I pulled my purse from the bed, opening the side pouch and carefully taking out what I knew was always there.

The tiny blade, patiently waiting for me.

Which brings me to here, now.

With my free hand, I pull my jeans down to my knees. I pick the phone up again. I know exactly where to go. I navigate to photos, scroll to the one I'm looking for.

It was a beautiful Saturday at the garden party. You with your dapper smile, me with a bright grin. I can almost smell the green again, my legs cool against the stone bench we sat on. Eleanor hated those shorts. *Why do you want to flaunt your legs like this?*

I look down at my legs, thick from ankle to waist, and I can almost hear my mother's words. *You should have checked if it was chilli powder.*

I try to remember the fragrance of the flowers in the garden. They call to me, reminding me I am not in this place. It's dangerous territory to wish for another life when I've just started a new one. But here we are.

I think of Alma's face and stiffen.

If there was anything to salvage before, it's receding fast. I'm losing my grip. I'm doubting.

We're trusting you here, Lisa, Eleanor warns again. I drop the phone on the floor. I press the blade against my inner thigh. Blood appears, a thin line crimson, accusing. I let out a deep sob-sigh. I try to conjure images of Seb. Of him and me together, planning a future.

And I try to forget how much I want to be with *you* right now, instead.

It's a while before I get up, tracing the line of blood with my finger. I wash the blood off, cleaning the blade. Breathing deeply, I put everything back. The blade, the phone. I remind myself to put some concealer on the wound, in case Seb wants to touch me. But he hardly has since we've been here.

I make my way down the stairs again, and find mother and son in the dining room.

I can't wait to leave this place.

CHAPTER 9:

CAT

Present Day

"Is Cat short for anything?" the woman on the phone says.

I lean against the empty desk, peering out through the glass walls into the academy's hallway. "Nope," I say. "Just Cat."

I got a call last night about the teaching job in Spain. A British man called Greg asked me a series of questions about my teaching qualifications and experience. He said he worked at the academy in Gexta. He sounded tense as we spoke.

Before he hung up, he told me they'd be in touch. Whoever *they* were.

And now we're here.

"Odd," says the woman on the phone. "I would have thought your name was Catherine, or something exotic like Caterina!"

She gives a short laugh.

"Right, *Cat*," she says. "I'm Deborah, but you can call me Deb."

I make a mental note not to call her that. Something about her gets my guard up. I remind myself this is an interview, and I shouldn't get too chummy with her.

"I spoke to Greg, and I wanted to ask you a few questions of my own."

"Sure," I say, taking another glance out into the hallway. I'm huddled in an empty room at the academy, and since I don't have a class right now, I have every right to be on my phone. And yet, I keep waiting for Sam's head to pop around the corner.

"Great!" says Deborah. "So, as you said to Greg—and keep me on the straight and narrow here—you're a part-time teacher, right?"

"Yes," I say. "I teach at Pennyhill Academy in Johannesburg. Six classes a week."

"Great. Good. And what do you do for fun?"

I open my mouth, close it, then open it again. "I like to read."

More like binge on Netflix shows, but no potential employer wants to hear that.

"Anything else?"

"Uhm," I turn on my heels, walking from one side of the room to the other. "I like hiking."

That's a lie. I barely go for walks. Why did I just say that?

"Do you like wine?"

Now this I finally have an answer to. "I used to," I say.

Deborah's voice rings with disappointment. "Oh."

Damn. Wrong crowd.

There's an awkward moment, but she soon fills it again. "No matter," she says. "Let's go back to your teaching. Would you say your students *like* you?" She emphasises the word and I'm surprised. Do they *like* me? I don't even know if *I* like me. But I let out a forced laugh. "I hope so."

My nostrils flare in disgust. *You sound so lame.* Deborah is quiet on the other end of the line, and my fingers fidget. "I try to make every student as comfortable as I can."

"Fantastic," she says. "That's always important. We enjoy likeable people over here. The friendlier, the better."

I nod. "How big is the academy there?"

"Oh, I don't know. Didn't Greg tell you about that?"

I think back to my brief conversation with Greg, how he told me in a rushed fashion that I'd be teaching a few classes alongside him and another teacher from the UK. He didn't talk about the size of the academy, but he told me it was fairly new, and that it was growing because of the demand for more English courses in the region.

"He did," I say to Deborah. "He spoke about the classes I'd be teaching."

"Good, good," she says. "And from what Greg's told me, you seem like you're a highly competent teacher."

I feel my head jerk a full 180 as I take in what she says. The man said *that*—about *me*?

"That's good to know," I say. "I'd love the opportunity to work with your team over there."

Deborah chuckles. "Oh no, I don't work at the academy."

"Oh?"

"I'd be your host here in Gexta," she says. "You know, the person you'd be living with while you work here."

I rack my brain for past information, mentally scanning the paragraphs I'd read on the ad from before. And then I remember the phrase. *Accommodation with a host family in town.*

"I should have mentioned that at the start of the call," she says, chuckling again. "Greg has already screened you for the teaching position. I just wanted to have a call with you to make sure you weren't—you know—"

"Unlikeable?"

A burst of laughter. "Exactly!"

For a moment, neither of us says anything. I feel so awkward I almost wish Sam would appear and pull me away.

But then I remember InCheck and my clients.

I remember that Instagram message from yesterday, threatening to expose my counsellor profile. *I know you're a fraud, Alice.*

But above it all, I remind myself that I really, really want this job. I want to get on a plane and go to a foreign place, and live in this foreign woman's house. Because maybe if I can get away, I can clear my head. Figure out my next move.

Desperate to get out of my head, I say: "Do you live close to the academy?"

"Oh yes," Deborah says nonchalantly. "I live just down the road. It's a lovely walk in the mornings."

The words are out of my mouth before I can stop them. "I've never stayed with a host family before. I've never left South Africa, actually."

Really building your case there, Cat.

"That's all right," she says, almost maternally. "We were all new to travel once. You'll enjoy it here. It's a different type of Spain. But since you've never been, you wouldn't really know the difference, would you?"

I hear that deep chuckle of hers again.

"True," I say. "But still, I'd love the opportunity."

"Well look, Cat, I'm happy to give this a go. And so is Greg. Everything looks fine on paper and it would be good to have someone with a fresh perspective here. And talking to you today makes all the difference. Sometimes hearing someone's voice just puts you at ease, you know?"

"Yes," I say. "I completely get what you mean."

If only she gave me that feeling too. One minute she's warm and the next she's so condescending. I can't get a handle on her.

"Am I right in thinking you'd need a visa to travel here?"

I nod, even though she can't see me. "That's right."

Deborah makes a humming noise like she's thinking. "All right, well, here's what we'll do. We'll organise a Schengen tourist visa to get you here, and then once you are, Greg and the gang will arrange a student visa through the academy. Does that sound good?"

I pace the room, facts from the past few days popping into my head. There is a range of visas that TEFL teachers can use to teach English in Europe. From the articles I read, the majority are aimed at Americans, Canadians and the British. Not so much for South Africans. There's no reason not to trust what she's saying. They're the experts. So why is there a sickly feeling in the pit of my stomach?

"I'm not familiar with the visas," I say. "So the academy will handle it?"

"Yes, exactly. The academy will convert the tourist visa to a student visa once you're here."

"Are we allowed to do—"

"We'd send you all the details," she says. "Everything you'll need to apply for the Schengen visa at the embassy."

"Sounds like you've done this before," I manage to say, noticing that my breathing is strained, like I've climbed some stairs.

But Deborah is cheerful on the other line. "The academies here do it like that. It's common practice, really. Do you have a bank account?"

"Yes, I do."

"Good. You'll need a certain amount in there, I think, but no worries, you won't have to spend any of it. It's standard."

The gnawing feeling in my belly grows. "Okay, if you say this is how it works, then we can do it."

For a moment, I think she's hung up, but then she speaks again. "Listen, it's just a paper hurdle we need to get over. But Greg knows what he's doing. It'll be fine."

I nod. "Okay, that's good to hear."

For a second, I think of how stupid I'm being. Shouldn't I be asking questions too? I take a deep breath and remind myself that this is good news. That I got the job.

"How's Gexta?" I ask Deborah. "As a town, I mean. Sorry, I'm just curious since it'll be so different. It's exciting."

"Oh, it's lovely," she trills. "It's usually quite relaxed, I'd say. I work in Bilboa, which is just a few minutes away. My husband works there too—you'll meet him when you arrive."

"Sounds—"

"It's not very touristy, and it doesn't attract much attention," she says. "Well, except for…"

"Except for?"

"Yes," Deborah says, her voice trailing off. "Actually, you wouldn't have heard about it, would you?"

A few people walk past through the hallway. I watch their legs move. Deborah's talking too fast, and I don't know where she's going with any of this.

She must have picked up on my confusion, because she's talking again, and it's like sunshine through the phone. "Sorry, love, I don't mean to spring so much information on you. But it's best to tell you everything up front. So you know all the facts. Not like it's a big deal—I just want us to start off on a good footing."

"I understand," I say, shifting my focus to the empty desk in the room. I grip the phone closer to my ear. "You were saying?"

"Right, yes," she says. "It's all fine. There's just one more thing."

* * *

"So you're going," Sam says.

"I'm sorry."

I expected this. When hearing the news, Sarah and Ben were happy. But Sam was different. Even a round of cocktails after work—virgin mojito for me—wouldn't make it easier.

"When are you leaving?" she says, eyeing me over her Aperol spritz.

"When my Schengen comes through," I say. "I'm applying this week. And when you've found a replacement for me, of course."

She shrugs and I fill the awkward silence. "I'll help you look."

"Okay."

She sips her drink, not meeting my eyes. "Are you excited?"

"I am."

She looks up, a faint smile appearing. "Well, I hate that you're leaving. But I'm happy you're finally doing *something* with your teaching."

I return her smile. This can't be easy for her, and I'm grateful for the effort. It makes me wonder if I shouldn't just be honest with her about my feelings. Everything Sam does is by the book, and she doesn't like cutting corners. When I told her about InCheck, she was pissed for a few days, and since then she's refused to talk about it. But if I actually decided to become a counsellor—a legal one, that is—what would she think?

"Thank you," I say.

"Who knows," she says, with a mischievous glint in her eye. "Maybe you'll end up with Adam in Shanghai."

Maybe now's not the right time to bring up the counselling thing. I raise my glass. "Thanks for everything, Sam. You're a good friend."

We sip our drinks and fill our mouths with the complimentary popcorn to mask the awkward silence.

"So you're applying at the Spanish consulate?" Sam asks after a while.

"Yes," I say. "It's weird, though. I'm going in with a Schengen visa and then they'll convert it to a student visa when I'm there. I didn't know that was possible."

Sam shrugs. "Every country has a unique process. In the Middle East they do it all the time. Border runs and all."

She talks from experience. Experience she's secretly dying to live, but can't. Being the owner of a language academy has its perks, but it also has its chains.

"So tell me more about this town you're going to," she urges.

We talk about Spain. She orders another drink, and I tell her about Deborah, and how I'd be living with her and her husband.

I tell Sam everything except the last part. The *one more thing* Deborah had mentioned on the phone. As we talk, the conversation plays out in my head again. Deborah's tone had changed, like she was being careful with her words. "Have you read any news? News in Spain?" she'd said, like she was tiptoeing across glass.

I'd thought back to my Google searches. I couldn't remember anything that jumped out. But then again, I didn't look for news stories when I searched the town.

"No, nothing," I told Deborah. "Why?"

"Right. Well, we had an incident a few months back," she said, her voice subdued. "I just thought it would be good to mention."

"What kind of incident?"

She took a breath. "There was a girl here from the UK. She was here with her fiancé. His family lives in town."

Deborah paused, and then her words came, sending a chill down my spine. "She died. Drowned."

I said nothing, listening as she searched for words to fill the awkward space. "She was only twenty-two," Deborah said, as if she was talking more to herself than to me. "Only twenty-two."

CHAPTER 10:

LISA

Six Months Ago

Alma's fallen down the stairs. I'm not sure what happened. I keep wondering if I pushed her. Maybe I dreamt it. I can clearly see her terrified face as she falls backwards. The image is vivid in my mind.

We heard the commotion. Seb was in the bathroom, me lying on the bed. We heard the sickening thump-thump-thump, followed by a guttural shrieking. We found her crumpled at the foot of the stairs, Seb rushing to her side.

Time passed slowly after that. The interminable ride in the back of the ambulance, the series of faces blurred into one, endless streams of gibberish, hospital rooms with their antiseptic smells.

The doctor said she broke her hip, but looking at her lying in the bed, it's likely she broke every bone in her body. Her face is yellow, the rest of her body pale and brittle, like the slightest touch could turn it to dust. She needed a hip replacement, they said. She'd need all the support we could give.

I sip the stewed coffee, the hospital cafeteria empty. Touching my nose, I feel the greasiness that comes with twelve hours of no washing or sleeping. I hear footsteps behind me and sit up straight.

Seb sits down, takes his coffee and gives me a lopsided smile.

"How is she?" I say.

The circles under his eyes are dark. He looks five years older and shabbier.

"Sleeping now. She'll need her energy for tomorrow."

"What time is the surgery?"

Seb presses his palms to his eyes. "Five in the afternoon."

That's over twenty hours from now.

"After the surgery, they need to monitor her for a few days. Then we can take her home."

His words sound soft, like he's talking about a sick puppy. I remind myself that this woman is his mother. His first source of love. He sips his coffee, then puts the paper cup down. "Listen," he says, his eyes not meeting mine. "My sister's coming to town tomorrow. From Barcelona."

Since I've known Seb, we've spoken briefly about his mother, his father, their legacy. But never his sister. Never more than a mention. Whenever I probed, he brushed it off.

"That's great," I say, brightly. "I mean, I wish it were under better circumstances, but still."

He nods, but under the table, his legs are jittery. Like those kids at school that just couldn't sit still. When he meets my gaze, his eyes look tired and faraway.

And a hint of something else, something that makes me speak up.

"Is that a problem?"

"What do you mean?"

"It's just... well, you don't seem too happy about her coming."

He sits back in his chair, sips his coffee, his nose wrinkling at the taste. When he speaks, he shakes his head. "It's fine. Ana and I aren't really close. I guess she's just worried about my mother."

"Which is understandable," I say, placing my hand over his. "Everything is going to be okay. That's what the doctor said, right?"

"Yes."

He looks so tired, and it makes my insides hurt. I'm out of my element here. Hordes of Spanish doctors and nurses, and signs I can't read. "Can I get you anything?"

Eleanor pops unbidden into my head. *A good wife takes care of her husband.*

He's quiet, contemplating. "I'd like to change my clothes." He pulls on his sweater. "I feel dirty."

"Me too," I say with a weak grin, trying to lighten the mood. "I can stop by the house. Grab some clothes for you?"

"That would be great," he says. "I just don't want to leave her right now."

"Leave it with me," I say with newfound conviction. "Who can I call?"

"I'll call our driver to pick you up. You can take my car when you come back."

Out of his pocket, he pulls his keys, places them on the tabletop. "Do you know the way?"

"Google Maps," I say, motioning to my phone. I take his keys and drop them into my handbag.

Because I've got a mission to accomplish. To help my fiancé.

* * *

The driver dropped me off as the sun slipped beneath the horizon.

The light was dancing on the still waters. I could almost reach out and touch the last orange rays.

I walked to the dock at the end of our street, half hidden behind some trees where the road ended. As I faced the walkway, I hesitated. Everything was quiet. I ran my hands over the worn wooden railing, coat pressed to my body to stop the cold seeping through. It was something to behold, this changing of the world from day to night. And as the warm glow of the afternoon disappeared, I walked back feeling lighter.

I showered, packed a bag for myself and Seb, and got into his car. When I turned on the ignition, my hands trembled.

Don't worry, I told myself. *You can do this.*

And I did.

The roads were empty, my phone directing me efficiently back to the hospital. I scanned the open parking spots, calculating which one was the easiest. But as I parked his angry-looking BMW and locked it, I felt newfound confidence.

Seb was sitting next to a sleeping Alma when I arrived. He put his arms around me and I breathed in his familiar scent. While he went to change, I sat next to Alma, watching her breathe.

Seb looked better after a change of clothes. "I'm going to stay here tonight," he said, "You should go home and get some rest."

I looked at him defiantly, as if leaving him was unthinkable. But he insisted. And I didn't really want to be there. Something about being back in the sterile environment of a hospital unnerved me. The sound of sensible shoes shuffling on linoleum floors, and the smell of cafeteria food mixed with sickness brought back terrible memories. Memories that ought to be locked away forever.

"Please," Seb said, holding my face. "I'll be fine."

And so I'm back at the house. Walking the empty hallways, wine glass in hand, feeling restless.

I move from room to room, lighting a lamp in every room. It brings some comfort to the eerie silence. I open the cabinet in the study. It's filled with papers, birthday cards and crocheted items.

I did this as a child. I'd walk around other people's houses, looking at their belongings. I tell myself it gives me a sense of control. Of knowing that everything is where it should be. Sometimes I wonder if this need for control was the beginning of the end for you and me. Not like it matters now.

I find an old picture of Seb, those same eyes glowing in a younger face. He can't have been older than ten. Next to him stands a girl in pigtails, a head taller. His older sister.

And I get to meet her tomorrow.

I put the photograph back in its pile, arranging everything as I found it. Sipping my wine, I sit by the bay window, my expression reflected back at me. What a contrast. The hopeful day and the gloomy night. I think of Seb's face, his palms pressed against his eyes in the cafeteria. *Ana and I aren't really close.*

There was something behind his eyes. Like worry or fear. Maybe he's

just tired. Emotionally exhausted. But maybe there's more to it.
And it's got something to do with Ana.

CHAPTER 11:

CAT

Present Day

At the airport, I'm supposed to look out for someone tall. It's like finding a needle in a haystack.

Deborah's not a specific one, I can tell. She uses too many emojis in her texts and types *lol* when there's nothing to *lol* about.

Eighteen hours ago, the plane took off from Johannesburg, my anxiety flaring as we gained altitude. I clutched my passport to my chest as I moved from gate to gate in Zurich, feeling scared and excited at the same time. All the way to Madrid, I tried not to think of InCheck. I'd taken a day of counsellor leave, in line with the app's policies. But I kept thinking of Fred and his shower. Susana and her baby. What were they doing right now? Were they as scared as I was? Flung into the deep end.

I'm aware of someone shouting.

The words come thick and fast. I look up and see a white taxi with a red stripe ahead. The man behind the wheel is looking for an answer, a tanned arm gesticulating through the window.

"Sorry?" I say.

He speaks again, a torrent of words.

"No hablo español," I say, and pull my suitcase closer. Barajas airport is bustling with people. The word reminds me of *baggage*, the physical kind. But then again, the emotional kind works too.

I think of the few possessions I have in a locker somewhere back home.

Ben and Sarah's apartment standing empty now, awaiting its new tenants. I think of Sam, and how her face fell when I told her I was leaving.

But I had to. Not for a new adventure, but to get away. That Instagram message from weeks ago still ingrained in my mind.

I know you're a fraud, Alice.

I fidget for a cigarette in my suitcase, and as I take one out, I hear my name.

"Cat?"

The voice is deep and resonant. Cigarette and lighter in hand, I turn, and there's a man behind me. Broad-shouldered, big, bald-headed. His cheeks boast dark stubble. Late forties, maybe fifties? He could be Deborah's husband.

"Yes," I say, gripping the cigarette between my fingers, careful not to break it. Who knows how much it'll cost to replace cigarettes here.

As the man moves closer, I internally curse Deborah for her vague instructions.

When you get there, my husband will be waiting. He's tall and you won't miss him. Lol.

I wonder if she gave her husband similar instructions. Maybe she was more descriptive in my case.

Look for the redhead wearing sweats. She'll be carrying baggage. A lot of baggage. Lol.

"I'm Richard," the man says, and I relax. It's the husband.

"Oh," I say. "Great. Nice to meet you."

"You too," he says with a deep dip of the vowels. He casts his eyes to my suitcase. "I'll take that."

One hand grabs it, lifting it clumsily and dropping it back down with the handle pulled up. It makes a thud on the concrete, and he rolls it as he walks past me. "We're this way."

We walk past the arrivals terminal to a parking area lined with taxis and tour buses. I take in the smells and sounds. There's a beep as we approach a black Audi. The rims look worn, and the car's exterior has lost its shine. Richard places my suitcase in the boot and leans against the car. "You should smoke that now," he says, pointing at the cigarette in my hand.

He takes out a pack of his own, the stems yellow like the strong cigarillos we have back home. He lights it and takes a deep drag.

"It's warm here. I didn't expect it to be this warm," I say.

"It'll cool down after August. You've never been to Europe, have you?"

I take a drag of my cigarette. "No. Never left South Africa."

"It's a different world this. Don't expect to understand a lot."

His *rs* rasp earthily. "I've heard. But hey, it's still Spain."

He snorts, eyebrows raised. It's a chance for me to take a closer look at him. He's wearing dark jeans, a black t-shirt. A no-fuss look. He barely talks as we smoke, but then his eyes meet mine as he takes a last drag. I wonder if he's looking at me like that too; taking in this stranger.

"Let's go," he says.

We flick our cigarette butts onto the concrete and get into the car. It smells of cheap air freshener. I shift the passenger seat forward. As we exit the airport, I study the faces of passengers in the taxis around us.

Where are you off to? I ask them silently. *Are you running too?*

When we're on the highway, the airport receding in the rearview mirror, I sit back. "So this is Madrid?"

Richard smirks. "Not a chance. Madrid is a few kilometres that way," he says, pointing to his left. Through his sunglasses, he gives me a sideways glance. "You won't see much of Madrid. We're heading up north."

"I Googled the roads, but it's different seeing it in person."

"Did you use the loo at the airport?"

"Sorry?" I say, pulling the sun visor down.

"The loo. The toilet."

"Oh, no. I didn't think about it."

"It's a four-hour drive. Can you hold it?"

"Yeah, I can hold it."

With his right hand, he fiddles in the back of the car like he's hunting for something. When he finds what he's looking for, he slings a plastic bag onto my lap. "Some snacks."

As we drive, I eat potato chips and take in the scenery. I had pictured bulls, dusty landscapes and bright blue oceans. But all I see is a lot of brown with the occasional splash of green.

"Thanks for picking me up," I say. "And for the snacks."

"It's fine. It was Deb's idea."

I don't ask him which part, but I study his stubble, the freckles on his light arms. "How long have you been in Spain?"

He readjusts in his seat. "About twelve years, I think. Always been up north. Close to Bilbao."

"Deborah said you came here for work?"

"Yep, contract work. Buildings."

"You're an architect, right?"

"Yep."

There's silence, and I wonder if I've asked too many questions. But then his voice breaks the quiet, louder than before. "So, what's the deal with you?" he says. "Why Basque? You're a long way from home, aren't you?"

"That's a lot of questions."

"I should know who I'm living with."

I shuffle a leg over the other. The car feels small and Richard's too big for it. As if the smallest bump in the road will send his head through the rooftop.

"The short answer is I'm looking for a change. And this was a great opportunity."

"And the long answer?"

I look at him and wonder if he'd have the patience to listen to it. But it's not a story I tell anyone. "Too complicated for a car ride."

"Is there a boyfriend in the picture?" he says, his tone tinged with amusement.

I open my mouth, but close it again. My mind wanders to early mornings in bed; her thighs wrapped around mine. Her fingers between my hair, eyes searching mine. *It's me, open up.*

"Or maybe it's a *she*," he says, his words gentler, like he's treading carefully. But there's a hint of a smile there.

"Well, it's in the past now," I say, grabbing for the soda. "Anyway, who wouldn't want to move to Spain? You only hear good things."

I open the bottle and drink deeply, the cool liquid a relief. It's half the truth. I'm sure lots of people would travel to Spain if they could.

"It's just another country," Richard says.

"Maybe, but it's exactly what I'm looking for. New and exciting."

"And you can't find that back in Africa?"

"No," I shake my head. "My life's too planned there. Too much routine. I don't know what I want to do with my life yet."

Richard sinks back into his seat, one hand on the steering wheel. "So you teach English instead."

"So I teach English instead."

"I hate to break it to you, but life's all about routines."

Richard, what do you know, really? Probably more than I do, looking at his worn hands. They're enormous, and I wonder when's the last time I saw a man with hands that size.

And then I remember.

My father would drive in the same way, one hand on the wheel, the other pointing outwards to the sky. *Look bud, up ahead!*

My stomach clenches.

"So how much do you know about Northern Spain?" Richard says, changing the topic.

"I read it has a unique language. Serves different food. And a lot of celebrities go there."

"That's mostly San Sebastian. Not like the rest."

"Guess I'll learn on the job," I say, trying to lighten the mood. "I read Gexta is pretty small. Only like 1,000 people."

He nods. "It's small. There are a few decent bars. But that's about it. It's got great views, though."

I think of the images I'd seen online. Small houses perched beside calm waters, green hills painting a vivid backdrop. I couldn't compare it to the lightness of the Cape Winelands, but also not to the roughness of the bush. It was like nothing I'd seen before.

"Why did you decide to move there?" I say.

"It's thirty minutes from Bilbao. And better value for money. Spain's not as cheap as you think."

I take another sip. "I didn't think it was."

"A lot of foreign investments in the area. Families with big houses and even bigger pockets."

"I can imagine."

"Very secluded, too. Friendly people, but everyone keeps to themselves." Richard clears his throat. "Especially since the incident."

Other images fill my head; search results with headlines serving as clickbait.

British girl drowns in small town in Northern Spain.

Possible suicide by young Brit in Spanish coastal town.

Chelsea family calls for investigation of daughter's death in Northern Spain.

I'd read the girl had gotten drunk, taken pills, then jumped or fell from the dock in town. Reports say the current either took her, or she was too drunk to call for help, the water pulling her under. A rich girl from London with a Spanish fiancé, on their first trip abroad together. A perfect life gone wrong.

"Deborah told me about it," I say. "Did you know the girl well?"

Richard shakes his head. "No. She stayed down the road from us with a Spanish bloke and his mum."

"I read there was an investigation. Did they find anything?"

"Nah. The police suspected foul play, but looking at the bruises, there was no way to tell. No one saw her jump or slip. So they called it off."

"That's awful," I say.

Death doesn't discriminate. It comes calling for us all at some stage.

"Something doesn't add up, though," Richard says. "A young girl like that, got her whole life ahead of her, comes here for a few months and then offs herself? By jumping off a dock?"

"How high is the dock?"

I don't know why I want to know that. I shouldn't be thinking about this girl, or her death, or the way she died. Maybe I'm morbid. Or maybe I'm just curious.

If Richard notices, he doesn't show it. He just sighs. "About four metres."

"Damn," I say. "And what does her fiancé say?"

"Barely talks. Just drinks in the pub, or stays in the house with his mum."

"That's horrible," I say, knowing that a drink seems like the only thing that can save you when you're that low.

"But that's the way the world works, right?" Richard says, "Something tragic happens, we stop for a second and notice, and then move along."

He sighs again. We drive in silence, and I watch the terrain change from flat and dry to hilly and verdant. As we pass through a tunnel, the surroundings are suddenly greener, more pristine.

"It's beautiful here," I say, but Richard just nods, his eyes focused on the road.

For the rest of the trip, I try to fill the void with words. But Richard's not talking much anymore. He opens his window like my father used to, letting the air wash through the car. Flap, flap, flap.

Come bud, open your window. Ride with the breeze!

As the silence expands, the fresh air the only comfort, I think of her.

Lisa. The dead girl.

I used to think that death follows you. But in reality, death doesn't follow me. I seem to follow it.

CHAPTER 12:

LISA

Six Months Ago

Alma sees her first.

I glimpse thick chestnut hair as Ana rushes across the room to her mother's side. They embrace, exchange words thick with emotion. I watch as she kisses Alma's cheek, her red lips contrasting with her mother's pasty complexion.

When she lifts her head, I see her eyes. The same warm, chocolate brown as her brother's.

"Hi. I'm Lisa."

She presses her lips together and for a moment I think she'll say nothing. Then, she's embracing me. Her hair smells like citrus.

"It's so nice to meet you," she says, her voice surprisingly deep. When she pulls away, she's smiling. "Thank you for taking care of my mother. This is so terrible. That you're here under such bad circumstances."

I open my mouth, look at Alma. "I didn't do anything, really. It's all Seb. But they say she's doing well. She'll make a full recovery after the surgery."

Ana nods, grips my hand. "Yes, I'm very thankful." She smiles and turns back to her mother. It can't be easy seeing your loved ones deteriorate. I can't imagine Eleanor decaying, slipping away. She'll either be here or she won't.

"Seb's just gone to the bathroom," I say, motioning to the door.

"He should—"

"Hola," his voice calls from the doorway. I look at Seb's expression. It's blank, a thin line where his lips should be. His eyebrows look thicker, close together. *Like a frown.*

As if in slow motion, he walks over to his sister and gives her a stiff hug. His face barely changes.

If this bothers Ana, she doesn't show it. "I was just telling Lisa how glad I am that you were here to take care of her."

"Everything's fine," he says. "You didn't have to come." Seb speaks in a monotone, looking at Alma, then at the window beyond.

"It's my mother," Ana says, eyes wide. "Of course I'm going to be here."

She shakes her head and looks at me like Seb just told a bad joke.

"Are you staying at the house?" Ana asks, looking at me.

"We are," Seb says, his arms crossed. They stand side by side, neither looking at the other. It's only been a minute, but the room's buzzing, the air thick with tension.

"I'm going to get another coffee," I say, needing to leave the room. "Anyone want anything?"

Brother and sister decline, both smiling. But they're tight, forced. I can't leave the awkwardness fast enough. I walk through the hall, past the cafeteria, down to the hospital's courtyard. Outside, I sit on a bench opposite a fountain, a stream of water spewing from a fish's mouth. I take out my phone and dial Ruth's number.

Relief floods over me as she picks up.

"Hola, señora."

Her voice is low and there's background noise, like pans clanging together.

"Hey, is this a bad time?" I say.

"Does it matter?"

There's a muffled sound, like she's talking to someone else.

"Can you hear me?" I say, my elbows on my knees, frowning.

"Never mind," she says. "What's up?"

"What are you doing?"

"Just off with the boys. Early brunch. Hair of the dog and all that."

"I remember those," I say, glancing up at the sky. "They were the best."

The times we had at uni felt so carefree, so devoid of any worries about the future. About the dangers ahead. Yesterday's sunsets seem so far away now, a suffocating grey taking their place.

The silence drags, and then Ruth speaks again. "So what's up?"

"What do you mean?"

"Well, you called me," she says. "It's not like I mind the chat, but what's going on?"

I don't know where to start, I want to tell her. *My fiancé and I aren't having sex, his mother hates me, she's fallen down the stairs and his estranged sister's shown up at the hospital and it's all so very, very weird.*

But I don't say any of that.

"I know, I'm sorry, it's been…" I trail off.

"How's Sebastian?"

The way Ruth says his name takes me back to our evenings together in the flat, drinking cheap wine, smoking cigarettes and dancing like we didn't have a care in the world.

"His mother had a big fall. She's at the hospital. We're here now."

"Is she alright?"

"Yeah, she's fine. It's just a little… it's… it's a bit much."

Silence. I take a breath. "I don't know. Things are just so *different* here. And not really in a good way."

I look to the inside of the hospital, the cafeteria empty apart from a man at the vending machine. "She doesn't seem to like me much."

"Did she say that?"

"No, but Seb's like a translator. We don't speak if he's not there. And there was this one day where I cooked and she gave me the wrong spice. It was a whole thing. I don't really know where—"

"Okay, hold on," Ruth says. "I have no idea what that means, but take a breath. Just breathe."

I breathe deeply, the emotion swelling up.

"I love him, but I want… I want to come home."

"Then come home."

"What?"

"Lisa, what were you looking for? If you're fed up, come home. If you're going to make it work, then stay. I don't know what else to tell you."

I stand up, walk towards the shrubs at the corner of the courtyard. My eyes scan their unruly ends, creeping out towards the concrete. "Yeah, maybe."

Guilt tinges my fingertips, but I brush it away. *Not here.*

And then the words tumble out.

"There's so much more to married life than I thought, you know? And we're not even married yet. Coming here with him was fine, but being in that house with her... I don't know. It's not easy."

Ruth's voice is softer. "I can imagine. She speaks no English, right?"

"Exactly, and I swear, sometimes I catch her watching Friends on the TV and she's *laughing*. Like she understands it."

"Come on, I doubt that's true."

"No really, you should see her."

"Didn't this woman just have a fall?"

The shame rises to my cheeks. "Yes, I know that. It's not her fault, of course, it's—"

"Then what is it?"

"It's like she's going out of her way to make me look bad," I say, my frustration breaking through. "And she's constantly talking. It's like a never-ending flood. I don't get a word in with Seb because she's always around. I know she's old and frail but honestly, she's insufferable sometimes."

I turn my eyes away from the sun. But they catch something else. A figure. The same one I saw just minutes ago in the hospital ward.

Ana. Here, in the courtyard.

Looking right at me.

CHAPTER 13:

CAT

Present Day

"I hope you like potatoes," Richard says as he rounds a bend, the ocean ahead of us.

"They're my favourite food group," I say, my eyes drawn to the glimmer of the water.

It's late afternoon and Gexta looks exactly like the pictures, but more pristine. An explosion of greens, blues, yellows and reds, mixed with textures of wood and flora.

"Good," Richard says. "And fish too. There's a lot of it here."

We pass by taverns, tables lining the pavement. The locals are drinking beer and eating baskets of rustic bread with tiny plates of olives. I'm practically salivating as I hone in on the amber liquid. I quickly move my focus to the plates of food instead.

"Can't blame them," I say. "If I lived by the ocean, I'd probably eat fish all the time too."

"It's small, but look," Richard says, motioning to the landscape in front. "The view's worth it."

His one hand is on the wheel, the other out of the window. A thought springs to my mind. *What would dad think of this view?*

"There's a market down the road and a pub that way," Richard says, pointing out the window. "Good for a pint."

My stomach drops. He doesn't know I don't drink, does he? Would

Deborah have told him? It sucks being that person—the one who doesn't drink. In a normal world, Richard and I could have been drinking buddies. Had a pint in a new country together.

I swallow again. It doesn't matter how much I crave a drink, I can't go back. Not after *that* night.

The car slows towards the end of a road, a cluster of trees up ahead. On the left, there's the water, undisturbed and silent. On the right, double storied houses stand in line.

"That's the house," Richard says, pointing.

He rounds a bend at the end of the road and drives into a small garden at the back of the house, the view of the ocean gone, replaced by brick walls and window sills. The interior is small, pot plants lining the perimeter. In the corner is a tiny bench made of brick.

"Here we are."

Richard's out of the car before I can catch my breath. I hear the boot open and as I step out, the cool breeze tugs at my skirt. Even without a view, I can smell the ocean, a ripple of freshness taking me back to summer holidays on the Dolphin Coast.

"You're here!"

The voice ruptures the silence, my suitcase clunking on the pavement behind me. My eyes follow the sound.

I raise my eyebrows. Deborah's much taller than I expected. From her light jeans to her oversized purple blouse, she's vibrant. She opens her arms wide and I take it as my cue to move in for a hug.

"Hi," I say, my voice higher than normal. Her hair is frizzy as it grazes my cheek, the colour dark and shiny. When we lock eyes, hers are a soft green and I breathe a little easier.

"I can't believe I'm here," I say.

"Me neither," she exclaims, hand to her chest. On the phone from thousands of kilometres away, I was picturing a lady close to sixty. But in person, she's probably ten years younger.

"I'll take this upstairs," Richard says, standing behind me, my suitcase in hand. He looks at us, then towards the doorway that we're blocking.

"We'll get out of your way then," Deborah says, stepping through the doorway leading into the house, motioning for me to follow. I step inside, the house dark.

"And hello to you," Deborah says to Richard as he passes us in the tiny hallway, planting a kiss on his cheek. But his large frame moves past her, barely acknowledging the gesture.

"Well," she says, turning to me, hands on her hips. "Shall I give you a tour?"

I nod. "Good idea."

She leads me through the hallway into a large space with much more light. From outside, the house's design is unclear, a rectangular block giving nothing away. But from inside, everything is illuminated, the ocean on full display through the bay window to the left.

"This is the kitchen and living area," she motions. It's open plan, with the kitchen towards the back of the house, an island facing the living area. The walls are egg white, with flecks of orange and deep maroon from the chairs and pillows dispersed across the space.

My feet are soft on the wooden floors as I step forward. I see new cabinets in the kitchen, the Medallion grey rug in the living area.

"Wow," I say. "Great place."

"Clean too, I hope."

I sniff and catch a whiff of peach. I think of Richard, the scented room a direct contrast to the cigarette smoke on his fingers.

I look out at the ocean, shimmering gently in the sunlight. "I can't get over this view."

"We're quite chuffed with it," Deborah says. "Come, I'll show you the kitchen."

It's filled with top-end appliances, including a stainless steel oven. "For all that baking I'm not doing," she says, giving a wink.

"And here," she says, leading me down the hallway again. "Is our study. But Richard mostly works here. I'm either at the dining table or at the office."

"So you work from home then?"

"I used to," she says. "But we've got an office space in town now. But I still like working from home some days."

I look at the wooden dining table facing the view. "Yeah, I bet."

"We bought this place ages ago. It's been a real project. When we first got it, it was a disaster. The kitchen was a whole other room," she says, striding back to the centre of the room.

"Well, it looks fantastic."

We walk up the stairs. For a moment it's crowded, as Richard squeezes past us. "I'll be in the garden," he mutters.

When he's out of earshot, Deborah leans into me. "Was he grumpy on the way here?"

"Not really. We were fine."

"He's a teddy bear once you get to know him," she smiles.

"Up here, we have the bedrooms. Again, a complete mess when we got here," she says, leaning against a doorway opposite a small bathroom. "This is your room."

The space is darker than the master suite at the end of the hallway, light streaming in from the ocean side. But the room is large and has a double bed. There's a desk, an upholstered maroon chair and bed sheets that look crisp.

"It's not much, but it'll do."

I see my suitcase in the middle of the room. "You mentioned it's the first time you're doing this hosting programme?"

"That's right. The academy wanted to attract more English teachers. But there's almost no accommodation around here."

I think of the paperwork sent through to me by a woman named Charlotte. Onboarding documents, information about the academy, the course material. All the things usually found in Sam's binder.

"That's nice of you to do that."

"I get a few pennies out of it. Also, it gets a bit lonely here sometimes," she says, crossing her arms.

"What made you move here?"

"Oh, that's a very, very long story," she says. "We first lived in Bilbao for a few years. Richard came here on business and I followed. Picked up some odd jobs here and there. Then we decided to put down some roots, and here we are."

The scenario starts coming together in my mind. The clean kitchen with new appliances, the suede couch, the soft finishings. A spotless home. A home without children.

"Do you have any family here?" I say.

"No, it's just the two of us."

Her expression falters, the smile narrowing. "We travel to the UK often. But we like the peace of living here. Even if it's windy and wet a lot of the time."

"So I came on a good day," I say.

Her face cracks open in a grin. "You did."

I think of Deborah's warm demeanour, her talkative nature. They say opposites attract. That must be true for her and Richard.

He's a teddy bear once you get to know him.

"Well, I'll leave you to it," she announces. "We'll start dinner soon. Come down when you're ready."

Before she leaves, I stop her. "Can I have the Wi-Fi password?"

After Deborah helps me connect, she heads back down the stairs. Closing the door behind me, I haul my suitcase on the bed, the few possessions I have all pressed against each other in the rectangular box.

Your life fits in a suitcase. What does that say about you?

I take out some clothes, fling them in the drawers. When I'm done, I stand at the window, eyeing the garden below. A rich green, with splashes of colour. I crave a drink. The adrenaline from the journey is wearing off, and the world is sharp around the edges again. In my six months of sobriety, I didn't expect to still get these types of cravings. It must be the travel, being in a new place.

I open my phone and log in to InCheck, distracting my mind from the drink craving. On the app, I find a message from Fred.

Call tonight?

My response is instant. *Yes.*

We schedule a call for later in the evening. From Spain, there's barely a time difference, which makes me breathe easier. *Everything's fine. Still fine.*

This is what I wanted. This is what I came for. A chance at something new. Something different. And from the ocean views to the smell of peach in this house, it's exactly what I need.

And far from danger.

Again, that Instagram message, the words engraved in my mind. *I know you're a fraud, Alice.*

But no. Here, I'm safe. Only a handful of people know I'm in Spain, and only Sam knows about this small town. I'm completely off the radar.

I freshen up and head down the stairs, finding Deborah at the counter.

"All settled?" she says, looking up from her reading glasses.

"All settled."

I spot a glass of white wine beside her, and instantly, she sees what I'm looking at. "Would you like something to drink?"

It's an open-ended question. Maybe she thinks I'm not really sober, and I might have one glass. She walks to the fridge, opens it. I stand, my voice slightly too loud. "What do you have?"

She raises an eyebrow, her hand gripping the bottle of wine in the fridge door. But something in my expression must show that I'm not interested in that, because she turns to look inside the fridge and says, "I have Coke and some mango juice. But the juice is probably expired."

"Coke, please," I say, watching her grab the wine bottle in one hand and the plastic bottle in another, nudging the fridge closed with her shoulder. She pours me some Coke, then pours herself more wine, the golden liquid dangerously close to the rim. I practically gulp my drink down.

"Would you mind if I go out for a cigarette?" I say.

"Sure! I'll come with you."

"You smoke?"

"No," she says. "I stopped ages go."

We walk to the garden, glasses in hand. I spot an ashtray in the corner by the brick wall and perch against it, Deborah at my side. The kitchen is bright from here, the overhead lights a warm glow.

"There you are," we hear Richard's voice from the hallway.

"You've got a smoking buddy," Deborah says, sipping her wine. He gives a forced smile, like he's got other things on his mind.

"What's for dinner?" Deborah says as Richard lights a cigarette.

"How does frozen pizza sound?" He looks at us both, eyebrow raised.

I sip my Coke, lift my chin. "Like a dream."

"The real gourmet experience on your first night," Deborah beams and we chuckle, the cool air soothing against my neck, the smoke delicious in my lungs. I can finally feel myself relaxing.

And yet.

I look to Deborah, then to Richard. Both a little buzzed from the newness too, their bodies shifting energy from one leg to another. The thought gnaws deeper, harder.

Something's off.

It's not their looks. They're fine on their own, but odd side by side. People love who they love. I should know that. But it's their flow, the way they mesh.

It's off-balance. Like mustard and custard mixed together.

CHAPTER 14:

LISA

Six Months Ago

"I should go," I hurriedly mutter to Ruth. "I'll call you later."

Ana's looking at me, her expression stark. The hospital courtyard is dead still.

How long has she been standing there? Did she hear me?

I stuff the phone into my pocket. Ana flicks her hair across her shoulders. She takes a packet of cigarettes from her pocket and puts one between her lips. My nails dig into my skin.

"I, uhm, I—"

"Do you want one?" she says, offering me a cigarette.

I hesitate, but then take one. "Thanks."

Smoking's another thing Eleanor doesn't like. Despises, actually. But like a lot of things, I do it anyway, the guilt lingering.

Ana lights her cigarette, passes the lighter to me. "Here."

I grab it, my fingers shaky. Blood rushes to my face and stings my cheeks. She watches me as I light mine. When I inhale, my stomach lurches with panic.

"Ana, about that phone call—"

"Don't worry about it," she says, waving the words away. "My mother, she doesn't speak English. So I can imagine it must be difficult to talk to her."

My brow creases. Ana's calm, the lines of her mouth pulling upwards, like she's about to smile.

She's just trying to be nice.

I shake my head. "Still, I… it was out of line. I'm so sorry if I offended you or your family. It's all been so stressful."

My hands keep shaking, the words sounding lame in my head. "Being here in this new environment. And the language. It's all just very foreign to me. But that's no excuse."

"Hey," she says, leaning in. "I get it. Spain's a strange place. It's very welcoming, but also stuck in its ways."

She shrugs her shoulders. I see no sign of disdain or anger. If someone had spoken about Eleanor like that in front of me, I don't know what I'd do. Possibly agree. Possibly scratch their eyes out.

My eyes flicker to the floor, then back to her, smoking the cigarette like it's my first time. Holding it like a newbie. "Sorry, I still feel so awkward."

"What you say in private is your business," she says, the cigarette in her hand poised in the air. "Anyone would feel awkward."

"Bad luck then," I say, trying to sound funny, but it feels like my heart is in my shoes.

"I bought these at the station," she says, holding the cigarette pack. "But I'm not supposed to smoke. Do you want it?"

I shake my head. "I usually don't either."

She beams, the silence spreading between us.

"I'm happy I got to meet you," she says. "I'm not sure I would have. If not for this."

I think of Seb. How cold he was to her in the wardroom, barely looking in her direction. *Ana and I aren't really close.*

But why is that? Why can't he get along with someone who seems so warm? So kind?

"I'm glad I got to meet you too. I've wanted to for a while," I say.

Ana shrugs, takes another drag. "I'm surprised my brother mentioned me to you at all."

Her eyes are downcast, mouth pulled to one side in contemplation. But before I can say anything, she's smiling again. "I guess we both got lucky then."

I think of the picture in the salon. Ana with her pigtails, a head taller than Seb. Within her smile, there's depth of spirit. Traces of nostalgia and resignation.

There's pain here.

"He talked about you. Told me you work in consulting. He was so proud when he mentioned that," I say, glazing the truth with a lie.

Good wives support their husbands, my mother echoes again. *Even with little lies.*

Ana chuckles, but I only half believe it. "We were close, you know."

She stubs her cigarette out against the bin. "When we were young. He was always looking for the next big thing. Moving from one thing to the next."

"Well, then he hasn't changed much."

Ana looks to the sky, her face soft. She wraps her beige coat closer around her, meets my gaze. "Listen, I don't know if Seb told you, but there's a British couple that lives down the road from our house."

I nod, my brain circling the minor detail from when we just arrived. "He did actually, yeah."

"You should meet them," she says, standing taller. "I'll introduce you. The woman, Deborah, she's great. You'll like her. We can walk over this week."

Relief floods me, the panic faltering. "I would love that."

Hope rises through my body, the message clear. *Just hold on a little longer.*

Since arriving in Gexta, everything has been a challenge. A new obstacle to overcome. The language, the isolation, seeing Seb in a new environment. Alma falling down the stairs. It all pushed my boundaries, maybe a little too far. Making me think that Eleanor was right. Maybe I couldn't cope on my own.

But hope arrived today. Ana, offering me a lifeline.

"So, should we go back inside?" she says.

We walk back towards the cafeteria, my body buzzing with energy. But this time it's good. It's not driven by fear or self-loathing, or accompanied by a primal urge to grab at the razor in my handbag. It's driven by hope.

It might actually be all right.

CHAPTER 15:

CAT

Present Day

Deborah has a lot of energy. She's constantly on her feet, splashing more wine into her glass and more Coke into mine. I don't need to ask for a refill. And she drinks like a sailor. Just like I used to.

Half an hour and three frozen pizzas in, we've covered the basics. Richard's taking a break from his job as an architect, designing buildings only when he feels like it. I can't imagine a life where a person can choose when to work or not, but it sounds good. Deborah also doesn't work full time. She works part-time from home, in subcontracting. They've been married for almost half my life.

The pizza is chewy but tasty, remnants of the crust powdering our hands. We get through the awkward part about why I don't drink as soon as we sat down. It's Deborah who asks the question.

"I just didn't like what it did to me," I tell them. "Drinking made me feel like I was out of control."

"So you drank a lot then?" Deborah says, and even though it comes out light-heartedly, it feels like an attack. Richard is quiet, his face giving nothing away as he looks at me. I sit back, trying to physically show how uncomfortable I am talking about my sobriety, and say, "I did, yes."

Luckily, that changes the tack of the conversation. Soon, Deborah is explaining how she only drinks 'a few glasses every now and again'. But by the look of how many refills she's pouring, and how Richard raises his eyebrows when she says it, I doubt it.

But hey, I drank for my own reasons. I'm sure she does, too.

As we finish the last of the pizza, I sit back and take a closer look at them. Deborah with her wine glass, talking animatedly. Richard nursing a beer, sprawled back against his chair. Seeing them side by side, it's impossible to not see the difference.

This is what happens with marriages, the voices inside my head probe, tugging me back to childhood. My mother in her room between meals. My father spread out on the couch, miniature whiskey bottles hidden beneath the cushions. How strange it was, watching them drag a lifeless relationship through our home. Day in and day out.

Neither ready to let go.

Until one could.

"So," Deborah says, "apart from teaching and dog watching, all of that, what do you like doing in your spare time?"

The question feels loaded. She's asked me this before. It's like we're strangers again, me and her, on that first phone call, our voices foreign to each other. I hesitate, wondering what to start with. A lie or the truth?

"I used to have a lot of hobbies." *Truth.* "But these days I feel all I do is teach." *Lie.* "I want to get back to doing more things again. Maybe being here," I say, motioning to the house, the view beyond the bay window. "I'll get to do that." *Truth.*

"What kinds of things?"

I shrug and take a sip of Coke, my breath fogging the glass. "Maybe a combination. Reading, taking walks, maybe writing?"

It's strange how faking can bleed into being real. A fake counsellor can only give advice for so long without following it. Or trying to, at least. The same mantras I've told my clients on InCheck, over and over again, pop unbidden into my head. *Be kind to yourself. What have you done today that's only been for you?*

Contemplation isn't hard. It's the acting that is.

"I've got some books there," Deborah points to hardcovers lined up neatly on a shelf under the television. "Not sure if they're your type of read, but feel free to have a look. As for the walks, there are great hiking trails around here. We can get you a map." She looks over at Richard.

"Thanks," I say.

My gaze shifts to Richard, who juts his chin, suddenly more present. "That girl, she used to like writing too."

Throughout dinner he's been quiet, uninvolved, scoffing down slice after slice of pizza, sipping on his beer. Maybe we wouldn't have been drinking buddies after all.

"Who?" Deborah and I say simultaneously.

He raises an eyebrow. "Lisa. The girl that drowned."

He turns, points his beer bottle towards the bay window, as if we can see the dock—the apparent scene of her drowning—from here. When we arrived, I barely had a chance to look for it, imagining a tall structure, violent waters beneath. But nothing about this place screams terror, fear, or even death.

That is, until Richard brings it up again. It's the second time he's brought up her death since I arrived. Why is he so interested in her? Especially since he told me he didn't even know her that well?

"So she was a writer?" I say.

Deborah shakes her head. "No, an *aspiring* writer. But from what she told me, she didn't get very far."

Deborah knew her too. Richard said so in the car. I guess by the size of this town, everyone knows everyone, and if someone died the way she did, the story would linger. But still, why tell all this to someone who doesn't live here?

"Were you close?" I say. If there's something they want to talk about, I'll let them talk.

Deborah shrugs. "We know the Levientos. Spaniards don't usually socialise with foreigners, but that family did. They live a few houses down from us, well—the mother does. The father died years ago. So we watched their kids grow up over the years. The son, Sebastian, was engaged to Lisa."

She rolls the wine around in her glass. "I knew Lisa. But not that well. She was British, so we connected on that front, but what would a woman like me have in common with a twenty-two-year-old?"

She almost chuckles, but there is sadness beneath her eyes, and I shift in my seat. This whole situation feels uncomfortable. How much they're telling me about this dead girl, and how much I keep listening. The articles I'd read online flash through my mind. Newly engaged. The alcohol and drugs found in her system when her body washed up. A sudden, unexpected death.

"Did she show any signs?" I probe. "You know ... that she was unstable?'

Deborah meets my eyes and suddenly, the atmosphere shifts again. When she speaks, her tone is dark. "Now why would you ask that?"

I catch my breath. I have no idea why I just asked that. My eyes shift from Deborah to Richard. He's also looking intently at me.

"I," I start, unsure of where my words will take me, "I—"

I have to save myself here, give them a nugget of information. Something that's *true*. I can't afford to lie again. If I'm going to stay in this house, I shouldn't look so damn suspicious. It's InCheck that's making me feel this way. The fact that I'm pretending to be someone I'm not and know that someone is on to me. I just flew across two continents to escape that reality.

I have to tell the truth, even though I'm going to hate it.

"I'm sorry," I say, lowering my eyes. "I guess I'm interested because..." I look down at my fingers. My chipped nails. "I've got a family member with mental health problems."

A truth, kind of.

I keep talking. "Every time I hear something like that, I guess I attach to it. To someone else's story. I think it's because I'm looking for solutions to my own problems. Maybe because I want to fix it or understand more about why people do what they do. Something like that."

It's a vague explanation, but it's painful to say it out loud. Because it's all true. It's why I like InCheck so much, and the thought of being a counsellor. I want to help. But in my case, the one time I really needed to help, I didn't. I did the opposite.

I look up, shift my gaze from Richard to Deborah, their expressions blank. "I didn't mean to sound insensitive."

For a moment, Deborah says nothing, and then her expression softens. "Oh—oh, I'm sorry to hear that. I really am. We understand," she looks towards Richard, placing a hand on his shoulder. "Don't we?"

He nods, gives me a half smile. One that says *I don't talk about feelings.* But there's a hint of gentleness in him, something I can't put my finger on. He's curious, but also holding back. What is it?

"Lisa had problems adapting to life here," Deborah says. "She came over to the house a few times, helped me to buy some clothes online. She told me she and Seb were having relationship problems. But everyone has, don't they? I didn't think it was serious."

She sighs again. "I think she was just lonely."

My eyes move to Richard, who's sitting closer to the table now, focused on the conversation.

"Did you know her?" I ask him.

"Not really," he says brusquely. "I was in the UK most of the time."

There it is again. One moment he's fully invested in the conversation, the next he's completely checked out.

In my mind, Lisa's life spreads like spilled wine on fabric, the liquid seeping into every fibre. Who was she? What did she think about? The questions come one after the other, puzzle pieces scattered, all waiting to be put together.

"Did she have any friends here?" I find myself asking.

"One that I know of," Deborah says, her face pensive. "You've spoken to him. Greg, from the academy."

Immediately, I recall the man on the other end of the line during my interview. How tense he sounded, like he didn't want me or anyone else to get this job.

"Anyway," Deborah says, "They were pretty close. *Too* close, if you know what I mean."

"No," I say. "What do you mean?"

There's a glimmer of something in her eyes, but I'm not sure what. Disgust?

"He fancied her," she says. "Flirted with her quite a bit."

Richard's looking at Deborah like she's spat in his beer. It bothers him that she said that. But why? Oblivious, Deborah keeps talking. "It's all so sad, really. For someone so young to take her own life. It's a real tragedy."

The words pierce the air, like someone's cranked the volume up too high. There's a tremor inside me. But I shift my attention back to Greg. Another puzzle piece. My first class at the academy is in two days, which means I'll get to meet him.

"But enough about that," Deborah says, draining her glass. "I'm going to bed. I've had way too much for a school night."

She gets up from her chair and I check the clock on the oven. It's just past nine. I've got some time before my call with Fred on InCheck. Wanting to go back to my room, I say, "Me too."

I help them clear the plates, offering to do the dishes as a thanks for dinner. As I clean, Richard gives us a quick goodbye and retires to the study, barely looking up from his phone.

"Always burning the midnight oil," Deborah says, her elbows leaning on the island counter. "Even when he's trying to cut back on work. He practically lives in that study."

When I'm done washing the dishes, Deborah walks with me up the stairs, stopping just short of my bedroom door. After we've said goodnight, she closes the door behind her. It feels like I'm being put to bed.

She doesn't trust me alone in her house yet. I sense that. But as I sit on the bed and open InCheck, I can't blame her. People lie all the time.

Especially me.

* * *

"Tell me about your day."

My voice sounds croaky. Not at all like how Alice usually sounds. How *I* usually sound. I'm on the floor and leaning against the bed, hoping it muffles the sound of our conversation. I can't tell if Deborah and Richard are asleep, but I'm hoping they are.

If Fred notices anything different, he doesn't say.

"My day started off okay," he answers. "But then we went to this brunch. And that's when it kicked off, really. Have you ever been to Dubai?"

His question catches me off guard. He's never asked about Alice before. I will my voice to come out older, more professional. "No, tell me about it."

"Well, here we have these crazy brunches. Nothing like you know it," he says, and I imagine him sitting upright, like he's telling a story to his friends. "It starts around midday. Hours of unlimited booze and food. Since the country can't serve alcohol in normal restaurants, it's usually in a hotel."

"Sounds lavish," the Alice in me responds. But on the inside, I'm like a monkey with banging cymbals. My body is tired, hazing my thoughts and slurring my words. I shake my arms to stay awake. Refocus on Fred.

"Yeah, it's great though. Anyways, that's where it started," he says. "We were a big group, so at some point, I was sitting next to this prick—sorry."

"No problem."

"He started going on about reincarnation. You know, the idea that when you die, you come back again? So he was saying that when that happens, he wants to come back as a bird. But not any bird. He wants to be an eagle."

"Did he say why?"

"He wants to be the hunter, not the hunted," Fred says. "And also, he wants to fly. Be free and all that shit."

"And what do you think of that?"

A hesitation, then his voice comes out thinner, higher. "When he said that, I… I didn't like it."

Fred's breathing is strained. I keep my cadence gentle. "Tell me why."

A deep inhalation. "Because, I kept thinking, sitting there, while everyone was getting sloshed on cocktails, how much I didn't want to come back as an animal. Imagine," the breaths ripple through the phone, his voice cracking between words. "Imagine coming back a worm. Or a *pig*. And getting fried, I just …"

"Fred."

He's spiralling, the thoughts digging a hole for him.

"Fred, can you breathe for me?"

He breathes in. "In for four," I say, but his breathing is jagged, like he's running down a bumpy road. "Let's go again," I say.

He tries, but his lungs are straining, sending out great gusts. I hear a thud. His hand against a table.

"This will pass," I say.

Finally, his breathing slows.

"I'm here. Just keep going."

And then a groan. Deep, agonising.

"Still here," I say.

Silence. Softer breathing. *You can do this*, I silently encourage him. *We've done this before.*

Fred's been down here before. In this pit. Within the midst of his panic attacks, trying to manoeuvre through the dark to the light at the end of the tunnel. Which never seems to come until it does.

"You're coming down from it," I say. "I can hear it. And your heart rate is slowing. Your muscles are relaxing. It's going to be okay."

I read somewhere that visualising the body's movements helps. As if seeing it will help you climb out of the deepest part of yourself. See it for what it is. Your body reacting to terror.

I imagine Fred with his head between his knees.

"Almost there," I say. "Just keep breathing."

When I hear him give a sigh, I speak again. "Do you want to talk through that?"

And then I hear it. The small whimper. The released tension. He cries like a child. I keep the phone by my ear, focus my eyes on the corner of the room. It's his moment, his space. So I make myself scarce until he invites me back in.

"It's so weird how that happens," Fred says, sniffing.

"It is."

"It's like, I know it's coming now, but I also know it'll end."

"That's right."

"I just can't get used to how fast it came. I mean, we weren't even on the phone for what, two minutes?"

"Your body knows when it is safe to release and break down. Has this ever happened when you were out in public?"

Another sniff. "No."

"There you go."

"Well," he says, a half-hearted chuckle hanging from his words. "I guess that means I feel safe with you."

"I hope you do."

The real me wants to jump through the phone and be there with him. Tell him he's not alone.

"Thanks," he says. "Look, I need to go."

"If you'd like, we can talk about it more this week," I offer. "If you feel ready."

"I'll let you know."

His voice is clipped, detached from the conversation and what just happened here. It's what Fred does. Compartmentalise.

"Whenever you want," I say.

We hang up and I drop down onto the bed, burying my head in the sheets. He got through that quicker than the last time. And yet, there's no getting used to hearing another person go through hell on the other end of the line. Keeping calm. Hearing the anguish as their bodies attack. Sending signals of mortality.

A never-ending cycle of existential terror.

My mind propels me back to what Deborah said about Lisa.

For someone so young to take her own life. It's a real tragedy.

It spins around and around in my head. The questions come in quick succession. *Who were you before you weren't anymore? What drove you to do it?*

And then I think of my father.

Just me and him. Here, in this room. I shift my face to the side, eyeing the corner of the room. And there he is. Motionless, like always.

But I remind myself that he's not there. Because he's not anywhere, anymore. And then I recoil, pulling the covers from all sides over and around me.

Like a cocoon. Hidden. Safe.

CHAPTER 16:

LISA

Six Months Ago

It's been two days since I met Seb's sister, Ana.

Two days since I called her mother insufferable and shared a cigarette with her. It's also been two days since Seb's been home from the hospital, only coming back for a change of clothes or to catch a few hours of sleep.

After Alma's surgery, Seb and Ana remained at their mother's side, working on their laptops in the cafeteria while she was sleeping. Any outsider would think they were strangers. The distance between them, the stilted conversation. Even in their family home, their paths rarely cross.

The whole thing feels awkward, unnatural.

Now, I'm standing outside a house I don't know, hoping for some type of normal. It's built in the same style as the rest of the houses on the street. Wooden front door, large bay window. The walls are freshly painted, giving a feeling of newness.

The door opens. It's a woman with dark chestnut hair, her bosom hidden beneath a dark green sweater. It looks bulky, making her look bigger than she is.

"Hello!" It's a surprisingly deep voice, with a lilt. "So sorry, my hands were a bit full."

She's holding two sweaters in one hand, seemingly shapeless like the one she's wearing. *I like her already.*

"Welcome back," Ana says. "My mother said you were on a trip?"

The woman shuffles her feet, moving the skewed doormat into place. "Yes, I only got back from the UK this morning."

Her accent is thick. Probably from up north.

"How are you? I didn't know you'd be in town," she continues, her eyes moving from Ana to me and back again. Ana's hand grazes my shoulder. "This is Lisa, by the way."

I step forward. "Nice to meet you."

"Oh, lovely to meet you! Please, call me Deb."

She extends her free hand. "Come in."

As we move past her, I can smell her floral scent. The house is open, a direct contrast to Ana and Seb's down the road. There's no division between the kitchen and the living space, with light wooden floors. The stairs are wooden, with a modern glass railing.

Everything screams 'new'.

"Have you heard from my brother recently?" Ana says.

Deb frowns. "Not a peep. Why?"

Ana fidgets. "My mother had a fall a few days ago. She's in the hospital."

Deb's eyes widen, and she brings a hand to her mouth. "Oh my—that is, oh my."

"She's fine now," Ana continues hastily. "She had a hip surgery."

"Oh my. She broke her hip?"

"She's in recovery. We'll be able to bring her home soon."

"Please send her my regards. I'll visit her once she's home. Is there anything I can do?"

Ana opens her mouth, looks in my direction before closing it again. She shakes her head. "No, it's fine. I just wanted to introduce you to Lisa."

Deb and I lock eyes. She smiles. "So glad you did. Come, I'll put the kettle on."

"I need to go back to the hospital," Ana says, her feet anchored to the ground.

"Of course," Deb says. "And you, Lisa? Staying for a cup of tea?"

I think of going back to that hospital. Surrounded by fingers typing away on keyboards.

"Yes," I say, "If that's all right."

As Ana drives away, Deb pours boiling water into two empty cups and adds tea bags. Handing me a cup, I cradle the warmth, letting out a small sigh of relief.

Home. As close as it gets.

Deb sits down across the island. "It's terrible what happened to Alma. Did you see it?"

I shake my head. "No, we just heard the fall. Seb found her at the foot of the stairs."

"Just awful."

My eyes drift to a packet of Sainsbury cookies on the counter. My stomach yearns for them. Triple Belgian Chocolate. The same ones I used to virtually inhale when Eleanor wasn't home.

"I see you've spotted the good stuff," Deb says, pulling the biscuits closer. "I never leave the UK without them."

"Where are you from?" I ask.

"Manchester. You're from London, aren't you? Originally?"

"Yes," I say, cookie crumbs falling onto my lap. She takes one too, gobbling it down.

"They're good, aren't they? Can't find anything similar around here."

I wipe my mouth with the back of my hand. "I haven't really looked for any since I got here. The supermarkets scare me, to be honest."

"They can be intimidating. But we're not in Spain to have British food, are we?" she says with a deep chuckle.

I let out a half-hearted laugh. "True."

"How are you getting on here?"

The question is vast, expanding throughout the room. I don't know where to start, so I focus on something tangible. "The language is hard. I'm having a tough time understanding it."

"I've given up," she waves her hand in the air. "Learnt the basics just to get by. But that's about it. I'm sure you'll catch on. Seb can teach you."

I nod, taking a sip of tea. The warm liquid runs through my body.

"How long are you here for?"

"I have no idea," I say truthfully. "We're only supposed to visit for a few weeks. Seb would see his mum and I'd try to do some..." the words trail off. "Some writing."

I feel my cheeks flush.

"A writer, are you," she says, sitting back. I wait to hear some joke about writers, but it doesn't come.

"Well go on then, what are you writing?"

"I haven't started yet," I say, a tremor in my voice. "But I've always wanted to write a novel."

She doesn't ask me what type. And since I don't know, I'm grateful.

"But so far, I've got no clue," I say. "There's been a lot of adjusting and now with Seb's mum—"

"That poor woman. And at her age, too."

Deb looks concerned. But her expression tells me she's exchanged as many words with Alma as I have.

"So that's that. Now I'm not sure how long we'll be here. Or where we'll go next."

"Are you thinking of moving here permanently?" she says. From this angle, the sun hits the side of her face, casting light on her sunspots.

"Oh no, no," the words tumble out before I can stop it. "It's never been a discussion point. I always figured we'd go back to the UK or someplace else. Barcelona, maybe. I don't know, just somewhere else."

As I say the words, I realise how stupid I sound. I look at Deb and imagine her thoughts. *This woman doesn't talk to her fiancé. She's got no clue.*

It's a good thing Eleanor isn't here to see it. The conversation, or the cookies.

"Plus, I'll want to start work soon. I'd imagine we'd look at a bigger city."

If Deb doubts me, she doesn't show it. "Well, it's better that way. There's not much happening here," she says. "Unless you have your own things to keep you busy."

"I've gone a bit crazy," I say, lowering my voice. "Doing nothing."

Deb looks up at the clock. "Tell you what, how about we turn this into a boozy lunch? I could do with a cheeky glass of wine."

The corners of my mouth lift in a smile.

Wine's become a constant these days. A companion. But it's no match for the real thing. Genuine conversation. I think of Ruth, the nights out with her drama friends. Of Seb, the two of us high on love and drunk on beer. I've missed that feeling of connection. Of letting go and just talking.

So when I respond, I try to hide the flood of joy seeping into my words. "I would love that."

Deb pulls a bottle of white wine out of the fridge. As she pours, I feel myself relax. I take a wine glass, feeling more comfortable than I have in weeks.

She clinks her glass against mine. "Now, tell me all about you and—"

A ding. From her handbag. And then another. *Di-di-ding*. Almost jubilant. *Di-di-ding*.

"Hold on," she says.

She pulls her bag closer, fiddling for the phone. Her body slouches as she types away, eyes focused. I glance around the room. The grey sofa in the corner, the row of books below the TV. The rug parallel to the wooden dining table, piled high with papers. It feels inviting, chic like a showroom, yet personal and cosy. The smell of tea and cookies lingers in the air.

Deb puts the phone on the counter and lifts her glass to her mouth.

"Everything alright?" I ask.

"Just my husband. Checking in." She crinkles her eyes like she's conspiring with me.

"Where is he?" I say, realising it's just her in the house.

"In the UK," she says. "But he'll be back next week. I'll introduce you two then."

CHAPTER 17:

CAT

Present Day

There's a dull pounding in my head as I shower, the aftermath of overthinking. About InCheck and the Instagram message. About my new host family. Their lack of interest in each other, but their big interest in the dead girl, Lisa. All these thoughts collide in my mind, tangling like a knot of thick hair.

As I get dressed and head down the stairs, the morning sun welcomes me through the bay window, its rays beaming down on the ocean outside.

A great day for a fresh start.

"Good morning," Deborah says. She's got a hand to her ear, adjusting her jewellery, radiating a fresh cloud of floral perfume. She's wearing a dark print dress with a brown leather belt. Chic.

"Hi," I say. "Are you going somewhere?"

"Into the office. Meeting a client."

Her handbag is on the kitchen island, with a notebook and wallet. "Do you need anything from me today?"

I shake my head. "I'm just going into town. To look around."

"You can try one of the hiking trails," she says, walking towards the shelf under the TV. She picks up a well-worn map. "There are multiple routes you can follow. The blue one is closest to our house."

I eye the map, with the routes spiralling out from the centre of town like a spider web. She jabs her finger where the house is. I take the map from her, and she places her notebook and wallet in her handbag and walks towards the back door. "If you need anything, just give me a ring," she says. "Richard is around all day."

All day.

I picture him yesterday, his arm hanging out of the car window, his expression stern. At dinner, gripping his beer like it was his only friend. Detached. Uninterested.

He's a teddy bear once you get to know him.

"Sure," I say. "Thanks. And good luck with your meeting."

Once Deborah's gone, I brew a pot of coffee. I walk to the bay window and stare out at the ocean. A few minutes pass. I could sink into the view. Nature has a way of making time stop.

But today, I plan to do more than just look out this window. I have a day off to enjoy the town before I'm expected at the academy. Walking over to the couch, I open my phone to find a WhatsApp notification. Before I can read it, there's a commotion behind me. I whirl around.

"Sorry," Richard mutters, standing by an open kitchen drawer, the cutlery still rattling.

"Didn't see you there," I say.

"People rarely do."

I return his curt smile. From the fridge, he grabs a tub of yogurt and plants a spoon into it.

"I made some coffee," I say. "Freshly brewed."

He takes a spoonful of yogurt. "Already had a cup, thanks."

For a moment we're quiet, and I wonder how we made it through a four-hour car drive without things getting this awkward.

"I'll be in the study," he says, turning on his heels, little yogurt tub in hand.

And just like that, he's gone again.

I exhale. What is it that's changed? When he picked me up from the airport he seemed so laid-back. A normal guy. But in his house, with his wife, something feels wrong. Like he doesn't belong amongst his own things. Plus, his constant references to Lisa have my brain going in circles.

I take a sip of coffee and shift my attention back to the WhatsApp message.

I open the chat, read the message, and press the call icon. She picks up on the third ring.

"I see you got my message," she says.

"Hi mom," I say, crossing my legs.

"Thanks for calling me back. Are you safe?"

"Yes, very safe."

"Good," she says.

But it's not good. The last couple of years haven't been good between us at all. It's been a world of eggshells, populated by two inhabitants who don't know how to navigate it.

"I honestly don't know where to begin," she says.

I sigh. "Me neither."

Ever since her divorce from my father, my mother has been a shadow of her former self. It's as if a cookie-cutter sliced her in half and kept the agitated, bitter half and discarded the warm, hopeful woman I once knew.

"I'm doing fine, mom. There's nothing to worry about." I add. "This job is just for six months."

"You could have told me. For God's sake, I don't even know where you're staying. Where *are* you staying?"

"I'll send you my location after this call."

"I mean—yes, okay. But Cat, *Spain*? You could have at least told me. You could have let me and David talk—"

"What does David have to do with this?"

"David is my husband," she says, her voice clipped.

"Yes. You don't need to remind me."

"You're being reckless, Cat."

And so it begins.

I hold my breath and sink deeper into the couch.

"Telling me you're going to Spain over a *voice note*. Running away like this—it's typical Cat behaviour."

"Thanks for the observation."

"Can you stop being childish for one second?" she almost shouts. "You're being just like him."

98

There, she's said it. It's always there, so easy for her to grasp at.

"You love saying that," I remind her.

She breathes through the phone. Then, a more hesitant voice. "I, I don't mean it like that."

And despite everything in me wanting to hate her for it, I don't.

"I know," I say.

Another few beats pass, a game of chicken between us.

"I have one favour to ask," she says. "Please tell me you'll consider it."

I wait for her to continue, bracing myself.

"Please consider going back on something. Just as a stabiliser."

My jaw tightens. My mother, the believer in modern medicine. *There's a pill for everything.*

My words are blunt. "I don't need medication."

"I really think you do," she says. "It's just chemical. You need something to balance you out. You're making rash decisions. Not thinking straight."

Her tone is calm, like a doctor delivering the news that my brain isn't wired right.

"I don't agree," I say. "I'm doing fine without it. All it does is make me feel like a zombie." As I speak, there's a voice in my head telling me to stop, to give up this battle with her. *It's not worth it.* It's not worth it because she never listens to anything I say.

"Cat," my mother continues. "How is taking meds different from drowning out the noise with wine?"

"I don't drink anymore."

"For how long?"

Silence. I should shout back at her that it's been six months since I've had a drink. Then I remember her last marriage was to a man who also stopped drinking, only to start again a few months later. My father was a human yoyo like that.

"I should go," I say, ready to forget this conversation already.

"Okay," she sighs. A sigh I know all too well. "But before you go, please can you tell me more about where you are?"

"I told you I'd send you my location."

"In your own words, please. Just so I can hear that you're safe."

So I tell her. I tell her of the flight here, the car ride through the landscapes. The classes I start teaching tomorrow. I tell her about everything except the British girl who died here, and my dead father I keep seeing in the corner of my bedroom.

No amount of pills can take that last image away.

"I'll call you soon," I say.

We hang up and the moments tick by, flashbacks of this same fight, over and over again in my head. My mother and I fight—throw words at each other we don't mean—because we hate being here. But we've been here for years. And neither of us knows how to get out.

I send her my location, as promised. Seconds later, there's a message from her. *I love you. I'm sorry for saying that again.*

My heart grabs at it. But my eyes focus on the word *again*.

She's always sorry, but it's the one card she loves to play. Like any vice, she knows it's wrong. But she can't stop doing it.

I grab the map, study the blue route. Stepping outside the house, the wind gusts across the water. Everything smells different here. Feels different. The blue route is furthest from the ocean, leading me up the hill to a viewing point, then back down to town. Twigs break beneath my feet, and birds chirp overhead. I listen to nothing and everything, the sound of nature seeping into my bones.

But the voice in my head keeps calling. *Soon this will turn dark too.*

In town, I order a juice at a cafe. I snack on the free bread basket as I read over my curriculum papers. In between bites, I watch the pretty brunette serving tables around me. When she walks by, my eyes inadvertently drop to her breasts, soft and sun-kissed beneath her blouse.

It's been so long.

Walking back to the house, I look towards the cluster of trees, the dock behind them. I walk closer, then step out onto the wooden structure, the waters calm beneath me. When I'm at the edge, I look down, a whiff of ocean breeze playing in my nostrils.

It's a long drop. You'd need to be brave to jump.

I wonder what Lisa thought about, standing out here.

And then my mother's words are in my ears. *You're being just like him.*

I close my eyes and try to picture my father, piecing together the fragments that made up his face. I remember his smile, the smell of his aftershave, the way he would call to me. The softness in his voice.

A lump forms in my throat. *Not here. Please, not here.*

I walk back to the house, spotting the bay window dark against the sunlight. The shutters are drawn on the smaller window, the one to the right of the front door. The study, no doubt. Where Richard works or is probably *still* working.

Inside the house, it's quiet, like I never left. I head upstairs, grab for my phone, and log in to InCheck. There are no messages, no requests for calls. But to get my father out of my head, I scroll through my previous messages. All the times I've given advice, lend an ear. Just been there for someone.

And for a moment, I don't feel like such a monster.

CHAPTER 18:

LISA

Six Months Ago

"Hola chicos!"

The teacher grins. I look around the classroom and notice there are only three of us—a Brit with lanky hair, a Filipino woman, and me, wondering what I'm doing here.

"¿Que tal?" the teacher says, and I shrink in my seat.

It was Seb who suggested I take Spanish classes. He brought it up over dinner two days ago. It was the same day I came back from visiting Deb—drunk from the wine we had, feeling young and free. There wasn't a thing in the world that could knock me off my feet.

Until I got home that night.

I went through different stages of wanting to learn Spanish—from a definite yes to a resounding no. But Seb's suggestion wasn't the weirdest thing that happened that night. The memory still rages in my head like an ulcer. Irritating. Constantly there.

* * *

Deb promised the third bottle would be our last. As I walked home, legs like jelly, I kept thinking that if she offered a fourth, I'd have said yes.

The air felt less suffocating. It was the booze talking, and I knew it. But I welcomed it anyway. From the street, the house was dark. I fiddled with the key in the lock, taking off my shoes in the foyer. If I was lucky, Seb and Ana would only be back from the hospital later, giving me time to freshen up.

But as I climbed the stairs, it hit me. It wasn't quiet in the house.

There was a gentle chatter in the background, like someone had left the TV on. *It's the booze*, I told myself, hand firmly on the banister. I stood on the landing, listening. For a moment the sound was gone, and I shook my head. My vision was blurry, the hallway coming in and out of focus. *It's nothing. You're drunk.*

But the sound returned, and with it a new realisation. I was hearing voices. Hushed and faint, but real.

Did I see a car out front? Was someone already home from the hospital?

I walked towards the sound, my heart racing, the blood rushing through my body.

It's Seb's voice. At the end of the hallway. In Alma's bedroom. He was probably getting her a change of clothes, but who was he talking to? And his voice sounded strange. *Strained.* The frustration hung from his staccato words.

I edged closer to the bedroom door.

This is stupid. Just call out to him.

But my body didn't listen. The bored little girl from my childhood inside was in charge, playing house. Seb's voice blurted out again, a sense of urgency rippling through the room.

"Por favor," he said, and I pressed my ear to the wall, willing my breathing to stop. I heard a woman's voice. *Ana.* Her words falling over each other.

And then a bang. Like objects colliding.

My heart wanted to jump out of my ribcage. I tiptoed back down the hallway. Whatever they were discussing, I wasn't going to ambush them with my presence right there in the doorway. When I stopped shaking, I stomped my feet on the landing and called out. "Hello?"

Silence, followed by rushed footsteps.

I turned on the light switch by the stairs and their faces came into view. Brother and sister, on the landing.

"Lisa!" Seb walked closer to me. "You're back."

"We didn't hear you," Ana said from behind him. He planted a kiss on my cheek, the stubble grazing my skin. I tried looking at Ana, but his frame blocked her face. My head continued to spin.

"We thought you were still at Deb's," Seb said.

"Why are you in the dark?"

"We came to get something from upstairs," he said.

"In the dark?"

"We wanted to be quick."

"Let's go downstairs," Ana called from behind her brother. "It is too dark up here."

We made our way down the hallway, Ana switching on the lights, bringing everything into focus. My eyes had to adjust to the bright light. I spoke slowly, trying not to slur as I told them about my afternoon with Deb.

Soon, Ana returned to the hospital, leaving in a rush. Seb asked me if I'd eaten. We left the lights on in the house, heading to the tavern down the road for dinner.

"Is everything okay?" I asked him. He ate his meatballs almost ferociously, hardly taking a breath.

He responded between bites. "Yes. Why?"

I didn't know what was bothering me. It could have been the hangover forming, making me paranoid. But something about his voice back at the house—the frustration and urgency of it. It wasn't right.

"Did you and Ana have a fight?"

He shook his head, took another bite of meatball. "She needed to get some clothes for my mom. And I came to find you."

I stared at his hand, suddenly noticing his knuckles. They were angry red, the skin irritated. *The bang.*

"But she seemed upset," I said. "Ana."

"That's just how she is."

I frowned. That couldn't be true. In the short time that I'd known her, Ana was rarely upset. She didn't seem like the type. As if sensing my disbelief, Seb continued talking. "I told you—we don't get along. That's all."

"So it *was* an argument."

"Kind of."

I sighed. "What about?"

He broke off a piece of baguette, dunked it in the sauce. "Ana and I don't see eye to eye on a lot of things, especially when it comes to our mother."

I sat silently, waiting for him to continue.

"She's never around, but when she is, she tries to control everything."

You're never around either, I thought, remembering our time in the UK together. A time that felt so far away now.

"Was the argument about your mother?" I asked.

He nodded. "About who will look after her when we bring her home. Ana wants to stay, but I said I should."

"For how long?"

"A month or so."

Or so.

I placed my hands on my temples, elbows on the table, a headache roaring. Through jagged breaths, my mother chimed in my head. *Be a good wife. Be a good wife. Be a good wife.*

"I know it's longer than you expected to stay here," Seb said. "But you can have more time to work on your book. And it'll give me some time to take care of business at the vineyard. Which means we'll have more time to spend together when we leave to go somewhere. Wherever we decide."

A sharp pang shot through my stomach. A remembrance. *The book.* The one I told myself I'd write with all this time that I now had.

"I've barely written a few words," I told him, knowing how pathetic I sounded. "I don't even have a story yet."

"Maybe take the pressure off?" Seb said. "The idea will come to you. Find something else in the meantime to take your mind off it."

And that's when he suggested Spanish classes.

* * *

The Spanish teacher takes us through the basics. Introduce ourselves. Ask how someone is. Her smile is big, but it feels empty. I try to remind myself that this is better than being back at that house. Staring at the blank laptop screen. The class is extensive, and by the end of it, my notebook is filled with words.

"First time taking Spanish?" the Brit asks me, flinging his backpack across his shoulder. During class he was taking notes furiously, his pale skin turning red when asked to read a passage aloud.

"Is it that obvious?" I say, glancing around.

"You did pretty well. But I guess it's just the start."

"Lord help us all then."

He laughs, runs his hand through his auburn hair. It's long and wavy on top. His eyes are hazel and something flickers inside of me. They're like *your* eyes.

"Do you fancy getting a beer?" he asks as we leave the building. I think of walking back home in the cold, to a house full of commotion. Seb and Ana scurrying around, preparing the house for Alma's return.

And despite my mother's probable advice, I look into his eyes again. "Sure, why not."

We head to a bar down the road, taking a table inside. The wooden chairs creak as we sit down and fling our coats beside us.

"Do you live close to here?" I ask.

"Oh no, I live about two bus rides down. In Vallican."

He doesn't look like you. His jaw is less pronounced, his nose much broader. And he's got freckles.

But the eyes.

I shake my head. "I don't know where that is. I haven't seen much, to be honest. I'm a ten-minute walk from here, in Galicio, apparently."

"Nice, that's a pretty area," he says. "Right by the water. Are you an English teacher?"

"No, I'm not."

He opens his mouth like he's about to ask me what I do. But then the beers arrive and I feel relief.

"Do you teach English then?" I say, steering the conversation back to him.

"Yep," he says, taking a sip of beer. "Moved here a week ago. I'll be teaching English up in town in a month and need to work on my Spanish before then."

"That's a challenge," I say. "Teaching while being taught."

"It gets easier. I was in Lithuania before, and languages follow a similar teaching structure. Think of the class we just had. How many times did the teacher speak to us in English?"

I think back. "Almost never."

"Exactly," he says. "You don't need to be an expert to teach a language."

His voice is deep, sure of itself.

"You like it," I say.

He smiles and leans back in his chair. "I do. I like the change of it."

There are potato crisps on the table. I take a few.

"I'm not very good with change," I say, my eyes downcast.

"Well, you're away from home, aren't you? That's a step."

Glasses clink in the background, the bartender bringing in a load of freshly washed glassware. I think of Deb—of last week—how the wine smoothed our edges.

"Can I tell you something?" I'd said to her in a whisper. She'd raised an eyebrow, leaned closer to me over the island counter. "What?"

I'd looked around, as if making sure that we were alone. The words were barely audible. "I don't think I'll ever get used to this place."

"It's not really like that," I say to the Brit now.

I tell him why I'm here. Newly engaged with the hope of a rewarding marriage—bewildered and alienated by the language and the people. A story that screams how sorry I feel for myself. Eleanor would be appalled.

When I'm done, his arms are crossed, his face in contemplation. He sips his second beer, then places his elbows on the table.

"I once heard a story," he says. "I don't know exactly how it goes, but it's something like this. Imagine you've booked a ticket to Italy. You're pretty excited to visit. So for a month, you're looking forward to it. You pack, get on the plane and pace yourself for the landing. But when you get off the plane, you're in Holland."

He moves his fingers over the table. "You can either be sad about the fact that you're not in Italy, or realise you're in Holland."

I raise an eyebrow. "So, Spain is Holland?"

"Holland is your whole situation. You can be sad. But also, Holland is pretty great. Why not enjoy it while it lasts?"

My mind propels me back to last week, to Deb's house, to where she asked me a question I wasn't prepared for.

"Why are you staying?" she'd asked.

At the time, I caught hold of the only sensible words. "For Seb. Because he's my fiancé. I don't have a choice."

"There's always a choice, love," Deb had said, casting her eyes out the bay window.

I had thought about what she'd said, wobbling home after we'd said our goodbyes. And sitting here, in this bar, with this man with eyes like yours, I think of it again. We have choices. Or rather, we believe we do. But not everyone does. I definitely don't.

Eleanor's words sound in my head again. *We're trusting you here, Lisa.*

If I leave now, go back to comfort and security of the UK, what would I be losing? My marriage. My family's approval, and our hold on stability. I picture Eleanor's face in the coffee shop before I left for Spain—a look of disdain and worry. A fear of something. *Shame. More shame.*

"I'll need to make this my Holland, then," I say now, new conviction bubbling to the surface.

The Brit smiles. "That's the spirit."

As we leave the bar, I pull my coat closer to me, the wind sweeping in.

"This was fun," he says. "We should make this a weekly thing. I'll see you Thursday?"

"Definitely."

He smiles and turns toward the bus stop up the street. But as he walks, something flickers in my mind.

"Hey!"

He turns, his face open.

"Sorry," I say, the heat flushing my face. "But I completely forgot your name."

There's a grin, and beneath it, there's that hint of *you*.

"Greg," he says. "My name's Greg."

CHAPTER 19:

CAT

Present Day

The academy is small, the blocky exterior not giving anything away. Climbing the stairs, there's an A4 paper with a bright red arrow pointing to the left.

Gexta English Academy, it reads.

There's a girl behind a wooden desk, her chestnut ponytail high on her head. When she sees me, she jumps up. "Cat?"

I didn't know I was expected. "Yes, that's me," I say. "And your name is?"

"Charlotte," the girl responds. She looks young, but as she steps away from the desk to shake my hand, I see why. She's a foot shorter and her entire royal blue dress can fit around one of my thighs.

"Nice to meet you," I say.

She smiles, her teeth crooked and her makeup thick, eyes peering out from caked mascara. "Come with me."

We walk down the carpeted corridor, her ponytail swinging from side to side. *Swish, swish, swish.*

We pass glass cubicles, each with a printed A4 sheet with a name on it. Manchester, Birmingham, Leeds, London. She leads me into the Liverpool room, where charts and phrases of the English language line the walls. The room smells stale, but there's a coffee machine in the corner and my mouth goes dry.

"Do you mind?" I ask.

"It's not very good," she says, shaking her head. "But feel free."

I fiddle for coins buried in my bag, the product of a cash withdrawal and an expensive sandwich at the airport. I feel her eyes on me as I watch the coffee drip into the paper cup. When I turn, there's a new face at the door.

He's tall with dark stubble lining his chin. His hair is thick, a wave curtaining his eyebrow. His dark grey jeans and navy sweater make him look older, like a figure of authority.

"You must be Cat."

He motions me to a plastic chair, pulling one closer. As he puts a pile of books and papers on the table, I think of Sam. Of how she could teach him a thing or two about organisation.

You need a binder, dude.

"Welcome to Spain," he says. "I hear you got in a few days ago."

"Fresh off the boat and happy to be here," I say, giving my best smile. He turns his attention to the papers, shuffling through them. "Did you fly in from Cape Town?"

Charlotte's standing with her hands folded like she's about to take our order. "Johannesburg," I say.

"Nice," he says, like he just scored a goal on FIFA. "I've always wanted to go to South Africa. I'm Greg, by the way."

Somehow, I must have known he would be. But the man who conducted my interview doesn't reflect the guy sitting across from me. He seems more awkward in person. But friendlier. Maybe he was having a bad day when we had our call.

And for a second I realise who I'm meeting. It's not just Greg, my interviewer, my colleague. It's *Lisa's* Greg.

Curiosity boils inside me, my ears buzzing as he tells me about the academy, the British curriculum, all the things I already know from the material I read online. But I don't want to talk about any of this.

I want to talk about Lisa. Even though I know it's a bad idea.

"Are you the core team?" I ask.

"Basically," Greg says. "We're small and only teach a few classes. Mostly to people living outside Bilbao looking to practise some English."

"Any specific age groups?"

He shrugs. "Working class. People in their twenties to fifties, really." There's something attractive about him, and I wonder if Lisa saw it too.

"Anyways, Charlotte will take you through the course material today and then you can start sitting in on classes tomorrow."

"Sorry, sitting in?" I ask, confused.

He raises his eyebrows. "Yeah, sitting in. You'll watch us teach before giving it a go yourself."

The way he says *giving it a go* sounds like I'm in kindergarten, about to throw a frisbee for the first time. But it's his turf, so I go along with it. "Whatever works best."

My instincts want more information. More dirt. I take a sip of coffee to bide the time. "Are there any gatherings for new members?"

Silence. Charlotte stares at Greg, not meeting my gaze as I look from her to him. *Weird crowd.*

"You mean—like what?" Greg asks.

"Like get togethers. Drinks after work. That sort of thing."

I'm fully aware that I won't be having a drink, but if I'm going to be working with these people, I should at least get to know them better. Over a juice, or something.

Plus—and again, I know I shouldn't—but I want to know more about Greg.

He scratches his chin. "We haven't really had a lot of outings. It's just me and Charlotte. We're a small team."

I try to smooth the edges of the conversation. "It would be great to grab a drink after work sometime. If you guys are up for it?"

"We went to San Sebastian once. You should visit," Charlotte says brightly, but as soon as the words are out she steps back, like a frightened bird.

Weird, weird crowd.

"I'd love to," I say, looking back at Greg. My mind weighs my next words, decides to let it out. "There's a nice place by the water where I'm staying. In Galicio."

There's a flicker of something, a change in his face. He knows where I live.

Who I live with. The paperwork shared by the academy before I arrived here shows as much. Which means he probably knows that I know about Lisa.

But he gives nothing away.

"There's a bar around here," he says. "We can go there one of these days."

I smile, but something tells me Greg isn't going to stick to what he says. He leaves Charlotte and me in the Liverpool room, taking his papers with him. The next hour passes quickly, the curriculum familiar. As we move through rules and practices, Charlotte's shoulders relax.

"You seem like you know all of this already," she says.

"I've had some practice. I used to work with a friend who has an academy."

"Well, the pace is much slower here, so you'll be fine."

Questions rise in my throat. I start with the most relevant. "Who can I speak to about my visa?"

Her eyebrows come together, a deep crease of foundation forming. "Your visa?"

"Yeah. I'm on a Schengen right now, but it expires in three months," I say. "My host family told me the academy was working to extend it to six months."

The way she looks at me tells me it's the first she's heard of it. "I'd need to check with the admin team."

She says it like there's more people in the building, but from what I've seen, it's just her and Greg. In a town this small, where everyone seems to know everyone's business, I'm sure that Charlotte knows more than what she's telling me.

Perhaps I'm looking for answers to calm myself. After all, many parts of my life are up in the air right now. InCheck. Family. Career. Somehow, clarifying the specifics around this town, my host family—how Lisa died—makes me feel like I'm in control.

I clear my throat. "My host family also told me about what happened here a few months ago," I say, preparing to ask Charlotte a question I wasn't planning to. "Did you know the girl that drowned?"

She looks battered, like I've hit her across the face. "You mean Lisa?"

"Yes."

Her mouth opens, then closes. Then opens again. "No. I only saw her once, but we never spoke.'

I look at Charlotte's tiny hands. She's picking at her fingernails, flakes of soft pink nail polish falling on her dress. A few seconds later, she's out of her chair, barely making a sound as her tiny feet hit the floor.

"I haven't shown you our canteen yet," she says. "Come, I'll show you where we keep the good tea."

As we walk through the hallway, the swish of Charlotte's dress is accelerated as she moves with determination. My thoughts jump from my visa to Lisa, then back again.

But one thought remains constant.

Something's off. There's something my new colleagues aren't telling me. This morning I felt excited to meet them. But just like Richard and Deborah, they're odd. Holding something back. And if I'm going to stop my anxiety from getting to me in this foreign town, I need to find out what it is.

CHAPTER 20:

LISA

Six Months Ago

"I think I found an idea for my book," I say, smoothing the foundation across my forehead.

"What are you thinking?"

Seb walks into the bathroom and for a moment I feel exposed, my blotchy skin on display. But he takes his cologne and sprays it across his chest without looking at me.

I apply blush to my cheeks. "A romance. About the impact of culture and language on a relationship."

He meets my gaze, blinks a few times. "Say that again?"

I draw a breath, my confidence faltering. "A love story about how language and culture can affect a relationship." I turn the words over in my head, wondering if saying them twice helped.

Seb walks to the bedroom, his voice trailing through the room. "Are you sure it's a novel, babe? It sounds a bit... formal."

I follow him. "They say a book needs a theme. If someone had to ask you what it's about, you should be able to sum it up in a sentence."

His torso is bare, the skin tight with his dark hair forming curves on the canvas.

"But what's it about?" he asks, eyes probing. "You know, like what it says on the back of the book. What do you call it?"

"The blurb."

"Yeah, the blurb."

I bite the inside of my cheek. "It's still a work in progress. But it needs a theme and I think I got that."

"It's definitely progress," he says, grabbing a striped shirt from the wardrobe.

It's the first time we've woken up together in weeks. I stayed in bed until mid-morning, but Seb was up before the sun rose. But this morning feels different. Like there's a purpose to the day. An invisible force willing me to get moving. To write.

Make it your Holland.

"I can use Spain as the setting too," I say. "And the main characters can be from two very unique backgrounds."

"Sounds a bit like us." Seb winks at me and it sends a rush through my body. When last did we touch, and not just share a bed?

"A little," I say. "But we write about what we know. So, for example, you speak fluent English, and that's what we speak to each other. When I met you, I was attracted to your accent. But then when you started speaking Spanish here, it felt completely different to me."

"So what you're saying is, you don't like my Spanish accent after all."

He buttons his shirt, a grin spreading across his face.

"I do," I say. "But you sound like a different person. It's like that night you and Ana were in Alma's room. I didn't even know it was you at first."

The grin disappears from his face. "How long were you standing there?"

"Uhm, not very long."

The silence drags. He grabs his shoes, sitting down on a chair. "You were saying?"

"So," I say. "I think the best love stories have hardships. Not just things like unrequited love or forbidden love, but the everyday things."

Seb ties his shoes, and from this angle he's either frowning or focusing. "Sounds relatable. I'm not sure where you're going with it yet, but I'm sure you'll figure it out."

I perch on the bed. Seb's not wrong. It sounds a lot like us. Greg's anecdote about Holland really got me thinking. Isn't it true that great writing comes from experiencing hardships? If that's the case, then being here—feeling this alienated and alone—is all for a reason. I could write about my doubts and fears. Put them on paper. Make something of it.

Seb walks over and plants a kiss on my head. "I'm going downstairs."

He leaves the room and I take a shower, my thoughts racing through my head. As I get dressed, I picture the setting for my novel. A town on the coast. A honeymoon by the water. A historic villa. The heroine would be bold. Like Ruth. Kind, like Ana. Flawless, like a young Eleanor. She'd look nothing like me.

The hero would be tall, dark, broodingly handsome. Like Seb. Funny and smart. The book could encapsulate my own journey. Hardships overcome and real love found. People would devour it. The critics would call it the best thing they've read in a while.

You might even read the book and curse the day you let me go.

My thoughts are disturbed by a commotion downstairs. Raised voices.

I hurry down the stairs, almost bumping into Ana as I round the corner into the foyer. Her face is hidden behind her hair, a dark wave of chestnut darkening her features. She grabs her coat from the rack, murmurs a basic greeting to me.

I look towards the dining room. Seb's at the table, his arms crossed and his mouth downcast.

"Is everything okay?" I ask.

When I look at Ana, her eyes are red, tears brimming. "Ana, what's—"

"I'll see you later," she mumbles and opens the front door. Before I can say anything more, she slams it behind her and darts towards her car.

"What's going on?" I say to Seb. Despite the urgency in my voice, he's leaning against the chair, his expression plain. "She's overreacting. She'll get over it."

I blink. "She'll *get over it*?"

"Yes. And hopefully leave us in peace."

My mouth hangs open. Seb's demeanour right now reminds me of a rebellious schoolchild.

"Your sister just left the house crying, and *that's* how you respond?"

When he shrugs, I feel the heat rise to my cheeks. "You're behaving like a child."

The way Seb looks at me tells me I've crossed a line.

"It's none of your business," he says, jaw clenched. Getting up, he storms into the kitchen, closing the door behind him. I stand alone, the scene replaying in my head. A memory surfaces—me as a child, crying on the floor of a supermarket. Throwing a full-blown tantrum. Eleanor watching in horror.

This feels strangely similar to that memory.

When it's clear Seb isn't coming out of the kitchen, I sit behind my laptop at the dining toom table, the blank screen staring back at me. Seb's face keeps popping up in my mind. His clenched jaw and crossed arms. A grown man turning into a child. A transformation I didn't think was possible.

I pull a notepad closer, jotting down the ideas I had while I was getting ready this morning. When I get to the main characters, I picture the tall, dark and handsome male protagonist again. The hero has all of Seb's traits. All except for the way he treats his sister.

* * *

"Will I be in your book?" Greg asks, taking a sip of his beer. We came to the bar after class, and his eyes are sparkling more than usual today. So much so that I need to remind myself that it's him and not *you.*

"Maybe," I say. "You could inspire a B plot character."

"I've no idea what that is," he grins. "As long as I'm not the bad guy. And if I am, at least make me a tormented soul."

Greg's funny. He's always cheerful these days, joking with the Spanish teacher. On his first day he was shy, but now he seems comfortable in his skin. But part of his appeal is his ability to talk to you about anything and everything.

"Last week you had no book idea," he says. "And here you are with characters already."

It's like what Seb said this morning. But somehow, Greg's words sound better.

You're just annoyed, I remind myself. Annoyed at Seb's childish behaviour this morning. At seeing that side of him. I don't care if he and Ana aren't close—they're family. And family means everything, doesn't matter what.

"Your hair looks nice today, by the way."

My cheeks tingle at Greg's compliment. "Thanks."

His face changes, like he's amused. "I probably shouldn't be saying this, but you look a lot like my ex."

As he takes another sip of beer, and I hold my breath.

"Uh oh," I laugh, but inside, my heart is climbing out of my ribcage. "What happened?"

"Ah, you know," he says nonchalantly, "Growing apart and going to different unis."

There's a hint of something in the way he presses his lips, as if he's remembering.

"Well, if it's any consolation, you look nothing like my ex," I say. "Which is a good thing."

Which is also a lie.

He lets out a laugh, those pearly whites showing again. "What did the poor bloke do?"

It takes a second, but then I'm back to that day. The breaking of glass, jazz music still blasting from the speakers. The stares. My fingers find my inner thigh and my eyes trail in the direction of the bar's bathroom.

"Forget it," Greg says, picking up on the tension. "You've found your fella now."

I nod, force a smile and plant my face close to my wine glass. Nobody's asked about you in so long. I wasn't ready. I never am.

"I'm going to the loo," Greg says, getting up.

"Another?" I say, motioning to the almost empty drinks.

"Trying to get me tipsy, are you?"

There's that grin again.

"Maybe," I say, the guilt making its way up my throat.

When he leaves, I motion to the waiter and order another round. As I wait, I glance at the iPhone Greg's left on the table. With a quick look around, I pick it up. Tapping at the screen, I see a picture of Greg and two of his friends. Smiling, a pub as the backdrop. I stare at Greg standing between them and smile at how carefree he looks.

A real lad's lad.

The phone prompts me to enter the password. I think of all the different things I might find if his phone was unlocked. Who's he texting? What would be saved on his notes? What would his search history look like?

"Here you go," the waiter says, placing a beer and a wine on the table. I jerk, dropping the phone in my lap. When he walks away, I hurriedly put it back where I found it. Suddenly I'm twelve again, in my aunt's dressing room, looking through her things. Eleanor finding me there, her words like daggers. *You need to stop this snooping. One day it'll get you in real trouble.*

When Greg sits back down, I get up.

"Everything alright?" he asks.

"Fine. Just freshening up," I call as I stride to the restroom.

My fingers find the razor in my bag long before I find an empty cubicle.

CHAPTER 21:

CAT

Present Day

It's been a week since I started at the academy, but I'm no closer to teaching. Between watching Greg and Charlotte do their jobs, I'm more of an assistant than a teacher. It's like they're afraid to let me contribute.

The days have gone by in a blur, each one bleeding into the other. Some nights, it's like I have gauze over my eyes. Deborah and I watch mindless British reality TV while Richard lurks in his study. If he's not in there, he's eyeing me like I'm something stuck to the bottom of his shoe.

I've given up on trying to be his friend.

As I walk back to the house from the academy—from yet another class I just listened in on—there's a message from Susana on InCheck.

I climbed into the cupboard today, it reads. *I just needed some alone time. It feels overbearing, being here with the kids sometimes.*

I shield my eyes from the sun and type a response: *It's normal to take time for yourself. You taking a break could be the best thing for your kids.*

Her response is immediate. *Do you have kids?*

Thoughts run through my head. It's policy not to divulge personal information to clients, but there's another thought there, somewhere deeper.

Maybe she knows you're a fraud.

I shake it off, reminding myself that the app keeps all information confidential. I'm just paranoid, thinking of that Instagram message I got almost a month ago. Since then, the account has been deleted, and I haven't received a similar message.

Turning Susana's question about having a kid over in my mind, I choose a response that feels the safest. I want to be relatable, but not too much.

Yes, I type. *One child.*

Her response comes again: *Have you ever done something like this?*

She's wondering if she's alone in this. If Alice has ever sat in a cupboard while her kid has a tantrum. I doubt she would have—if she were a real, that is— but what I know for sure is that Susana is not alone in her struggle to be a good parent.

"I don't have all the answers, bud," my dad used to tell me. He always called me bud—like a rosebud, or a buddy. Memories flash through my head: the drives around town listening to The Beatles, the ice creams mom never knew about. The countless times other people thought I'd be better off with another father, or none at all.

I start typing a message to Susana.

Yes. I've learned that taking deep breaths helps.

It feels flat, but I send it anyway. No sharing of personal information. As I stand on the corner of the street, I jot down another message to her. *You're a better mother to them than you think,* I type. *They are lucky to have you.*

I have no clue if Susana *is* a good mother. And then again, what makes a good parent? But what I *do* know is that words carry more power than we give them credit for. What you say—or don't say—can bring a lot of joy. Or pain.

Her response appears again: *Thank you. I needed that.*

I crack a smile. It's moments like these I feel less guilty about taking someone else's name on a counselling app. I picture what a real psychologist would have said, how much weight it would carry. How different would it be from what I just said.

My own therapy sessions from years ago float around in my head. Talking, analysing. Talking, analysing.

The fact is, everyone likes to talk. And the more they talk, the more can be thrown back at them to dissect. But sometimes, people need more. They need answers to the fundamental questions that they wrack their brains about. They need to be guided to where they want to go.

The sun's sinking beneath the water now, a soft orange glow staining the sky. It's so beautiful I almost don't see the figure walking towards me. We're on the same pathway, one going up the hill, one going down. He's got a black hoodie on, and his face is downcast, distorted.

But something tells me I already know who he is.

There are only so many people on this street. And they're all older. Deborah and Richard's house is one of the last before you hit the dock.

As his tall frame gets closer, I see the hands in his pockets, the thick hair masking his face. And then, dark-rimmed eyes meeting mine for a second. I try to say hi, but he's already walked past, a whiff of alcohol following in his wake.

That's him, I think. *That's the fiancé.*

I glance back, his hunched form making its way to town. My eyes trail back to the dock. I can picture Lisa standing there. No wonder he keeps his hood over his head. I wouldn't want to see that dock ever again, if I were him.

The house is quiet when I enter. But as I climb the stairs, there's a muffled noise. Deborah's voice. The walls are thin here, and when I'm on the landing, I can hear her clearly.

"I will bloody stretch this out if I want to," she shouts. "I have no problem with it, Richard."

I weigh my options. Either I walk to my room or go back downstairs. But before I can decide, she's shouting again, louder this time.

"You must be out of your *fucking* mind if you think I'll allow that *whore* to live in my house!"

All I can do is stand there, frozen. When my limbs finally decide to move, I edge closer to the stairs. I'm about to take the first step when Deborah's voice comes through again, deeper.

"You've taken everything from me."

My foot slips and I reach for the banister, legs hitting the stairs with a loud thump.

"Hello?" Deborah calls.

Great timing, Cat.

"Who's there?" she calls out again.

I steady myself, rushing downstairs. I stand up straight and roll my ankles, checking for pain but finding none. "Hi," I call, my voice hoarse. "It's me—Cat."

There's a hushed commotion, followed by a friendly shout. "I'll be out in a sec!"

I throw my bag on the couch and sit down. Hearing her footsteps on the stairs, I pull a curriculum book from my bag, paging aimlessly through it.

"Hi," she says, her breathing ragged. "How was class?"

It doesn't take much to see that she's flustered. "Yeah, good." I nod. "How are you?"

"Great," she says, trying to sound casual. She fiddles with her hands, then strolls to the kitchen. Her words from upstairs still sound in my head, and I crane my neck to look down the hallway. The door to the study is closed, like always.

"Is Richard home?" I ask.

"Fuck knows."

I blink at her response. "Sorry?"

"What?"

Deborah's angry tone is soon replaced by one of confusion.

"I was just asking where Richard is," I say, getting up and walking to the island. Deborah's face drops like she's forgotten something. "Oh, h-he's gone for some errands," she says. "I'm sure he'll be back soon."

The silence drags, and I shift my weight from one foot to the other.

"Sorry about that," she croaks, pulling a wine bottle from the fridge. "I was just on the phone with some realtors for our property back in the UK. They really get me wired up."

She shakes her head, lets a small laugh escape. But her lips are trembling, and when she licks them, she looks away.

A lie.

Unless the realtor's name is Richard, I'm pretty sure she was on the phone with her husband. By the look on her face, she's more than wired up. She's depleted, like someone's slapped the life out of her. If she was talking to Richard, it was a fight. A bad one.

A part of me is relieved. If Deborah and Richard are having problems, then that would explain their weird chemistry. The thing I can't quite put my finger on. But what was she talking about on the phone—about the house and the whore? Was she referring to this house? And what about the whore—who was that?

Deborah looks at me, then at the bottle of wine in her hand. "Want some?"

I say nothing, opening then closing my mouth like a fish. How hard is it to say *no*?

"Uhm—"

"Oh shit," she says, "Right. Coke then?"

"Sure," I say, my cheeks brimming with heat. Without saying a word, she pours a glass of wine for herself and a Coke for me. As she passes the drink to me, I can feel the tension spreading to the corners of the house. Like an oven working overtime. Sipping the cold liquid, my body cools down, but my muscles remain tense.

First Greg and Charlotte, then the hooded man in the street. And now this.

What is up with the people in this town?

CHAPTER 22:

LISA

Six Months Ago

We arrive at Deb's house for dinner. As Seb rings the doorbell, I huddle close to him, with Ana close behind. The ocean breeze adds an icy bite to an already cold evening. It's only six, but it's dark out, the fog hovering over the water. It's so close I can touch it.

"Here you are!" Deb exclaims, brimming with energy as she opens the door and ushers us in. The house smells like food and my belly rumbles. *A proper British roast,* Deb promised. We hang our coats and follow the smell coming from the kitchen. There's a different feel to the house at night. In the daylight, it's stark and modern, a direct contrast to its ancient, gloomy surroundings. But as the darkness settles, the house is filled with a soft, warm glow.

Or I might just be excited to be here. To drink wine, banter and eat familiar food.

We enter the house, and there's a man standing by the kitchen island.

"Welcome," he beams.

Deb's husband is large. Probably a foot taller than her. He's handsome, too. As handsome as a man double my age can be, anyway. There's an edge to his features, striking and bold, with piercing blue eyes.

"Richard, how are you?" Seb says, walking over and shaking his hand.

"I see you brought the good stuff," Richard replies, taking the bottle of red from Seb. *What a party trick*, I think. Bringing wine made from your own vineyard to a dinner party. How many people can do that?

Richard greets Ana like he's known her since she was a child. When he introduces himself to me, I catch a whiff of his minty cologne. His gaze lingers on my face for a moment too long, then down my chest. I should be mildly rattled, but my cheeks flush instead.

We pour the wine and take our seats in the living room, the men standing.

"How is Alma doing?" Deb asks Ana.

"Much better. She's at home resting. They say she'll make a full recovery in a few weeks." Even Ana seems happier tonight, her eyes dazzling. Seb's smiling too.

It's like they've never argued before.

"Richard, Deb tells me you've been travelling a lot," Ana says. Her posture is perfect, thin legs elegantly folded over one other.

"Yes, it's been back and forth to the UK. But some interesting ventures. It's all very exciting."

"So, no more Bilbao?" Seb asks.

"God no, that's far behind me," he chuckles. But as he speaks, Deb's eyeing her wine, her lips thin.

"And how's Barcelona been, Ana?" Richard asks, standing with one hand in his chino pocket.

"Busy, always busy with the kids. They're adorable, but a handful."

"Next time you should bring them along!" Deb exclaims, and I watch the wine sloshing around in her glass. I try to picture Ana as a mother. Looking at her tiny body, it's impossible to imagine two children came out of her.

Richard's question brings me back to the moment. "How are you adjusting to Spanish life?"

"It's interesting," I say, and everyone laughs like they were expecting me to say that. "I've never been to Spain, but this isn't what I expected. Not in a bad way, just not what I expected."

"Not a Brit on each beachside corner, you mean," Richard smiles. "At least you get some quiet here. And privacy."

"It's like nothing has changed," Seb says. "I see they still haven't fixed that dock."

He motions out the bay window into the darkness, and all our heads follow.

Deb shrugs. "It's a hazard waiting to happen. They should just block it off and be done with it."

I think of the dock, the overgrown grass hiding the worn-down wooden walkway. The timber railing shattered into splinters.

"I still remember when a few people tried to fish down there," Ana says, looking at me. "Since it's so secluded, we had people bring fishing rods. But I don't think they ever caught anything."

"It's better like that," Richard says. "I don't like having strange people on our street."

Deb gets up too fast from the couch, sending a ripple through the couch cushions.

"Whoops," she says as she straightens her dress, a loose yellow fabric hanging from her body. "I should check on dinner."

Seb and Richard start discussing the family winery, so I walk to the kitchen, finding Deb's face buried in the oven. She's scraping potatoes from the sides of the baking dish, the edges burnt.

"Need any help?" I ask.

She takes the pan out with an oven mitt, places it on the counter. "You can keep me company."

I watch her turn the vegetables and put them back in the oven. She stirs the gravy. When she speaks again, she's eyeing me up and down. "I love your dress. You always look so good."

I grin. "I do most of my shopping online. It's a struggle to find my size in actual stores."

Deb shrugs, looks down at her sack of a dress. "I've been struggling with that for years."

"What are we talking about?" Ana asks, placing her wine glass on the island.

"I was just complimenting Lisa on her clothes. We were discussing how hard it is for women like us to find clothes our size."

Women like us. She thinks we're the same size. I've never been small, but then again, I didn't think I was as large as her. It shouldn't bother me, but now I can hear *your* voice in my head again, saying those awful words. The ones you said at the wedding.

"Lisa's clothes are fantastic," Ana says, appreciation spreading across her face. "Didn't you tell me you buy everything online?"

I nod, burying my face in my wine glass. It's not a complete lie. Eleanor often sends me links to things online, but in a way, I'm still the one completing the purchase. In an effort to try and forget about my size, I say, "Deb, I can help you buy some clothes. I know ASOS sizes pretty well."

Her eyes widen. "Would you?"

"Sure," I say. "I can come by this week, and we can pick out some things together."

Elation spreads across her face. "We can use the computer in the study and—"

"Excuse me."

Richard's voice is a surprise as he passes through the hallway and out of the backdoor. From the window, we watch him in the garden. His profile is dark and his back is turned, phone clutched to his ear. When we turn back to Deb, she's still looking at him. The elation is gone, her features darkening.

"Deb?" I ask. "You were saying?"

Ana and I share a glance, then look back at Deb, who seems to have not heard my question, her eyes still locked on Richard.

"Business never sleeps for him, does it," Seb says, making his way to the island, his handsome grin sitting comfortably on his face. But as the quiet extends, the grin fades.

"Just give me one second," Deb says.

She plants her glass on the counter. She storms towards Richard in the garden, his back still turned. She grabs the phone from his hand. We avert our eyes as the muffled shouts start. Ana sips wine as we share awkward glances, the background of yells impossible to ignore. I look to the oven, the chicken glistening. Deb's words break through from the garden and make me flinch.

Embarrassment. Disrespect. Twat.

"Should we leave?" Seb asks, scratching at his knee.

Ana shakes her head, her voice a whisper. "I don't know."

"Let's give them a few minutes," I say.

There's a thud and we turn our heads to the garden, but there's no sign of either Deb or Richard.

"Okay, maybe we should go now," Ana says, putting down her wine glass. But then Richard's back in the kitchen, a gleam of sweat on his brow.

"Apologies, guys." He leans his elbows on the table like he's about to confide in us. When he speaks, the words come out controlled. "I think Deb's had a little too much to drink."

"Is she okay?" Ana asks, her eyes darting to the garden. "Where is she?"

"She's getting some air—out back."

Richard turns to the oven, switches it off. "I'm afraid she's not well enough to join us for dinner. I hope you don't mind."

Pressure mounts as we exchange quick glances, looking unsure of who should speak first.

"That's all right," Ana finally says. "Is there anything we can do?"

Richard shakes his head, smiles. "We'll be all right." He glances at the glasses still in our hands and takes a deep breath. "Well, it was great having you three over for some wine, at least."

My eyes dart to Seb as I realise what's happening. *He's expecting us to leave. Right now.*

By the look on Seb's face, he's just as surprised as I am. Like a sheepdog guiding sheep, Richard leads us to the front door, leaving our half-drunk wine on the island. The smell of the roast still fresh in our nostrils.

Richard slams the door, leaving us on the street. We stand there for a moment, then Ana that starts walking down the street first.

"What was that?" I ask.

Seb's hands are in his pockets, his shoulders hunched. Without answering me, a torrent of Spanish flows from his mouth, aimed at Ana. We keep walking and she's silent, her heels click-clacking on the tar.

"Seb, what are you saying?" I ask.

"I'm saying that was rude."

"They clearly had a fight," Ana says, turning on her heels. "I wonder what about?"

"Whatever it was, Deb wasn't happy," I say.

"I'll make us something to eat at home," Ana offers.

Seb and I nod. As we walk home, he places his arm around me, something he hasn't done since I scolded him for shouting at his sister a few days ago. It feels good, having him touch me again. In this moment, we're like a team, pairing up against something strange that's just unfolded before us. Even Ana seems to share this newfound camaraderie.

But the energy is dissipating quickly, the cold dragging it from my bones. I stop and turn back to Deb's place, eyes searching for a sign. A movement, a sound. Anything to know that she's okay.

"Lisa," Seb calls from the house, a few feet ahead of me. "Come inside, it's freezing."

I wait for a beat, then two, then three. Then I turn and walk towards my fiancé.

CHAPTER 23:

CAT

Present Day

"What does he do all day?"

Deborah shrugs at my question, then reaches for her wine glass. We're sitting at the dining room table, and she's on her fourth glass of wine already.

"Don't know," she says. "Seb's been closed off to everyone since it happened."

Hearing his name feels foreign, out of place. I don't know him or Lisa, but their story keeps me intrigued. What was their relationship like? Did he notice signs of his fiancé's instability? And how must he feel now?

"What about his mom?" I say, trying not to think of my own mother, sitting somewhere worrying about me.

"Alma's frail," Deborah says. "She barely left the house in the past few years. Now, even less."

I think back to when I passed Lisa's fiancé on the street, his eyes red-rimmed and haunted. Before I can say anything, Richard clears his throat. He's been so quiet I've forgotten that he's at the table with us. "I see him down by the tavern," he says. "Goes there almost every afternoon."

Throughout dinner, I kept looking for signs that something was off between Richard and Deborah. Her angry words from the afternoon still ringing in my head.

You've taken everything from me.

My eyes and ears are alert, looking for evidence of the fight they had just hours ago. But Richard's as he always is. Silent, observing. Nursing a beer. It's as if nothing has happened.

"It's so morbid," Deborah says. "This whole situation."

"Are you going to start teaching next week?" Richard asks, suddenly changing the topic.

I shrug. "I hope so. This week's just a trial run. They're probably making sure I'm up to speed with everything before I start."

But in the back of my mind, the doubts sit. My work visa, which, according to Charlotte, the *admin team* is sorting out. If there even is an admin team. Plus, the averted eyes whenever I pass Greg in the hallway.

But I'm in a foreign country with people I don't know. Of course I'm doubting, overthinking everything.

Deborah looks pensively out of the window. "I couldn't do that," she says. "I can barely communicate with contractors, let alone teach someone."

"It's a skill—being able to teach, to take someone's thoughts and train them to change it," Richard says, eyes on me. "Do you feel confident in doing that?'

The question feels loaded. Like he's been waiting all night to ask me this.

"I don't know," I say. "But I think you can learn by doing."

He lets out a snort of a laugh. "Okay."

"This one," Deborah says, shaking her head at him. "Always with the questions."

But I'm still focused on Richard. Apart from the car ride here, he's barely spoken more than a few words to me. Before, he seemed nice, but now it's as if I annoy him. He's always cooped up in his study, or out for errands, or smoking in the garden. Keeping to himself. Maybe that's just how he is? What was it Deborah said about him before? *He's a teddy bear once you get to know him.* Sounds like bullshit to me.

"So here's a question," I say slowly. "Do you think there's a secret to having a happy marriage?"

Let's see what he says to *that*.

There's a shift in the room's mood. I watch as Deborah's face drops, how she brings her wine glass to her mouth. It's like a zig-zag, the glass swishing from side to side. But Richard's still, his expression unchanged.

"Patience and consistency," he says. "And showing up every day to put in the effort."

I wonder if he's building a best case or if he practices what he preaches.

"Very nice," I say. I turn my attention to Deborah. "What do you think?"

She sighs. "Marriage has its fair share of ... challenges."

There's a scuff as Richard repositions his chair, leans forward to look at her. But she's caught in a haze, her eyes faraway. "I don't think anyone knows the secret. If we did, things wouldn't fall apart."

"But you guys seem to be doing a good job," I say encouragingly, even though I don't believe my own words. Fishing for information, that's what I'm doing.

The air feels tight and there's a tingle in my stomach. As if oblivious to the energy, Deborah sighs. "It's so much more than just that."

"Okay..." Richard says, leaning back and stretching. "This has taken a turn."

He stands up, patting his pockets for his cigarettes. "I'm going for a fag."

When he's gone, the stillness remains, Deborah's eyes glued to the table. I lean forward. "Is everything okay?"

Her posture is slumped, and when she raises her eyes to meet mine, they're teary.

I hesitate. "I know it's not my place, but—"

"I just don't know how we got here," she whispers. I turn to see if Richard's in the garden. When I don't see him, I speak in a hushed voice. "I heard you arguing today."

"What?"

"I know you said you were talking to a realtor. But I heard Richard's name. You were speaking of a... of a—"

"A *whore*."

The word is charged with hate. I tread carefully. "Yes. That."

As if she's found a new conviction, Deborah grimaces, her eyes narrowed. "Like I said, marriage is complicated. You never know who you're getting into it with. Or who they're bringing into your bed."

The spectre hovers around us. Infidelity. A childhood memory.

"How long has this been going on?" I say, my hands inches from hers on the table. For some reason, I feel like taking hold of them. Maybe it's the fake counsellor in me, looking to reach out and reassure her.

She shrugs. "Months, maybe even years."

My father cheated on my mother many times. Almost always with the same woman. The colleague. The person he shared his hungover days with, snuggled together in the tiny boardroom in an office block just off the highway. I still remember car rides with her on the odd day out. She was a redhead, just like me.

It seems fitting now. She, a cheater in love. Me, a cheater in life.

"What about the house?" I say. "You were talking about the—person—living in your house."

I realise I've just told her I heard her entire conversation. But if she minds my snooping, she doesn't say it.

"We've got a property back home," Deborah says. "In the UK. And him being him, he likes the girls young. And poor. So they always need some support."

"So… she's living in your other house?"

"Yep."

"Right now?" I ask, looking around for Richard again. "While he's here with you?"

Deborah's face goes blank, then she nods, does a nosedive into her wine. I think of what to say, studying her eyes for what she wants to hear. But they're swimming in booze and everything falls short.

You should leave. He's an idiot. You deserve more.

But I settle on the truest thing I feel. "I'm so sorry this happened to you."

If she wants to rage, she can rage. If she wants to cry, she can cry, too. If she wants to leave now, I'll help her pack. But by the look on her face, she doesn't want to do any of those things. She sniffs, and a tear trails down her cheek.

Witnessing pain causes pain. So I dive into the collective of it, hoping to dilute hers. My hands edge closer to hers and I place one over the other.

135

Her eyes meet mine as she tries to hold in a sob. "I've made a mess of my life."

"It's all a mess," I say. Even the best of words fail sometimes.

"Thank you," she says seconds later, her voice a whisper.

We hear the back door slam and instantly, she's off her chair, wine glass still clutched in her hand. "I think I'm going to lie down."

"Are you all right?" Richard says to her as she stumbles to the kitchen. From here, he almost looks like he cares. Like he's really worried about her. But the dislike in my stomach stops me from believing it.

"Yes," she says. "Just going upstairs."

"I'll clean up," I say, collecting the empty plates.

Deborah refills her glass close to the brim. She leaves the bottle on the table and as she stumbles past Richard, she mumbles words of goodbye. He places his large hand on her shoulder. "You sure you're all right?"

No, she's not. And you're the reason.

"Just tired," she says, heading for the stairs.

When she's gone, Richard turns to me. "Did she say anything to you?"

There are so many things I can say. In anger, in spite. But Deborah's fallen face strips me of it all.

"Just that she was tired," I say.

And before he can respond, there's a shattering of glass. A loud thud from the stairs.

And a scream.

CHAPTER 24:

LISA

Six Months Ago

I get no writing done, the scenes of last night's disastrous dinner playing out in my mind like a film.

Richard's eyes lingering on my breasts.

The look on Deb's face when she saw him talking on the phone.

The words they shouted at each other.

Alma is in front of the television on a recliner. Which leaves me here, between Seb and Ana in the dining room, aimlessly typing away at characters and thoughts. All hazy and one dimensional.

I message Deb, ask if she's okay. Then I stare at the chat, willing the blue tick to appear. Time seems to pass extra slowly as I wait to leave for Spanish class.

When it's finally time, I hunch up against the breeze outside, the fog blanketing the water. On days like these, the ocean somehow feels less vast, like it's slowly ebbing closer.

As I walk up the hill, the air scratches at my throat. Halfway, I stop as I see a figure in the distance. A runner, dressed in black.

Richard.

My mind tells me to turn around or cross the road, but I keep walking. When he sees me, he slows and pulls an AirPod from his ear. "Lisa?'

"Hi," I say.

He's breathing heavily, his face sweaty. But his minty cologne lingers, creating a bubble around him.

"Listen," he says. "I want to apologise for if I was rude last night. I was caught off guard and might not have acted in the best way."

At least he's apologising.

"I would hate to have left a bad impression," he continues. "Especially on you."

That last part is a surprise. "On me?"

He smiles, and suddenly he doesn't feel twice my age. Since meeting him I've been on the fence, feeling creeped out by his looks and yet liking them at the same time. What is it about him that's so charming?

"You left a good impression," he tells me. "I would have liked to have done the same."

My memory jumps back to last night. How confidently his eyes swept across my body. Like he's used to doing it. How often does he do this, and more?

I brush the thought away. "It's fine. I'm sure we'll have more get-togethers to make up for it. As long as Deb is okay."

Part of me wants to have a redo of last night, a proper flashback to home. But another part of me simply wants to *go* home. My excitement about a simple roast dinner just showed me how unhappy I really am here. Despite trying to make it my Holland, like Greg recommended.

Richard nods. "Yes, you're right. Deb feels much better now, thankfully."

He looks out at the fog, as if deciding something, then turns back to look at me. "It's nice to know Deb has someone here for company. I can tell she values you."

He takes his phone from his armband, the material sticking to his skin. "How about we stay in touch? It'll be good to know I have someone here looking out for her while I'm gone."

"Are you going somewhere?" I ask.

"The UK. Later today."

"But you just got back."

He smiles, holds out his phone to me. "I've got work to do."

I take the phone, tap in the digits of my number. When I hand it back to him, I feel like I've given a part of myself away without wanting to.

"Great," he beams, adjusting his AirPod in his ear again. "Appreciate it."

I watch him jog down the road, pivoting at the dock and up the adjacent street. I scan my phone for a message from Deb, but there's nothing.

* * *

"I think he was flirting with you."

As usual, Greg and I are at the bar, in the same spot as last time. Our Spanish books firmly in our bags filled with notes from class.

I scoff. As soon as we sat down, I told Greg about last night. "I don't think so."

But he doesn't look convinced. "No guy acts like that if he doesn't have an agenda."

He takes a sip of beer, his shirt sleeves rolled up to his elbows. "But hey, I can't blame the guy for trying."

Heat rushes to my cheeks, and I smirk. The more I drink, the closer those eyes resemble yours. They say we shouldn't dwell on the past, but how can I move forward when it keeps catching up with me?

"It's just *weird*. Everything about it," I say. "You should have seen Deb last night. She was so happy, then so angry when she saw him on the phone. And then she just disappeared."

Greg raises a brow. "Maybe he was talking to his mistress."

The idea doesn't surprise me. "Maybe."

"It could be anything. Cheating, family issues, money prob—"

My phone vibrates on the table and my heart lifts. There's a text from Deb.

Hello, stop by tomorrow if you like xx

"She's okay," I say, typing back that I'll see her tomorrow.

"There we go," Greg says. "See? Nothing to worry about."

"Thank God," I say, putting the phone back on the table. "Now I can at

139

least check on her. Hear her side of the story."

"I'm a bit disappointed, to be honest," Greg says.

My brow creases. "Why?"

"I thought it was the husband. Texting you already. Now *that* would be interesting."

I gape at him as he grins. "You're *bad*. I hope he never does."

Greg raises an eyebrow, again confirming that he's not convinced.

"What, you think I *like* drama?" I ask.

He leans in close and gives me a tease of a smile. "I think you *love* drama."

CHAPTER 25:

CAT

Present Day

It's been a few days since we found Deborah at the foot of the stairs, surrounded by splattered wine and shards of glass. Richard and I were careful to avoid the mess as we carried her, her left knee an angry red. She didn't stop apologising as we helped her to her bed.

Since then, she's been a different woman. She barely talks.

It hasn't stopped her from drinking, though.

It's almost like she's turned into a cat. She's lethargic, either sprawled on the couch or the bed for most of the day.

With Deborah mute, the house is silent. The academy isn't any better. The online reviews weren't kidding when they called Gexta a sleepy place. The scenery is beautiful—just like the ad promised—but apart from the green landscapes, the place isn't lively at all. It's more like a ghost town, with hushed voices and closed-off faces.

Lisa's fiancé is the only constant. Every day, he treads the same path uphill to the tavern. Then he stumbles back to the house hours later, his hood hiding his face. I watch him from the window sometimes, feeling anxious. I've considered going back to South Africa. After all, if my colleagues *and* my host family don't talk to me, what's the point of being here?

But then I stop and think of the alternative. Going back to Sam's academy, working a job I don't like, and having to face my mom. Stopping InCheck.

And so, I decide to stay.

Richard watches me like a hawk. He thinks I don't notice. Just like he thinks I don't notice the hushed conversations between him and his wife.

But I do.

I've tried listening in, my ears pressed against the walls of my bedroom whenever he goes into the master bedroom to talk to Deborah, but her voice seems to lose its strength whenever he's in the room. Like he's a silencer. Plus, I don't think I've ever heard Richard go up to bed. Either he sleeps in the living room, or in his study.

If that isn't strange, then I don't know what is.

Speaking of the study, Deborah never seems to go there, either. And whenever Richard leaves the house, he locks the door behind him. Why would you lock a room in your own house? If you ask me, it's only if you have something to hide.

But apart from all that, there were some interesting developments tonight.

I was upstairs in my room when I heard a knock. Deborah popped her head in, dark circles beneath her eyes. "I'm heading to bed. Richard will start dinner soon."

"Everything okay?" I asked, even though I knew the answer.

She tried to smile, but the act looked painful. "Just tired."

"You sure you're not hungry?"

"Positive," she said, already turning down the hallway to her bedroom.

Passing the time until dinner, I logged on to InCheck, reading a message from Susana.

I had a glass of wine at lunch today. I watched as the kids rolled around on the carpet. It was very mellow. I feel like a bad parent.

I sunk back into my pillow and typed a response.

Only you know your limits. Do you feel incapable of taking care of them after a glass of wine?

I listened as Richard fiddled with pots and pans downstairs. I didn't hate my father for being a cheater. So I couldn't hate Richard for cheating on his wife, either. If morality had a line, I'd crossed it ages ago.

Susana's response was sudden. *I don't know.*

And I didn't, either.

Richard and I ate dinner in silence, the pasta sauce straight from a bottle.

"Are you sure Deborah's okay?" I asked. "I don't think she's eaten anything."

"She gets like this," he said. "She gets too active and then hits a downer for a few days."

Even though the words made sense together, it didn't feel right. As if reading my mind, Richard spoke again. "You think I'm doing too little about it, don't you?"

"I—I", but there were no words. His tone was accusatory, and I didn't know where it came from.

"Tell me," he said in that tone again. "What do you *really* think?"

I pursed my lips. "It's not my place to say."

"I couldn't agree more."

He banged his beer down on the table. "Do you reckon other people know best?"

I shook my head, not understanding. "What do you mean?"

"Let's say I have a problem. Who do you think has the best solution—you or me?"

He leaned forward, as if the world depended on my answer.

I shrugged. "It depends on—"

"Nah, theoretically now," he said. "Would it be you—a total stranger—or me, who's known *me* for my entire life?"

He sounded patronising, and I felt the dislike rise in my throat. "You. But if you're in too deep, you might not see things clearly. Someone else could show you another perspective."

He let out a scoffing laugh. "How neutral can an opinion be? We're all biased."

I couldn't argue with him on that. I wasn't sure I was as neutral as I wanted to be when I advised people on InCheck. If my mother was neutral, trying to push pills my way. If my previous therapist was neutral, or if she was simply imparting her own beliefs on me.

"See," Richard said. "I think we're born to know what's best for us. Call it fight or flight, or what have you, but we don't need anybody to be giving us advice. By doing that, we're letting others play with our lives. You can't play God like that."

I looked at him, a vivid picture in my mind of people on strings like puppets, being played by others. I thought of Susana. Of Fred. Whether I was leading them towards outcomes that suited them, or me. Whether I was giving advice or purely counselling.

Whether I was playing God.

"You're biased too," I told him. "Even what you just said is biased."

"Exactly, but I'm not giving you advice, am I?"

He seemed happy when he made that point. The way he looked at me, like he wanted to teach me a lesson, made my stomach churn. *What was this guy's problem?*

I kept talking.

"I think there's a difference between giving advice and showing people what they can't see for themselves. It's a fine line."

"Good point. It's a very, *very* fine line," he said, his eyes narrowed.

"People need people," I croaked. "We're only as smart as those we surround ourselves with. We can't do this alone."

Richard nodded, looking at me like I was trying to explain a math equation to him. "I'm going for a fag."

He walked down the hallway, turned, then smirked. "Good chat."

He'd made it clear that he didn't like me, that he thought I was poking my head where it didn't belong. And on the flip side, I didn't like his arrogance or the way he was talking to me.

He wasn't a fan of me? No problem—the feeling was mutual.

As I rinsed the plates, I heard the familiar *click* of the study door. Richard was back in the place where he seemed to spend most of his time.

Now, back in my bedroom, I can't stop thinking about the past few days. The dinner we just had. I think Richard knows Deborah told me about his infidelity. He's clearly trying to make a point. To tell me to stay out of his business. And who knows, maybe he's told Deborah to stop telling me about their personal life. Maybe that's why she's retreated into herself.

But why does he lock himself in his study—and maybe even sleep there too? Why does he talk about Lisa so much, and why is it like he's on a mission to call me out in conversations?

If he didn't want me here, then why was I *still* here?

And despite all of this happening, it's not the worst thing about tonight.

What *is* the worst thing is this power outlet. Here, in my room. It's above the dresser, across from the bed.

On the day I arrived in Gexta, I connected my charger, but the outlet didn't work. I've been charging my phone in the kitchen ever since, but tonight after dinner, I tried the power outlet again.

As I looked closer, that's when I noticed it. The tiny aperture, half hidden beneath the plastic surface. A reflective element. And for a second, I saw a flicker, as if it moved.

Exactly like a camera would.

CHAPTER 26:

LISA

Six Months Ago

Deb looks awful when she opens the front door. Her face is ashen, the circles under her eyes deep.

"Hi, love," she says, and I can feel the darkness behind her words. Like she needs a thousand naps to recover from whatever she's going through.

When I enter the house, I smell something off. Like food left out too long.

"Tea?" she offers, walking to the kitchen. She's dressed in an oversized blue shirt, the fabric of her black jeans folding on itself by her ankles.

"No, I'm all right," I say.

She grabs a cup for herself, puts the kettle on. I walk towards her and hold out my hand. "Let me."

She hands me the cup, then sits down at the island, eyes staring out of the bay window. When it boils, I pour the water from the kettle into her cup. "How are you?"

She shrugs. "Fine, I guess."

I leave the tea bag in the cup and turn to her. "Are you sure?"

She raises an eyebrow, then drops it like she's too tired to keep it in place. "You mean from the other night?"

I look down at her fingernails. They're cut short, the cuticles red and swollen. I nod.

Another shrug. "Yes, well, I can't imagine *that* could have been ignored, could it?"

I hand her the steaming cup with sugar and milk. "I'm just worried," I say. "Richard said you were a bit flustered—"

She looks startled at the mention of his name, and I quickly explain. "I ran into him yesterday. On my way to Spanish class. He told me you had a bit too much to drink but…" I take a breath. "I don't believe him."

She leans back. "Yes, I'm sure he said that."

"If there's anything I can do, please tell me."

I look at the overflowing garbage bin in the corner of the room, the source of the foul smell. "I can help around the house? Anything."

She glances over to the bin, then splats out a chuckle. "Oh, it's a mess, isn't it?"

All I want to do is hug her. "It's fine."

"Did he say anything else?"

Heat rushes to my cheeks. I can tell her everything Richard said yesterday, but something about the way he asked for my number—and the way I just gave it away—makes me decide not to. No good can come from that.

"No," I say. "Nothing else."

Deb grunts. A few beats pass before she says, "Thanks for stopping by love, but you can't help with this." She takes a sip of tea. "Love is more complicated than it looks. You think it's hard now, but trust me, it only gets worse."

She sees the frown on my face and her face softens. "Not to be morbid about you and Seb. You're lovely together, I just…", she fumbles for words, "I just mean that young couples worry about the small things. When you're together as long as we've… well, there are other things to worry about."

"I can imagine."

"But you don't have to worry," she says. "Not at all."

I place my hands on the island. "Are you? You know… worried?"

She twists her mouth, gives a small nod. I feel the unspoken words hovering between us, the truth coupled with the pain.

"Is he cheating?"

"Is it that obvious?"

I drop my gaze. The silence builds. When it's almost too painful to let it continue, Deb's voice shatters the quiet.

"Right, well, that's that." She slams her hands on the island. "Let's do something else, shall we?"

"How about some shopping?" I offer. "Shopping always makes me feel better."

It's not really true, but anything will do to get her in a better mood. She agrees to let me set up an ASOS account for her. We sit together, hunched in front of her computer in the study. And before I can scroll for outfits, she's off her chair. "Wine?"

I doubt for a moment, looking at the time.

"Come on," she says. "It's past twelve."

She pours us two glasses, and looks visibly more relaxed. We choose clothes that Eleanor would call *easy grabs.* Items that can look good on any shape, especially the bigger ones. Flowy dresses. Adjustable belts. Deb becomes enthusiastic, watching the online videos of plus-sized models in printed winter dresses.

"We're not trying to hide your shape," I say. "We're trying to accentuate what there is, and hide what you feel uncomfortable with."

By the time we're done, we have four items in our checkout basket. Our trial clothes. Once we know her fit based on these, it'll help us to expand her wardrobe.

Deb's putting in her credit card details when I get a message from Greg. *These reflexive verbs keep falling from the sky, don't you think?*

He's sent a picture of him pulling a sad face next to his Spanish textbook. I can't help but smile.

"And that?" Deb asks.

"It's just Greg," I say. "From class."

She looks at me questioningly. "He's British," I continue. "He's in my Spanish class. We've gotten pretty close. He's really funny."

I tell her about our weekly outings to the bar, his story about making Spain my Holland.

"Careful," she says. "Seb is a lovely gent, but I doubt he'd like another man moving in on his lady."

For a moment, I feel embarrassed. Am I spending too much time with this guy? I've been so lonely here, so alienated, that I've grabbed any opportunity for a friendship. Deb included. Apart from her, Greg is the only friend I have in this town.

But then I remember who he reminds me of, and I suddenly feel unsettled. So maybe there *is* some casual flirting. But that's normal, isn't it?

"I have a question," I say, eager to change the subject. "How well do you know Ana?"

"She's a sweetheart," Deb says. "Why do you ask?"

I think of Seb's sister, with her soft eyes and warm demeanour. How friendly she's been to me ever since I met her at the hospital. "I'm just curious," I say. "Seb doesn't talk about her a lot."

"When we moved here, we only saw the Levientos during the holidays," Deb says. "Alma and Manuel mostly stayed in Madrid when the children were growing up. It was closer to schools. But when they were here in town, Ana was always such a friendly young thing. Much like her father, bless his soul."

"Seb must have been young then," I say, remembering the photograph I found in Alma's house of the siblings together, Ana with her pigtails.

"Much younger. And very different," Deb's brow furrows like she's recalling a memory. "He was more reserved back then."

"But were they close?"

"Who?"

"Seb and Ana."

She tilts her head. "I think so. Maybe more so when they were younger."

"Seb told me they weren't close. Even now, they don't seem to be."

"Well, they would play together all the time when they were little," Deb says, taking a sip of wine. "Maybe some sibling rivalry started to surface."

"What do you mean?"

"Well, from what I remember, Ana was always the golden child. Alma wasn't a big talker. She still isn't. But Manuel—he would parade his daughter around every chance he got. She was clearly his favourite. Seb was a bit more troublesome, by the looks of him."

Questions spring to mind. "Do you think Seb disliked Ana? Because he knew his dad preferred her?"

Deb raises an eyebrow. "I don't know. We rarely went to their house. But when they came over to ours, Ana was the star of the show. And it was pretty clear that Seb didn't like it."

I picture a disgruntled, jealous child. An image so far removed from the handsome, successful man I sleep next to at night. But then I remember that morning—Seb at the dining room table, arms crossed and lips pouting. Like a child about to throw his toys out the cot. Sending his sister off in tears.

"But actually," Deb says, "Come to think of it…"

She bites her lip, looks deep in thought.

"What?"

"No, it's just—now that you mention it, I do remember one summer where things might have changed. I told you they came over a few times during the holidays? But one summer, they didn't. We invited them, of course, but Manuel kept making excuses. He looked angry, now that I think about it. They left early for Madrid, too. Ana must have been a teenager then. Seb a little younger. The two of them were never around again after that. At least not together, from what I can remember."

"So something must have happened, right?"

She shrugs. "Maybe, but then again, maybe they just had a falling out. Children grow up and leave the nest, you know."

I look at Deb's nest—empty. Is there a reason she never had children? Was Richard against the idea, or was it her decision? I look at her and offer a polite smile, thinking of Seb. The faded photograph resurfaces again, Seb standing beside Ana. Deb's right: families argue all the time. I can attest to that.

But what if something else happened that summer? Something more than just sibling rivalry?

"Family is complicated," Deb says, shaking her head. "You never know what's lurking beneath the surface. And once you finally do, it's too late. Maybe that's why we're all such a mess."

CHAPTER 27:

CAT

Present Day

The dream always starts in the same way.

There's a knock at the door. I'm instantly awake. I stay curled up under the duvet. But my eyes are wide open, waiting for the next knock. And then the voice. It used to be so authoritative and warm, but now it's whiny and whimpering.

Bud. Bud, pleeease.

The knocking continues for what feels like an age. I hear a thud on the carpet, like someone sitting down on the other side of this make-believe bedroom door. I don't know how long he stays there, but the ticking in my head tells me it'll be over soon.

I wait.

Wait for the drop. Wait for the thud.

And then the quiet that stretches out for so long, it feels like I'm falling.

Wake up, wake up, wake up!

And I do.

My chest heaves as air enters my lungs in a heated rush. My hair is drenched with sweat. I take a moment to adjust to where I am, realising it's the same dream, all over again.

I breathe in. *You're in Gexta.*

I breathe out. *You're fine.*

I look at my phone. It's close to 3am.

My throat is dry, dry with an unslakable thirst. I swing my feet onto the floor, trying to forget the dream that's been a recurring nightmare for a year now. The dream that transports me back to that awful day.

I walk past the dresser in my room, the vanity bag covering the power socket. The one with the camera I think is there, but don't know for sure. Seeing the socket in the dark gives me the creeps. Maybe it's the panic of the dream still pounding in my heart, or it's the simple thought that someone in this house is watching me. Filming me.

For a moment, I consider drinking water straight from the tap in the upstairs bathroom. Instead, I open the door of my bedroom as quietly as I can, looking around. The hallway is dark, the door to Deborah's room closed. There's a steady snoring on the other side.

Alcohol used to make me snore, too.

I use my phone's torch to navigate the stairs and tiptoe to the kitchen, my socks slippery on the floor. There's a low hum from the fridge. The living area is eerily still. The moon is bright through the bay window, casting reflections across the room.

Even the ocean is quiet.

I open a cupboard, grab a glass. I wince as the water whooshes from the tap, breaking the silence. But I try to remind myself that no one's awake.

I drink fast, swallowing air with water. The glass makes a thud on the metal bottom of the sink as I put it down. My heartbeat slows as I stand with my eyes closed, focused on nothing but the calming of my mind.

I'm about to move back towards my bedroom when I hear it.

A stir. Movement. Footsteps.

I realise the noise is coming from the study. Richard's study.

I walk towards it, my socks barely making a sound as I cross the hallway. I stand in front of the study door and hold the torch of my phone up to it.

I'm about to put my hand on the doorknob when it opens.

Seeing his face in the dark sends a chill down my spine.

"What are you doing here?" Richard grunts.

"Sorry," I whisper, my heartbeat racing. My flashlight's still on, casting light onto his torso. He's in a sweatshirt, his hair tousled in all directions.

The light falls on the drawn window shutters, the Mac on the desk with its screen shining bright. In the corner of the study, there's a mattress, a few pillows and a duvet cover.

I strain my neck to look closer into the room, but Richard's body looms over me.

"Turn that off," he says, pushing me away as he steps over the threshold and closes the study door behind him. I fumble with my phone, my fingers scrambling as I turn the light off.

"What are you doing here?"

"Getting some water," I say, my voice croaky. His gaze is intimidating, his eyes heavy like he hasn't slept in weeks.

"Is everything okay?" I ask, knowing full well that if he's sleeping in that study, then clearly things are not okay.

Richard leans forward so our faces are on the same level. The sourness of his breath makes my eyes water. "I'd be careful about sneaking around down here."

I open my mouth, then close it. Tiny particles of matter float between us, soft like snow.

"I wasn't sneak—"

I stop. Maybe I *was* sneaking. But then again, I was half asleep and recovering from a nightmare. I wasn't thinking straight.

His face darkens, and with his brow furrowed, he looks almost menacing. "Go back to bed."

Without a word, I head to the stairs, a sense of urgency jolting me forward. I don't look back to see if he's behind me. When I'm finally alone in my room again, the door closed behind me, I take a deep breath. I sink down onto the bed, Richard's face playing through my mind. So aggressive. So *scary*. All because I was outside his study? Even if he's sleeping in that room—working through the night—his reaction to me finding him there was all wrong.

There must be more to what just happened.

My eyes skip to the power socket again, and I'm hit with a reminder of the *maybe-there-maybe-not* camera in this room. Suddenly, it's very clear. I don't feel safe here.

It's like I'm a kid again, being chased by the Bogeyman.

Except this time, the threat feels real.

CHAPTER 28:

LISA

Six Months Ago

Seeing Seb's face this morning was painful.

We've been underwater for what felt like so long, the two of us. Grasping for each other, desperate to come up for air. Being in this town has done something to us. Made us into strangers. And the weekend was the chance for us to get back to who we once were. People who could laugh together and share their dreams with each other.

But it didn't turn out the way I expected.

On Friday, Ana packed her bags and left.

"My daughter's sick," she told us. "I'm sure it's nothing, but I'd feel better being there."

And off she went to Barcelona, leaving Seb and me alone with Alma for the weekend. But he was quick to make a reservation at a restaurant close to San Sebastian, a place on the brink of receiving a Michelin star.

"Will your mother be okay?" I asked, remembering the evenings he'd insist on staying in or close to the house, in case Alma needed anything.

"We'll go for lunch, so we'll be back in the evening," Seb replied.

When we arrived, the restaurant looked like a giant mushroom from a child's book, startlingly white against the backdrop of green.

Seb took charge in ordering the wine, talking to the waiter about the menu. The man smiled at me, as if knowing I was just a prop.

The food was ridiculously over-elaborate, Seb's eyes shining as he pointed out the hint of this, the tang of that. From octopus in a sweet vinaigrette to lamb with an arugula foam, each dish was more colourful than the last, an ode to our magical surroundings.

Seb was almost like I remembered him. Almost.

Behind his eyes, I saw the young boy in the photograph, in the shadow of his sister. Ana in her pigtails. Each time Seb grasped his wine glass, his fingers gripped lazily around the stem, I could hear Greg in the back of my mind.

Posh lads. I like to cup my wine when I drink.

As we drove home after dinner, I lazed back in the passenger seat.

"How about some dessert when we get home?" Seb teased, putting his hand on my knee. I kept the corners of my mouth in a tight smile, trying to keep down the nausea that was forming in the pit of my stomach. I hid the feeling as we got home and had coffee with Alma. My fingers were tingling when I took our empty cups to the kitchen, feeling Seb's arms around my waist, his breath on my neck.

When he shut the door to our bedroom, I was quick to take off my clothes, pulling in my stomach as I lay on the bed. I'd applied concealer between my thighs, covering the thin lines of my little secret. The one even Eleanor didn't know of. Seb's torso towered over me, his head nestled in my neck, groaning with each pulse inside of me.

I wanted to be in the moment with him. But my head was far off, with you. With Greg.

I'm not sure when it happened. In my dreams, or on my walks to class. But there was a merging. Somewhere Greg's face turned into yours and you disappeared into him. It was no longer just the eyes that pulled me, but the scent from his body and the thought of his hands on me.

It was too much to think about.

So when Seb kissed me goodbye this morning, I wanted to cry. Because I had hoped for this for so long. This connection between us again, the connection that had been lost the moment we arrived in Spain. But somehow I'd been pulled into the deep waters of you. *Again.*

When I arrived for my Spanish class, Greg was standing outside the building waiting for me like he always did. I had half a mind to fake an illness and turn back. Run back to Seb. But I hesitated.

"So I was supposed to write that passage in the past tense, but I didn't," Greg said as he approached me. "So it's all improvising today."

The afternoon clouds were gathering when class finished. As soon as we stepped outside the building, Greg set off towards the bar. "Coming?"

"I'm not feeling well," I said. "I think I'll take a rain-check."

"Sure? A beer might make you feel better."

I should have listened to my gut. Gone home. It's what Eleanor would have done. But I proved again that I can't be trusted. That despite everything that's happened, I still make terrible decisions.

I took my seat at our usual table. "I ordered patatas bravas. It'll oil your stomach and make you feel better," Greg said, sitting down.

And here we are, two beers in.

His ears are red, his expression warm in the haze of the bar. I take another sip of beer, splashing some onto my arm.

"Whoops," he chuckles. "You know, spillage is an offence. Normally, you'd get a fine for that. But I'll be easy on you today."

I curse, lick the beer from my arm.

Greg seems impressed. "You make a great day drinking partner. I reckon you're a good plus one at weddings too."

The mention of a wedding sounds like a loud church bell in my ears.

"I don't like weddings."

He raises a brow. "Don't women love weddings?"

I used to, I think. Until the last one I went to. I can still remember the look on your face when you saw me in that red dress, the utter shock in your eyes. Like you'd seen a ghost.

I don't even try to force a smile as I look at Greg. "The last time I went to a wedding, it didn't go very well."

I shouldn't be talking about this. Eleanor would *hate* that I brought it up. But something about being here with Greg makes me throw caution to the wind.

"Oh—some more drama," Greg teases, leaning in. "What happened?"

"Well, I guess I was uninvited," I say. "But I rocked up anyway."

"A proper wedding crasher, were you?"

It's not the only thing I ruined that day. But he doesn't have to know that.

"Another drink?" he says, but he's already gesturing to the waiter.

My sips soon turn into gulps, and by my fourth beer, everything seems irrelevant.

"You know, I lied to you before," I say, leaning in so close I can feel Greg's breath on my face.

"About what?"

"You *do* remind me of my ex."

"Uh oh," he says, but his expression tells me he's listening more intently.

"No, no, it's a good thing," I explain, nearly sending my drink tumbling off the table. "He was nice."

"He couldn't have been that nice," Greg says. "Since he's not in the picture anymore."

His voice is soft. Something about him feels like home. Like a path I was meant to take. A path so different from the one I'm on now.

When we step outside, it's dark, the sky a deep charcoal.

"Fun as always," I say, bowing in Greg's direction, the booze making every movement languid. He laughs, hands in his pockets, his chest outstretched. But there's a moment where his face looks contorted, like he's wrestling with something. He steps forward, and for a moment my mind doesn't register as his hands come to rest on my waist.

And before I know it, his lips are on mine.

A beat passes, then two. By the time it's three, it's too late. I've taken too long to pull away. I stumble backwards, creating the needed distance between us. When I look at Greg, his eyes are wide.

"Fuck," he whispers. His hand wipes at his lips, smudges of my lipstick on his fingers. "Lisa, I—"

But I'm already gone, darting down the road, my handbag bumping against my hip. The light of day seems to fade faster, the darkness creeping in. It's like the clouds are circling me, suffocating me. The contempt builds, bringing tears to my eyes. How had I kept this going for so long? Even

Deb warned me. But I'd convinced myself otherwise. Let it go too far. Let thoughts of *you*, of Greg, fester in my mind.

Seb and Alma are in the living room when I enter the house. There are cookies on the table and seeing them hunched together, oblivious to the outside world, makes me sick.

My voice is croaky, and I force a smile. "I'm just going to shower, then I'll be right down."

I close the bedroom door behind me, lunge for my purse, fishing out the tiny blade. But instead of sinking to the ground, I walk to the shower, strip down and step under the water. My knees crack as I crouch down, bringing the razor to my thigh.

I go deeper this time, the tears mixing with the stream of water as the blade cuts into me. The blood flows in crimson streaks down my skin, towards the drain. I repeat the action, wondering if I shouldn't do more damage.

Bring an end to the shame.

CHAPTER 29:

CAT

Present Day

I need to figure out what's going on. *Today*.

Waking up this morning, I list the things that are bothering me. The weird energy in this house. Deborah's stilted conversations. Richard sleeping in the study and working at three in the morning (on *what*?). The sidelong glances from Greg and Charlotte at the academy. My work visa, which no one seems to have a clue about.

Not to mention the camera in my room. Richard's behaviour last night has convinced me that the power socket does indeed house a tiny little bulb. A gateway into my room, with someone watching on the other side. But why? And for what?

This morning, Alice—*I*—have a call with Fred on InCheck, and his bad mood oozes into my psyche.

"I just don't see the point," he says. "Why bother trying to address our feelings when we're just going to die anyway?"

It's a statement more than a question. It makes me wish Alice was real—a legit counsellor who has her shit together. One who can advise people like Fred when they're feeling morbid. Despite me feeling like an imposter, I try my best to talk him out of his pit, telling him that tomorrow will be a better day. I ask him to go and do something he loves, to take his mind off his temporarily hopeless thoughts.

I wonder if actual therapists feel this way too. Burdened by the words of their patients.

My coffee's gone cold by the time Deborah makes her way down the stairs. After that slip she had, she's careful with her knee, keeping it as straight as she can.

"Need help?" I say, getting up from the chair at the kitchen island.

She waves a hand, her eyes on the stairs. "I'll manage."

The kettle boils and she prepares two cups of tea. Barely a minute passes before Richard's footsteps sound on the stairs, and I watch him across the brim of my mug. When his eyes meet mine, his face is expressionless, like he has no memory of last night. I wonder what time he snuck back up from the study to take a shower. It must have been while I was on my call with Fred. I look at Deborah, study her face for a sign. Anything that gives away that *my-husband-and-I-don't-sleep-in-the-same-room* vibe. But there's nothing.

"Sleep well, Cat?"

Richard has a tiny smile as he asks me the question. *No, I didn't sleep at all. You scared the shit out of me last night.*

"Fine," I say. "Not too bad."

He nods as Deborah takes a sip of tea. But I don't allow the silence to build.

"I was wondering if you could help me with something," I say, looking him right in the eyes. "The power socket in my room doesn't work. The one by the dresser in the corner? I tried checking for a power source, but I can't find one."

If he's surprised, he's hiding it well.

"I think I know which one you're talking about," Deborah says. "It's been faulty for ages."

"I could have a look," Richard says, eyes not straying from mine. "See what the problem is."

And there it is. That same look he gave me last night. One that's accusatory and threatening all at once.

"How about I just call an electrician?" Deborah offers, seemingly unaware of the sudden tension building around her kitchen island. "It'll be safer. I don't like the idea of you shocking yourself."

She places a hand on Richard's shoulder, and as soon as she does, his body tenses. Not so much that it's obvious, but just enough for me to see.

"Well, I'm off," she announces, gathering her handbag. "Jam-packed with meetings today. I'll see you both later."

When she's gone, I shift my full attention to Richard. "How did you sleep?"

He adds two spoons of sugar to his tea and gives me a smirk. "Like a baby."

My nostrils flare as he heads for the study, which I now know is also his bedroom. Slumping down on the couch, I try to think of a plan. A way to find out what's going on. My eyes scan the dining room table, the stacked books below the TV. Now that I think about it, there's not much space to store anything. Even in my room, the dresser is filled with linen. I've seen no paperwork or boxes (like ones for hidden cameras) anywhere in this house. My mind circles back to last night, the Mac in the study with its screen bright against the darkness.

If there's something Deborah and Richard are hiding, it's in the study. On that Mac, or maybe in the desk drawers.

I turn and look towards the hallway, eye the closed door of the study. Richard will have to leave the room at some point. But when he does, he'll lock the door, like he always does.

Except—just maybe—he won't, if he thinks I've left the house.

I open my phone, type a WhatsApp message to Richard. *Going for a walk. Need anything?*

The blue tick appears almost immediately, and a frisson of excitement builds.

His response comes. *No thanks.*

I grab my purse and head for the front door, making a point of shutting it with a bang. I walk towards the street, careful not to turn around, in case he's watching me from between the window shutters. When I turn the corner up on the hill, I dart to the back road. It's a longer path from here, but it's the way to the walking trail.

I reach the back gate of the house and peek through the gaps in the wood. No sign of Richard in the garden. My best bet is to wait until he takes a smoke break. Which, considering how much he smokes, won't be long.

I go over the plan in my head. I'll wait until I know he's taking a smoke break, then sneak through the back garden to the front of the house, entering through the front door. Hopefully, he'll have left the study door unlocked, and I can steal a few minutes inside.

I unlock the back gate, slide it open a crack, and close it behind me. I crouch, keeping to the corners of the yard, staying out of view from the kitchen window. Keeping my head low, I move slowly, the grass tickling at my ankles. If I'm caught now, I don't know how I'd explain it.

I reach the corner of the house and sit down. From here, no one can see me, and if the backdoor opens, I'll hear it. For now, I'll just wait. As soon as Richard is outside, I'll turn the corner and sprint to the front door.

It takes a while, but soon I hear the back door creak open, the footsteps on the grass.

I scuttle around the house and to the front door. Richard's a chain smoker. He'll probably have two cigarettes. Still, that doesn't leave me with a bucket load of time.

I slide the key into the lock. A slight pull and thud and I'm in. Dropping to my knees, I slide on the floorboards, particles of dust accumulating on my clothes. From this vantage point, I'd hear him if he comes back inside. I have a few minutes.

But barely enough.

I get to the study door and my fingers tremble in fear of it being locked, but as soon as I turn the handle, it clicks and opens. *Yes!*

I lift myself to a hunched position and shuffle into the room. My eyes flit from one thing to the next, the room a blur as adrenaline pulses through me. I only have a minute or two to find something. Anything. I'm about to head towards the Mac on the desk, but then my eyes catch something on the left side of the room, something that was hidden from view in the dark last night. Something that Richard's frame was blocking.

I stop, look closer at it. And my blood runs cold.

163

CHAPTER 30:

LISA

Six Months Ago

"You okay?" Seb asks. We're in bed, our legs entangled. But despite our physical closeness, we feel more distant than ever.

"I'm fine," I lie. "Just didn't sleep very well."

I nestle closer to him, as if the act of our skins touching will erase what happened. And for the millionth time since yesterday, the memories come back.

Cheater, cheater, cheater.

My stomach contracts. Thinking back, it's impossible not to have seen the signs. There's been a steady tension building, a frisson of sexual energy, between Greg and me. As soon as I saw *you* in his eyes, I should have run for the hills.

"Do you need to work today?" I say, hoping for the answer I need to hear.

Seb smiles. "Well, it's a Tuesday, so yes."

"Could you take off?"

The words sound needy, but I can't stop them from coming. "We could go on a trip. Just you and me. Drive around the area."

Seb sighs, arching his back and sitting upright in bed. "I'm sorry. I know I've barely shown you anything since we got here."

He turns to face me. "How about I take you to the vineyard this weekend? I need to be there at some point, and we can make a trip out of it."

In my mind, I'm going over the logistics, wondering if Ana will be okay with taking care of Alma while we're gone. She arrived back from Barcelona last night, exhausted but relieved that her child was no longer sick. But I don't want to bring any of that up right now. All I want is to focus on the future. Seb and I together at his family vineyard.

I sit up straight. "Sounds perfect."

He smiles and wraps an arm around me. I bury my head in his neck, knowing that in a few seconds he'll get up and leave. So I savour the moment for as long as it lasts.

Here, in this bed, I tell myself, we're safe.

* * *

The misty haze of the shower swirls around me like a blanket. It's funny, but in the steam, I breathe easier.

But something's nagging at me. Gnawing at my stomach. My hand is careful with the shower gel, barely touching the wound on my thigh. The pain is deserved, I tell myself. But I hate how it reminds me of what happened yesterday. What I failed to put a stop to, before it was too late.

As I wipe the mist from the mirror, the feeling in the pit of my stomach grows. It's almost like a premonition. I know something is about to happen. Something that will change everything. And my body is busy warning me of the threat.

I get dressed in the bathroom, trying to forget about the sinking feeling. But when I open the bathroom door, I know what's waiting.

Seb is on the bed, and when he meets my gaze, he's wearing a look I haven't seen before.

I hold my breath. *He knows.* Call it collective unconscious, but if there's something to hide, you can trust life to shed light on it. I stand there, unable to say anything. For as long as we're quiet, it isn't real yet.

But Seb breaks the silence.

"Is there something you want to tell me?"

165

I blink, say nothing. Then, hating myself for it, I say: "What do you mean?'

I can sense the disappointment before it shows on his face. "Do you know where your phone is?"

"My phone?"

"Yes."

I can feel the heat rising to my cheeks, my heartbeat loud in my ears. "Uh, in my bag, I think."

But I know it's not. I can see my phone there, next to the bed, plugged into charge. But I don't remember plugging it in. I'd been in such a rush yesterday to get home and bring the blade to my thigh that I'd dropped my bag on the floor, the phone either still inside or slipping out.

Seb must know what I'm thinking, because he says, "I found it on the floor. It was basically dead, so I put it on charge for you."

Dread spreads through my body, the warmth shooting down my limbs. The seconds pass in slow motion until Seb utters the question. "Who's Greg?"

I visibly flinch. "He's—he's a classmate."

Seb nods, his gaze on the floor. It's like he can't look at me. "You should check your messages. He really wants to talk to you."

"Seb—"

"Fucking unbelievable," he says with a snarl. His eyes lock on mine and they're wide and fierce. Angry, like I haven't seen him before. "All this time, I knew there was something going on. You come home drunk every time from that class." His eyes are narrow. "If there even *is* a class."

"Of course there's a class!" I counter, my voice shrill.

"Obviously, from all the Spanish you can clearly speak."

The words are sharp. He's never spoken to me like this before. I try to speak, but I realise I'm in the dark here. Seb must have seen some sort of message from Greg that I haven't. My stomach drops again. *Oh God, what did Greg say?*

"Nothing happened between us, I promise. I—"

"Please, stop," Seb says, holding out a hand. "I don't want to hear it."

"Please," I say. "You're right. You're completely right. I *have* been drinking too much. But I promise you I didn't do anything, and that kiss was an accident, it was—"

I immediately realise my mistake. Seb's face crumples. "Kiss?"

Fuck, fuck, fuck.

"He was drunk," I say, fumbling for words. "He just leaned in, I—"

Seb holds out his hand again, eyes cast to the floor. "I need some air."

"Let me come with—"

"*No.*"

His words stilt me, loud and angry. Without looking at me, he's out of the door. I stand still for a minute, as if waiting for Seb to change his mind and come back, but he doesn't, so I dart for my phone. It feels like forever for the device to recognise my face, my hands shaking as I hold it. Suddenly—just like the guilty would—I regret granting Seb access to my phone. Setting facial recognition up for him. Without it, he might not have seen anything.

The phone unlocks and there, open for the world to see, is the thread of texts from Greg.

I'm so sorry. We drank way too much.

I feel like a twat.

I couldn't help myself.

I sit on the ground, bringing my knees to my chest. I scroll further up the chat. Flinching, I cringe at the messages dripping with flirtatious energy. Not one mention of my fiancé.

The two Spanish musketeers! More like the two drunkards.

Is it weird that our bar crawl is the highlight of my day?

I throw the phone across the room. Closing my eyes, I picture what Seb must have thought as he went through the texts. Reading that last message, then scrolling up through the thread, curiosity taking hold. I would have done the same.

And now he's seen it. All of it.

A sob forms in my throat as the next thought hits me.

What happens now?

CHAPTER 31:

CAT

Present Day

There's a board against the wall.

I walk towards it, my eyes still adjusting to the darkness of the study. It's a corkboard, with red linen lines stretched across the surface, connecting handwritten notes. Newspaper clippings with headlines I can't make out. Yellow and green push pins hold the notes and clippings to the board. Beside them, I see photographs. They're all a blur of colour, but when I walk closer, there's one that leaps out at me. One that caught my attention in the first place.

It's a picture of me. From Facebook, taken years ago. It's pinned to the top right corner of the corkboard. I walk closer, tracing the red lines connected to it. The first line connects to the top left of the board, a newspaper clipping with a picture of a blonde woman. The headline reads *British woman commits suicide in Northern Spain*.

I've seen this article before. I scan the other newspaper headlines on the board. They're all like the ones I'd seen online. About Lisa. Her suicide. I study her face in the picture, her smile that doesn't look natural. Almost like it's forced.

In the middle of the board, there's another photograph. This one more intimate. It's of Lisa and a man. It's a selfie, and in this picture her smile is genuine. For a moment I don't recognise him—his dark brown hair and stubble. But seeing his eyes, I remember.

The fiancé.

At the bottom right of the board, there are scattered notes stacked atop each other, a green push pin trying to hold them together. I don't recognise anyone in those images. Lastly, on the bottom left, there's an older photograph of two children standing next to each other. A young boy and a girl. She's taller than him, with pigtails.

The dread swirls in my stomach as I step back and take in the full board. I'm breathing so loud I barely hear the footsteps. It's only when I hear the click of the study door closing that I know I'm not alone.

And I've run out of time.

I turn, the stench of cigarette smoke surrounding him. In this light, he looks like a ghoul, cut from the dark cloth of the shadows.

"What the hell is this?" I ask, motioning to the wall.

Richard's face is blank. "It's a corkboard."

I point to my photograph. "Why is my picture here?"

His lips shift like he's eaten something sour, and his gaze moves past me, scanning the board. Finally, as if he's decided something, he looks at me. "Why do you think it is?"

I blink, my mind racing. All at once, I think of InCheck, the Instagram message. The camera in my room. Every single bad thing that has ever happened. Everything including—

"There's a good reason it's up there," he says. "I just wonder if you can figure it out."

"No, no—" I say, jabbing a finger at my photograph again, "Why is this here? What *is* all of this?" My voice turns hysterical. "Are you spying on me?"

"I wouldn't call it spying."

"Were you spying on *her*?" I say, shifting my finger to Lisa's picture. Richard has been talking about her since the day I got here, and here are pictures of her pinned against the wall—along with one of me—like in some crime drama on Netflix. This, the camera in my room and Richard's Bogeyman behaviour last night. It's all painting a picture, and I'm not liking it one bit.

"You were spying on Lisa," I say. "And now you're spying on me."

Richard shakes his head. "No."

"Then what about the camera?"

His face twists. "What camera?"

"Come on," I say, my voice quivering. I'm trying to sound tough, but it's clearly not working. "I've seen it. In my room. Behind the power socket."

Richard raises his hand, closes his eyes under furrowed brows. "Hold on—we're going off track here." When he opens his eyes again, he brings his index finger and thumb together. "There's no camera in your room. I can assure you of that."

"Then what about all of *this*?" I say, pointing at the wall. My eyes fall on the newspaper clippings again, the headlines of Lisa's suicide sounding like a drum in my ears.

"You were involved, weren't you?" I say.

Richard's face crumples. *"What?"*

"In her death," I continue. "You had something to do with it. And now you're what—trying to cover up for something? Think *I* know something?" I shake my head. "I don't."

I'm making things up as I go. I don't believe half the things I'm saying, but what other explanation is there? My mind's on a mission to find an answer. A reason for why I'm here in this room with this man, trying to find a connection between me and a dead girl.

"Okay, back up," Richard says, his voice louder than before. "None of that is true. This isn't about me. This is about *you*."

I shake my head again. "I don't know what you're talking about."

"I'm an investigator," he says, the words articulated so clearly his teeth are showing.

"But you told me you were an architect."

He shrugs, rubs at his neck. "That's not completely true."

"So why should I trust anything you say? If you've lied before?" For a second, I feel proud of myself. Standing up to this giant. But then again, I'm completely in the dark about what's going on. He could be right, and I could be wrong.

"Look—let's turn this around, okay?" Richard says. "Do you think there's any reason someone would investigate you?"

"*Me?*"

"Yes."

The same thoughts rush through my mind again. InCheck, the Instagram message. Except now, they're coming the other way, fast and aggressive. Towards me.

"So I'm being investigated?"

"You are."

"By *you?*" I say, not quite believing my words. Here I was, thinking I was onto *him*. He's been suspicious from day one. But thinking about it now, maybe he's been suspicious because he's been silently observing me.

"You might want to sit down," he says, motioning to the chair behind the desk.

Nausea rises in my chest. Suddenly, I'm aware again of how alone I am. Alone in this room with him, alone in this foreign country, with almost no one knowing where I am. Even if my mom has my location now, who is to say I'll be here tomorrow? Or in an hour from now? What if this guy thinks I'm someone I'm not? Or worse, what if he's found out about InCheck somehow and is about to report me? Who will save me then?

"You really need to sit down," he says.

The thoughts keep coming, and the more I think about the possibilities, the more they seem so obvious.

He's onto you. He knows about InCheck.

I think of the Instagram message. *I know you're a fraud, Alice.* A simple warning. One I ignored.

But there's one thought I hold on to. One thing that can save me. *What does any of this have to do with Lisa?*

I sit down behind the desk as Richard leans against it. "We're going to talk through this, all right?"

I don't nod or shake my head. I trust nothing right now. My breathing is harsh and jagged. Maybe I should run. But where would I go? I have no car, and I haven't seen one taxi in this town. Plus, with Richard's car, he can easily follow me. Stuck—that's what I am.

I look up at him. "Why me? I didn't know Lisa. I wasn't here when she died."

"You need to breathe," he says.

"*Breathe?*" I say, hands motioning to the wall again. "My photo is pinned to a board!"

"Yes, but look," he walks around the desk, crouches down. "I don't think you did it."

My face crinkles. "Did *what?*"

I look back at the corkboard, at the scattered photographs, recalling the news articles I read about Lisa's suicide. According to the police, there was no foul play suspected. But there's a shadow of doubt surrounding the circumstances. It's in the way Richard keeps talking about her, how Charlotte seemed shocked when I brought her up.

Like there's more to the story.

I suck in a breath. "But she killed herself," I say, forming my mouth around each word, the question desperate. "How could I have anything to do with that?"

CHAPTER 32:

LISA

Six Months Ago

Seb and I didn't go to the vineyard.

The more I tried to talk to him, the more he recoiled from me. After storming out that morning, he came back hours later, letting me explain the texts between me and Greg. And the kiss.

"I swear, he only kissed me. And then I left," I pleaded, trying my best to get close to him.

But he didn't budge.

"Where were your other classmates?" he asked.

I couldn't bring myself to lie to him again. Each moment with Greg was a type of betrayal. Not just against Seb, but against me. With Greg, I was reliving my past. Moments I shared with *you*. Without knowing it, I was breathing them into Greg.

And for my own sanity, I couldn't go back there. To the past. It was that realisation that brought me to tears.

"I'm so sorry," I said to Seb.

He paced the room. He looked hurt. We'd barely started our life, and here I was setting it on fire already. If people cheated, it was later down the line, years into their marriage, right? Not whilst they were still engaged, on the brink of starting their journey together.

Was it really cheating? A small voice called to me amidst the chorus of self-loathing.

I'd pushed Greg away and fled. Back to Seb. I'd stuck around for him in this strange town. But here I was, pleading guilty. Eleanor was right. I cause havoc wherever I go, but I also seem to have no backbone.

"What happens now?" Seb had asked. "Was it just a drunk moment? I need to know."

Beneath his grim expression, there was something. A need for the truth, so he could make a decision about our future.

"It was nothing," I told him. "It meant nothing. I promise you."

He nodded. "Where does he live?"

I replied with the truth, ignoring the pit in my stomach. "Somewhere uptown."

Seb walked to the window, staring out at the ocean. But when he turned to face me, his eyes were different. Dark. "You're not going back to that class."

"I won't."

It's the least I could do. I think of the bar Greg and I kept going to, the blurred faces passing us by. How many of them had known Seb? His mother? What must they have thought? Seeing this foreign woman hanging out so much with a man that wasn't her fiancé?

Shameless, Eleanor squawked in my head. *You're completely shameless.*

"I'll make this better," I told Seb. "I promise."

I took a cautionary step towards him. He didn't smile, but the frown faded. And when he spoke, it was like I could hear Eleanor in his voice. The disappointment laced through the words.

"I hope so, Lisa," he said. "I know it's been hard, but I'm counting on you to keep it together. For us."

* * *

Days pass slowly. The house is quiet, despite my mind whirring away.

With Ana back from Barcelona, Seb and his sister have fallen back into a familiar rhythm, the dining room simmering with barely-disguised annoyance as they work. Seb watches my every move, as if waiting for me to make a mistake again. I try to keep my head down, writing empty words, the characters hollow and sad. To make up for my guilt, I make Seb and Ana constant cups of coffee, and stand by as the physiotherapist performs small, strained movements with Alma. The only relief is that Seb didn't tell his sister or mother about our fight. About what I did. That would be horrible.

I wonder when we'll leave Gexta. If we'll ever leave, now.

This morning offers some relief, though. Deb's WhatsApp message lights up my phone on the dining table. My eyes trail to Seb's, watching if he's noticed. But he barely looks up from his laptop.

"Deb's ASOS order arrived," I say.

"Hmm."

"She wants me to come over."

I wait, split seconds dragging. *Please don't make me ask.*

"You should go," Seb says, eyes still on his screen.

Minutes later, I'm out the door and up the street. I must look awful, because when Deb opens the door, her eyes widen. "Are you all right?"

She makes me tea while I spill my woes, telling her about the kiss with Greg, and the last few days of solitude I've had in the house.

"Just give it a few days. Seb will calm down," Deb says, sliding a packet of biscuits towards me. I inhale them like I haven't eaten for days.

"So, where's the ASOS pack?" I say, wiping the crumbs from my mouth.

"Oh right," she says, as if she's forgotten. "It's upstairs. Shall we go have a look then?"

I wait in the spare bedroom as she tries on her new clothes. The sheets on the bed are freshly changed, like someone's slept here.

Maybe Richard.

I remember the fight they had a week ago, sending us out before we'd even had a chance to eat the roast dinner. I look around the room—at the few personal touches. I wonder how many times Deb has sat here, wondering if little feet would patter across these floorboards.

175

"How does it look?" Deb says, standing in the doorframe. The floral dress she's wearing is wrinkled, the fabric falling like a sheet over her.

"Where's the belt?" I ask.

She pulls it out from behind her back and I walk over to her, adjusting the belt around her waist, and letting her check the mirror in her bedroom. As I follow her into the room, I notice the contrast between the bedside tables. Hers is scattered with books, reading glasses, and vials of pills. The other table is bare, like no one uses it.

"There," I say, looking at Deb's frame in the mirror. "See how the dress now creates an hourglass shape? The belt completes it."

She swings around, the dress shimmering. "I love it."

She tries on the other dress and blouse, each fitting well. When she tries on the black trousers, they're tight around her middle. She gives me a look of disappointment as she takes another look in the mirror.

"It's okay," I tell her. "Now we know what sizes work for you. Perhaps the Tall collection, but a size smaller."

Deb changes in her bathroom, coming back out with a frown, holding up the trousers before she places them on the bed. "But what do I do with this?"

I take the trousers and put them back in the plastic bag they came in. "We return them and get a refund. I'll do it for you at the post office."

It's not much, but it's *something* to keep busy. And it feels good, helping a friend. There's a shine to Deb's eyes as she takes her new clothes down to the washer.

My stomach churns at the thought of going home, so when Deb offers wine, I accept. It's only when she pours the liquid that I feel the guilt settling in. "Not too much, please."

She raises a brow and hands me a glass. "You know, Richard isn't around a lot. As I'm sure you can see. If you ever need a place to escape to, you're always welcome here."

We sip wine and watch the fog spread across the ocean, as it does every afternoon. But when she offers me a second glass, I turn it down.

"I need to get back."

Her lips tighten, but something tells me she understands. I'd love to stay here with her. To bask in the familiar. But I need to be home with Seb. And drink less.

The wind tugs at my coat as I walk the few steps down the road, playing out ideas for the evening. Perhaps Seb and I could cook together. Talk about the vineyard. Talk about anything, really. But when I get home, Seb's not there, his car gone. I check my phone for a message, but there's none. Sound scrambles from the kitchen, and when I enter, Ana's at the stove, reheating soup.

"Do you know where Seb is?" I ask.

"He's gone to the vineyard. He'll be back tomorrow," she says, a smile on her face. But her eyes reveal how tired she is. "Didn't he tell you?"

She doesn't need me to answer. My dismayed look says it all. She shrugs, waves it away with a hand. "He was in a rush. Is soup okay for dinner?"

I nod and crack a weak smile.

After dinner, Ana and Alma hunch together on a video call with her family in Barcelona. I say a brief hello to Ana's husband, his face barely visible behind two sets of white teeth, smiling at the camera. Ana's kids are adorable, a genuine reflection of her.

I make my excuses and escape from the living room. Laying my head against the pillow in the bedroom, I reread the message Seb sent me right after dinner.

Urgent meeting at the vineyard. Will be home tomorrow morning. Hope you're okay.

I think of how different his message is to previous ones. No *I love you* or *thinking of you.*

But it's like Deb said. Give it time.

Hearing Ana and Alma's laughter from downstairs, I pull the laptop onto the bed, my fingers urging me to find something to type. Anything to distract me from the sounds of laughter. The voices of a happy family.

I look at what I've typed into Google. *How to stop being lonely.*

CHAPTER 33:

CAT

Present Day

I felt calmer after a cigarette. Or two.

Richard, if that's even his real name, offered me one. Then another. We stood outside as we smoked, and with each breath my heartbeat slowed, the fog in my mind starting to lift.

"So what happens now?" I said to him after a while.

He put the lighter back into his cigarette pack. "Now, we talk."

So now we're back in the study. I take the big seat behind the desk. From here I have a clear view of the corkboard, my picture still there, exposed. From behind me, a ray of sunlight breaks through the shutters.

No wonder he kept this room locked. If only I knew what was in here all along. Then again, would it have helped me? It makes me wish I'd never come to this weird small town in the first place.

Richard sits down opposite me, taking out his phone. He starts a recording and my senses go on high alert.

"Hold on, what's that for?"

"I'm recording this conversation," he says. "For evidence."

"Could you not?"

I still don't trust him. Even if he is an investigator, I don't know what I'm being investigated for. I should be cautious. Protect myself.

There's a standoff as we stare at each other. Richard sighs and grabs for a notepad on a cabinet against the wall. He puts his phone back in his pocket.

"Fine."

"Thank you."

"You pulled a sly move," he continues. "Sneaking in here like that."

His expression is stern, but there's a tugging at the corners of his mouth. It's like he wants to smile.

I shrug. "You didn't hide what you were doing very well."

"Guess not," he says, eyes scanning the room.

"So who are you?"

"I'm Neil."

"*Neil?*" I reel back. "Really?"

"Like I said, I'm an investigator. Some of the things I told you about me before were a front."

"You mean like a cover."

"Exactly," he says.

My mind scrambles to make sense of it all. "So if you're not Richard, then what's all this?" I gesture around me. "The house, Deborah, your architect job?"

"A front."

I place my elbows on the table, hands tugging at my face. "So Deborah, she's—"

"Not my wife."

I look at him, my eyes narrowed. "I knew something was off with you two."

He raises an eyebrow, says nothing.

"So, is Deborah your investigating partner?"

He lets out a little laugh. "No, God no. She's just cooperating."

I scratch my forehead in confusion.

"Let me explain," he says. "Everything Deborah told you about herself is true. About this house and the Richard bloke, it's all true. Richard is Deborah's real husband, or rather ex-husband, now."

I shake my head. "So are you saying you're acting like the real Richard? Deborah's husband?"

"*Ex*-husband," he says. "They're separated. And yes. He used to live here and is a real architect. And a piece of shit, from what Deb told me."

I shift in my chair. On the surface, all of this information is crazy. But somehow, it doesn't shock me as much as I thought it would. My mind flashes back to the night when Deborah fell, how she told me about Richard's cheating. And the house they have in the UK where he's keeping his new fling. Suddenly, it all makes sense. The real Richard used to live here. It explains why Neil sleeps in the study and his relationship with Deborah seems off. They're strangers to each other.

"But don't people notice?" I ask. "In town? That you're not the real Richard? And why use a cover? Why would Deborah allow you to do this?" I bury my head in my hands again. "What the hell is going on?"

"Hey, *hey*," Neil says, leaning over the desk. "It's a lot to process, I know. But it'll all start to make sense."

I look up at him. That threatening look he's been wearing for days is gone, and in its place is a look that makes me feel slightly more at ease. Even if I can't fully trust him yet, I believe he's telling the truth. That somehow he means well.

I nod. "Okay."

Neil takes a breath. "I needed a reason to be in Gexta for the investigation. The townspeople know about it. So Deb offered me a place to stay. And then, when you came here, well—"

"You thought it was a good idea to trick me?"

"I thought it was a good idea to make you think that nothing was going on."

I sit back, cross my arms. "But now I know."

He sighs. "Yes, now you know. And maybe it's better like this. I haven't been getting very far with anything, but—look, you can't tell Deb you know about the investigation. It'll complicate things."

"Complicate it?" I ask. "It seems pretty complicated already."

He's not impressed. For the first time, I can picture him as a policeman. "Deb and the people in town only know that there's an investigation. I don't want them to be involved in the details. It's important that we keep everything the way it is."

"Completely in the dark, basically," I say.

"Yes."

For a moment, I think of agreeing to his request. He has a new air of authority to him that makes me think he knows what he's doing. But then I remind myself that this could be another one of his lies. And me keeping quiet could be a bad call.

"I'm not promising anything without knowing what the investigation is about. And how I'm involved."

Neil purses his lips. He walks to the corkboard and unpins a series of photographs. From the corner of the room, he rummages through a box filled with papers. He sits down again and slides a photograph across the desk to me.

The photo of Lisa.

"Then let's start at the beginning," he says. "Do you know this girl?"

"Yes," I say. "From Googling her."

"So you know she lived here. A few houses down the road."

He doesn't wait for me to answer.

"She came here with this bloke, Sebastian." He puts another photo down. The hooded man I've seen on the street. Neil takes another look at the photos. "His mother lives here. They're locals."

"And what's all of this got to do with me?"

"We'll get there," Neil says calmly. "Long story short, Lisa didn't like it here. From what people were saying, she was having problems adjusting. Things took a rough turn. She started hitting the bottle, drinking a lot with this one."

He motions to the hallway. Deborah.

"Lisa started withdrawing more and more. Then one night she goes missing. Her body washes up two days later on a beach not far from here. The last anyone saw of her was on the dock."

"The dock down the road," I say.

"Yep, that one." Neil takes a breath and from this view, he looks almost reverent. "The autopsy said she drowned. They found alcohol and narcotics in her system, which all point to her being drunk or high or both. They say she fell into the water. That it was an accident."

There's a pause as his gaze shifts just behind my shoulder. He looks different to the other times he's spoken about her. Before, it was as if he was angry, but now, he seems genuinely touched by the loss of this young woman's life.

"But they found a note," he says. "Addressed to her fiancé. They reckoned it was a suicide note. Some friends of hers also came forward after her death with some odd texts she'd sent them. It all started to indicate that she ..." he trails off.

"Killed herself?"

"Looks like it."

I fold my arms and sit back.

"The British police got involved," he continues. "Took matters into their own hands. They looked into Lisa's past and found things that pointed to her... *instability*."

He makes a point of emphasising the word, enunciating every syllable clearly. "Some drama with an ex-boyfriend. The police then looked into Sebastian, the fiancé. They wanted to cover all angles. You know how they say the husband always does it? Well, they wanted to cross that possibility off the list."

"And did they?"

Neil takes a breath. "Yep. He had a solid alibi for when she went missing. Was with his sister, who backed up his story."

"So?"

"So they ruled it as suicide," he says. "All the facts pointed that way. And the case was closed."

My brow furrows. "But if it's closed, then why are you here? And why am I the one being investigated?"

If Neil's impatient, he's not showing it. "The girl's family is wealthy. Too much money to know what to do with, really. And they weren't happy with the outcome of the investigation."

My mind connects the dots. "So *they* hired you?"

"Yes," he says. "For a second look. And after some digging, I've found something the police overlooked the first time."

He takes a piece of paper from the stack on the table. Slides it towards me. "Take a look."

I take the paper, sentences swimming in front of me. It takes me a while to see it, but when I do, heat rises up my neck and my stomach lurches. I scan the first page, flipping it over to the second, third, fourth. My hands start to tremble.

"Do you recognise the name?" he asks, tapping his finger on the page. "This one here, in the corner."

The words die in my throat. I want to say no.

But I can't.

CHAPTER 34:

LISA

Six Months Ago

I quickly fall down the search engine rabbit hole.

I find numerous articles on relationship health, dozens of YouTube videos on loneliness. What anxiety feels like. As I read, the same phrase appears in a million different variations. *Depression is normal, normal, normal.*

It's funny, but not funny ha-ha. Because it's not what I've been told all my life.

Terms like *depression* and *anxiety* weren't permitted in our house. Whenever I talked about how I felt, instead of what I thought or did, my father would leave the room. And when I had that brief episode that ended with me in hospital, he wasn't there. Only Eleanor was. I still remember her hand patting mine, chalking the situation down to fatigue. I'd be better tomorrow, she'd said, and I just needed time to lick my wounds.

But we're not going down that road. The wedding, my red dress. *You* in your tux, rigid and shocked at the sight of me there.

I think back to school and uni. How the topic of mental health was largely talked away. There were conversations about it. But I never took part in any of it, because why would I have? I was surrounded by lively, high-on-life people who were drunk on life and love, and had the education and money to carry them. As Eleanor kept telling me, I had everything to be grateful for, and nothing to be sad about.

And yet, I keep scrolling. Googling symptoms. Everything feels so ... *me.*

Lost. Alienated. Self-harming (can't deny that one). Self-loathing. Stressed. Tired.

All of it is me.

You should seek help, they say. Talk to someone. But who would I speak to?

A friend, they say. A family member, a lover. So I take inventory of the people in my life. Eleanor, the mother who I've disappointed time and time again. Ruth, the best friend who I keep bothering with my problems. Seb, who I've hurt. Deb, who drinks her problems away, just like me. Greg, who's off-limits. And Ana, a friendly face, but one that makes me hesitate.

No, talking to anyone in my immediate circle wouldn't work.

I type in *find someone to talk to,* and watch the results flood in. I avoid the ads, and find an article linking to a directory for counsellors and therapists in Spain. The more I see, the more lost I feel.

There must be a better way.

I settle on a woman therapist in Bilbao with experience in self-esteem and depression. But when I look at her profile, the logistics of my expedition become clear.

How would I get to her office? What would I tell Seb?

I type *online therapist* into the search bar.

The headline jumps out at me. *Start Being Happy Today.*

I keep reading. *Speak to a licensed counsellor anytime, anywhere. What are you waiting for?*

I never click on ads, but this one pulls me in. When I land on the page, the banner reads *InCheck—confidential and convenient therapy.*

I scroll down the page, ignoring a prompt to take InCheck's starter quiz. There's an animated section that tells you how easy it is to sign up, find a therapist, and start communication. I find the reviews next, each more positive than the first.

It's been a long journey, but with Sarah's help, I've started taking the necessary steps to achieve self-love. It's brought me out of a dark place and shown me how differently I can see the world, says Hannah from Boise, Idaho.

Then there's Jonah in Doha, Qatar: *Stress has always been part of my life.*

But with the help of my counsellor, I've found my balance and have learned that I'm stronger than I ever thought.

My curiosity piqued, I decide to take the quiz. It's supposed to help assess your needs and match you with a counsellor. The quiz starts out easily with a list of demographic questions. Gender. Relationship status. Age. I select from the multiple-choice options, and when it comes to religious beliefs, I hesitate. It's strange, answering a question you've never considered.

Religious, no. Spiritual, maybe.

The quiz presents a series of symptoms for me to choose from. I click on *depression*, *anxiety* and *self-esteem*. It asks about my eating and sleeping habits, how I feel most days and if I have problems with intimacy. As I click the relevant answers, images bubble up in my mind. The food binging, the drinking, the cutting, the self-loathing.

One question catches me off guard. *Have you ever considered suicide?*

The wedding comes into focus again, and I shake my head. No, surely that's not what it was.

I select *Never*.

When I'm asked how I'd like to communicate with my counsellor, I select text and phone calls only. My stomach turns at the thought of someone looking at me, analysing me across a screen on a video call. I want to stay as private as possible.

I'm prompted to create an account. I use a fake name. *Rachel MacMillan.* I quickly take out my card and pay the monthly subscription. A small price to pay for a friend.

Once I'm signed up, I stare at the welcome screen. I'm nervous, still feeling exposed. I take my old phone out of the suitcase and switch it on, fiddling in my handbag for my old sim card. Thank God I kept it. I log out of InCheck on the laptop and download the app on my old phone. The last thing I want is Seb or anyone else finding this.

I sit back on my bed, eyeing the welcome message from InCheck. *Are you ready to meet your counsellor?*

I'm buzzing with adrenaline as I click through. I think of how I'll introduce myself, what I'll say when they ask me the inevitable question.

Why are you here?

I barely know how to begin.

But I'm strangely excited.

CHAPTER 35:

CAT

Present Day

I knew InCheck would come back to bite me someday. Looks like today's that day.

Neil leaves me alone in the study as he goes to the kitchen. I reread the pages he's handed me, the typed words washing over me like a distant memory. One I don't want to remember. *Haven't* remembered. When he returns, he's holding a sandwich in his hand, the cheese on the brink of falling out.

"Are you really going to eat that now?" I ask.

Neil keeps chewing. "Are you ready to start?"

I sigh. I'm not ready to talk about any of this. But it doesn't feel like I have a choice. These pages—the ones I've been reading over and over again—are proof that Neil knows more about me than I thought. If I could look past my anxiety and think logically, I'd know that a private investigator hired by some family in the UK wouldn't have a hold on me. He's not the police. But the pages give him leverage. Something to use against me.

So I look at Neil, take a breath. "Sure."

He pulls out a napkin, puts his half-eaten sandwich on it, and grabs a pen. "So. InCheck. Let's start there."

My eyes search for his phone, for if he's planning on recording this, but it's nowhere. "I have a question," I say as Neil gives me that *this-is-not-how-this-works* look.

"How... how did you find me?" I say. "I mean, how did you figure out I was Alice? On the app?"

Neil clears his throat. "It's a long story."

"We've got time."

He sits back. "Tell you what. We can trade information for information." He lifts a brow. "And we'll start with you."

My eyes find my photograph on the corkboard again. "Fine."

Neil scribbles *InCheck* on the paper, underlining it. I'm looking at him like he's a movie playing on the TV. It feels distant. Because how can any of this be real?

"When did you start using InCheck?"

I think back to when I first met John. It all started with John.

"Almost a year ago. Maybe eight, nine months," I say.

"And how?"

"How what?"

"How did you start impersonating a counsellor?" Neil says, with particular emphasis on the word *impersonate*.

"Why are you interested?" I ask. "Am I being investigated for InCheck, or Lisa?"

My question seems to catch him off guard. He takes a deep breath. "Both."

"But you can't be," I say. "Because Lisa's family hired you."

My voice is shaky, but I keep talking. "You're just a private investigator."

Neil grips the pen. He's clearly irritated that I'm not following the script. But it means I have a point.

"I can report you to the authorities at any time," he counters.

We're silent for a moment, staring at each other across the desk. Inside, I'm terrified that what he says could be true. He knows I've done something illegal, and even if it doesn't relate directly to Lisa or her family, it can land me in a lot of trouble in a country where I don't even speak the language.

"So I suggest you work with me here," Neil says, breaking the silence. "And tell me how you started using InCheck. It might just help your case."

I could tell him some of the story. He might already *know* the story. I think back to the days leading up to it, a whole other time in my life.

189

"I had a neighbour," I say. "He gave me access to the app."

Neil raises an eyebrow, but doesn't seem surprised. Maybe he knows about John. I think back to how I met him in a local bar. The suburb we lived in, Melville, is perched atop a hill, and on a clear night, the blinking lights of the Johannesburg city centre are vibrant against the brooding African skies.

I think back to that tiny bar with a faux beach theme. The wallpaper was yellow and curling away from the wall in places, the wooden tables sticky with the residue of endless cigarettes and spilled beer. John saw me sitting alone in the corner, nursing my wine. As he approached me, he looked like a ghoul, his skin pasty in the dimly lit bar.

"Hey neighbour!" he called. I'd often seen him talking to people outside his house, but I'd never met him.

I let him buy me a shot, then another. I didn't really want the company, but I could do with the drinks.

"You know, my mother always trusted redheads," John told me. "Believed they were old souls. You should come over to my place sometime. It's a real funhouse."

And so I did.

"At first, I thought he was a small-time drug dealer," I tell Neil. "But when I went to his place, there was clearly more going on."

I remember the garden, with its unruly shrubs and yellow, patchy lawn. Inside, three or four computers lined the dining room table, a tangle of wires across the floor.

"He must have been some sort of hacker," I say. "Or worked with a few of them. Strange guys were always arriving at his house. Drunk or high most of the time."

I didn't particularly like John. Or his buddies. But it was an easy escape. I was a university dropout carrying dark clouds of guilt. All I wanted was to get away from my mother and my life.

Neil frowns. "So the guy was bad news. And despite that, you still hung out with him?"

"I didn't know what I was doing. I was in a bad place," I say. "By the time

I realised he was probably not a good guy, well—"

"You were caught up in the rush of being a counsellor," Neil finishes my sentence for me.

I narrow my eyes. "When do I get to ask my question?"

"Soon."

I clear my throat and Neil waves at me to continue.

"So one day he asks me what I do for a living," I say. "I said *nothing* because, well, I wasn't doing anything at the time. I only started teaching a few months later. And so he offered Alice's profile to me."

"*Offered* it to you?" Neil says, his brow furrowed.

"Yes. He was selling InCheck profiles. Plus profiles for other apps as well. He said it was common, especially with US companies. Something about it being less traceable to Africa."

"Plus, I found it interesting," I add. "Talking to other people about their problems. I went to a therapist before, so I figured I could do it."

Neil looks like he's really, *really* trying not to roll his eyes. Hearing my own words, I understand why. I must sound like an idiot.

I remember John and I smoking in his unkempt garden, a red kimono wrapped around him.

"You seem like a nice girl. A bit sad though," he told me. "I think you've got a painful story to tell. And make others feel better for it."

He said he usually sold the profiles to unemployed people who were proficient in English, but too lazy to look for work.

"But with you, I think I'll be paying it forward," he told me.

"Sounds like a pretty easy way to make money," Neil says now, scribbling notes on paper.

I tell Neil how payments worked on InCheck. The actual amount of money I made from the app was barely enough for a tank of petrol every month. But for someone who counted every cent for their next drink, it was fine.

"Can you answer my question now?" I ask.

"Right after you answer me this," he says. "When did you start talking to Lisa? Or as you knew her, Rachel?"

I feel that same sinking feeling that first hit me when I read the pages he gave me a few minutes ago. Proof of my connection with Lisa. Neil slides the transcripts over to me again, stabbing a finger at the name on the first page. I should have known Lisa was a previous client. It was the only thing that made sense.

The moment I saw my photograph pinned to that corkboard, I should have known, too. Because what else could it have been? And yet the idea felt too crazy, too far-fetched. Rachel was one of my first clients. It was a dark period of which I remember very little.

"Because Rachel is Lisa," Neil says now. "I can confirm that."

I clear my throat. "I spoke to her half a year ago. In January. She—*Rachel*—was one of my first clients."

"And how long did you talk for?"

I take a breath. "A few weeks, maybe a month." I meet Neil's eyes. "But you already know all this, don't you?"

He sits back in his chair. "And according to you, what was Rachel's main problem? Why was she using the app?"

"Anxiety or depression. That's what I—Alice—listed as my skills."

Neil's face barely changes, but I know he's judging me again.

I carry on. "We had an intro call on the first day. The app recommends that. Having a first call. It's better to hear a voice first before chatting over text."

Neils scoffs. "Sounds… *professional.*"

"I remember her saying she was lonely." I pull the transcripts toward me, scanning the first few chats laid out on the page.

"And how many times did you talk?"

"I don't know. A few times, I guess."

Neil pulls out another paper from his pile. He studies it, then looks up at me. "You had four calls in total."

I exhale. "Honestly, I don't see why you need me for this. You seem to have all the information already."

He's slow to respond, his fingers tapping on the table. "The phone calls weren't recorded. Apparently, it's against InCheck's policy. So even though

I have all the transcripts from your chats on the app, I don't know what you talked about on your calls. I need you to piece together everything that happened on those calls. Because the last call you had with her ..." he trails off, raising his eyebrows. "Well, it correlates to the last time she was seen alive."

My head swims. None of this makes any sense. I can barely remember Rachel, or anything we talked about. I try to sift through the memories, recollect anything, but that time six months ago feels blurred out by the alcohol-fuelled darkness in my head.

"How did you find out I was Alice?" I ask again.

He breathes in deeply. "I have some hacker friends of my own."

"Come on. I gave you more info than that."

"I identified your IP address from InCheck," he says. "As soon as I knew Lisa was Rachel, I found Alice on the app and then tried to track her down. Alice's profile says she lives in the UK, but the IP address kept showing South Africa. After some digging, I found you."

Neil looks at me. "The rest was just marketing. I had to bring you here, so I needed to create something to lure you in, and make you take the bait."

I think back to the web banner for visiting Basque. The website promoting the teaching job, the messaging that seemed to speak directly to me. The concept was straightforward enough. I'd been served enough ads to know that companies followed you around the web. I just didn't think it would go this far. That a person could be targeted by an ad like that.

"So the banner, the website—it was all you?"

Neil nods. "Yep."

"But how did you know I'd take the bait?"

"I didn't. But I had the time and the resources. Lisa's family is looking for answers, and they paid me enough to do everything and *anything* to find it. It was a long shot. But hey, it worked."

I twist in my chair, my skin crawling. "You didn't even know anything about me."

"No, I didn't," he says. "But I knew your IP address. Your location, roughly. I knew the websites you visited. And by monitoring your activity—and with the help of my friends—I could link it back to your email address. From there, we could find your social media profiles." He takes a breath. "You really should look into your privacy settings."

When I say nothing, he continues. "And like I said, I did some marketing. I watched a lot of videos on how to create offers enticing enough to get people to click on it. And you did. You filled in that form on the website, and that was that."

"You mean for the offer to teach in Spain," I say.

"Exactly. By then, I'd found out that you were an English teacher, and from all the young teachers I know, who doesn't want to teach abroad?"

I think of Sam, how she'd flinch at someone saying this.

"And so you made up the Spain offer," I say.

"I did."

"And the visa too? The spending money I got?"

"All of it," Neil says, leaning back. "But hey—you now have a Schengen visa, don't you? You're still here legally."

My annoyance builds. None of this makes me feel any better.

"Why go through all this hassle?" I motion at the papers, the pictures on the board. "Getting a hacker to help you locate me, bringing me all the way here, staging a fake family. Why not just question me in South Africa?"

"Because that wouldn't make sense."

"What?" I say. "*How*? Because what you did—all of *this*—seems like a really elaborate and sick way to get me here for questioning."

A few beats pass as I wait for Neil to answer. When he opens his mouth, his words seem resigned, like even he isn't convinced about any of this.

"When I came to Gexta, my priority was to investigate the fiancé and his family. Along the way, I found out about Alice and InCheck. About you. So while I investigated my leads here in town, I used those marketing tools to draw you—Alice—in from abroad. I waited for you and your IP address to take the bait, and it ended up working."

I cross my arms, and Neil knows I'm not convinced.

"Look, I might not be police, but I know how the law works," he says. "I can't just go to a foreign country and question you there. I needed it to be closer to my own turf. I would have been out of my element in Africa."

I lean forward, the heat gathering in my cheeks. "Or maybe you're just enjoying this. This little play pretend charade."

Neil's lips are thin. I keep talking.

"Aren't you supposed to take me somewhere neutral? If you're not the police, I can leave right now and you can't do anything about it, can you? Like you said just now, I have a valid visa. It might not be a *work* visa, but it's a *tourist* visa, and I can leave anytime I want."

"True," Neil says, "I'm not the police. And you could leave, but I wouldn't suggest that."

"And why not?"

He leans forward, eyes burning into mine. "Because then things will get really bad, really fast."

CHAPTER 36:

LISA

Six Months Ago

Sleeping alone without Seb last night felt wrong. His absence was a gnawing reminder that things aren't okay between us. And yet somehow, I feel more rested than I have in weeks.

As the sun spreads across the sea this morning, I make coffee and toast in the kitchen. Alma and Ana are in the living room with the physiotherapist. With my breakfast in hand, I make my way back up the stairs to the bedroom, trying to motivate myself.

Today you might actually write something.

I do. And it's all rubbish. After a few hours of trying—and failing—to write down words with meaning, I open InCheck on my old phone and scan my counsellor's profile.

Alice Huntington.

She looks American, and I feel a strange disappointment. Was I hoping for someone more... well, British? But as I look at her chestnut hair and blue eyes, I feel calmer. She looks kind, like someone who doesn't just judge.

According to the app, she's a certified therapist with more than 100 clients. Worked as a private practitioner for eight years. At the bottom of the page, a button prompts me to schedule a call, or send her a text.

My mind wrestles with the options. A call would be a good start, right?

I'm about to schedule the call when there's a knock at the door.

"Lisa?"

I shove the phone under a pillow. "Come in."

"Hey," Ana says, peeking her head in.

"Hi."

"How's the writing going?"

I glance back at my closed laptop on the bed, the heat rising to my cheeks. "Oh, slowly. But you know what they say… it takes time."

I hate my words. *As if you're a pro, right?*

Ana's smile doesn't fade. "I was wondering if you wanted to go for a walk? And get some lunch?"

"Right now?"

"If you're not too busy?"

"No," I say. "Not busy. I need a break anyway."

A break from doing nothing.

I take a quick shower to freshen up, and meet Ana in the hall. She walks into the living room and says a few words to Alma, who is watching TV from her recliner chair. From behind Ana, I awkwardly wave goodbye to her.

Outside, the sky is bright, the sun shining through a few desultory clouds.

"I asked Seb to meet us for lunch," Ana says, walking ahead. For a second, my body is rigid, like the act of saying his name is a sin. We haven't spoken since he sent me that text last night, telling me he won't be coming home.

"He's on his way back from the vineyard," Ana continues. "He'll meet us at Casa Lucio."

I nod like all of this is normal. Like Seb and I are fine, and he has a perfectly functioning relationship with his sister. "Great."

As we walk side by side, the cool breeze gives me goosebumps, even through my coat. Despite the chill in the air, the sun is warm on my head and shoulders. "It's nice out today."

"It is," Ana says.

She takes her sunglasses from her jacket pocket as I look out across the bay, the water glistening in the sun. "How was Alma's physio today?"

"Good, the physiotherapist is very hopeful," she says, sunglasses over her eyes. "He says she'll be able to use the stairs again in a few weeks."

"That's great news."

"I guess that means we can all go back to normal," she says. "Are you and Seb planning to go back to the UK?"

Despite myself, I frown at Ana's question. I don't know the answer, and I doubt Seb does either. It's like we're stuck in limbo, our future uncertain. There's a fork in the road, compelling us to answer the inevitable question—can we move on from this?

The kiss with Greg, the ugly parts of Seb I've seen since being here, the ever-growing distance between us. All negative points on our scorecard.

"I don't know what we'll do," I tell Ana.

What if my marriage is over before it's even started?

She takes a breath, hands jammed into her jacket pockets. The wind tugs gently at her hair. I find myself wondering how someone so beautiful can be so understated at the same time.

"My brother is stubborn," she says. "I don't know what happened between you, but I know that whatever it is, he's taking it too far."

It takes a few beats for me to register her words, but when I do, relief comes flooding in. Thank God she doesn't know what I did. All this time I've been wondering if she or Alma knows.

"He always does that," she says.

I shake my head. "I don't know if he'll be able to move past it." My eyes are glued to the road, the faded line on the tar my anchor.

"He will," she says. "He likes to sometimes—how do you say it?" she looks up and creates a *tsk* sound with her tongue as she searches for words. "Sit in his pain. Sulk."

I smile. It's something an older sister would say. But despite that, the words ring true. I remember us back in the UK, when Seb would catch a cold. How he'd wallow in his pity like he was on the verge of death.

And when he was upset over a business call, he'd often sit in silence for hours, refusing to talk. The memory of him sitting at the dining table the other day comes to mind. Folded arms and pursed lips, like a child on the verge of a tantrum.

"Give him some time, he'll get over it," Ana says. "And then you can leave."

That last part catches me off guard, and I stop walking. Ana notices and turns to face me. "What?"

"It's not that I don't want to be here," I say.

"I know."

"It's so beautiful here, really," I say, motioning at the scenery. My eyes roam across the docked boats bobbing in the water. I feel the fresh air rolling down from the hills.

"It is," Ana says, smiling out at the ocean like it's an old friend. "But this is not a place for a new life."

"What do you mean?"

"This place is stuck in time. It's old, and it's fading."

I suddenly think of Alma, sitting in that house for years. Of the tired faces at the taverns, the empty streets devoid of laughter.

Ana keeps talking. "And it's beautiful *because* it's old and fading. But apart from the nature, nothing else grows here."

I look out at the greenery, the distant peaks with their clusters of trees. From here it all looks so lush. The rich green, the deep blue of the ocean. An incubator of life. But I see the steady deterioration of the buildings, and how the people in town look at foreigners like me.

"Is that why you moved to Barcelona?" I ask.

Ana's lips turn up faintly at the corners, like she's smiling. "My mom is here, and she'll always be here. But my family is in Barcelona now."

Her words are filled with warmth and love. It makes me sad. Makes me wonder where my own family is—back in the UK, or wherever Seb is?

We get to Casa Lucio, with its name painted across the top of the wooden door, the smell of the ocean rolling in from the bay. Outside, wooden tables and chairs face the sea, the walls painted a light blue. Ana greets a man with skin like leather, the result of being seasoned by the sun for decades. He ushers us to a table.

"Are you okay to sit outside?" she asks.

"Of course," I say.

We order two beers. There's silence as she types away at her phone. "Seb will be here in a few minutes," she says.

When he arrives, I watch him park his car down the road. I'm not used to seeing him drive so much. Back in the UK, he was fine with walking or taking public transport. But here, it's different. Just like so many other things about him.

Seb strides over to us, looking calm and collected. It's only when he sits down at the table that I'm propelled out of the spell of staring at him, forced to act.

"How was the vineyard?" I ask.

"Busy," he says, unzipping his jacket. I can smell his aftershave. Familiar. "But definitely needed."

There's a hint of a smile on his lips, and my insides relax a bit.

The three of us make easy conversation. We talk about the weather and the changing seasons that Gexta experiences—often all in one day. When the waiter comes to take our order, Ana gives me an uncertain look. "I was thinking of ordering a few things for the table. I know you don't like fish, but maybe you'll like some of the dishes here."

I hold my breath, look at Seb. His eyes are soft.

"I'll try it," I say.

And instantly, there's a shift in the energy at the table. The sun breaks through the clouds, rays hitting the water. I move closer to Seb, and he doesn't move away. Instead, he's smiling, stretching out his arms like he's on holiday. Ana sips her beer with an expression that says, *I told you so.*

The food arrives, and I immediately grab for the breadbasket. Better line the stomach before trying the fish.

"Just try a little bit like this," Seb says, holding out a small piece of the fish on his fork. I lean in and take the bite, careful to chew and process the flavour. There's a briny tang, with a hint of lemony butteriness.

"It's all right, actually," I say. "I was expecting worse."

Ana and Seb chuckle. I join in, but move my plate closer to the potatoes.

"Good. But you don't need to eat more of it," Ana says, a grin playing on her face.

"She loves bread more, anyway," Seb says.

His words make my insides dance. *Yes, yes. You know me. You still love me.* And then I hear my name being called.

For a second, it's like I misheard. But then Ana turns and looks around. Something bubbles in the pit of my stomach, rises like heat in my throat. I look up and he's there, in the street, walking towards us.

Greg.

Seeing him here feels surreal, like a character from one movie jumping into another. Misplaced. I haven't spoken to him since the day he leaned in and kissed me. There's a girl with him. Skinny as a broom, her light hair faded in the sunlight. As he walks closer to the restaurant, my eyes dart to the wooden railing separating our table from the street, willing it to rise up and block us from view.

Greg calls out to me again, oblivious. "Lisa, hey!"

"Who's that?" Ana asks.

I say nothing, but that's all it takes for Seb to stand. My eyes dart to his face. He's frowning, suddenly on defence. "Is that him?" he asks me.

I nod. It's the only thing I can do.

The chair scratches on stone as Seb pushes it back, bolting for the street. Aware of what's happened, Greg stops, eyes focused on my fiancé. It's like I'm watching a speeding car head towards a pedestrian, a collision inevitable. Seb's hands are raised, like a cat about to pounce, and I can hear Ana speaking, but it's like I'm underwater.

Greg's eyes are wide. "Mate, look I—"

But Seb pushes him hard in his chest. Greg falters, steps back. "Mate, just—"

Seb's voice is a growl. "Get out of here, *mate.*"

He bares his teeth, and the image I had of him as a grumpy child is replaced with something darker, more intimidating. A full-blown, violent man.

Ana blinks, looks from me back to her brother. I steady my hands on the table, my breathing shallow. A wet bitterness takes over my mouth, acid rising in my throat. I swallow to push it down, but the more I do, the more it climbs.

The next thing I know, I'm retching on the floor.

CHAPTER 37:

CAT

Present Day

"What do you mean, things will get *really* bad, *really* soon?" I ask, my words feeling disjointed, like I'm listening to a voice recording of myself. But before Neil can answer me, there's a car engine sound from outside.

We both turn to the study window. *Deborah.*

"Damn it," Neil mutters, getting up from his chair. "You have to go."

"What, *now?*"

"Now."

A thought hits me. "You don't want Deborah to know?"

Neil's already out of his chair and standing by the study door, motioning me out. I walk towards him, keep talking. "I mean, you don't want her to know that I know."

"No," he says. "It'll complicate things."

I can hear Deborah's footsteps outside the front door as I whisper, "But it's already complicated."

Neil puts his large hand on my shoulder and propels me through the door. He locks it behind us and walks into the kitchen. I trail behind him, and as Deborah's keys sound in the front door, he turns to face me from across the island table, a bead of sweat glistening on his forehead. "She doesn't know a lot. Let's keep it that way, right?"

"But—"

"*Later,*" Neil rasps, right as Deborah walks in. I open the fridge door and hide my face behind it.

"I thought I heard some voices," Deborah says, sounding cheery as she throws her keys down on the island.

"You're back early," Neil says, his demeanour suddenly friendly. Warm, even.

I pull my head out of the fridge. "Good day?"

Deborah looks appraisingly at me, then at Neil, her lips curving faintly upwards. "I thought I'd drop by for lunch. It's been a slow day at the office."

"We don't have much in the fridge," Neil says. "I haven't gone to the shops yet."

Deborah waves a hand. "Oh, that's okay, I'm sure we can whip something together."

Deborah walks towards the fridge, and I move out of her way, standing next to Neil at the island. She squats down next to the freezer. "Let's see … what about these?"

She holds up a couple of boxes of frozen pizzas. "Dr Oetker. Always a solid choice. We can just put these in the oven."

"Sounds good," I say.

"Sure," Neil adds.

Deborah raises an eyebrow, and for a moment I wonder if she senses this new energy in the house. Can she tell something is different? That I have a tornado of questions swirling around in my head?

How are you okay with a stranger living in your house?

Where's the real Richard now?

I think of that phone argument I walked in on a week ago, when she was fighting with Richard. Was that her real husband—or ex-husband—she was talking to? When she told me about Richard, she painted a picture of a liar and a cheat, but I couldn't make the connection between that Richard and the one who locked himself in his study all the time.

Now, knowing that Neil is only pretending to be her ex-husband, things are making a bit more sense.

But only a bit.

Deborah takes the pizzas out of the boxes and puts them in the oven. As she wipes her hands on a cloth, I get a whiff of her perfume. I wonder—why all this pretending? Doesn't she get tired of playing the part of someone else?

But isn't that exactly what I'm doing with InCheck?

"Do you have more meetings today?" Neil asks her.

Thank God he asked. I thought of doing the same, but it might have sounded suspicious. The sooner she leaves the house, the sooner I can get answers from Neil. It's weird standing around like this and acting like everything's normal, when it clearly isn't.

Deborah shrugs. "One at five. With that contractor I was telling you about."

"Right," Neil says. "Here's hoping he's less of a twat today."

She lets out a laugh. "Exactly."

It's strange how they act around each other. From this vantage point, I can't tell who's a better actor. Neil, the taciturn fake husband who has these bursts of affection for his fake wife. Or Deborah, the talker, seemingly comfortable in any situation. I think of her drunken moments over the last few weeks. How she's kept up the facade all this time.

Why do this?

According to Neil, Deborah doesn't know much about the investigation. She offered him a place to stay when he came here. She must know about Lisa, but how much does she know about me? Neil must have told her *something*, because she was the one who called me for my interview.

Plus, Greg spoke to me too, so there must be multiple people involved here. People who know more than I do about this whole thing. And yet Neil doesn't want me to say anything to Deborah because—why? It'll *complicate* things? Wouldn't it be better if we all worked together on solving this? On clearing up this misunderstanding?

I need answers, and soon.

The three of us stand around the island and eat, like we're all too scared to sit down and have a proper conversation. It's impossible to not sense something is wrong. But none of us says anything.

"I'm going upstairs for a bit," I say. "I'll see you later."

As I climb the stairs to the first floor landing, my ears are pricked up. *Will Neil tell her that I know?*

But there's silence. And when Deborah starts talking about the weather, I curse and head to my room. I lie down on the bed, hands shielding my face. Fragments of information circling above me like vultures. InCheck and Alice. Richard and Neil. Rachel and Lisa. I shake my head to reset and start with what I know for sure.

Rachel is Lisa, and Lisa is dead.

Richard is Neil, and he's investigating her death.

And somehow—and I've still got no clue—I could be involved. Because I'm Alice from InCheck. And according to Neil, the last call Lisa had before she died was with me. But how could that be sufficient reason for bringing me all the way here and investigating me?

The last few months spin through my head, the chats and phone calls. Rachel was one of my first clients. She was lost. Had her own demons following her, just like I had. That period was a blur, the edges scrubbed away by the countless bottles of wine. I remember the blackouts, the ones I can thankfully still count on my fingers, throbbing reminders of the time right before I got sober.

And luckily I did. If I were still a drunk now, how would I manage this mess?

I look towards the dresser on the opposite side of the room and think of the *might-be* camera. Neil said there wasn't one. Maybe I was just being paranoid, picking up on the energy in the house. Because technically, I *was* being watched. Maybe not through a creepy camera, but by an investigator. A *might-be* investigator.

I log into InCheck, wilfully ignoring the text from Fred as I scroll down to Alice's chats. My eyes scan the screen for Rachel's name, but it's not there. Removed. I want to hurl my phone against the wall. It's the app's policy, I remind myself. Every three months, messages get removed automatically. And if an account has been deactivated, they get removed immediately.

Which is what must have happened with Rachel.

During my first few weeks of sobriety, I took inventory of my life, cleansing my system of the booze, but also going through my previous messages on InCheck. I remember thinking it was strange that Rachel's account wasn't on the app anymore, and that my messages to her no longer went through.

I had brushed it off as just another app drop-off. It happened all the time, didn't it? So what could Neil have found that incriminates me?

I picture the InCheck transcripts in the study. The chats all there, in the open. But was there something that I missed when I was going over them? And what about the phone calls with Rachel? The ones Neil needs my help to piece together?

The sound of a car engine brings me out of my trance. I jump up and open my bedroom door.

Silence.

I rush down the stairs and there's Neil, still standing at the kitchen island. I look around the room, making sure Deborah is nowhere in sight.

"She's gone," Neil says.

"So what now?"

He takes a breath. "You have a class to teach right now, don't you?"

I gape at him. "You're joking, right?"

"No."

I think of Greg, how he conducted my fake interview, how he's been avoiding me ever since I came here.

"The people at the academy know, right?" I say more than ask. "They know I was brought here to be investigated?"

Neil shakes his head. "They only know that you're part of some investigation. That's all."

"So the whole town is basically in on it," I say, sound like a child, but I don't care. I feel taken advantage of by these people, by Neil.

"Look, we'll continue all of this when you come back," he says. "We'll have time before Deb comes home. It's just important that you keep up the illusion of normalcy. I don't want anyone knowing more than they should before we have a clear direction."

"How much do they know?"

"Very little," he says. "As far as they know, I work for the police, and everything needs to be kept strictly confidential. And they're just cooperating. They might think I've brought you here to discuss a cross-continental case. No one was ever told that you are the suspect."

"But they might *think* I'm a suspect."

He shrugs. "They might."

Heat rushes to my face. I want to leave, to get on the next plane and leave Neil and his investigation behind. Even if it's a bad idea, there's technically nothing holding me here.

And yet Lisa's face pops into my mind. I connect her smile to Rachel's voice. Something tells me to stay. If not for me, for her. To close what should have been closed months ago.

"Fine," I tell Neil. "I'll be back in two hours."

"Good."

As I leave the front door, I open my phone and check the message from Fred on InCheck.

Call tonight?

I type fast, but as I click *Send* a thought hits me. Neil said he could report me to the authorities. Maybe that's why he's so confident around me, because he knows I won't leave. Because he knows I won't risk him reporting me.

I think of that Instagram message I received weeks ago. *I know you're a fraud, Alice.*

Could that have been Neil?

The message was unsettling then, like someone was watching me from a window. But things are different now. They feel scarier now that there's an actual human being who knows about me and InCheck.

I scan Fred's message again, and feel an indescribable sadness sweep over me. Glancing out at the trees up on the hilltops, everything feels like a prison.

I walk, each step away from the house feeling like a relief. My eyes scan for the hooded man. Lisa's fiancé. Weirdly, I feel closer to him now, because he's not the only one being watched. Neil said that when he arrived, he looked into the fiancé's alibi, and it checked out.

I shake the thoughts loose from my head. There's too much to consider right now. In a few minutes, I need to somehow teach a class. Or watch as Greg teaches and help if he needs me to.

To look like I'm okay, when I'm a hot mess.

If I think about it, I've been a mess all along. Acting like a real counsellor. I made—and continue to make—that choice every day. In truth, I deserve all the consequences I get. But if I go down for this, which could happen, what happens to Fred and Susana? After we've made so much progress? Will they be told that I wasn't the Alice they had trusted their deepest secrets with?

"You look like shit," Greg says when I enter the classroom. I feel like punching his freckled face, but then he grins. "I mean, you look tired."

And you look like a liar, I want to say, but don't.

I sigh and nod, sinking into a chair and gathering my notes. He hovers beside me and I turn. "What's up?"

"I spoke to Charlotte," he says, eyebrows raised. "We could grab some beers tomorrow. Like you suggested."

I cock my head to the side. "Really?"

"Yeah," he says, suddenly looking unsure. "You mentioned it, right? Something about team building?"

I nod slowly, but inside my head is spinning. Why would they be up for drinks now, all of a sudden? If they know I'm part of an investigation, and suspect I'm to blame in all of this, wouldn't they try to steer clear of me, like they've been doing for the past few weeks?

Maybe they can't help it. Maybe they're curious and want to know more. I force a smile. "Sure, let's do that."

In the back of my mind, I'm assessing the options. By tomorrow, I could either be in a bar with them, or in a holding cell somewhere. It's all up in the air. Plus, if we do go out for drinks, I'll need to explain why I don't drink. And honestly, a drink right now sounds pretty good. Just what I need to take the edge off. But I won't do it.

"Cool," Greg says. "I'll let Charlotte know."

He grabs his books and makes for the door. As he's about to step out, an idea hits me.

"Hey, Greg?"

He turns. "Hmm?"

"Is there any update on my work visa?"

There wouldn't be, of course. Neil told me it was all nonsense. I'm just interested to see how he'll react.

Greg's eyes widen a fraction, and a red flush spreads across his neck. "Uh, I don't think so. I'll have to check with Charlotte."

He's out of the room before I can respond. I sink back in my chair and let out a breath. This whole thing might be far from over, but at least seeing that look on Greg's face—the panic—was pretty amusing.

CHAPTER 38:

LISA

Six Months Ago

The phone rings four times before Eleanor picks up.

"Lisa," she says, sounding exasperated already. I can hear a buzz in the background. It sounds as though she's in a mall or a supermarket.

"Is this a bad time?" I ask.

The wind is mild, and the crisp air feels like it can whisk away any bad energy. I'm pacing on the dock near the house, each step sending a shiver through the wooden floorboards. The water is quiet, like it's listening in.

It's strange how being close to the water has grown on me.

"No," Eleanor says. "Just leaving lunch with the girls. I was wondering when you'd call me."

We haven't spoken in a few days. Usually, my mother and I text almost every day, the words bland and empty. Questions about what we're doing, or what we're wearing. But the last few days have been hard, and I've found it difficult to fake the formalities.

There's a clicking sound, and I imagine she's walking through a carpark, her heels echoing crisply.

"Lisa, is everything all right?"

I bite my lip, thinking of the past few days. Things are not all right at all.

When Ana and I walked to lunch yesterday, I'd felt hope again, the wish that I could rekindle my relationship with Seb. Ana's reassurance that *this too shall pass* made it even more plausible. Seb and I would be okay. And we'd go back to England together.

"I wanted to talk to you about something," I say to Eleanor, my voice shaky.

After the incident at the restaurant with Greg, Seb completely withdrew from me. He left abruptly, leaving Ana and me sitting there, my vomit on the floor between us. She was cool on our walk back, asking careful questions.

Who was that man? Does he go to class with you?

When I answered, she quickly worked out the rest for herself, and the remainder of our walk went deadly silent. As for Greg, he barely gave me another look after Seb shoved him outside the restaurant.

"Of course," Eleanor says. "You know I'm always here to talk."

I can hear her getting into the car.

"Things with Seb have become..." I trail off, trying to find the right words. "Difficult."

"Difficult?" She sounds bewildered. "How?"

"We've been fighting a lot," I say. "And I'm not sure how long we'll still stay here—"

"Are you coming back to London?"

"I—I might be, yes. That's what I wanted to talk to you about."

There's a slam of the car door on the other end of the line, but she says nothing.

"I'm thinking of coming back alone," I tell her. "At least for a while. Seb's mum is getting better, but he's been talking about staying for a while longer. For work. And with everything going on, I thought it might be good to come back home for a bit."

It was Seb's idea—me going back to England. It was a mere suggestion, but it felt like a command.

He cooled down a bit after his encounter with Greg at lunch. But there was a distance in his eyes. That night, I worked up the courage to ask him the question that had been sitting on my mind for weeks.

"Do you know when we'll go back?" I said. "To the UK?"

He seemed taken aback by my question. We were sitting at the dining

THE LAST TIME YOU CALLED

table, Ana in the living room with her mother. The way Seb looked at me showed that he didn't know how to answer my question. It was almost as if he'd forgotten about the UK. That it was a place where we used to live.

"I don't know," he said. "I need to go back to the vineyard. There are things I need to take care of."

He'd seen the concern in my eyes.

"You could always go and visit your parents," he offered. "Then you could either come back in a few weeks. Or I could, I don't know—maybe meet you there once I'm finished with my business here?"

It seemed like a good idea, but the way he'd said that last part—about coming to meet me once he was done with work—didn't sound very convincing. But the prospect of going back home sent a flutter of hope through me. It was an idea I felt confident talking to my mother about.

And yet now, the idea seems like a bad one. A forced decision.

Eleanor's breathing is measured across the phone. "Does he want you to leave?" Her tone is slightly on guard. Like she's getting ready for damage control. "Seb—did he ask you to leave?"

"What? No. He's fine, I'm just—"

"But you've been fighting?"

"Yes."

"So, is he unhappy?"

"I... I don't know," I say truthfully. "So many things have happened—"

"Like what?"

"Fights, mum. He's a different person here, it's like he doesn't even want to—"

"Look," she says, and I hear the car start. "It sounds to me like you're trying to run away. Your marriage hasn't even started and because of a few arguments you're ready to leave him high and dry?"

"No it's not like that, you don't know the—"

"Running away from problems is not the way we've raised you," she says. "If I were you, I'd stay there and work things out with Seb. Lord knows he's been patient."

I frown. "What's that supposed to mean?"

212

There's a sound of a flicking indicator, and I picture Eleanor connecting me to the car speaker. "I think you know what I mean, Lisa," she says.

"No. I don't. What do you mean?"

She sighs, and when she speaks, her voice is softer. "He's not Daniel. What happened with Daniel was an accident."

Hearing your name feels like a stab to my chest.

"Seb is a different man. He's about to be your husband," my mother says. "Sometimes I feel like you're holding on to Daniel. And because of it, you're trying to sabotage your own chance at happiness."

Tears well up in my eyes. "It's really hard. I don't know if I can do it."

"Sweetheart, you've chosen this," she says. "Remember, Seb's chosen *you*. And I think you know deep down what I was going to say when you called. You don't run from your marital problems. Ever. You stick it out and make it work."

I hold the phone away from my ear, wipe my nose. She's right—a part of me knew she would say this. Knew she would connect all of this with what happened in the past. But another part of me also wishes she would tell me to come home.

"I understand," I say, feeling deflated.

"Spend some time working on it together," she continues. "I was worried you might not be ready to be there on your own, but you are now. There's no point in running away. I don't know what you might have done, but try to see things from his perspective. Even if that means staying longer."

I nod as if she can see me. "Okay, I'll do that."

"You know I just want the best for you," she says with a tilt to her voice, like her finger is hovering over her phone, ready to end the call.

"I love you, mum."

We hang up, and I put the phone back in my pocket. I rest my arms on the wooden railing of the dock, careful not to put my full body weight on it. To my left, a piece of splintered wood shows how easily it gives way.

I breathe deeply, feeling the crisp air on my face.

I need to stay. It will be hard, but I need to make it work, despite Seb not wanting me here. My chest tightens at the thought. *Not welcome here, not welcome there.*

From my jacket pocket, I pull out my old phone. I brought it along in case I needed it. Turns out that I will after all. I navigate to the InCheck app and decide to text Alice.

Hi Alice,

Great to meet you. Can we have a call? I'm free tonight or tomorrow. I don't know how this works, so hope this is fine. Thanks!

I reread the message, then press send.

I was hoping I wouldn't need this app. I've been so distracted since that afternoon in the restaurant with Seb and Ana that I barely had time to think. But hearing my mother talk about the past feels like the final straw. Change has to happen. I need to stop this self-sabotage and forget about you—once and for all.

And I'll need all the help I can get.

CHAPTER 39:

CAT

Present Day

I'm dripping with sweat when I get back to the house.

"Ran back here?" Neil says as he sees me rush through the front door.

"How much time do we have?"

"About an hour."

I grab a glass of water from the tap and follow him back into the study. Since leaving the academy, my mind has been circling back through all the details, ready to dive in.

"So you said Lisa's family hired you, right?" I start.

"Yes."

"Because they were unhappy with the first police investigation?"

"Correct," he says, putting his elbows on the desk.

"And you think there's more to it?"

"Look." He folds his hands. "They refuse to believe that she committed suicide. So they've hired me to find out what happened."

He tightens his lips, like he's uncomfortable. "So it doesn't matter if I agree. It gets the bills paid."

"But what if there's nothing to find?" I ask. "You said yourself that the fiancé has an alibi. And they found a suicide note she wrote, and alcohol in her system—"

"They don't care about that," Neil says, voice raised. "All they want is a name. They've got a lot of money to throw at this, so if they want to reopen the inquest, then they bloody will."

I look at the stacked papers on the table. My InCheck chats with Rachel. "And I'm the name?"

He nods, his face dark. "Looks like it."

The thought of it makes my head spin.

"But that doesn't mean I think you did it. You did some dodgy stuff with this app," he says, motioning to the papers. "But I don't think you made Lisa kill herself."

I lift my head. "So, you want to know what we discussed on our InCheck calls?"

"Yes," he says, "It's the only option we have."

"Because you've got no other leads?"

Neil narrows his eyes. "Not yet."

He takes his phone out of his pocket and starts recording. He looks up at me, as to see if I'll try to stop him. But I don't. Instead, I watch the seconds tick by on the timer and feel my heart race. Something inside me wants to stay. To figure out what happened here.

"Let's start," I say.

The next hour is gruelling. We talk about how I matched with Rachel—Lisa—on InCheck. Reading the transcripts has refreshed my memory a bit. I tell Neil that Rachel was a quiet client, that she didn't share much.

"She wasn't direct about anything," I say. "She was always vague."

Neil's taking notes. "Did she ever mention Spain to you? Or her fiancé?"

I shake my head. "No. She sounded British, so I assumed she lived in the UK. She didn't give more details."

I take Neil through the ins and outs of InCheck. How clients are assigned to counsellor profiles that match their needs using an algorithm. As I talk, Neil sits back, crosses his arms.

"Like I told you, Rachel—*Lisa*—and I had an introductory call. I didn't want to have a video call, obviously. And she asked for a normal call too, so yeah."

Neil sighs, barely hiding his disdain. "You say she had issues with anxiety and depression. And you had those listed on the app as your areas of expertise?"

I nod. "That's right."

Neil says nothing.

"Look," I say, "the app has helped loads of people. You'd be surprised how—"

"I doubt it," he says, eyes boring into mine. "I don't think anyone has the right to play God."

My defence dies in my throat. Somehow my opinion on InCheck has morphed into something else. Someone's dead and I'm involved. It doesn't matter what I did or didn't do. Or what intentions I had.

"Lisa told me about her mother, if that helps," I say. "On our first call."

Neil picks up his pen again.

"She said she made some mistakes."

"What mistakes?"

My mind reels over the past information, searching for something to hold on to. "A past relationship, I think."

"You *think*?"

I exhale. "I'm trying to remember."

"Try harder."

I close my eyes and think back. "She was in a new relationship, I—I'm guessing with the fiancé?"

"Sebastian."

"Yes," I say. "And she told me she spoke to her mom about it. There was some problem in her relationship. But I think there was more to it."

"More, as in?"

"As in, she was still holding on to the past." I tap my fingers against the desk. "Yes, yes—that's what she said. She was holding on to the past."

The corners of Neil's eyes wrinkle. "Anything else?"

I shake my head. "No. Not on that call."

"But she seemed troubled?"

Don't we all?

"I—I guess so?" I say. "Did I think she was going to kill herself? No."

217

Neil's lips are pursed, and he taps at the transcripts. "It's a good start. I think you should read over these again. Refresh your memory. The texts aren't a lot to go by, but they will hopefully help you remember the other calls, too."

I nod. Remembering pieces of our chats is like remembering parts of a book. But right now, there are still lots of blank pages. How much have I forgotten? The drinking didn't make me forget everything, did it? I have this feeling there's more beneath the surface, like a clue waiting to be found.

"Do *you* think it was suicide?" I ask Neil.

He shrugs. "I don't know. She could have just been drunk or high and fallen into the water."

The sound of a car sends us both out of our chairs. Deborah's back. We agree to meet the following morning to go over the rest of the calls. Neil hands me the transcripts as we leave the study, and I stuff them into my slouch bag.

Deborah walks into the kitchen just as I make my way up the stairs.

"Did your meeting go okay?" I ask her.

"Could have been worse," she says, giving a tired smile.

"I'll be down just now," I say.

I fall face down on the bed, my head a maelstrom of thoughts. Nothing feels real, and yet everything is real. I try to relax, scrolling aimlessly through Instagram. Neil said we're off to a good start. We're following whatever process he has.

But then I think of who Neil works for.

As parents, hearing your child committed suicide can't be easy. And from what Neil has told me, Lisa's family is pretty influential. I think of the rich families back in Johannesburg, and the doors that their status open for them. If Lisa's family is anything like that, they'll stop at nothing to save face. Because no one wants suicide attached to their name. It's a dirty term, a dark ugly smear.

I'd know.

I sink my face into a pillow, remembering Neil's words. *All they want is a name.*

My mind sifts through the broken fragments of my conversations with Lisa. *Who were you really?* The more I try to remember, the more the memories seem elusive, hiding in the recesses of my mind.

I look at the time. Six-thirty. Time for dinner, and then my call with Fred. I leave my phone on the bed and descend the stairs, my brain whirring.

I need to find out what Lisa said. What clues she left. Especially on our last call—*her* last call, ever, by the looks of it.

Because if I don't, it'll be my head on the block.

CHAPTER 40:

LISA

Six Months Ago

I'm scrolling through leather boots on the ASOS website when my phone vibrates. When I see the caller ID, my stomach does a little somersault.

"Hi," I say carefully.

"Hey," Seb says on the other line, his voice gentle. "Where are you?"

I swing around in the chair and look around the study. "I'm at Deb's. Just helping her do some online shopping. Why? Is something wrong?"

It's unusual for him to call. He's been at the vineyard almost every day this week, leaving home early and returning late. He's been friendly, but our conversations have been empty, his kisses rare.

"I was thinking we could go out for dinner tonight," Seb says. "I have some things to finish here, but we could leave at eight?"

I stand up. "Really? Just the two of us?"

"Yes."

The words flood out of me in an excited rush. "Yes! That sounds great. Should I do anything?"

"Just show up," he says with that tinge of charm I love.

I beam. "I'll see you later."

When we hang up, I walk to the kitchen, buzzing with newfound jubilation. Deb's still upstairs, sorting out her closet. I smile and do a little twirl. There's been a definite shift these past few days. We're still in winter, but I feel the seasons changing.

It all started when Alice from InCheck responded to my text. We agreed to have a call, and when we connected, the first few seconds felt loaded.

"It's nice to meet you, Rachel," she'd said.

Her voice sounded younger than what I'd imagined, but she was warm and comforting.

"I've never done this before," I admitted to her.

"That's okay. You're trying this out," she said. "Let's start with how your day went."

Her accent was hard to place. It wasn't British English. American? Australian? I wasn't going to ask. The less we knew about each other, the better.

"I spoke to my mother today," I told her.

"How did that go?"

I wasn't ready to divulge everything at once. I barely knew the woman. And I kept thinking what I was doing was stupid. That if my parents find out, they'd be disappointed.

Lisa's at it again. Convinced herself she's got mental problems.

"I'm married. Well, about to be married," I told Alice. She asked me some questions. How I met my fiancé. Had my parents met him. When she asked me how I felt about the upcoming wedding, I stopped.

"We haven't planned it yet. We first wanted to just..." I trailed off. "Sorry, this is harder than I thought."

"That's all right. There's no rush."

I remember feeling grateful for her patience. "Things have been difficult. And I feel a little ..." The tears welled and my chest heaved. "See, my parents, they look out for me. I was in love once, when I was younger. And—and I guess I can't let go of that."

"Let go of the past relationship?"

"Yes," I said. "But I'm worried. I can't disappoint my parents this time. I have to see this through."

As I composed myself, Alice sounded like she had all the time in the world to listen. Like all that mattered was this conversation we were having.

"Rachel, can I ask you something?"

"Yes, please. Sorry, I must be talking your head off."

"When you are with your husband—or soon-to-be husband—do you feel happy?"

I nodded. "Yeah. Not when we fight, but when I'm with him, yes."

"And when you say *'see this through'*, are you referring to him?"

"Yes. I need to make my marriage work."

She hummed as if she was considering this. "And do you feel he's doing the same? Putting in the effort to make this work?"

I had to think about that. And then I told her the truth. "I don't know."

But now, standing here in Deb's house, it feels like the tables have turned. Seb's asked me to dinner. He hasn't done something like this since before what happened with Greg.

I grab my phone and open InCheck to message Alice.

He's taking me to dinner tonight. His idea!

I drop the phone on the island and start picturing what I'll wear to dinner.

I'm so deep in thought that I almost don't hear the key in the door.

My head jerks up. I look at the stairs, but see no sign of Deb. I'm still frozen in place when I hear footsteps approaching. And then a familiar face.

"Richard?"

He's dressed in tailored navy trousers and a crisp white shirt. He looks handsome, and my stomach churns for thinking that.

"I didn't expect to see you here," he says.

His eyes examine me, that familiar slow scan of my body, then back up again to my face. There's a smirk playing on his lips.

"Is Deb home?" he says, pointing to the stairs.

"Yes."

He nods. "Right. Well, I'm just picking up some stuff."

I watch him as he moves to the study. He hasn't been home since that morning I ran into him on the street. Since then, Deb's been a mess, hanging aimlessly around the house.

"Do you need me to get her?" I call after him, but there's no response.

I walk quickly to the stairs, but Deb's already on the landing, her face ghostly white. "Is that—"

"Richard," I say. "Were you expecting him?"

But she's rushing down the stairs. I move out of the way and watch her hurtle towards the study. Her voice pierces the silence. "What in God's name!"

"Hello to you too," I hear Richard say, deadpan.

"What are you *doing* here?" Deb almost shouts.

"Well, if you have to ask, I'm visiting my house."

"You can't just come barging in here. Give me—"

There's a muffled sound, like a brief struggle. Then a shriek, a thud. I dart down the hall and approach the study door.

There, amidst scattered papers on the floor, is Deb. She's sitting on her backside, her eyes wide. Richard towers over her with journals and what looks like a hard drive in his hands. When he sees me, he's quick to move past, bumping my shoulder as he makes his way to the front door.

I take another look at Deb, then run after him.

"Hey!"

My yell ripples through the cold air. I stand in the open doorway, watching Richard as he walks to his black Audi, opening the trunk and throwing the files inside. As he closes it, he looks up at me.

"Hey!" I yell again.

He narrows his eyes, like I'm a stranger he's trying to recognise. And then his face changes. I watch the corners of his mouth turn up into a leering grin.

A shiver runs down my spine as he walks around the car. I'm suddenly aware of how alone we are here. Even outside, there's no one else around. This man's just pushed his wife to the floor. What could he do to me?

I gulp, frozen in place.

He opens the car door. "You ladies take care now," he says.

I watch him start the car, drive down the road and disappear around the bend. I clutch the door, my heart hammering in my chest. But something else builds amidst the fear.

Anger. At him and his actions. At me and my lack of.

I curse under my breath. *Bastard.*

CHAPTER 41:

CAT

Present Day

When I first opened my eyes, I almost convinced myself that yesterday was just a bad dream. That the whole investigation is just a nightmare.

But it's not a dream. Deborah will leave for work soon, and Neil and I will go back into his study. We'll read over the InCheck transcripts again, and crumbs of information will hopefully return to my memory.

I slowly smoke a cigarette in the garden, shielding my eyes from the morning sun. In the corner of the garden, the pot plants are wilting from a lack of water. I stub out my cigarette and grab a blue bucket from the garage, filling it with water.

I don't know much about gardening, but all those afternoons watching my mother watering plants must count for something.

Add to life. Don't take from it. That's the goal, right?

I trudge forward, the water sloshing in the bucket. I tilt the bucket, and the water seeps into the plants. Their leaves are brown and lifeless. I pour more water, and the soil soaks it up almost gratefully.

"You're up early," a voice calls.

I almost drop the bucket as I turn, seeing Deborah in the doorway.

"What are you doing?" she asks.

I motion to the plants. "They looked dry."

She walks over, her heels sinking into the lawn. "No need," she says. "I watered them the other day."

I look back at the shrivelled plants. They look desperate for water. But that glint in Deborah's eyes makes me put the bucket down.

"They don't need a lot of water," she says.

"Right. Okay," I say.

"You alright?" she asks, her perfume making me faintly ill. A smoke this early in the morning was a bad idea.

"I just need to sit down."

We walk back to the kitchen, and my head spins as I take a seat at the island.

"You went to bed pretty early last night," she says, checking her phone.

"I was tired," I say. And it's true. The past few days have been a rollercoaster, each more demanding than the last. After my call with Fred last night, it was lights out.

"Well, it's almost the weekend."

I smile at her. It can't be easy, playing pretend like this. Especially when your real life is in shambles. Looking at her now, the drinking and mooching around the house makes sense.

"See you later," she says, lifting her bag from the counter.

As I say goodbye and Deborah leaves, it hits me. It's Thursday.

I've been so wrapped up in my thoughts I've completely forgotten about drinks with Greg and Charlotte today.

"Morning," Neil says as he enters the kitchen, looking far fresher than I feel.

I eye him as he makes a cup of tea. He won't like the idea of me having drinks with the academy members. It'll complicate things, like he told me. It'll have to be something I keep to myself.

"Any luck on remembering those phone calls?" he asks, turning to me.

"A bit."

"Good. Let's go."

He carries his mug to the study, motions for me to follow. We sit down opposite each other, the dim room a refuge.

"So," Neil says. "Let's start with the second call you had with Lisa."

From the drawer, he pulls out a stack of the same transcripts I have in my bag and puts them on the desk. I frown. Somehow, seeing there is more than one copy gives me the creeps.

But I readjust in the chair, trying to conjure memories of that day with Lisa.

"She texted me the morning after we had our first call," I say. "She said her fiancé asked her to dinner. Like a date. Which was good, since they were having problems, remember?"

Neil nods, takes a sip of tea. "And what about this section here," he says, jabbing at the paper. I read it: *I think my friend is in trouble. Her husband attacked her. Should I do something?*

I look at Neil. "I thought about this last night."

"And?"

"I think she was talking about Deborah."

"Why?"

I look at him. *Come on, you must know.*

"Deborah's husband cheated on her," I say. "She told me over dinner a few weeks back. At first, I thought it was you, obviously. But she must have been talking about the real Richard. Maybe he was violent too? You said Lisa was close to her, right? Who else in town could it be? I don't think she had a lot of married friends here."

Neil's silent, considering. He lifts his eyebrows and sighs. "I think you're right."

"Did Deborah tell you anything?"

He nods. "She did. Her ex-husband was a right bastard. When they were getting separated, he came by and took things from the house without checking with her. He shoved her, too. Lisa saw it all, apparently."

A surge of sympathy runs through me as I scan the room. It must be bad for Deborah, living here among the remnants of a broken marriage. Memories all gone bad.

"Do you think that's why she asked you to stay here? For some company?"

Neil shrugs. "It was the other way around, actually. I asked her. I don't know if you've noticed, but there are no Airbnbs in this town."

I look at him. A fish out of water, a giant in a small town. So out of place.

227

"I told Lisa she should report her friend's attack," I say.

"Solid advice," he says, and there's a gleam of something in his eyes.

"But what happened on the call?" he continues. "She texts you in the morning to tell you about the dinner with Sebastian, then again in the afternoon about Deb, and then in the evening she calls you—what did she say?"

I take a breath. This is where it gets tricky. The memory is a little blurry, but I hold on to the small scrap of information I have.

"That dinner date Lisa had," I say. "With her fiancé? I think it went badly."

CHAPTER 42:

LISA

Six Months Ago

"How's Deb doing?" Seb asks.

He takes a spoonful of melted cheese, spreads it on a piece of baguette. The restaurant we're in is dimly lit, wine bottles adorning the walls, the smells of cooking in the air.

Deb's words from this afternoon ring in my ears. *Don't tell anyone.* After Richard left, she hastily picked up the scattered papers from the study floor, desperate to wipe the room clean of what had happened.

"I can't have people talking about me," she said. "Not about this."

"She's fine," I tell Seb.

"You guys have become close," Seb says in between chews. "Hmm. You really should have some of this."

He pushes the bread basket towards me and I take some cheese. It's almost sweet, the caramelised textures playing on my palate.

Seb takes a swig of wine. "Ana's leaving next week. She's going back to Barcelona."

"Like, permanently?"

He doesn't look up. "Yeah."

Despite myself, I smile. Ana leaving is the start of what I hope will be our own departure. If she's going back to Barcelona, it must mean that Alma is getting better. Which means Seb and I can leave soon, too.

Seb tops up his wine, then mine. "Did you speak to your mother?"

"About?"

"About going back to the UK."

My mind goes back to our drive up to the restaurant, how Seb had smiled as I spoke timidly about the landscape and the weather. Despite my best dress (picked by Eleanor) and fresh makeup, my confidence is low. Even now, our conversation feels superficial and forced.

This date was a bust before we even got here. And now, the look in Seb's eyes makes me nervous.

"Do you want me to leave?" I ask.

He frowns. "No. I didn't say that."

I shake my head. "But that's what you meant. You've been so distant. And yes, I know a lot has happened, but I don't know what else to do."

He sighs, sits back in his chair. "All I asked was if you want to go see your family."

"When are we going back?" I ask. "Your mum is doing much better."

"The vineyard needs me," he says. "I need to be here, but you obviously don't like it here, which is why I suggested you go back for a bit."

There's a pang in my stomach. When did we stop being partners and start being people who did everything separately?

"I want to be here," I say. "With you."

Seb swirls his wine, looks down at the tablecloth. "How's the writing going?'

The question sounds normal enough, but when he looks at me and lifts his eyebrow, I know it's not.

"What's that supposed to mean?"

"Exactly what I said," he says. "You've been here two months and you've written nothing."

"Because I don't feel comfortable showing you anything yet," I blurt out.

It's a mistake, raising my voice. Seb places a finger over his lips, shushing me. He looks around the room to see if anyone noticed my little outburst.

I take a breath. "A book takes time to write."

"Lisa, I'm worried about you," he whispers across the table. "You're having a hard time."

I want to scream, tell him it's his fault I'm like this. How it was his work that brought us here. I think of the last time I spoke to Ruth or any of my uni friends. It's been ages since I felt normal.

"I need to go back to the vineyard," Seb says. "For a week this time."

I pause, then say, "I'll come with you."

"Don't you want to go back to the UK instead?"

Eleanor's words are on repeat in my mind. *You don't run from your marital problems. Ever.*

"No, I'm coming with you."

Seb sighs. "You can't. It'll be too busy, and I'll be living with the workers."

I'm not surprised by his words anymore. *He's embarrassed by you.*

"Fine," I say, stabbing at the cheese with a fork. "I'll stay with Alma then."

We're quiet for what feels like forever, then finally, he says: "Next time, okay?"

The rest of the meal passes slowly. Our food arrives, and we eat in silence. When Seb pays the bill, I make a mental note to schedule a call with Alice when I'm alone.

"Maybe you should spend a few nights with Deb while I'm away," Seb suggests on the drive home. I catch a glimpse of my reflection in the window and I catch my breath. Me sitting here, next to a man who says he loves me, whilst Deb sits at home all alone.

"I'll do that," I say, turning my body towards Seb's and placing a hand on his lap. All the way home, I think of Deb. How she must feel.

And how I can't end up like her.

CHAPTER 43:

CAT

Present Day

"Lisa called me after her dinner date," I tell Neil. "She was down. Told me her fiancé was going away for work."

Neil's taking notes again.

"She was hoping the dinner would be good for their relationship," I continue. "But he clearly only did it to butter her up for the fact he would be away for a week. But I remember she sounded weirdly relieved, in a way."

"Meaning?"

"Well, it was as if she was happy to have a fiancé at all."

"So she was convincing herself," Neil says. "Rationalising."

"Exactly," I say. "So I asked her why she felt like that. Why she needed to feel so grateful about having someone."

"And?"

"She said she'd made mistakes in the past. Didn't want to make them again."

"What mistakes?"

I think back to Lisa's voice, suddenly clear in my mind.

"She..."

I rack my brain for the thread that holds the story together. And then I find it.

* * *

Rachel—Lisa—was hesitant to talk about her past. It was almost as if she was ashamed. I was sitting on the small balcony of my shared apartment in Johannesburg, a glass filled to the brim with cheap red wine. I remember lots of calls on that balcony, sipping away at my wine and listening to the never-ending drone of the traffic in the background.

"I had a boyfriend before," Lisa told me. I settled in as though I was listening to an audiobook, smoking one cigarette after the other.

"He was... beautiful."

She emphasised the last word almost wistfully.

"How did you meet?" I asked.

"At school."

"And you loved him?"

"So much," she said in a whisper. Then silence. She was quiet for so long that I thought she'd changed her mind about telling me. But she found her voice again.

"We dated for three years. Our friends got along, and our families too. It's necessary, you know what I mean?"

I nodded. "So, it was important that your family approved?"

"Not just mine. His too. It was kind of like a courtship."

"What happened?" I said, taking a drag of my cigarette.

"Daniel—that's his name—well, we spent summers together. We spent most of our free time together. We were inseparable. Like those couples who had a joint Facebook account, but in real life."

I frowned. Did people really think a love like that was healthy?

"One day, we had a fight. Just a fight," she said, her tone changing.

"About what?"

"He'd spoken to his mates. Something about *freedom*, about needing to spread his wings. Or something. It was crazy. He *was* free. I never held him back."

Lisa's voice became more animated as she flicked through her memories.

I had to remind myself that I was her counsellor, not a friend ready to gossip with her. "And then?"

"There was a wedding. Daniel's cousin's wedding. He was a few years older than us, but we moved in the same circles," she said glumly. "We agreed to go together. I was his plus one. I was his girlfriend. And I bought a red dress."

Something in my stomach felt uneasy. "And did you go?"

"Of course."

Silence. I checked my phone, wondering if we'd been cut off. But then her voice came through again.

"He embarrassed me. I showed up, and when I got there he just..."

She stopped talking. Her soft sobs echoed across the phone.

My words were a whisper. "This must be painful. I can hear how hurt you are."

Her voice was brittle. "After that, I just... faded. I couldn't function. My mother told me it would hurt, but it hurt too much. And the guilt of it—I couldn't."

"Where is the guilt coming from?" I asked.

"I let my family down."

"How?"

Lisa's words came out almost robotically. "Because it was humiliating. For all of us."

* * *

"And that's where she stopped," I tell Neil.

He sits back. "She didn't say anything else?"

I shake my head. "She didn't want to talk about it anymore. She said the breakup disappointed her family. But I remember thinking that didn't sound right. Families are supposed to support you, not bring you down, right?"

"You got that on a post-it note somewhere?" he says, eyebrows raised.

"All I'm saying is it sounds wrong."

A few beats pass, and then Neil perks up. "Hold on."

He takes his laptop from the drawer, flips it open on the table. We sit in silence as he taps away at the keypad. He turns the laptop around to show me a document. I start reading from the top. As I read the lines, my unease grows.

"Like she told you, her ex's name is Daniel," Neil says.

I say nothing, my mind racing as the words swim in front of me.

"And the cousin she talked about is Samuel. It was his wedding she was telling you about. And this," he taps the laptop, indicating the document on the screen, "Was filed a week later."

I lean back. "So this is—"

"A restraining order."

I blink once, then twice. "But why? How?"

Neil looks at me as if I'm stupid. "She was stalking him. After Daniel ended things with her, she kept showing up wherever he went. His cousin's wedding included."

My mind goes back to that phone call. I remember the tone of Lisa's voice. Fragile. Robotic. I shake my head. "Maybe it was a bad breakup, but a restraining order? That's bordering on—"

"Stalker behaviour. Instability."

Neil and I stare at each other. "She would have told me," I say.

"She told you what she wanted to believe. What put her in a better light."

I open my mouth to speak, then close it again.

"If you ask me," Neil says, spinning the laptop back towards him, "Lisa had some secrets she didn't tell anyone. Not even you."

CHAPTER 44:

LISA

Six Months Ago

I didn't tell Alice about the restraining order. Admitting it would mean admitting it happened. And as my mother said, it's best to forget it ever did. She called it 'a lapse in judgement', saying I was stressed, with my uni finals coming up.

"It was just an accident," Eleanor said at the time, when I was just a shell of a person for the first few days after the wedding. The hospital was cold at night, but when she came to visit, she never took off her sunglasses. Luckily, I was discharged a week later.

Not like *you* cared. Or even knew about it.

My mind kept going back to Samuel's wedding, thinking about what made you do what you did. To say what you did. Maybe you were just scared of looking like a fool in front of your mates. Or maybe it was a power play, like your father taught you.

So many maybes.

You clearly didn't think we belonged together. That was a mistake. To this day, I think you chose wrong. I know you chose wrong. Didn't you see it, Daniel? How we were meant to be together? We could have been free, like you wanted. But together.

On the day you left, I kept telling myself you were wrong. That you didn't know what you were doing. And so I'd continued as if nothing had happened. Calling you like I always did in the mornings. It was our routine.

236

Me asking what you had for breakfast, what plans you had for the day.

"Lisa, you need to stop calling me," you said after a week. "I told you. We need space apart from each other."

I didn't care. You were clearly still brainwashed by your mates. They didn't understand, and you seemed to have lost all perspective.

And then you just stopped answering my calls. So I went to your house.

You didn't like that either. In fact, you were pretty rude. You even pushed me away one evening, your breath reeking of beer.

You never apologised to me for that. Or for anything, for that matter. And I guess a part of me still hates you for it.

I didn't tell my parents about the breakup. And from what I heard, you didn't tell yours either. Because how could you? We were the perfect pair. The pretty couple at garden parties. If your parents knew you'd replaced me with binge drinking sessions with the boys, what would they think?

So when Samuel's wedding rolled around, I figured you'd had your fun. You'd come to your senses and be ready to go back to how we were.

But you weren't.

Instead, you looked at me in horror when you saw me. I had put so much effort into looking good for the wedding. I'd bought a red dress—your favourite colour on me. But you didn't seem to care. You screamed insults at me, as the rest of the guests stood frozen, their eyes wide and their champagne glasses paused halfway to their mouths.

To this day, your words still ring clear in my mind. *You're a lunatic. You fat, crazy bitch! Don't you listen? You need help. Just leave me alone.*

I don't know if you noticed, but I clutched the champagne glass so hard that it broke in my hand. Blood ran freely down my arm and dripped on the floor, matching my crimson dress. Little did I know it would start a whole new series of events involving my little razor.

The pain felt strangely good.

It was like something snapped. You never called me *fat*. It was a word reserved for the chubby girls. With Eleanor's help, I dressed my extra pounds away. You said you loved my body. You called me *curvy*, said you loved to cuddle me.

237

You lied.

So I walked out of the wedding and got into a taxi, bloody hand and all. All I could think about was sleep. I just wanted to sleep. The house was empty, my parents out at some luncheon, so I walked up the stairs to Eleanor's room. In her drawer, I found the Diazepam she took every night. I tipped the whole bottle into my mouth.

The pills didn't make me sleepy, at first. Instead, I was buzzing. The events of the day were too loud in my head. So I walked back downstairs and took one of my father's bottles of whisky from the drinks cabinet. I remember the TV being on in the background. Images moving soundlessly across the screen. But all that sounded in my head were your words as I took large swigs from the bottle.

Fat, crazy bitch. Fat, crazy bitch.

The next thing I remember was the fluorescent lights in the hospital. I had the worst headache I ever had, and spent most of the day vomiting noisily into a bedpan. Apparently, Mary, our housekeeper, had found me on the floor and managed to make me vomit. When my parents got home, they dragged me into the car and took me to the hospital. I don't remember a thing.

A week later, the restraining order came.

"This is ridiculous!"

My father never yelled, and he rarely turned red, either. But there he was, crimson-faced in the living room, his voice booming as Eleanor and I sat on the couch, me still in my pyjamas. I'd been summoned to our front door, the letter delivered into my hand by a man with acne wearing an ill-fitting suit.

"You need to call Bill," my mother told my father, trying to keep her voice from getting shrill. "Clear all of this up."

But your father didn't budge. Apparently, the love your parents had for me was as fake as yours. The restraining order stayed and with it, a stain of shame that spread throughout our circle.

"They're overreacting," Eleanor said. "But Lisa, next time—"

"There won't be a next time. Pick a better bloke! Or at least keep yourself in check," my father yelled again. "We'll never live this down."

You crossed a line, Daniel. You brought the law into our failed relationship. I crossed the line, too. Somewhere deep inside, something unhinged, removing the buffer that was there to protect me from bad decisions. It's my fault my parents don't trust me. If it had to happen again, I don't think I'd survive. Even thinking of it now makes me sick.

Which is why I can't tell Alice about any of this. I can't open that wound again and show her that streak of crazy. Even if she is my counsellor.

Because if I open all this up, history might repeat itself. And there's too much at stake here. It's not just my reputation on the line—or my family's. It's my sanity.

CHAPTER 45:

CAT

Present Day

As I walk to the academy, Neil's words run through my mind.

Lisa had some secrets she didn't tell anyone. Not even you.

After dropping the bombshell about the restraining order, Neil told me how Lisa's friends had described her. Self-absorbed. Ditzy. Unambitious. Not things you'd say about a friend. But my mind keeps going back to the restraining order. Why did she lie to Alice—someone who was there to help her? What narrative was she trying to build for me, or for herself?

I scroll through Facebook as I walk, finding her profile: *Remembering Lisa Hawthorne*. The page is filled with posts from so-called friends. The cliches practically leap off the page.

Gone too soon.

One of the most vibrant people I knew.

An angel on earth and in heaven.

Even in death, people can't be real. I curse aloud. I hate the fact that Lisa didn't tell me, and I hate what it's made me question about my own life. About InCheck. How much do I really know about my clients? Are Fred or Susana who I think they are? If I had to see them in a coffee shop, would I recognise them by their voices? Would I see Susana with her baby, or Fred with his eclectic clothes and camera, as I've always pictured him?

In reality, I don't know a thing about them. And I'm lying to them about who I am.

But one thought keeps nagging away at me.

"Lisa had a breakdown after the wedding," Neil had told me. "Did she tell you that?"

"No," I sighed, increasingly less surprised at how little I actually knew. "What happened?"

"Nothing official. But off the record, she took a handful of sleeping pills and washed them down with the best part of a bottle of whisky. Was admitted to hospital to have her stomach pumped."

I said nothing. What could I say? She didn't tell me.

"We think she tried to kill herself," Neil said. "They kept her in hospital for a week, monitoring her. And then she went home and it was like nothing had happened."

"But … hold on."

I frowned, piecing everything together. "If that's true, then she clearly wasn't okay. If she tried to kill herself before—then it could have happened again, couldn't it?"

I tried keeping my voice calm, but my annoyance was building. Neil had brought me here to find a way out for Lisa's family. But it wasn't my fault. She just didn't have the support or treatment that she so clearly needed. Neil had scared me into thinking I was stuck here. That he could keep me in this godforsaken town. And for what?

"So what if I talked to Lisa?" I asked, my confidence building. "It's not like it's a—"

"A crime?" Neil said, taking the word from my mouth.

"I'm not responsible for her death."

Neil shook his head. "You don't get it. The family won't take suicide as an answer."

"Not even if it's true?"

He took a breath. "I told you, these people want to protect their reputation. And they're not going to admit to the world that their daughter offed herself. Not then, not now."

And at that moment, the problem became obvious.

Lisa's parents needed a scapegoat. Someone to blame for their daughter's death. They tried—and failed—to pin it on the fiancé. But with the help of money, Neil offered them a second chance. A second investigation. Whether or not it was suicide, someone else needed to hang for Lisa's death.

And that person is looking more and more like me.

I need to remember what happened that night with Lisa. And fast.

CHAPTER 46:

LISA

Six Months Ago

Deb's in her pyjamas when she answers the door.

"Hi love, come in," she says.

I close the door as she moves over to the couch and sits down. Some reality show is playing on the TV. Real Housewives of wherever.

"Can I get you something?" I ask.

She barely looks up. "All good."

I want to give her a hug. It's been three days since the incident with Richard, and since then, she's totally retreated into herself. "I'm going to check on the ASOS order," I say. "I'll be back in a bit."

She nods and I walk to the study. It's painfully neat, as if nothing ever happened. But there's an eerie feeling to it. Like Richard's about to barge in. I sit down and type ASOS into the browser. The shipment has arrived in Spain, but there's no sign of where it is.

If I think about it, Deb and I are helping each other. I shop for clothes for her, and she breaks my loneliness. I suspect she likes having me around as much as I like being around. Right now, I can't think of anything worse than going back to the house, wasting the days away.

I'd much rather stay here.

I browse the *Daily Mail* online, the bold blue headlines holding my attention for a few minutes. I log onto Facebook, and familiar faces pop up in my feed. Friends of friends. People I used to be close to, but barely talk to at all now. It's all I can do not to miss home.

I realise I haven't checked my email in weeks. I open Gmail, but it's already logged into an existing account.

Richard Taylor.

I should click away, but I can't stop myself. I skim through his inbox. Old friends asking to meet up. Facebook notifications. All signs of a normal human being.

One subject line catches my eye. An order confirmation from Interflora. Whatever he's ordered, it's certainly not for his wife. There are no flowers in this house. I check the order, and wonder if Susie Davies in Camberwell knows about Deb. Or vice versa.

My fury builds. Not only is Richard abusive, but he's a cheater too. And Deb probably knows. My mind goes back to the evening of the dinner party. How she grabbed the phone from his hands. How angry she was. She definitely knows. Whether she knows about the flowers is another thing.

I continue scrolling furtively through his inbox, glancing at the door. I stop when I read another subject line. *Thank You For Your Latest Donation.*

I narrow my eyes and open the email. It loads, and there's a banner of an African girl beaming up at the camera. *Your donation brings a brighter future,* the strapline reads. I keep reading.

Hi Richard,

Thank you for your ongoing support! Your latest generous donation has helped to feed the people of the village of Dhakiya, and is giving their children hope by providing them the resources they need for a world-class education. With your help, we're building a better future for our children.

The Save a Village Foundation

I frown. *What?* I read the message again, leaning forward and blinking at the screen. *This is surprising.* On the one hand, we have an altruistic man, donating to the less fortunate. On the other, we have Richard.

It doesn't add up.

I sit back in my chair. Maybe Richard assuages his guilt through charity? Or perhaps Deb convinced him to donate? They don't have kids, so maybe this is their way of paying it forward.

I scan the email for more information, but there's nothing. I click on the web link at the bottom of the email and open a site that looks like it's from the early 2000s. I know funds are tight at NGOs, but a website revamp is seriously overdue for this one.

I type in *Save a Village* in the search bar, and a whole series of emails pops up.

Thank You For Your Latest Donation.

Thank You For Your Latest Donation.

Thank You For Your Latest Donation.

There must be more than 100 here. At least one every month.

My curiosity is piqued. How much are Richard and Deb donating? The emails don't say. And without access to a bank account or bank statements, there's no way of telling.

Unless.

I look over at the cabinets in the corner of the room. What are the chances they still get their bank statements delivered?

No. I shake my head. I'm not going there.

I think of the empty bedroom upstairs, the softness of Deb's eyes. It had to be her idea. But why is the email addressed to Richard, then? I search for another Gmail inbox, but Deb's isn't there.

You should stop snooping, I tell myself.

I close the browser and shut down the laptop.

I make lunch, but Deb barely says a word. She's like a tipsy ghost, her second wine of the day already in hand.

"The order's in Spain already," I say. "It should be here in a day or two."

"Nice."

She stabs half-heartedly at a potato wedge. I steal a glance at her. She must feel awful. Dedicating years to a marriage, only for it to collapse. I look at the house. Beautiful as it is, it's empty. Devoid not only of children, but family and friends.

She must be so lonely.

I think of their unexpected charity habit. I have no doubt they can afford it. But I can't help but wonder how much of this life Deb chose for herself. I wish I could get inside her head, check for warning signs. So I decide to try something.

I scroll through my phone, then abruptly plonk it down on the table. "I really don't like these ads."

She looks up. "Hmm?"

"I keep getting these ads on Instagram," I lie. "To adopt a polar bear."

"I don't use Instagram anymore," she mutters into her wine.

"Right, well, there are a lot of ads going around asking you to adopt a polar bear, or some other charity. Honestly, how much will it really help? Am I awful for thinking that?"

Deb's face is blank, but then she shrugs.

"Do you ever donate? You and—", I swallow fast, forcing the name out, "Richard?"

She takes a swig of wine. "I've donated clothes a few times. But him?" Deb shakes her head, lips curling in a sneer. "Never. Nothing is ever free with him."

I watch her drain the rest of her glass.

"Why don't you go back to the couch," I say. "I'll clean up."

She doesn't argue, slouching over to the TV. As I wash up, I run through it in my head. The outdated web page. The numerous, regular donations. Deb's belief that Richard doesn't give anything to anyone without getting something in return.

Maybe I'm wrong. Maybe Richard has a softer side.

But my gut tells me otherwise. And I won't let it go.

CHAPTER 47:

LISA

Six Months Ago

"Sunny side up?" I ask.

I'm cooking eggs. It's pretty much all Deb has in the house.

"That's fine," Deb says.

She's standing at the kitchen counter, her hair still wet from the shower. When the eggs are ready, we eat in silence in front of the TV, our plates balanced on our laps. We've taken to eating on the couch now.

"Those boots will look good with anything," I say, trying to make conversation. Deb's ASOS order arrived this morning.

She says nothing, so I try again.

"The great thing about ankle boots is you can keep wearing them in autumn."

Still, nothing.

I sit up straighter. *Come on. Talk to me.*

It's like I've said it aloud, because she puts down her knife and fork. "Sorry, I'm in a bit of a daze today."

"Do you want to talk?" I tread carefully. "About anything. As long as we... talk."

She blinks, her expression blank. But then she sighs. "Okay."

I take a mouthful of egg, then ask the question that's been on my mind for days. "Is he coming back?"

She shrugs. "I'm not sure. Probably not."

"Is that what you want?"

Deb looks at me like I've just asked her to sign away the deed to her house. "What?"

"What do you want from this, Deb?"

She stares at the coffee table. "I don't know. It doesn't matter anymore."

"Why not?"

She sighs. "We've been discussing divorce for years. Well, he's been screwing around and I've been threatening."

Her eyes turn to mine. "I never thought we'd actually go through with it."

I hold my breath. "How do you feel?"

She sinks into the couch, places a hand over her eyes. "I don't know. Angry. Sad. Scared."

I put my plate next to hers on the coffee table. "Scared?"

A small, bitter laugh escapes her. "Because I know what he's capable of."

Memories come flooding back. How Richard barged into the house. How he'd left Deb on the floor after pushing her. No remorse. That smirk on his face as he sensed my fear right before he left.

"You know, you could get the locks changed," I say.

Deb shakes her head. "That's not it. What you saw the other day, that's harmless. It's the other bits I'm worried about."

An uncomfortable chill runs down my back. She turns to face me, her eyes dark. "He's a resourceful man. If we get divorced, he'll try every trick in the book to take my life away from me."

My emotions overwhelm me for a moment. Anger at this man. Sadness for this woman. Hopelessness for this house, this life. All crumbling. But there's something else gnawing at me.

The charity. If something felt off before, it's ringing alarm bells now. Before I can stop myself, I ask the question.

"Sorry to ask this, but you have a prenup, right?"

She shakes her head. "We never got one."

"So it's fifty-fifty?"

She nods.

I sit back, thoughts pouring in from my uni days. Conversations in pubs.

248

The endless case law we had to memorise between tests. Debates running long into the night.

"I hate how biased our system is to a fifty-fifty split," one girl from our class had said on an evening out. "If you ask me, prenups should become the standard. The world's changing. Things shouldn't be divided equally by default."

"I think half of the UK will disagree with you," another classmate, Emma, had said. "And even if prenups become standard, you'll still have spouses hiding assets. People are changing, but they're also getting smarter. Financial infidelity is a thing."

The notion had stuck with me. Financial infidelity. Among my Commercial and Tax law courses (Criminal was not an option, according to my parents), this topic was by far the most interesting in that first year.

And just like that, the shady charity website turns more suspicious. If Richard doesn't donate like Deb said, why are there consistent donations to an outdated charity? Something isn't right.

"It's *supposed* to be fifty-fifty," Deb says, "But with him, you never know."

"You think he might try to get more out of the divorce?"

She turns to me, her expression stern. "Of course he will. If he hasn't already."

"Do you have a lawyer?" I ask.

Deb's face crumples. *"We* had a lawyer. So, I guess not."

I wish I could tell her about the flowers for Susie in London, or the charity. Surely this could help her in any divorce proceedings? But if I do, I'd be admitting to snooping, and that could harm our friendship.

Plus, the information I have on Richard is only a grain of doubt. So what if he's donating to a charity? Even if Deb thinks he doesn't, he could be. Sure, the charity could be some type of front for something else he's hiding from Deb. But it's all just a hunch. I need something concrete.

"I need a nap," she announces.

I stack the plates and stand up. "Sure, I'll just wash up. Do you want me to go?"

"I'd like it if you stayed."

I don't have to ask her if she's sure, because I know that look. Loneliness. I give her a sympathetic smile and my heart hurts for her. "Of course."

I put the plates in the sink as Deb slowly walks up the stairs, leaving me alone with the TV. I switch it off, and when I'm sure Deb's in her room, I dart to the study.

I walk to the cabinet. If I need something to build on this shred of suspicion, I'll find it here.

"But how do they do it?" I remember asking Emma from uni all those years ago. "Surely there's a process to check for hidden assets."

"It's the system. Some are really efficient in hiding it," she'd told me. "Some don't bother because their partners don't understand the paperwork behind it. And when it comes down to it, it's a matter of getting caught or not."

I open the cupboard, pulling open the first drawer. *A matter of getting caught or not.*

There must be something here that can help Deb. There's no way that charity can be legit. It just feels sketchy. Maybe Richard's been making a fool of Deb for years. And if it's not the charity, then it's something else. I believe Deb when she says he'll try to milk her for everything she's got. Even if he's the one whose caused this mess.

Luckily, Deb has me.

Because she might be too weak right now to see through her cheating husband's lies. But I'm not.

CHAPTER 48:

CAT

Present Day

It's been running through my brain all day. One question. Over and over.

What happens next?

I've tried to play out the different scenarios. Maybe a fine for using InCheck? Maybe jail time? Gross negligence or manslaughter?

I've thought of running so many times, but Lisa's face keeps stopping me. I need to know the truth about what happened to her. I must get to the heart of what really happened in this godforsaken town.

If I look at it with a neutral hat on, it's karma at its finest. You can't go around impersonating a trained professional—and examine people's deepest thoughts and feelings—and think you'll get away with it. Karma always wins.

Of all the things that life throws at you, handouts isn't one of them.

I wipe down the whiteboard, watching the rules of English tenses disappear. It reminds me of something else I need to erase from my life. InCheck.

It doesn't matter how I look at it, but I just can't justify using it anymore. Fred and Susana will be fine. They'll find themselves genuine counsellors, and move on with their lives.

When the last student leaves the class—taught my Greg, not me—I sit down at the desk. I lean forward and cradle my head in my arms.

"You all right?"

Greg's voice cuts through the silence.

I glance up at him, massaging my temples. "Feel a headache coming on."

"Chickening out of drinks already, then?"

He's grinning and seems awfully cheerful, considering how he's avoided me since I arrived in this town. Maybe he's truly clueless about the investigation and is just following Neil's orders.

"I think I'll take a rain check on the drinks," I say.

There's a glimmer of surprise on Greg's face. "Oh, that bad?"

"Yeah," I say, getting up. "I think I'll go home and lie down."

What I'll actually be doing is going straight home to go over those last two InCheck transcripts with Neil. The more information we have to work with, the sooner we can conclude this investigation.

The sooner I can get out of here.

I'm about to leave when I hear Greg's voice again. "I'll walk you out."

As we walk down the hallway towards the street, I look around for Charlotte. "She's gone home already," he says.

"She wasn't going to join us for drinks?" I ask.

Greg holds the door open for me. "But we're not going for drinks anymore, remember?"

As we step outside, the sun is unexpectedly bright. It quickly turns my made-up headache from a few moments ago into an actual one. We walk in silence for a while.

"I'm over here," Greg says, pointing up the street.

"Me too," I say.

"Aren't you down the road?"

I point towards the hill. "I like the route through the trees."

Greg looks like he's just stepped in something. But there's that flicker of courtesy, or curiosity, that makes him smile. We labour up the hill together.

"So how do you get around in South Africa?" Greg asks, breathing heavily.

"What do you mean?"

"I heard you guys don't use public transport there."

"It depends who you ask," I say on a breath. "Some people take the bus every day, and some drive."

"What about trains? Metros?"

I can't believe we're talking about public transport when we could be talking about Lisa.

"We don't really use them," I say.

"I hate metros," Greg says. "Back in London, I took the tube every day. Getting across the city could take you two hours on some days."

We're nearly at the end of the road. "I can't imagine that."

"Ask anyone from London and they'll tell you the same," he says, looking around. "So this place is… refreshing."

From up here, the ocean stretches out endlessly, the mountains behind us green and glorious. The air is ripe with the salty tang of the sea, and it makes me think of summer holidays.

"What's the pull?" I ask as we stop to take in the scenery and catch our breaths. "Of Gexta?"

Greg shrugs. "Seclusion, maybe?"

I give him a sideways glance. He's still staring out at the landscape.

"I'm sure there are downsides to a small place like this," I say. "Everyone knows everyone's business."

Greg nods, saying nothing.

"Like what you get up to," I say. "Who you hang out with."

He turns on his heels, ready to walk again. I inhale and say, "At least you had Lisa, right?"

Greg stops. There's a moment of silence, and then he turns to me, the gravel crunching beneath his feet. His face is deadpan. "I didn't know her."

"I think we both know that's not true."

His brow furrows, and I continue. "You know who I'm staying with, right? Deborah told me you knew Lisa. You guys were friends."

He mulls this over, chewing on the corner of his lip. "So why are you asking me then?"

"Why did you lie?"

"Can we stop with the games, please?" he says, his voice agitated. "I know you're part of an investigation. You shouldn't even be talking to me about this."

Finally, some truth.

"I was wondering when you'd bring that up," I say, struggling to keep my voice even. "If you know I'm part of the investigation, why are you even talking to me?"

He looks confused. "What do you mean?"

"Neil told you not to talk to me, right?"

He looks past my shoulder into the distance. "No more than necessary."

"But here you are," I say. "You were even going to have drinks with me. Why would you do that?"

He leans forward, his voice gruff. "I'm trying to cooperate, okay? And I have. I helped create this bogus teaching job for you." He brings a hand to his temple. "I thought this whole investigation was over with already."

"So why did you stop cooperating?"

Greg looks down at his feet, his nostrils flaring.

"You were curious," I say.

He looks up. "Yeah."

"Me too," I say. "So why lie to me about knowing Lisa?"

Greg takes a breath. "I panicked, okay?" The back of his neck is turning red. "But yes, I knew her. We were friends."

"A bit more than friends, from what I've heard."

It's like I'm holding a match, about to burn a bridge I might need. But something's got to give. Someone needs to start telling the truth.

Greg locks his hands behind his neck and rolls his head back against them. "I didn't know her *well*. So it's not really that much of a lie."

"We hung out," he says. "While I was taking Spanish classes. And yeah, I fancied her, alright? I also knew she was getting married, but…" He shakes his head. "Her bloke was a twat. She was clearly bored."

"How was he a twat?"

"Well for one, he was never around," Greg says. "And if you met Lisa, she's not exactly low maintenance. Anyways, he wanted to get into a fight. Nearly hit me."

"He wanted to hit you?"

He nods. "I was a bit tipsy and made a move on her. He found out and

254

wanted to have a go at me. Which I would have done too, to be fair." He takes a breath. "But something just seemed off about him. You must have seen him around, right? He's suspicious. And Lisa also once—"

He cuts off abruptly.

"What?" I ask. "She once what?"

Greg closes his eyes. "Ah, fuck sakes."

"What?"

"I don't want to get into this. It's none of my business."

"But this could help with the investigation," I say. "If there's anything that might have been overlooked, it could—"

"How are you involved, anyway?" Greg asks, his tone turning accusatory. "I still don't know why you're here, or why we had to make up this teaching job. It's freaking people out. Charlotte doesn't know what to do about it."

I open my mouth, then close it. There's no reason for him to believe anything I say, and do I really want to tell him why I'm here? About InCheck? It's better I don't.

"It's complicated," I say. "I'm legally not allowed to tell you."

He shakes his head. "Look—I'm not debating what happened. It doesn't matter what issues Lisa had with her bloke, but she called me one night. This was a while after we started hanging out. She was…" He swallows hard. "Hysterical."

I feel a knot forming in my stomach.

"She called and was talking a bunch of gibberish," Greg continues. "Telling me she misses me, that I'm her only friend, things like that."

"Did she say anything else?"

He breathes deeply again. "She said something about catching him. Her bloke, I'm guessing. She said he was a liar. She was beside herself about it."

Greg's words dance around in my head. What could her fiancé have lied to her about? What did she catch him doing?

"Did you tell the police?" I ask.

Greg brings a hand to his face. "No. I should have, but it felt stupid. Half of what she said made no sense, and Lisa was dramatic. Honestly, I just wanted to put it behind me."

I take a breath. "When was this?"

He frowns into the sun. "A few days before she went missing."

"You should have told the police."

"I know, okay?" He sighs. "Look, I don't know why you're here. And yes, I'm an idiot for not telling anyone then. But I'm telling you now. And just so you know, I don't think everyone told the police the truth about Lisa, either."

"What do you mean?"

Greg shifts his weight from one foot to the other. "I barely knew her, but she didn't *look* suicidal. She still laughed and cared a lot about stuff. I didn't think she was unhappier than most girls I knew."

"You can't see depression like that," I tell him.

But Greg keeps shaking his head. "I don't know. When the police said it was suicide, I couldn't believe it. I still don't. Someone else—like that bloke of hers—could have had a hand in it. It happens, right?"

My stomach tightens. "What does?"

He takes a breath. "People killing their other halves. Love gone bad."

CHAPTER 49:

LISA

Six Months Ago

It takes me a while to find it. But when I do, it's impossible to ignore. Sometimes you just need to know what you're looking for.

I open the cupboard in the study to find piles of bank statements. *Do people still keep paper records like this?* I start laying the pages on the floor. Soon the entire floor is covered. Then I start looking.

The first thing I notice is the sizeable sums of money going in and out every month from a bank account. It isn't clear whose it is—Deb or Richard's—but the sums are substantial. Suddenly, the revamps on their house in Gexta and Richard's frequent trips to the UK seem miniscule by comparison. They're far better off financially than I'd thought.

The next thing that jumps out at me is the sheer number of transactions. There are too many for just one person.

I narrow down the dates of Richard's donations to *Save a Village.* The third of every month. There it is. *SAVE A V.* A transaction of five hundred pounds. I go back through the statements for months. The same amount, every month, like clockwork.

As I shuffle through the pages, Eleanor's words sound in my head. *You need to stop this snooping. One day it'll get you in real trouble.*

But this is different. I'm helping a friend. And so I continue sifting through the statements, listening for any movement, just in case Deb wakes up from her nap.

I count up over two years of donations. In that time, Richard has donated more than twelve thousand pounds to this so-called foundation. A foundation that raises a lot of red flags. Is it even legitimate? I put everything back and let my thoughts run free.

When Deb wakes from her nap, we drink wine together, the silence heavy between us. But I don't let it last long.

"What will happen to the house?" I ask. "You know, if you..."

She sighs. "This is my home. I won't leave without a fight."

I reach my hand out to hers. "It'll be okay. We'll make it okay."

We eat oven-baked fries and half-heartedly watch *Friends,* its canned laughter rippling through the house. Now, as I walk back to Alma's house, the gravity of the situation hits me. Deb could lose her house. Her safe space. I remember Richard's charm, his ability to take anything he wants and deem it his. Unapologetic. How he pushed Deb in her own home. A home they built together. How different that ugly image is to the altruistic one of a man who donates to a village in Africa.

People do uncharacteristic things. But also, people lie.

The street is quiet. I pull my coat tighter across my chest. Just a few more steps to the house.

I think of the dodgy donation website. The order Richard placed to Interflora for Susie in London. The gravel is loud against my shoes. It's dark, but the moon peeks through the clouds, illuminating the tops of the parked cars. I'm almost there, the house in sight. From here, I can see the lights are on.

Seb will be home by now. Back from his vineyard trip. He hasn't messaged, which isn't surprising. I'm sure that if it were up to him, I'd stay at Deb's all the time.

Then something stops me.

Shadows in the bay window. And then I see him.

It's Seb, standing by the window. He's wearing something dark. I squint and see it's the black polo neck I got him on Cornmarket Street. I walk forward and I'm about to wave to him, but I stop myself.

There's someone else there. Another shadowy figure in the window.

I keep my distance. From here, Seb can't see me. The second person is turned away from me, too. I take a step closer, trying to see clearer.

Before I know it, Seb is pulling the shadow closer to him. His face merges with the dark. It lasts for only a second, but the image is there. I blink, the realisation seeping into my bones.

A kiss. My fiancé, kissing someone.

Time slows as I try to process the scene. The shadow has pulled back, and I can finally see who it is. My legs propel me forward, my feet crunching loudly on the gravel. She turns, and we lock eyes.

Ana.

I blink, and she's still there.

Ana.

I blink once more, the image replaying again and again.

Ana. Kissing Seb.

Ana. Kissing my fiancé.

Ana. Kissing her brother.

CHAPTER 50:

CAT

Present Day

I leave Greg at the top of the hill. As I make my way through the trees towards the house, I keep thinking of how passive he has been in all of this. He didn't tell the police everything he knew, and he thought Lisa's fiancé could have killed her. And despite thinking this, he's done nothing about it.

Greg also thought Lisa was crazy—hysterical, he said. And isn't that part of the problem with the world today? Too many passive people doing too little to help those around them.

When I step inside the house, I do a double-take to see if Deborah's home. There's no sign of her in the living room or kitchen, and no sound coming from upstairs. I walk to the study and open the door to find Neil sitting at his desk.

"How much do you know about Lisa's fiancé?" I ask.

"Where have you been? I've been trying to—"

"Are you sure his alibi checks out?"

Neil's eyes shift from mild irritation to confusion. "What do you mean?"

I take a seat across from him, my feet tapping against the wooden floor. "I spoke to Greg. He told me something interesting."

"You did *what?*" Neil's voice raises sharply.

"Don't worry," I assure him. "I just asked him some questions. He doesn't know how I'm involved."

Neil grits his teeth. "You're the one being investigated here. You realise that, right?"

"Didn't you say that you believe me? That you're on my side?"

He sits back, his face deadpan. "I never said I was on your side."

He stands up suddenly and towers over me. He brings a finger close to my face. "One wrong move and you can expose everything. And I don't have to tell you that when that happens, you're in a pickle."

I say nothing as he sits down again, rubbing his face wearily. "Tell me what happened then. With Greg."

I tell him how Greg lied about knowing Lisa before admitting that they were friends. About the phone call Lisa made to Greg a few days before she went missing, and how he thought her fiancé could be involved.

"This could be a lead, right?" I ask. "Can't we re-look at Sebastian's alibi?"

Neil crosses his arms. "This is just one guy's opinion. There's not much to go on."

I look around. There must be *something*. And then, that something pops into my mind. "Do you still have the transcripts? From the next call I had with Lisa?"

He pulls the dog-eared stack of papers from the drawer. "Here," he says, sliding the pages over to me. I scan through them, chunks of information flooding back into my memory.

"Lisa went quiet for a while. She stopped requesting calls with Alice." I look at Neil. "It happens a lot. App drop-offs."

He's silent as I read the transcripts again, the messages drawing me back in time. I remember now that days would pass with little to no interaction with Lisa. When she did speak to Alice, it was all by text message, asking one vague question after the other.

How far should you go to help a friend?

When is a relationship irreparable?

Maybe some people are just born bad. Do you think so?

The questions had confused me back then. I was used to people laying their problems out on the table, looking for tangible ideas of what to do. I could handle that. But her general questions gave me nothing to work with.

Her questions also felt loaded, as if she was trying to catch me in a contradiction. Expose me, even. I remember that Instagram message like it was yesterday. *I know you're a fraud, Alice.*

I keep reading. Then I stop at a statement Lisa made.

I feel like my past keeps coming back. It's like a ghost that follows me around. Do you ever feel like that?

My insides tighten at the memory. I hated her for asking that, because it was a question I couldn't answer. For any other topic, I could detach myself emotionally. Step away and put on my counsellor hat. But for this, it felt too close. Too threatening.

I put the pages on the table.

"Anything?" Neil asks.

"She was in her own bubble, jumping around with different ideas. It was hard to keep up or get through to her."

He leans in, reading the passages of the transcript. I don't know why. He probably knows the contents by heart by now. He looks up, his eyebrow raised. "You played it safe. I didn't expect that."

I nod. For every fairy dust question Lisa threw at me, I hit back with a similarly vanilla response.

We go above and beyond for our friends. But don't do it to your own detriment. And keep it legal.

It depends when you feel you've given all you can give. Do you feel that way? People have all kinds of reasons for doing things.

I'd felt a bit like a magic eight ball, shooting out whatever life quote came to mind. It was annoying. I wanted to talk to her. Try to help her. But it felt like a game of tennis, an interminable back and forth.

Maybe my chats with her showed my genuine desire to make a difference. To do something good, no matter how small. But I knew it would catch up to me, eventually. Giving people advice had become a drug—and I know what happens to addicts.

"I know I'm not a real counsellor," I tell Neil. "And I know I can't play God. But people want advice, or at least someone to talk to. So yes, it frustrated me that I couldn't be that person for Lisa."

"Can I ask you something?"

"Okay," I say. He'll ask me anyway.

Neil takes a breath. "You're still young. But you clearly like this," he motions at the pages. "And without sounding like I'm encouraging you—which I'm not—you don't seem like you're that bad at it."

I say nothing, thinking back to that one time I *was* bad at it. That one time with Lisa, where there was too much booze involved, which is probably why I'm here now.

"It's just interesting," Neil says.

I don't need to remind myself how much this man knows about my life. Where I live. How I got onto InCheck. What my interests are. But there's something else. It's like he's reading me. It feels useless even trying to lie to him.

I respond with something a previous therapist once told me. "I struggle to stick with things. To see them through."

Neil folds his arms. "I can see that. I think you're running away. All these things you're doing on the side. Dog walking, house watching, teaching."

Funny, I don't remember telling him about the dog walking.

"It's all just stuff to keep you busy," he says. "Keep you occupied."

I hold my breath. It's like a game. The longer I stay quiet, the more points I win.

"You're like those snow globes," Neil continues, making a shaking motion with his hand. "All shook up and too scared to let the snow actually settle."

I wonder when the scared me will come out and start throwing punches. And then Neil's voice turns softer. "Your father... I read about what happened."

My mind doesn't register the words right away, but my body does. Before I know it, I jump up, sending the chair skittering across the floorboards. My heart pumps wildly as I rush for the door, Neil's voice echoing behind me.

"What—where are you going?"

"Out."

But he's right behind me, following me out of the study. "Could you stop running for once?"

I freeze, my feet glued to the floor. Neil walks around to face me and puts his hands on my shoulders. I don't dare look at him.

"Sorry," he says. "That came out badly."

My breath comes in ragged gasps.

"I just mean that life happens," he continues. "You seem like the type that understands that. Life's full of horrible situations. I've had them too. People get sick, they do bad things, they die."

The room spins in front of my eyes. All that's keeping me upright are Neil's hands. But it doesn't stop the nausea. I never talk about this, and with good reason.

He loosens his grip on my shoulders, pats his pocket. "I'm going for a smoke. Want one?"

Without waiting for an answer, he turns and walks outside.

When I'm alone, the tears pool in my eyes. I replay the scene in my head. Why can't I ever just speak up about this? Instead, when Neil said what I didn't want to hear, I immediately looked for an escape. He's right. I'm running.

I walk towards the garden, my breathing settling. It's baffling how Neil knows all this stuff about me.

It makes me wonder what else he knows.

CHAPTER 51:

LISA

Six Months Ago

I blink so hard that my vision blurs. The shadowy figures entwined in each other just moments ago are gone. Like they were never there.

Did that really just happen?

I swallow, my mouth dry. I try to recall what I just saw. An embrace. A kiss. My stomach lurches strangely just thinking about it. It couldn't be. People don't kiss their siblings. Not like that.

Had Ana seen me? And I could have sworn Seb turned and saw me too. And then there was no-one, the bay window empty, the curtains standing as mute witnesses.

I stand frozen, my breath little puffs of water vapour. *What happens now?* If they were there, they'd surely have opened the door by now.

I wait for the front door to open. Wait to unsee the scene.

Did that really just happen?

I need a plan. I need to do something. Do I wait for them to act? Do I take charge and confront them? The house seems intimidating now.

Real or not, it can only be one course of action. Take your pick.

I move to the door and put the key in the lock. It clicks as I push it open. The house feels warm, the smell of fried potatoes lingering faintly in the air. As I step inside, I keep my coat on and peek around the door. Living room, empty. Dining room, empty. It's silent. And then there's a clang from the kitchen. Metal on metal.

And I hear my name.

"Lisa."

His voice sends a jolt through me, my heart beating faster. Seb's at the top of the stairs, dressed in a cream turtleneck. I blink a few times, my eyes refusing to believe what's in front of me. When I saw Seb at the bay window a few minutes ago, he was wearing a black turtleneck—the one I'd bought him.

"I was just going to call you," he says, moving down the stairs. "I got back a few minutes ago. Dinner's almost ready, too."

He's smiling, and when he kisses my lips, his mouth is warm and dry. "I hope you're in the mood for *pisto* and potatoes."

I say nothing.

"How's Deb?" he asks, walking to the dining room table.

My words come out in a croak. "Where's Ana?"

"In the kitchen."

He says it nonchalantly, his eyes on his laptop screen.

"Were you …" I trail off. When he looks at me, my ankle gives way under me and I have to catch myself before I slip.

"Woah." He moves over to me, puts his hands on my shoulders. "Are you okay?"

He looks genuinely concerned, but I'm still shaking. I try to get the words out again. "Were you—"

There's a voice coming from the kitchen. "Voy a poner—"

Ana's standing in the doorway with plates in her hands. There's a confused look on her face.

She's wearing black.

I open my mouth, close it.

"Are you okay?" she asks me.

Putting the plates on the table, she walks over to me, arms crossed. My eyes dart to Seb—to her—then back again. I shake loose from his grip, pointing a trembling finger at the bay window. "You were there."

"Sorry?" she asks just as Seb says, "What?"

"You were standing at the window. There." The words sound more like a question than a statement, and I feel myself faltering.

Seb frowns. "At the window? When?"

"Now. A minute ago."

I place a hand on the wall. Ana's still got her arms crossed when I look at her. "I saw—you."

She looks at her brother. I do too. I see his cream turtleneck, the plates on the table. I smell the cooking food.

Did that really just happen?

"Hey," Seb whispers, his face close to mine. "What's going on? What did you see?"

The words run through my mind, refusing to sound reasonable.

I saw you kissing Ana. I saw you kissing your sister.

I shake my head, but his eyes don't leave mine. He looks truly concerned. Like I've gone mad.

"Do you want to sit down?" he says in that tone I love. The one that says he's only talking to me. Like he's only ever talked to me. "Let me take your coat."

I let him peel the coat from my arms and hang it by the door. When he turns back to me, tears sting my eyes. "I, I—"

But the words won't come.

Seb leads me to the chair, holds my hand as I sit down. Ana disappears and reappears with a glass of water.

"Tell me," Seb says, kneeling down and rubbing his hand over my thigh. Up close, his cologne is musky and sensual. His voice is barely a whisper. "What's going on?"

I meet his teddy bear eyes. Where would I start? What would I say? I close my eyes, picture the house from outside, the fog behind me. The memory now drifting away on the water. I manage a word. "Nothing."

"Is it Deb?" he asks.

I think of Deb, sitting in her home alone, unsure what her husband is capable of, memories of their past corrupted by his behaviour. I compare her to me, sitting in this warm house, Seb's hand on my knee, a worried look on his face.

But I saw it, didn't I?

I nod through a sob. Seb wraps his arms around me, the fabric of his turtleneck soft against my cheek. When he lets go, he wipes away my tears. "We'll have some dinner and you'll feel better, okay?" He leans in, placing a kiss on my forehead. "I missed you."

He stands, walks to the kitchen, then turns. "Do you want some wine? A cup of tea?"

I shake my head.

"Have some water," Ana murmurs. I've forgotten she's been here all this time. She motions to the glass on the table, her arms still crossed in front of her.

I do as she says. It's only when I put the glass down that I notice my hand is wet. I look back at the glass. It has water splashed all over it, like it was poured in a rush. I turn to look at the window. It's dark outside, and my face reflects back at me. From here, I can see my eyes are swollen and puffy.

And then I look at Ana's reflection in the window.

She's standing behind me, but something's off. And when I look closer, I see it.

She's shaking.

I turn back to look at her. She's frozen in place, her eyes downcast. From the kitchen, I can hear Seb shuffling around with the cutlery. She looks up and meets my gaze. Her eyes are stricken, like she's seen a ghost. I want to look away but I can't. It's like a story's about to be told. That if I look for a second longer, all will be revealed.

Please, I want to say. *Tell me I'm not crazy.*

But Seb walks back into the room, a platter of vegetable stew in his hands. Ana moves to take a seat at the table, eyes still downcast. In his haste, Seb drops a fork onto the floor, and in those few beats where he bends to pick it up, Ana looks up and stares right at me. I can see clearly what's behind her eyes.

Fear.

CHAPTER 52:

CAT

Present Day

Neil and I smoke in silence for a while. With every puff, the feeling burns in my chest. Embarrassment. For not speaking up. For always running away. For getting myself into this situation.

Neil's calm, clearly comfortable with the silence. When I build up enough courage to speak again, the words feel stupid. "How did you become an investigator?"

He takes a long drag, exhales slowly. "Just fell into it, I guess."

"Were you in the police before?"

"Yep."

He stubs out the cigarette on the wall. "My father was a copper. So I became one too. At least for a while."

"What made you leave?"

Neil squints at the sun, and for a second it feels almost like the sky could turn cloudy if he willed it to. "I don't handle authority well."

"But don't you still have a boss now?"

He gives me a look.

"Lisa's family," I say.

"I pick my projects. And the money is good."

I nod. "We could all use more money."

He lounges back on the brick wall. "What would a kid know about money?"

"A few things."

He doesn't ask me what things, and it speaks volumes. Strangely, it's been ages since I've felt this comfortable around someone. It's as if I can almost forget why we're here. He says it as it is. He doesn't wear kid gloves when he talks to me.

"I got some inheritance money," I say, looking down. "A while back. Did you know that?"

He takes out another cigarette.

I take a breath. "I could do a lot with it."

"But you can't."

I eye my burnt-out cigarette, flecks of ash floating lazily to the ground. Neil's right. The inheritance is mine, but it only exists since someone else doesn't anymore. How can I spend money that is tied to a human life?

"You know, my dad died when I was your age," Neil says. "His life insurance didn't even pay out. It all went straight to the debt collectors."

I remind myself that I started this conversation. On some weird level, I wanted this talk to happen.

"I'm sorry," I say, and a moment later. "How did he die?"

I don't bother with euphemisms. Like Neil, I prefer a person to say it as it is. Not *moved on* or *passed away*. Just dead. Like they are.

"Behind the wheel while he was on a binge," Neil says, taking a drag.

I say nothing.

"Yours?" he asks.

I look at the grass in the corner of the garden. There's an ugly yellow ring where a pot plant used to be. A remnant of something gone forever. Soon the grass will grow over it, leaving no trace of its existence. Make way for new life.

The words burst out of me before I can stop them. "Hanged himself."

Perhaps Neil just wanted me to say it. People do that. They're drawn to tragedy. It's human nature. We're morbidly curious about other people. As if death has a smell. It's the same reason I'm here, chasing death again.

"You can't blame yourself," my second psychologist had said. I'd been doing the rounds of grief counselling. She'd tried her familiar tricks, encouraging me to spill the beans of my life. Like my head was a mystery and she couldn't wait to climb into it and dissect it. Pull out the wrongdoer.

It would make everything better if those parts of ourselves could be removed. The ones that hurt others. Whether we're aware of it or not. How many lives would it save?

For me, it might have saved my dad's.

"Do you want to talk about it?" Neil asks carefully.

"No," I say, abruptly. Too abruptly.

I could tell him how it happened. How my father drank his last glass of whisky, watching tennis on TV. How something had compelled him to take a rope and shape a noose in his living room. The space where we'd shared countless meals and memories. A noose which he eventually put around a ceiling beam, and the other end around his neck.

There's something deliberate about setting up your own death. It takes real drive. You really need to want to die.

I could tell Neil all of this. But he still wouldn't get it.

Because it's not the full story. My father didn't decide to off himself that night. The drive to end his life had come from somewhere else. I think back to that day, feeling the old raging sensation surface. It makes me want to knock my head against something until it all goes away.

Fathers often kill themselves. It's a fact. But how many daughters kill their fathers?

CHAPTER 53:

LISA

Six Months Ago

I stare at the bowl of cereal in front of me. It's gone soggy. The bran has turned into a murky paste.

"Not going to eat?" Seb asks. We're in the dining room, playing house. But this morning I don't feel like pretending.

I shake my head and stare out of the window. The sky is clear, which means it's probably freezing outside. But if I look only at the sun, it's the Spain I was hoping for.

"I'll make you a coffee," Seb says, walking to the kitchen.

I bring my hands to my temples. If I could only switch off my brain. Stop the images from last night playing on repeat.

Two shadowy figures. Brother and sister. Kissing. *Did it really happen?*

Ana's leaving for Barcelona in two days. And then it'll just be Seb, Alma, and me.

I look at my cereal, willing the brown sludge to part, like Moses parted the sea. To make way for something. Anything.

They say you see the things you want to see. If that's true, what does that say about me? I can hear Eleanor's disappointed voice in my head again. I can hear *you* in my head again—calling me crazy.

Seb walks back into the room and puts a steaming mug next to me. "Be careful, it's hot."

He smiles and I force one back. I look for a trace of something dark, a clue that he's lying. But if he is, he's doing it well.

"Are you going to Deb's today?" he asks.

Deb. I've forgotten all about her since last night.

"Yes, a bit later."

He nods. "It's nice that you're looking after her. I never thought Richard would turn out to be an asshole."

"Me neither."

"It's a shame," he says, turning his attention back to his laptop screen.

I stare out of the window again, thinking back to this morning. How I watched Seb get out of bed, afraid to stir and let him know I was awake. He went to the bathroom, and when he returned, he sat on the bed and greeted me happily, asking me how I'd slept.

As if nothing was wrong.

I just smiled and told him I was fine. His concern for me last night felt real, believable. I almost bought it. Until Ana gave the truth away with her shaking hands across the dining room table. I can still see those eyes, full of fear. But fear of what?

I felt she was trying to tell me something. She looked torn. But she said nothing for the rest of the night, and she's been gone all morning. I hoped for clarity today. I even prayed for it last night, as if the universe would give me a sign that Seb was lying. But looking at him now, I'm so conflicted.

Everything feels wrong. Seeing him at the top of the stairs last night, dressed in his cream turtleneck. He was so handsome, like the Seb I knew. But I had seen the black turtleneck in the bay window.

I know I did.

"I'm going to get ready," I say, getting up and taking my coffee with me.

"I'll be here," Seb says, his words feeling more like a reminder than a comfort.

I walk up the stairs and close the bedroom door behind me. Heading to the bathroom, I put my coffee on the basin and stare at my reflection in the mirror. *Am I going mad?*

I whisper the words, watching my lips move. *Am I crazy?*

I half expect to cry, but my face refuses to crumple. Before I can ask the question again, my insides tug at me. It's the same visceral feeling you get when you're standing too close to the edge of a cliff, or a balcony.

"I'm not crazy," I say out loud. Because I know what crazy feels like. It feels like you can't believe who you are. Like everything you've ever known is a lie. Like that day the restraining order arrived, and I saw my name in print.

That's what crazy feels like. And this doesn't feel like that.

I sip my coffee and look at my hands. A part of me wants to reach for the razor again, but even that doesn't feel right. Because this time it doesn't feel like my fault.

So instead, I do something else.

I put the mug on the basin and walk over to the washing basket in the corner. I rummage through the dirty clothing. Searching. If I'm right and I'm not crazy, then there will be evidence of what I saw. Something to prove that it wasn't all in my head.

I fling the contents out onto the floor. Blue jeans, emerald dress, black stockings, cream turtleneck.

And then I find it.

A piece of clothing at the bottom of the basket. The black turtleneck.

* * *

"Something wrong?" Deb asks.

It's past two, and she's still in her nightgown. Even from across her kitchen island, there's a musty smell to her.

"I think I'm getting a cold," I say.

She walks over to a cupboard and takes out a tube. She puts a glass of water and a tablet beside my cup of tea. "Here, vitamin C."

I want to tell her the real reason I'm sick—I'm living in a house full of liars. But I drop the tablet in the water and watch it fizz.

"You sure you're all right?"

I meet her gaze. "Are you?"

Her lips compress into a thin line. "Sorry," I say, "I didn't sleep well either."

She fiddles with her mug. "It's okay. You're right. I'm not doing too well."

She chuckles weakly. We stand like that for a while, silent. Sometimes stillness between two people is the strongest remedy. A way of recognising each other's pain without verbalising it or touching it.

"I might as well go and shower," Deb announces, putting her mug in the sink. "Staying for lunch?"

I can't think of anything I'd rather do. "If that's okay?"

"Macaroni and cheese?" she says with a grin. I love her for it, but I know she's got none of the ingredients for that in the fridge. I give her a smile.

As Deb goes upstairs, I stand by the island until my tea is cold. The questions keep bashing around in my head, each heavier and more hurtful than the one before.

Are you going to confront Seb? What makes you think he'll admit to it? And what would he be admitting to? Changing his sweater?

And then, almost unbidden, a word bubbles to the surface. *Incest.*

I walk around the island. Once, twice. I need to keep busy, keep my mind from spiralling out of control. The old photograph I found in the house comes to view again, the one of Seb and Ana when they were children. Her pigtails, the frown on his chubby face. *It can't be, but what if it is?*

I look at the study door. From here, it's half-closed. Like a relief, my mind recalls yesterday's thoughts. The charity email, the bank statements.

Without thinking, I walk to the study. I hear the water running upstairs. I switch on the Mac and listen to it whir to life. I type the charity's name into Google's search bar. Suddenly, the page returns no matches. *Has it been taken down?*

I navigate to Richard's Gmail, new messages in bold taunting me to read them. I type *Save a Village* into the search bar and click on the emails that appear. The African woman grins toothily as I scroll down the letter to the website link.

It loads slowly, and when it's done, my breath catches in my throat.

If the website looked suspicious before, it looks even more so now. Apart from the outdated layout and colours, the latest posts on the site are from 2013. *Did I notice these before?* No wonder Google hasn't found it. The site looks dormant. Even the URL name has a series of numbers behind it.

I click on the *Donate Now* button, but nothing happens. I click again. Nothing.

I'm scrolling through the *Our Vision* page when I realise there's a silence from upstairs. The shower has stopped. If Deb finds me here, I'll have no excuse. No ASOS order to check this time. My finger clicks hastily, navigating to the *Contact Us* page. It's blank with only a phone number and email address. I open my phone and take a picture of the page.

I switch off the Mac and straighten the chair. Before I leave, I find the bank statements in the cupboard again. From the pages, I find the line with the charity donation, take another picture of it. The last shot is of the bank account number at the top of the page. I can hear Deb on the stairs by the time I leave the study, striding over to the kitchen.

"Let's get our Italian on, shall we?" she says, a towel wrapped around her head.

I watch her walk to the fridge, examine its contents, then close it. She looks almost comical. "On second thought, how does oven pizza sound?"

I break into a smile. It's good to see her in a better mood today. "Perfect."

She preheats the oven as she pours us wine, her eyes sparkling as she talks about some of the delicious meals she's had in her life. The falafel in the Middle East, the prawn curries in Sri Lanka, the stamppot in the Netherlands.

"You've seen so much," I say. "I've barely left Europe."

She brushes the comment away. "You've got time. I did most of my travelling in my thirties."

"Don't you miss it?"

"The older you get, the more you want something of your own. Put down roots. Well, at least for me it's like that."

I nod. "I get that."

She gulps some wine, takes a pizza out of the freezer. "But like I said, you've got so much time."

Why do people always say that? It feels like a warning. A reminder that one day you won't have it anymore. That you'll be like them, nostalgic about the days when they had the luxury of time. I think of Seb, of all the places we haven't been. How we might never get there. How he could end up just like you did—stuck in my brain but not in my life.

And somehow, it doesn't hurt as much as I expected it to.

"Have you thought of taking a trip?" I ask. "It might be good to go away. Especially now?"

Deb raises her eyebrows. "Maybe. I wonder where I'd go. Got any ideas?"

We list places, slurping more wine. Bali, Maldives, Morocco. "Maybe I'll even find someone to rub lotion on my back," she says, winking. We chuckle, and talk of the adventures she could have.

But it's futile, because we both know it's just a dream. Like me, Deb has other problems to worry about. An impending divorce, a separation of lives.

As the wine loosens my limbs and my worries, I think of telling her. But the words sound awful in my head. *I think Seb kissed Ana.*

I also think of telling her about the charity, and showing her the pictures I took of the website and the bank statements. But something inside me holds it close. Tells me not to. Not yet.

I need to do more than tell. I need to show.

And this *Save a Village* charity—whoever they are—might just be the right people to help me do it.

CHAPTER 54:

LISA

Six Months Ago

When I walk through the front door, there's a familiar suitcase standing in the hall.

"Hey," I hear Seb call.

"What's this?" I point to the suitcase.

"I have to go to the vineyard," he says. "There's a problem with our storage unit. If I leave now, I can be back tomorrow evening."

It's strange. Whenever he announced these unexpected visits to the vineyard before, I'd be burning to join him. Sad to see him go. But that was before all of this mess. Before he started lying to me.

I give the smallest of shrugs. "Okay."

"Ana's here if you need anything."

"Oh-*kay*."

That came out snippy, and I can see that Seb thinks so as well, because he takes a step towards me, but it's cautious. He thinks better of it, and takes a breath. "Are you sure you're okay?"

"I just want to lie down," I say, not a total lie.

"You sure?" His eyes look concerned again, but they don't tug at my heart the way they did last night. "If there's anything you want to talk about, you'll tell me—right?"

But you'll just lie again.

"Of course I will," I tell him.

Seb tries to smile, but it comes out as an odd twist of his lips. To save us both from the awkwardness, I walk towards the stairs. He steps aside, and there's an infinitesimally small part of me that hopes he'll stop me. That he'll pull me to him and tell me everything he's been keeping from me. That he'll give me a believable explanation for what I saw last night, and promise me it'll be okay. That we can fight this darkness together.

But without another word, I'm up the stairs.

I close the bedroom door behind me and lean against it as I try to gather my thoughts. Thinking of Seb and Ana together will only be torture. I need to focus on something else.

The charity. That's where my focus should be right now.

I fish my old phone out of my suitcase and put it on the bed. I find the picture I took of the charity's contact details when I was in Richard's study, and type them into my old phone. Then I delete the picture on my new phone. I don't want photos like this to be found and linked back to me.

I dial the number. The phone rings once, then disconnects. No longer in service. I create a fake account on Gmail, and write an email to *Save a Village*.

Hello,
I want to follow up on some billing information. My husband and I have been making regular donations. They are reflecting on our bank statements, but we haven't received any receipts from you for the past few months. Can you please resend?

I press 'send'. Then I double check that everything is deleted from my phones, and lie down on the bed. Now, we wait.

Any information will be of value. Maybe a confirmation that Richard's been truthful about his donation, or a suspicious email response from the charity that I can take to Deb. She won't be happy that I snooped, but if her husband is hiding money ahead of their divorce, then this would help her.

I scroll aimlessly through Instagram. I must keep busy. I listen for sounds downstairs, indicating that Seb has left for the vineyard or is still here, but there's nothing. And come to think of it, I haven't seen Ana since yesterday. Where is she?

I see a picture of Ruth. She's sitting next to two men, holding a beer. She looks happy. How I wish I was there with her rather than here. Without thinking, I find her number and press *Call*.

"Hello?" Ruth answers.

"Hey."

"Hi," her voice is high-pitched, curt.

"How are you?"

"I'm all right, thanks."

There's an awkward silence, and I feel the unease build. "Good," I say. "I was just scrolling Insta and saw you were out for beers. Just made me miss you. So I thought I'd call."

"I'm sorry to hear that." There's that tone again.

"Is something wrong?" I ask.

She sighs. "No, there's nothing wrong."

"You sound… off."

"I'm not off. I just don't have the time right now."

I frown, sit up straighter. "Time for what?"

There's a loud thud and I can picture her throwing a handbag down on a counter. "To be here for your needs."

"My needs? I don't—"

"What's it this time? Are you bored? Had a fight with Seb?"

I flush, struggling to find words as she goes on. "How many times have you asked about *me* lately? Or asked how I'm doing?"

My voice comes out small. "I just asked how you're—"

"Did you? Did you *really*? That's just small talk, Lisa. You call because you want to talk about you."

Bubbles of air escape my mouth. "I'm sorry you feel that way, but I don't—"

"No—you know what? *No*. I was fine dealing with this selfish shit when we lived together, but I don't have to anymore. I've got a lot going on and I really don't have time for this."

I scramble to find words. What's happening? How is my closest friend saying these things?

"I don't know what to say," I start. "Look, I'm thinking of coming home."

She gives a curt laugh. "Sure, you do that," she says coldly. "Do whatever you want."

Before I can say anything, the line goes dead.

I let the beep carry on until it fades. And then all at once, the thoughts break over me like a tsunami. Was I such an awful friend? She never told me she was unhappy. Or was I just not listening? I sift through my memories, questioning everything. A snide comment, an ignored text, nights out without me. She barely spoke of her family, her childhood. She always livened up a room, but didn't get into the nitty-gritty of her emotions.

Unless I didn't see it. Had I been so caught up in my own life that I'd completely skimmed over her? Who does that?

A horrible person.

For once, it's not Eleanor's voice in my head. Not yours either. It's deeper, darker. The same one that comes out whenever the razor does, saying things I try to bury.

Eleanor's biggest sadness is having a fat child like you.

Daniel dated you out of pity.

You're never going to amount to anything.

You don't deserve to be here.

Even now, I've made this about me. I never had a lot of friends, and maybe that's why. I can't seem to get out of my own head and into others' shoes.

I had people I took pictures with, hid behind before the flash. Facebook friends. But then again, weren't they all *your* friends? After our breakup, all that remained was Ruth. My happy-go-lucky friend who always fitted right in with my life.

But even she's had enough of me.

Everyone's had enough of you, the voice says again.

Except for Deb. Surely with her, it's different. She trusts me. Opened up to me. And I took care of her, kept her company. That's what friends do, right?

I sniff, picking through my contacts; a friend from uni, the girlfriend of your mate. All people who'd barely remember me.

I find a name and press *Call*.

"Hello?"

Greg's voice is hoarse, like he's just woken from a nap.

"Hi, it's Lisa," I say, feeling the heat rise in my cheeks. "Sorry to call, I just…"

I don't know why I called. Loneliness, the need to speak to someone who once cared. A reminder that my life's not in shambles.

Several seconds pass. Then Greg says, "I don't think this is a good idea."

His words make my stomach drop. I think back to that day at the restaurant, Seb shoving him on the street. How I'd retched on the floor.

"I know," I say. "But I don't know what else to do. I just wanted to talk to you."

And it's true. I've missed the familiarity of him, his softness.

He says nothing, and I continue. "It's been the strangest couple of weeks."

I gulp, the tightness growing in my throat. Without warning, tears rush to my eyes. "Things have gotten worse."

"Worse how?"

My voice is a rushed whisper. "Crazy things have been happening. You wouldn't believe me if I told you."

I hesitate, but his breathing on the other side reminds me of how I used to feel being around him. Wanted. There's sudden anger that burns and the words start to flow. "But I caught him. I saw it. And they're making me think it's all in my head, but it's not. He's a liar. It's all just lies."

"You're not making sense."

"I know," I say, placing my head in my hands. "It doesn't make sense to me either. Everything's a mess …" I take a breath, my voice a whisper. "I can't make it my Holland."

Silence, and just when I expect him to say something comforting, he sighs. "You shouldn't be calling me."

I can't stop myself. "I miss you. You're my only friend here."

"Lisa, we're not mates."

The words reverberate in my head, and he speaks again. "I'm sorry, but we weren't. And you should be talking to your boyfriend about this."

I clasp the phone closer to my ear, my body shrinking.

"I'm going to hang up now," Greg says.

When I open my mouth, the line's gone dead. The phone falls from my hand and I sink to the ground, sobs wracking my body.

Who are you going to call next?

The voice is back, taunting me. I think of Eleanor, and how she'd respond to my crying over the phone. *Embarrassing.*

I want to scream that I've tried. That I've stayed to make things work, to build some sort of life here. To make this place my Holland. But it's like the fog from outside has seeped into my head.

Perhaps I was never going to get out of this place with something good. Maybe my relationship with Seb—my freedom and trust in myself—was always meant to fail. If there's nothing to go home to, and nothing to stay here for, then what is there?

I lie on the floor, listening for any movement downstairs. When there's nothing but the sound of my breathing, I focus on that. I focus on that until sleep finally takes me.

CHAPTER 55:

CAT

Present Day

I stare at the screen.

Delete it.

But what will they think?

I press and hold down the InCheck logo on my phone and watch it jiggle.

Delete it.

But I don't. Instead, I throw the phone on the bed and curse out loud.

Fred and Susana. I've been thinking about them all morning. They won't miss Alice, not really. They'll move on, as normal adults do, and find another counsellor. A real one this time. But then I think of Lisa, and I pick up the phone again. I have to do this today.

"Cat?" Deborah calls from downstairs.

"Coming!" I reply.

I jam the phone into my pocket. I'll delete InCheck later, come hell or high water.

After yesterday, I'd felt like crawling into a small space and never coming out. Neil and I were still smoking outside, our dead fathers the elephants in the garden, when Deborah opened the back gate. I wiped my eyes and tried to look as calm as Neil. When she waved and went inside the house, I asked, "Did you know she was coming home so early?"

He shrugged. "No."

"Don't you guys keep tabs on each other?"

"We keep to ourselves," he said. "It's better for the investigation that she doesn't know what I do all the time."

As usual, Deborah was in the mood for wine last night. I watched her throw back glass after glass as I sipped on my Coke. Despite not drinking, I felt unhinged. One wrong look from Neil or Deborah, and I'd probably break down. Talking about my dad brought emotions like that dangerously close to the surface.

This morning, I find Deborah at the kitchen island—ready for work—and Neil standing across from her.

"Morning," I say.

"Morning, love," she says, "I wanted to ask you something."

My eyes dart to Neil, but he's not looking up from his phone. I look at Deborah again. "Yes?"

"A colleague of mine is going to South Africa in a month," she says with a smile. "He's done his research on safaris, but since I know a local, I told him I'd ask you what's best."

My ears ring as the words sink in. "A safari?"

"Yes," she grins. "You know, to see lions and rhinos. Those things."

"He should go to the Kruger Park," I say. "It's the biggest game reserve in the country."

She shakes her head, wags a finger. "He knows Kruger. He says you sometimes wait for days to see any action. He wants to see lions up close, you know? Almost touch them."

"Maybe he should go to a zoo," I mutter.

For a moment, she's stunned. Then, she lets out a cackle. "Ha! Well, I'll pick your brain on it later."

But she looks at me for a moment too long, something else hidden behind her eyes. It's the same look she gave me last night.

Dislike.

Maybe she senses my panic. Knows what's happening on a deeper level. What do they call it? The collective subconscious.

"I need to get going," she says, picking up her handbag. But as she walks past me, she slips and crashes to the floor.

"Damn!"

Neil's by her side before me, taking her by the elbow. She's rubbing at her knee.

"You need to be careful," he says.

She nods, her face twisting in pain. "Bloody knee. It's still not healed."

I remember the day she tripped, the shards of glass scattered across the wooden floor, red wine splashed everywhere.

"Can you walk?" I ask.

"I'm all right."

She brushes us off and walks out of the house with a slight limp. A few moments later, her car disappears down the road. My phone pings.

Mom. *Can we call today? Miss you.*

I wish she'd stick to texting only, but today the thought of hearing her voice brightens my mood. *Sure, I'll call you tonight?*

"Ready?" Neil says.

"Let's do it," I say.

It's straight down to business. We walk to the study and sit in our usual spots. The room is stuffy and I remember how claustrophobic I felt in here yesterday. But today I'm ready. No classes to interrupt me, no personal surprises bubbling to the surface. I'm ready to dive into the hole of my blackouts and dig up what we need.

"Two more calls," Neil says, taking stacks of InCheck transcripts from the drawer. "Both on the same day. I went over them this morning."

My mind tries to find something familiar, but it's useless. I've been over this before, trying to pinpoint the last time I spoke to Lisa. I take the papers, scanning through them. A familiar dread washes over me. Only two pages, the last with barely any chats.

How are you feeling today? It's been a while. Alice's opening seems normal enough, but when I see the timestamp of the text, it turns my stomach into a hard knot of trepidation.

14 January.

I read on. According to the transcript, Lisa responded a few minutes later. *Not sure.*

I try to piece together the puzzle in my head. 14 January. I had classes at Sam's academy in the morning, and had the rest of the afternoon off. Getting through the morning was gruelling, but Sam needed me that day. Luckily, she didn't remember the significance of the date.

14 January. The anniversary of two years prior, the day my life came crashing down. The day I started feeling like a murderer.

"You okay?" Neil asks.

I scratch at my head. "Just trying to remember."

I draw the pages closer again. I shouldn't have called Lisa that morning. Alice should have been professional enough to know that her own mental state was shaky. Especially on that day. Lisa was in an awful state too, judging by her curt responses on InCheck.

And yet, I—Alice—still asked her if she wanted to talk.

Ok. 30 mins? Lisa had responded. She was usually a talker, but how much did I really know about her? We'd only spoken on the phone twice, and she'd been vague in her chats ever since. Not at all like Fred or Susana.

I think of them again. Do they ever wonder where Alice went? Why their counsellor simply abandoned them without so much as an explanation? Have they reported Alice for breaching the app's terms of service, for not replying to them on time?

Neil brings me back to the moment. "So you and Lisa had a call that morning. January 14th. Do you remember what she said?"

I sink back in my chair. I should be able to remember this call. The one in the morning. Not the second one, later on. The one where I'd come home from the academy and started drinking midway through the afternoon. That one feels like I'm staring into a pot of blackness.

Slowly, little shards of memory start coming back to me.

I had a break between classes that morning. It was enough time to fit in a phone call with Lisa. I close my eyes, trace back my steps. I'd used a private room at the academy, sitting at an empty desk. And then, suddenly, it all comes back to me.

"She sounded terrible," I say. "Lisa."

"How?"

I tell Neil how empty and hopeless she sounded. Her sadness seeped through the phone, coating the walls. I remember how hard it was. I felt out of my depth, trying to build some positive energy where there was none.

But I was living through a horrible day myself, and I had little to give.

"Would you say she was suicidal?" Neil asks, eyes searching.

I shake my head. "She sounded depressed. But she was engaging." Inside me, the dread builds again, fluttering up my throat like angry butterflies. I feel now like I did then. Scared. Like trying to paint a picture with only one colour. Walking a tightrope with just one foot. How can you give advice to someone when you barely know them? When you need all the advice you can get yourself?

"She wanted to make some… changes," I say.

"What kind of changes?"

"She wanted to get out of her situation."

"Are you sure she didn't want to check out of the world?"

I frown at Neil. "No, I just told you she was engaging. Sad, but engaging. Why would you say that?"

He opens the drawer again, this time putting a stack of pictures on the table. He takes one from the middle of the pile and slides it over to me.

"Like I told you, the police found a suicide note."

I swallow hard.

"Take a look," he says.

My heart's in my throat. But I look down. It's a scanned picture of a handwritten note. I read through it line by line, the bile rising as I do. I try to remind myself that it's not like before. That this has nothing to do with what happened then. What happened on January 14th, two years ago.

And as I read, a calm descends over me.

"They found it in her bedroom," Neil says. "At the house down the road."

I keep reading, the words coming together. I read every sentence twice, just to be sure. And then I meet Neil's eyes, a newfound conviction growing in my chest.

"You've got it wrong," I say, flipping the photo back to him. "This isn't a suicide note at all."

CHAPTER 56:

LISA

Six Months Ago

Morning wakes me rudely, like an uninvited guest incessantly ringing the doorbell. I pull the bedsheets over my head and lie in the dark for what feels like hours. When I can't pretend to sleep anymore, I pull my old phone from the bedside drawer and scan for an email from the charity.

Nothing.

But there's a message from Alice on InCheck. I tap my finger on the old touch ID, but the biometrics don't register. Another sign that I should get rid of this phone. I enter my password and navigate to the app.

How are you feeling today? It's been a while.

I bring a hand to my face, thinking of what to say. I settle on what's most true. *Not sure.*

Alice is quick to respond. *Do you want to have a call?*

I wonder if I'm capable of saying anything at all. I feel like falling asleep and waking up as someone else. But I will my fingers to type. *Ok. 30 mins?*

When she agrees, I walk to the bathroom and stare at my reflection. My face is pale and sickly looking. After a quick shower, I'm back to sitting on the bed, exhausted. When did doing everything become so hard?

Alice's call comes through, but when I pick up, it disconnects. I try again, but I'm locked out if my phone, the touch ID vibrating at my failed attempts.

"Dammit!" I exclaim.

I enter my password again and call Alice, the phone warm against my cheek. Her voice is soft when she answers. "Rachel? Are you there?"

"Sorry, my touch ID is acting up. Old phone."

"It's okay. How are you?"

I wonder where she is right now. Maybe she's sitting in a grand study overlooking rolling woodlands, with a glossy grey cat snoozing in the corner of the room. I picture her life: a loving husband, a successful career, well-behaved children, supportive friends. All the things I'd ever dreamed of for myself.

"Honestly, I don't know how I am," I say.

I wonder how she'll approach this. Surely there's a guidebook counsellors follow. Words they need to say during every session.

"Why is that?" Alice asks.

I don't respond, stare out into the room.

"Did something happen? Is it your fiancé?"

I shrug. "It's a lot of things."

"Can you tell me more?"

"I feel like there's so much built up," I tell her. "So much has happened and I don't know which way to go. I feel like I'm drowning."

"Okay. Do you want to be more specific?"

I swallow down the lump in my throat. "Not really."

How could I tell her? The kiss. The *incest*. Me snooping through my only friend's financial information. It's cringeworthy. I can't go there.

"It's like everything I think and do is wrong," I say. "Like I'll just mess everything up again. And I have—messed things up, I mean. Big time. Have you ever wanted to take back the things you've done?"

Alice is silent, and I wonder if I've spiralled beyond her ability to respond to me. Finally, she speaks.

"One of the best things we have is the ability to trust ourselves," she says. "That doesn't mean we don't make mistakes. I've made them too."

She takes a deep breath. "But they don't justify giving away your power."

I think of Eleanor, of you, of Seb. Of all the people who I've relinquished control to, handing over the steering wheel to my life. How, ever since I've been here, I've wanted it back. Wanted to drive off by myself, leaving it all behind.

My tears well up. "I've given my power away."

"So let's take it back," she says. "I want you to do something for me. Can you?"

I take a breath. "Yes."

"Think of what you want more than anything right now. Something only you want. You don't have to tell me. Just think about it."

I don't have to think long for the image to surface. Leaving this place, getting away from all of this. Going back home on my terms. Live with myself and my decisions. Decide which wounds to lick, and when.

"Got it?" Alice asks.

"I do."

"Good. Do you have a pen and paper?"

I look around the room. There's a wooden armoire next to the drapes. It's not vintage. Just old. I rummage through the drawers and finally find a piece of paper and a pencil. "Got it."

"Good. Now I want you to write what you want in a letter. Is there someone you can address it to?"

So many choices, so much to say. "Yes."

"Great. Now, this isn't a letter to them. This is just for you. But sometimes you can process things better if your thoughts are directed at someone. Does that make sense?"

I nod like she can see me. "And I just write what I want?"

"Exactly. Tell them what you know. Deep down. The things that you want and need right now."

"Okay."

"But Rachel, there's no blame here. No blaming yourself for how you feel, and no blaming others, either. This just makes it real. It puts you back in control."

I nod. "Okay, but I just feel like I've let so many people down."

"I doubt that," she says softly. "But if you have, apologise and move on. Don't dwell too long in this dark place."

We talk for a few more minutes, my mind focused on the letter. When we hang up, I write Seb's name at the top of the page.

Seb, this is too difficult to say, so I'm writing it down.

The words form in my head before I write them, my tears threatening to drop onto the page. But the thought of taking back control propels me forward.

Here are four reasons why I'm done:

1. *I thought I was adaptable to change, but I'm not. Change is something I have never dealt with well in my life. I don't think I can this time.*
2. *I've broken all the relationships I've had, including this one. I don't think we can move past this.*
3. *I've let everyone down, but mostly myself.*
4. *I want out. Out of all of it.*

I stare at the page, wanting to add *"you are a liar"*, but then I remember Alice's words about not blaming others. Even if he did what I think he did, blaming him for the failure of our relationship wouldn't help.

I end the note simply. *I'll always love you, somehow. Lisa.*

I sit for a long time staring at the words. The truth on a page.

Alice was right. Putting it down on paper makes it feel more real. This is the first time in a long time that I've been honest with myself. Everything since the wedding, the hospital, has been a blur. I've barely been there for any of it. And when Seb came along with his proposal, his idea to come here, I went along happily. Never asking myself the questions I needed to.

Is this the right thing for you? Is this what you really want?

Not Eleanor's idea of right. Or Seb's. *My* type of right.

So, what's next?

I think of Alice again. *Apologise and move on.*

I pick up my phone and type a text message to Ruth. *I'm so sorry that I hurt you. I was a bad friend. Please know that I am sorry.*

We'll see how she responds and take it from there. Next on the list is Greg.

I'm sorry that I put you in a difficult position, even if we were never friends.

I'll always remember our fun times together. You saved me in a lot of ways.

And it's true. If it hadn't been for what happened with Greg, who knew where I'd be?

I stare at Deb's profile picture, taken in a meadow somewhere in the Cotswolds. I could tell her about the charity now, send her the screenshots and never see her again. But I owe her more than that. It's an in-person thing to do.

I scroll on, seeing the contact I've been dreading, but who I need to tell the most. I start messaging Eleanor.

Mum, I tried to make it work here, but too much has happened that's blurred my vision of what's real. I've needed help for a long time. My own help. You might not see me for a while, but know that wherever I am, I love you and I'm sorry for how my actions affected you.

The message feels too long, so I rewrite it.

Mum, I'm afraid I'm going to let you down again. But please know, it's the best decision for me. I love you. It'll all be okay.

I press send.

Standing up, I eye the room and make a mental list of the things I need to do.

Pack a bag.

Book a flight.

Talk to Seb.

That last item makes my stomach drop. I think of giving Seb the letter, but it's too vague for him to understand what I'm really trying to say. For me to take full control, I need to face this head on. Talk him through my decision. I pace the room, wondering if there's anything missing from my mental checklist.

I'm about to pull my suitcase closer when my phone lights up with a notification. An email.

It's from the charity. The entire message fits in one line.

Can I call you? Here's my number.

I copy the digits in the email over and hit dial on my old phone, my heart beating in my ears. Before I go, this is another thing I should take care of.

CHAPTER 57:

LISA

Six Months Ago

"Is this Rachel?"

The woman's voice is raised, like a scolding mother's.

"Yes, that's me," I say, pacing the room.

"Okay," she says. "So I got an email about a donation you made?"

"Yes, my husband and I, we made a donation—"

"A donation every month?"

"Yes."

"Right. Well see, that's impossible."

I clutch the phone closer, standing by the window. It's only early afternoon, but it's already dark outside. From here, the fog blankets the ocean all the way to the shore.

"I ran the charity back in 2017," the woman says. "But it's closed now."

"Really?" I say. "When did it shut?"

The woman takes a breath, and I swear I can hear the impatience in her voice. "Save a Village was a foundation that operated for a few years, but since then we've merged with another organisation. So it's not possible to make a donation. Our bank account is shut."

"But I have an email from you," I say. "I have emails from the last five years."

I'm searching for crumbs of truth, but deep down, I know what's coming.

"You can forward it to me," she says, a frustrated lilt to her voice. "There are a lot of charity scams going around. Sometimes they use the name of an existing one. If you send me the email, I can confirm it."

I wonder if this has happened to her before. Judging by her voice, I bet it has.

"You said you and your husband have made these donations together?"

I take a breath. "Yes."

There's silence. She's holding back. But she doesn't have to say anything, because we're thinking the same thing.

"I have the bank statements too. Would that help?"

"Yes," she says, her voice suddenly softer. "We can share it all with Action Fraud."

I nod. "Thank you. I'll send those today."

"Sorry about this," is the last thing she says before we hang up.

I sit on the bed and think through my next move. It's a tricky one, but hopefully the right one. Everyone deserves a chance to make things right. Even bastards.

It takes a few minutes to find his number. My old phone's practically overheating, but I quickly scroll to his LinkedIn profile and find his architecture firm's website. On the team page, below his name and experience, is his mobile number. It's crazy how people do that: give the world access to their lives so easily. It's like anyone can call them.

Anyone like me.

He's quick to pick up, sounding in a hurry. "Richard speaking."

I end the call, my heart pounding in my chest. He doesn't call back, so I type out a text, my fingers shaking with adrenaline.

You have a day to tell Deb. I have the emails and bank statements to prove it. Show her how you've been stealing money, or I will.

I press send, dropping the phone on the bed. Pacing the room, I wait for a reply. Time seems to stand still, with nothing but a black screen.

And then it comes. The first message.

Who is this?

I try to ignore the twisting knot in my stomach as the second message comes through.

You should be careful.

And finally, when it feels like my heart can't beat any faster, the last one.

You don't know who you're dealing with.

CHAPTER 58:

CAT

Present Day

I tell Neil everything I can remember. When I'm done, his forehead is so creased a pencil can practically fit between the folds.

"You see?" I say, pointing to the piece of paper on the table. "It's a manifesto of Lisa's feelings, not a suicide note."

He looks it over, rubbing the stubble on his chin. "And you told her to write it?"

I nod. "Yes."

"Why?"

"I read about it online," I say. "Writing your feelings in a letter helps clarify things. To be honest, I was lost. And I didn't know what she wrote until… well, now."

Neil purses his lips. Then, as if deciding something, he pulls the page closer. "If you read this without knowing any of that, it could still be a suicide note," he says. "Plus, there are other things."

"Like what?"

"Lisa texted her friends and her mum the day she went missing. All apology messages." He raises an eyebrow like I'm supposed to be surprised. "Plus, the autopsy confirmed she had painkillers and alcohol in her system. A lot. And to top it off, she showed self-harming behaviour in the past."

I sit back, surprised. "Self-harming?"

"They found cuts on her arms and inner thighs," Neil says.

I lean forward again. "Some girls do that. Lots of girls, actually."

"Do you?"

"I used to," I say, thinking back to high school, when listening to Fall Out Boy and bleeding used to be cool. "It's not a sign of suicide. And those apologies Lisa sent? That was part of the advice I gave her. To apologise to all the people she had wronged."

My words all sound fine, but they don't feel fine. I feel as if I'm reaching, sliding backwards fast.

Neil stares at me. "So, she what—just fell into the water?"

He thinks I sound like an idiot too.

My fingers intertwine. "It could happen."

Neil studies the page in front of him, scanning it for information that's not there.

"Who was the last person to see her?" I ask, grabbing for another angle.

"The fiancé's sister. She saw Lisa that afternoon."

"And the fiancé?"

"According to his statement, he returned from work in the evening and was with his sister and mother the whole time," Neil says. "They only realised something was wrong when Lisa didn't come home that night."

I frown. Something about that makes little sense. "You don't find that suspicious?"

Neil shrugs. "He said he thought she was at Deb's. Or just walking around. Seeing people from her Spanish class, maybe. I couldn't poke holes in his alibi with the sister there to corroborate it. His mother went to bed early, so she couldn't confirm, but his sister did."

"And Deborah?"

"She texted Lisa that day, but didn't see her."

I follow his eyes to the transcripts on the page, and the dots start to connect. "So, that means..."

"You're the last person that spoke to her."

I stare at the transcripts. Our first call was at 13:21, our second at 19:37. What happened in between those times? And what did I tell her in the second call? A heavy sensation builds in my core, like spilled ink, seeping into every crevice of my body.

I stare at the second timestamp. 19:37 on the annual worst day of my life. 14 January. I'd done my rounds, called who needed to be called, and bought the vices I needed to pass the time. The sun would have set by then, my senses numbed by the wine.

"Do you think you said anything that could have…" Neil's face is careful again.

My brow furrows. "Could have what?"

"Lisa clearly listened to you. Could you have said something that she took the wrong way?"

"No."

"That might have pushed her over the edge."

"No."

"Cat."

Neil's eyes are on me, but I can't look at him. The room suddenly feels smaller. I want to get out.

"People say things," he continues. "And they're sometimes unaware of the effect it has on others. It happens."

Nausea crawls up my throat. I can taste the bitterness of the bile. Neil's voice is soft now. "I can only help you if you tell me."

It makes me wonder. Even if I knew for sure what I said that night, would I tell him? I say nothing, and so he takes a breath. "Do you remember where you were the night she called you?"

On my balcony, pissed out of my mind.

"Yes. I was home."

I can picture the bottle of wine at my feet, the cigarettes on the table. Watching the day fade into night. And then I remember the incoming call.

"I was on my balcony when she called me."

"And what did she say?"

I remember the cigarette smell on my fingers. The drone of the highway traffic in the distance. Like an accident in slow motion, the pieces start coming together.

I twist my face. "I don't remember what she said. It's all a bit fuzzy."

He brings a finger to his temple. "Alright. Let's take a break." He starts to pack away the papers when something catches my eye. "What's that?"

I point to a photo in the pile on the desk. Neil pulls it out. "These are shots of the house she stayed at," he says. "The one down the road. With the fiancé."

"Can I see them?" I ask.

He slides the pictures over. In them, the bedroom Lisa stayed in looks so sad. A suitcase on the floor. An unmade bed. An ancient dresser. And something else.

"Is this her phone?" I ask, pointing at a picture of an iPhone on the dresser. "Yep."

"Are you sure?"

Neil shrugs. A dumb question, no doubt. But my memory grabs hold of something and it solidifies.

"Lisa had a touch ID," I say.

"What?"

"On the first call we had, Lisa had issues with her phone's touch ID. And this—" I point to the phone in the photograph, "Is a newer model. It doesn't have it. The touch ID." I look at the phone on the photograph again, the clear screen devoid of a button.

Neil is staring at it too. He scratches his jaw. "Really?"

I nod. "She struggled to answer our call once because of it."

Moments pass, and then Neil's grunts, suddenly defensive. "The police only found this phone at the house."

"Maybe she had two?" I offer. "Didn't they find another phone on her? You know, when they… found her?"

Neil shakes his head. "There was no phone on her person when they discovered her body."

"Isn't that weird?" I ask. "I mean, if I was the last one she had a call with, and I'm telling you she had a different phone to the one the police found, wouldn't that mean she had a second phone?"

Neil doesn't look convinced. "I don't know."

His uncertainty sparks another question. "How did you find out Lisa was tied to InCheck? She used a fake name, so how did you know she had an account?"

"Monthly subscriptions on her credit card," Neil says. "And her login details for InCheck on her laptop."

"And the police didn't find that interesting? Or worth looking into?"

He shrugs again. "They were looking elsewhere. At more prominent evidence."

We're quiet for a while. In a way, I understand that the reasonable thought is to consider suicide. It's the easiest route to an open-and-shut case, but what if it's more complicated than that? Not so black and white?

I take a breath. "I think the second phone is worth something."

Neil says nothing. I thought he'd be happy. Finally, he has some evidence to work with. So why does he look so disappointed?

"Can't you reach out to her family or friends?" I ask. "See if she had a different phone or number before?"

His eyes are far away. I can almost see his brain whirring. Then he's back, fishing for his cigarette pack. "I'll look into it." He gets up and there's a whiff of stale sweat as he walks towards the door. "In the meantime, try to remember that last call with her. We can't choke on this final piece of the puzzle. We need all the facts straight."

A click. Something comes together in my mind. I turn in my chair and look at Neil, who's walking out of the room. "What did you just say?"

He turns. "About what?"

"That last part, about the call."

"That we need to get all the facts straight."

I shake my head. "No, the other thing. About the puzzle."

His face is blank, a cigarette dangling from his fingers. "That we need that piece of the puzzle. The call with Lisa."

"Yeah, but…" I trail off. He said a specific word. *Choke.*

"Never mind," I tell him.

"Want one?" Neil says, offering the cigarette to me across the room. But I shake my head. I need him to leave so I can be alone. When he's finally gone, I turn and put my hands on the desk in front of me.

Choke, choke, choke. As I whisper the words out loud, the memories come seeping back like strokes of watercolour on a canvas.

Neil wants me to remember what happened, and I think I just did.

For a moment, I wonder if I should race after him and tell him. But then I remember how upset he was when I spoke to Greg. It frustrated him how involved I got in the investigation. How close I got.

I stand up and pace the room, sifting through my thoughts. There's not enough time for a proper plan. There's not enough evidence to do anything concrete. But I need to act. It's the only chance I have.

Because right now, the main suspect in this investigation is still me. That has to change. Today.

CHAPTER 59:

LISA

Six Months Ago

My heart's still pounding in my chest when there's a knock on the bedroom door.

"Hello?" Ana's face peeps through. "Are you okay?"

I'm lying on the floor, where I've been for the last hour, worrying about the text message from Richard.

You don't know who you're dealing with.

"I'm okay," I say. Because, for the most part, I am. The letter Alice asked me to write is on the table, my newfound resolve buzzing in my veins.

"Do you want to go for a walk?" Ana asks. She's hovering uncomfortably, and I remember how we've been tiptoeing around each other for days.

"Aren't you leaving today?" I counter, remembering her expected trip back to Barcelona.

A faint smile plays on her lips. "Only tomorrow."

She's been avoiding me ever since that night I saw Seb and her together. This walk could be an opportunity for me to find out what really happened. Or to give her a chance to tell me. Judging by the way she's looking at me, there's more to this walk than just a goodbye.

"Give me five minutes?" I ask.

I splash some water on my face and go downstairs. Alma's bustling around in the kitchen. It's amazing how she's recovered from her fall. If only our minds could heal as fast as our bodies.

Leaving the house is like stepping into a freezer.

"Let's go this way," Ana says, turning towards a cluster of trees down by the water. I follow her downhill, glancing back towards Deb's house. I texted her an hour ago, asking if I could come over. There's evidence now. Proof that her husband is a liar, and I'm ready to tell her.

But her incoming text sends a shiver through me. *Can't. Richard's in town today. Tomorrow? xx*

There's no sign of his car in the street. Yet.

Ana and I walk in silence for a while. From here, I can barely see the dock behind the trees. It's like the fog's locked us in. At the end of the road, she sits down on a bench, burying her hands deep in her coat pockets. I stand beside her, gazing out into the gloom. How far we've come—from strangers to almost friends, then back to strangers.

"I think you need to leave."

Her words are soft, but I don't understand them immediately. "What?"

We lock eyes, and her face is expressionless. She holds my gaze, then looks to where the dock should be. "You're not happy here. And this place—my family," she says. "It's not good for you. And it won't get better."

I say nothing, and she stares at me. "It's going to kill you," she says.

My feet are rooted to the ground, but her words batter me harder than the cool sea breeze.

I breathe. "I saw you two," I finally say.

She doesn't look away. But her expression shifts, losing its hard edge. She's both thrown me a lifeline and made me question everything. The images from that night form again in my mind. A brother and sister. Kissing the way that brothers and sisters shouldn't.

I move closer to her. "I thought I was crazy," I say. "But I'm not, am I?"

She looks away.

"We used to come out here as kids," she says after a beat. "Seb never liked Basque, not like I did. We were in Madrid most of the time. But every now and again, we came here."

I perch on the edge of the bench.

"We didn't get along very well," she continues. "I was always out talking

305

to people and making friends. But my brother kept to himself. He was always in his room. He never wanted to be outside."

I imagine a younger Seb in his bedroom. Reading. Brooding.

"He didn't talk much either," Ana says. "My parents took him to doctors, but they said nothing was wrong. He just needed more time to process things. But I was different. Outgoing, curious, silly. I didn't know…" she trails off.

"Then there was this one day. I was up in my room." Ana's words come haltingly. I feel uncomfortable for her. "I was sixteen. Still getting used to my body. But back then we didn't feel so shy about stuff."

I look over her slender figure, her golden skin. A body to be confident about.

"I wanted to swim, so I was changing. I left my door open—just a little—and I didn't hear him." She leans forward, her hands on her knees.

"He was standing in the doorway. And when I turned and saw him, he was shocked, like he'd never… he wasn't supposed to be there. To see me like that."

She's silent again. I don't move.

"I should have yelled at him or slammed the door or… something. But he was always so passive." She gesticulates with her hands. "I just wanted him to *do* something. To *say* something."

Her eyes brim with tears. "So I let him watch me."

The silence spreads. We let it sit there, threatening to engulf us. I blink once, twice, and then Ana breaks the silence.

"I was stupid. Just playing around. I don't know why. Maybe I was waiting for a reaction. I didn't think any of it would have…"

She trails off again.

"He was only a child," she says. "But something about that day must have set him off. I've read so much about it since then. It's like something cracked inside of him."

My mind won't let her words land. All it does is circle around a nursery rhythm. *All the king's horses and all the king's men. Couldn't put Humpty together again.*

The tears are flowing freely down her cheeks now. "After that, he was different. At first, he watched me when he thought I wasn't looking. And then he stopped caring if I saw him at all. After a while, he started coming into my room at night, sitting on my bed, like he just wanted to..."

I want to reach out and grab her hand. But I'm frozen.

"...wanted to just *watch* me," she stammers. "And then I'd push him away and tell him to get out. But it was too late. It was all so wrong already."

My head swells. Beats pass with no words, and finally, I find my voice. "Did you tell your parents?"

Ana shakes her head. A violent back and forth. "No, no. I couldn't tell them. Never. I made him like that. I let him watch me that day. How—*sick* is that?" She reels back, her face twisted in disgust. "My own..."

Sobs wrack her body. Heart-rending, animalistic. I give her a minute or two, then speak again.

"And he's still doing it? Watching you like that?"

I want her to say *no*, but there's a need for a *yes*, too.

Her nod is almost imperceptible. "When we were older, he started cornering me when we were alone. I never let it go anywhere," she says. "I tried telling him we could fix it together. Talk about it. But he never wanted to. Not even when our father caught him."

She puts her hands over her face. I feel nauseous. "Your father?" I ask.

"Yes," she nods. "We were here, in Basque. He caught Seb cornering me in the house. He was still a teenager. I didn't think my father would know what was going on, but he did. He grabbed Seb by the scruff of the neck and dragged him outside." She points in the direction of the dock. "He took him out there. I don't know what he did or said, but Seb came back a different person."

"It was the last summer we spent together," Ana continues. "After that, we weren't teenagers anymore. We didn't keep in touch. I tried, but he kept his distance. He didn't even come to my wedding. He made up some excuse. The last time I saw him was two years ago."

I stare at Ana. She looks defeated. "Did your father tell Alma?"

"No. It would break her heart."

All the king's horses and all the king's men. Couldn't put Humpty together again.

"I thought time would heal it, make it go away," she says, the words rough in her throat. "And when I heard he was engaged, I was so relieved. I really thought we could put it all behind us. But I was wrong."

All at once, things start clicking into place. Alma's fall, how it brought Ana back here, how Seb changed. Something had happened to him to shape him into this person. A mound of complicated feelings triggered by one moment, a precedent set where there should never have been one. I swallow hard as the nausea rises in my throat again.

I wonder what his father had said on that dock. What he'd done to get Seb to see the world differently. Either way, it led him to me. A person barely equipped to handle her own broken life, let alone someone else's. Two cracked eggs together in a basket.

I stare into the fog. "So it happened. What I saw the other night."

"Yes."

"He kissed you?"

I can feel her shudder beside me. "Yes."

And all I can do is sigh. And as I do, I feel a strange relief. The last few years have been a series of made-up stories. Stories of my thin body, my circle of friends. Stories of you, stories of Seb and me building a life together. All fairy tales.

Finally, I'm not telling myself a story. I'm confronting the facts. And it feels good.

"But I pushed him away," Ana says urgently. "Nothing else happened, Lisa. What you saw... that was all there was."

"It doesn't matter," I say. Because none of it does. In my head, I'm already miles from here. "But you lied to me. I saw it happen, and you denied it."

She goes quiet, but I don't. "I know you wouldn't want to tell me. I'm basically a stranger to you," I say. "But why keep lying for him? Why keep his secret?"

The change is swift and astonishing. Ana's face morphs from fragile to determined in an instant. Her eyes harden and her shoulders tense beside me.

"Because I love my brother," she says, her eyes locking on mine. "And I have a part in this, and doesn't matter what happens, I'll always protect him."

CHAPTER 60:

CAT

Present Day

I lock the front door behind me, the afternoon's sudden chill giving me goosebumps. But it's not just the breeze. It's the adrenaline. After a late lunch, I told Neil I needed to go for a walk to refresh my memory. In reality, my thoughts are crystal clear for the first time in weeks.

The nugget of memory—what Lisa told me that night—burns in the centre of my chest.

I walk uphill towards town, and the road is quiet. The salt of the ocean hits my nostrils, and I'm struck by another memory out of the blue. A memory of a day many years ago. The sun was setting over the school parking lot. All the kids had long gone home. Except for me.

My dad was drunk when he finally arrived to pick me up. As he often was. I threw my bags into the back seat of his car, and when I got in next to him, the air was thick with cigarette smoke and whisky fumes. I refused to look at him.

"Sorry I'm late," he mumbled.

I looked out of the window, feeling more alone in the car than in the parking lot.

"Drive-through ice cream?" he asked.

I sat in silence as we drove. He cranked the window open. Maybe he was hot. Maybe he just wanted to save me from the funk of cigarettes and booze. As we waited for our ice creams, he turned to me.

"Bud, life is too serious for you to be so serious." He'd pulled a funny face at me. I couldn't help but smile. It didn't matter what happened. There would always be a drive-through to go to, and something to laugh at.

But none of that is here now. Including him.

I wish you were here now to tell me what to do, I whisper. But there's no answer, of course. So I keep walking, focusing on the one thing that can happen. That I can make happen.

When I get to the bar, I order a Coke and sit at a corner table. I scroll through my phone, avoiding InCheck. I say the words over and over in my head, like the sound of them will solidify my recent memory.

Choke, choke, choke.

My Coke is only half drunk when Sebastian walks through the door.

His shoulders are slouched and he looks smaller than I remember. The bartender pours him a whisky. He knocks it back, orders another. When he's on his third drink, the bartender calls across the room to ask if I want anything else. My eyes burn into Sebastian's back, hoping he will turn and see me. But he doesn't. So I order a coffee and wait.

When he leaves the bar a few hours later, I'm practically salivating. He's had at least five whiskies, and I could really use one right now. But I won't. I wait for him to walk out before I get up to pay and leave.

Outside, the street lamps create little circles of light in the fading daylight. The town is deserted, apart from Sebastian. As I follow him, I feel a sense of anticipation. I think of Neil. Whether he's looking into Lisa's second phone. If he even believes me. *You're going to mess up this whole investigation*, I imagine him saying. But for the first time in a long time, I feel like I'm doing the right thing. I'm about to fix something, not break it.

Choke, choke, choke.

"Hey," I call out. "Hey, you!"

He turns around. We're at the end of the road, just before the downhill. From here, the water shimmers below us. As he turns to face me, I'm suddenly reminded that it's just the two of us out here. That if something had to happen, I'd be all alone.

As I walk towards him, I dig around in my bag for my house keys. It was a move my father taught me the first time I wanted to go out alone to buy chocolate.

"Do you have your keys?" he asked me. "Keep them in your fist."

He took my hand in his and put a key between each finger, like a crude knuckleduster. "Like this."

My father looked at me with a rare seriousness. "Always be prepared for the worst, Bud. If someone grabs you, take a swing at them. As hard as you can."

Now, I scrabble for the keys that can protect me from the worst. I clutch them in my hand and hold them close.

Sebastian says nothing as I walk towards him, looking around us for a sign of life—a lit window, or an open door. But there's nothing. As I get close to him, I see the thin line of his lips, his furrowed eyebrows like caterpillars. He looks surprised.

My breathing is loud in my ears.

"I know who you are," I tell him.

His face is contorted. He takes an unsteady step forward, his hands still in his pockets. "What?"

I steady my voice. "I know who you are."

"And who are you?"

"A friend of Lisa's."

I try my best to stand my ground. We're a few feet from each other now, and suddenly he doesn't look as small as he did in the bar. He's a foot taller than me, with legs that look like they belong on a rugby player. He could pick me up—or knock me down—without a second thought.

He shakes his head loosely. "Lisa? I—I don't," he slurs. A few beats pass before he speaks again, his voice deeper this time. "What do you want?"

"She called me," I say, feeling the adrenaline rushing through my body. "The night she died. From the dock."

I don't move my eyes from his. But I carry on because if I don't, I might run far, far away from here.

I hold my keys tighter and take another step towards him. "I know who you are, and I know what you did to Lisa that night."

CHAPTER 61:

LISA

Six Months Ago

I didn't count on feeling this angry.

As Ana's words sink in, I feel a combination of pity and relief. But as she keeps talking, my anger brims to the surface.

"That's why I think you should leave," she says. "For your own sake. My brother's not well, and it's not fair for you to carry his burden."

I want to tell her that nothing is fair. Being born in a bigger body, growing up under the shadow of your parents, loving someone who won't love you back. But I suspect she already knows all that.

We walk back to the house, but I can't go inside. Not yet. So I leave Ana at the front door, telling her I need to think things through. I can tell she wants to be alone, too. This day has been too much for both of us.

I walk to the shop up the road. I spot a bottle of vodka on the top shelf, and motion to the shopkeeper. I don't wait for my change. Outside, I take large swigs, as if they can somehow burn away the resentment in my throat. The resentment at Seb. At myself. Vodka splashes onto the tar as I take another slug. How similar we are to liquid, slipping through the cracks of life.

Walking to the dock, I feel lighter. I sit on the bench under the trees and feel the thumping in my chest. My heart beats with rage, red and raw. I take out my phone, and see I've brought my old one by mistake. I must have left the new one in the bedroom. I think of calling Alice and sharing this newfound truth, but I don't.

I need to calm down first.

I sit until the fog rolls over the tops of the trees, and the sky turns a dark purple. I hear a car engine and turn, squinting into the darkness and seeing its headlights. I wonder if Richard just got home, but it's too close to Alma's house to be his. It must be Seb. I hear the car door open and close. I picture him talking to Ana—him reeling back in shock and fear as she tells him about this afternoon's happenings. I get up and walk onto the wooden boards of the dock. The fog swirls as I go, making me stronger, more confident.

I imagine Seb weighing his options. Tell the truth, or lie to me again. I wonder whether he'll come and look for me. I look back, but I can barely see the road now. It's like the fog's devoured me and made me a part of it.

And so I wait right here. No way forward, no way back.

* * *

It feels like an hour has passed, and I'm starting to think it was Richard's car that I saw after all. No one's come to find me. I've had too much to drink, and I can barely see anything around me. There's a violent throbbing in my head, so I swallow down two ibuprofens. Eleanor's rule: always carry something with you for a headache.

She wouldn't wash them down with vodka, but we're way past that now.

I sit cross-legged on the edge of the dock. I want Seb to see me clearly when he passes through the mist, like clarity waiting for him at the end of the path. The water swells gently below me, and I don't know why I was ever afraid of it before. It adds to the calm.

All the king's horses and all the king's men. Couldn't put Humpty together again.

It's funny how sitting here brings me so much peace. Even with all my broken parts, I suddenly feel capable of picking them up and carrying them with me. No more relying on others to put me back together.

Because some things remain broken, and it's fine that way.

I take another swig of vodka and feel the threads of my life ravel and unravel. But I'm getting impatient. Tired of waiting for the truth to come. I think of walking to Alma's house and confronting Seb. Of walking to Deb's house and exposing Richard and his lies. So many truths to uncover in this street.

But before I can decide what to do, I see a figure approaching through the mist.

CHAPTER 62:

LISA

Six Months Ago

When I stand up, the vodka hits me. It's Seb. My legs wobble on the dock as I try to stand up straight. My vision's blurry, but I squint to focus on him. Looking at his face, I remember when he used to be the person I loved most in this world. My golden ticket.

"What's going on?" he asks, confused. His eyes land on the vodka bottle. "You're drunk."

"I am."

The defiance vibrates through me. I don't mind his disapproving tone, because I know that the tables have turned. I'm ready to take my power back.

I try to keep my voice calm. "Is there something you want to tell me?"

He looks up at me, a frown forming. "Like what?"

I narrow my eyes, the words bitter on my tongue. "Ana told me everything."

For a moment he just stares at me. "I don't know what you're talking about."

I take a breath, the vodka making my tongue sticky, but I manage to get the words out. "I thought I was an idiot. You made me feel so guilty." I take a step towards him, lowering my voice. "But you were so much worse."

He says nothing.

"You lied to me," I almost shout. "You made me feel like *I* was the one who was ruining everything between us."

I move my weight from one foot to the other, and I lose my balance momentarily. Seb reaches out for me "Lisa—"

"Don't!" I yell, holding up a hand and regaining my balance. When I'm up straight again, I look at him and my voice breaks. "I saw you kiss her. You lied to me."

It feels like the world's spinning, and the naked truth hangs heavy between us. "You're a liar. And a cheat."

He opens his mouth, then closes it. He runs his fingers through his hair, the way I used to like it. But now, it just makes me sick.

"It's wrong," I say. "What you did is… wrong."

My insides heave with stifled sobs. I want the anger to stay right here, overwhelm the loss I'm feeling. The loss of a life together that could have saved us both. I'm unsure if I should ask the next question, but I know that if I don't, I won't be able to move forward from this.

"You never really loved me, did you?"

His face changes into something soft. Suddenly, it's like he's reaching for me. "Of course I did. I do."

But I shake my head. "It was just to keep you busy. You just brought me here to prove a point. To show that you were fine."

He looks at the wooden boards beneath us.

"For once—please Seb—be honest," I say. "Were you ever going to marry me?"

His eyes meet mine. A chill permeates the air, and I know it's the truth I've been waiting for.

"No."

The scene splits open in front of me, like someone's hacked at it with a blunt knife. My eyes well up so fast that Seb's in a dozen pieces, and I need to close my eyes to keep still. When I open them again, he's still standing there. Like he hasn't just blown up my entire life.

"I was going to leave you. Today," I say.

He gives a slow nod. "I understand."

But it's not the response I'm looking for. There's heat in my stomach and

I want to hurt him, turn his world upside down, too.

I speak the words with pure rage. "I wonder what your mother would say if she knew you wanted to screw your sister."

He flinches, and I take a step towards him. "You're disgusting, you know that?"

It's like he's a statue. But my words build and gather momentum, all the nastiness and sorrow flooding out. "Ana said your father caught you once. How did that feel? Knowing that he knew what you did?"

I want him to show some emotion. I want to break his mask of calmness. And until he does, I'll continue twisting the knife, deeper and deeper.

"I don't know how you can come back here," I say, my eyes not leaving his. He's eerily still, his face not moving.

"If I were your father, I'd be ashamed of you," I say. "I'd be so, so—"

I step forward and lose my footing. It feels like I'm floating for a moment, then I feel a sudden pain as Seb's hands grab at my neck through my scarf. I look at his face, his eyes blazing. I claw at his hands, digging my nails into his skin. My legs flap beneath me but it's no use. I'm battling to breathe, and it feels like the fog's in my head.

It's the worst few seconds of my life. I'm still grabbing at Seb's hands when he releases me, and I fall to the ground. I heave for breath, taking in a lungful of air. Seb towers over me for a moment. Then, without a word, he's gone.

I let out a cry. Pain sweeps through my body as I lie flat on my back. The images of the past few moments flash in front of me. How is it possible to feel so much pain—so much betrayal—in the space of a few seconds? I want to touch my aching throat, but I don't dare. It'll only make what happened real, and if I admit that, then I don't know how I'll get up from here.

I stare at the fog, wondering if he'll come back. I lie back and count my breaths. The more I count, the more I don't have to think about what just happened. I want to erase all of it.

I feel the tide move beneath me, how it ebbs and flows. More forceful than before. After a long time, I try to get up, but my body resists. I feel as if I'm tied to this dock, trapped in the fog. I watch for movement in the darkness, but there's none.

I feel for my old phone in my pocket, wondering who to call. Because I need to call someone if I'm going to get up from here. My finger taps nervously at the touch ID. It's as if it senses my desperation, and it works the first time.

She answers, and my throat burns when I speak. "Alice—are you there?"

CHAPTER 63:

CAT

Present Day

The colour drains from Sebastian's face. His eyes dart around nervously. He takes a few seconds to speak.

"I ... I think you have the wrong person."

I fold my arms in front of me, trying to hide my shaking hands. The keys I'm holding dig into my skin. "I don't. You were Lisa's fiancé."

I can almost feel his confusion. "I... I don't remember you."

"We were long distance friends," I say. "She called me sometimes. And sometimes we talked about you."

He looks as if he's afraid to ask the next question.

"What did she tell you?"

His question only fuels my frustration. "What did she tell me? How about what *you* didn't tell anyone?"

He winces, but I continue. "How long did you leave her there? Alone on that dock?" Before he can say anything, I speak again. "Before you went back and finished what you started?"

Sebastian's eyes meet mine and I can see his fear. "She called you? She called you after... after—"

"After you choked her."

The anger courses through my body as I picture Lisa on that dock. I can almost feel her shock, her distress. Her anguish at how the man who was supposed to love her above all else had hurt her. Neil's use of the word that reminded me of our conversation. The truth that makes me want to stab Sebastian with my keys anyway.

Choke, choke, choke.

Sebastian's eyes glaze over. He's like a wax figure, his body almost not registering my words. Then he sways, and it's like the breath has left his body.

"I—"

"You left her there," I almost shout, cutting him off. "You hurt her, and before you could come back and finish her off, she called me. And she told me what you did."

His face contorts, his jaw rocks back and forth. I'm not sure whether he's crying or grimacing, but I've never seen so much pain on a person's face. My rage eases slightly, but I keep my pose. The last thing I need is to feel is pity for a murderer.

Sebastian opens his mouth and tries to speak again. "I…"

He buries his face in his hands. He lets out a howl that sounds as if it comes from a wounded animal. He drops to his knees, and moans. I think of Lisa, and how she sounded that night. So desperate to be heard. And then she was gone. Silenced.

"You told no one what you did," I say. "You're a murderer and a coward."

Through his shuddering sobs, I make out his muffled words.

"I didn't mean it. I didn't mean to hurt her."

I move closer to him, his words sparking bolts of anger that shoot through me. He didn't mean to? How. Dare. He.

"You killed her," I sneer. "You thought no one knew what you did. But I do."

Sebastian sits down on the grass. When he looks at me, his face is ashen, hands shaking. "I—I…"

This time, I wait for him to get the words out.

"I got so angry," he says. "She knew everything."

His words surprise me. "Everything about what?"

He presses his palms to his face, his cheeks streaked with tears. I've never seen a grown man cry this much. "What I'd done. It happened so fast… my hands." He wipes his nose on his t-shirt. "One moment I was in control and the next I just—snapped."

"You wanted to kill her."

"I wanted her to stop talking," he says. "She was saying all these horrible things. And being out on that deck—it brought back everything that happened with my father. Lisa—all the things she said made me so mad. The next thing I know, it all went dark in my head."

"Your… father?"

He nods. "My father knew what I was. He saw me with Ana. He could have killed me that day. His hands were ready to break me in two."

I shake my head, trying to make sense of his words. I know Ana is his sister, but what does she have to do with any of this? Before I can interrupt, Sebastian keeps talking, almost more to himself than to me. "I just wanted the pain to stop with Lisa. He just wanted me to stop back then, too."

I cock my head and look at him. "I don't understand."

His words come in a fierce whisper. "I hated myself. I made her doubt everything. Lisa was trying to fix it. She tried so hard and I just couldn't…" He brings his hands to his face again. "If I only knew what she was going through."

Something stirs in me. "What do you mean, if you only knew?"

He takes a deep breath, his eyes downcast. "It's all my fault. I brought her here and made her live with me. I made her see me with Ana."

He keeps bringing up Ana. I picture the sister with her pigtails, the father long dead. It's too much to bring together.

"I lied to her," he says. "I made her think there was something wrong with her. And then I hurt her when she found out who I really was."

The nausea builds in my throat. Something isn't right. But he keeps talking. "She was so lonely. I made her life hell and left her with no choice."

His words are like a punch in my stomach. I back away from him, my eyes never leaving his face. "But you didn't—"

He looks up, his eyes red-rimmed. I feel like the air has turned to molasses around me. I try to say the words I don't want to say, but have to. "You didn't go back for her."

322

Sebastian stares at me, then looks down again. When he shakes his head, it feels as if the air is driven from my lungs.

"I drove her to it," he says. "I destroyed what we had—I hurt her—and then left her alone on that dock. I made her feel like there was nowhere for her to go."

I'm only hearing half of his words, because I keep getting stuck on one part. Before I know it, I'm repeating the words out loud. "You didn't go back for her."

His face is crumpling again. "No."

Which means...

Sebastian keeps talking, but his words turn into a cacophony in my ears. I turn and run, my heart pounding in my chest.

CHAPTER 64:

CAT

Present Day

I run back to the house as fast as my legs will carry me. From the street, I can see the lights are on. I stumble to the fridge and pull out one of Deborah's bottles of wine. I put it on the counter and stare at it.

Drink me. Drink. Me.

I twist it open and pour a glass, barely pausing before taking a massive gulp. Two seconds. That's all it takes to break my sobriety. I walk outside, replaying the scene with Sebastian in my head. His confession to hurting Lisa was genuine. Almost like he wanted to tell someone about it. It needed to pour out of him. I almost felt sorry for him.

But it wasn't the confession I was hoping for.

I gulp more wine and light a cigarette. My eyes glance over Deborah's car and the pot plants in the corner of the garden, fading in the early evening light. I think of how Sebastian said all the right words, but that there was a big black hole in his story.

The part where he went back and finished what he started. Or didn't.

If he choked Lisa the first time, and left her to call Alice, then he must have come back again. And that time, hurt her so badly that he had no choice but to push her off the dock to silence her. Or some version of that.

But he seemed to have remorse for *not* going back. *Which means...*

I think of Lisa calling me all those months ago, while I was drunk on my balcony. I'd told myself I wasn't going to answer her call—that I wouldn't be able to play professional Alice that night.

But something made me pick up that phone.

I made her feel like there was nowhere for her to go.

Sebastian's in my head again, and I wish he'd leave. Lisa did have somewhere she could go that night, and she came to me.

He believed he killed her. But not like I thought.

Earlier, I'd seen Sebastian's pain at taking someone's life, driving them to surrender. I saw it in his eyes. I recognised it, because I see it in my own eyes every day.

I believe him. He didn't go back to kill her, and he didn't throw her off that dock.

Which means...

The wine softens my edges, but not quickly enough. I take another gulp. How did I ever stop drinking? It. Tastes. So. Good. With my newfound courage, I take my phone from my pocket and dial the person I've been avoiding the most.

She picks up almost instantly. "Cat? Are you okay?"

Emotion bubbles to the surface, and my lips quiver at the sound of her voice. "Mom," I say. "I'm in so much trouble."

There's a rustling on the other end of the line, like she's standing up from her bed. "What's going on? Tell me."

I lean against the wall and feel my body cave in. "I wish I'd opened that door."

She says nothing.

"I can't stop thinking that I could have stopped him."

Fat droplets of tears course down my cheeks, one by one. I don't need to tell my mom what I'm talking about. She already knows.

She takes a breath. "Oh, baby."

Her voice is soft. "None of that was ever your fault. You know that."

"It was."

"No, baby. That's not how it works. People have dark thoughts, they—"

"No," I say. "You don't know. It was me. I'm the reason he's dead."

There's silence. Maybe she's waiting for me to come out and say something truthful to her for the first time in months. Finally, I'm ready to.

"I didn't tell you everything," I say, licking the salty tears from my lips. "About how dad died. But I'm going to."

* * *

Dad and I agreed to spend every second weekend together. The divorce left me feeling hollow, but the three of us dealt with it amicably. Well, as amicably as we could under the circumstances.

We sold the house. My mother moved into a townhouse, and my father moved into a shabby apartment block a few suburbs away.

On the weekends when I was broke—which was most weekends—I drove to his place, where we ordered takeout and watched TV as he sipped his whisky. Except now, he didn't have to hide the bottles between the sofa cushions anymore.

Every now and again, women would move in with him, their eyes blazing with the need to mark their territory. Their toiletries would line his basin; their underwear would dry over the shower door. But they left just as quickly as they came, and the apartment remained his, stripped bare and perpetually smelling of smoke and aftershave.

Along with the women, the jobs my dad had came and went, too. One day we'd eat burgers for takeout, the next day convenience store pies.

I didn't care. He was my dad. It was only during university that things started shifting. His inability to pay my tuition fees, his continuous jibes towards my mother, the emotional booze-fuelled scenes in restaurants. He seemed determined to break every relationship in his life.

And then, one day, it all came crashing down.

It was a seemingly normal weekend. We ordered pizza and watched a tennis match on TV. He tried making small talk. I was slumped on the couch, glued to my phone. With every whisky he drank, his agitation grew. Until he finally had enough.

"Hey, put that away." He grabbed drunkenly for my phone. He could barely stand, clutching his chair to stabilise himself.

I shrugged at him. "You're drunk. Sit down."

"Cat," he warned, his eyes bulging. "Don't talk to me like that."

That day, I felt daring. Thinking back, I was just plain stupid.

I looked him right in the eye. "Or what?"

He changed course, his tongue turning razor-sharp—as it did when he drank. "Do you think you'll accomplish anything in life by using people? You don't think I know you come here just for the food?"

"You're one to talk."

"Hey," his words slurring from the whisky. "At least I'm not a spoiled little brat."

"Do you like this?" I asked.

"Like what?"

"Ruining your life."

"Cat, I'm warning you—"

There was no stopping me. "Drinking away the days, letting mom go, losing your job. It's pathetic, you're—"

And then he grabbed my arm, his eyes blazing. "Stop it!"

But there was something else there. A lingering pain. The corners of his eyes were too red. I went to bed and shut the door behind me. I listened to him pour another drink. And then a few more. By the time he knocked on my door, it must have been midnight.

I hear his words in my nightmares.

Bud. Bud, pleeease.

I closed my eyes and waited for him to leave. It was just another drunken fight, another one of his calls for remorse.

What followed was a moment I'll regret for the rest of my life. My last words to him were brutal, spat out in anger.

"You know, sometimes I wish you'd just die."

After that, he spoke his last words to me, too.

"I love you, bud."

I found him where I left him. In the living room. Except he was hanging from the ceiling.

I felt confused, like I was dreaming. It wasn't real. Surely the beam couldn't hold him. And where did he get the rope? But as I kept staring at him, it became horribly real.

There was no way to get him down. He was too heavy. So I stood outside the front door, vomiting into a trash bin and counting from one to a hundred on repeat because I couldn't go back into that apartment while he was still there. The police arrived, and then Mom, her face white with shock. He'd left no note, no explanation.

But my father didn't need one. I'd given him the instructions.

My mom is silent on the other end of the line. Then she speaks.

"Cat... I wish you'd told me."

But how could I have told her? Where would I have begun?

"People fight," she says. "They say things they don't mean. There's so much we need to talk about. Your dad, he wasn't well. Not for a long time. He—can't you come home?"

And I wish I could. But home's never been the same since that night.

Neil's words sound in my head.

You're like those snow globes. All shook up and too scared to let the snow actually settle.

"I can't right now," I say.

Because I've gone and done it again. I said something that brought someone's life to an end. And this time, I won't run from it. Because Neil's right. I was the last person to speak to Lisa before she died. And what if I didn't say enough? What if I let her slip through my fingers, just like the last time?

Sebastian might have driven her to the edge, but what if I gave the final push?

CHAPTER 65:

LISA

Six Months Ago

"Rachel, are you there?"

Alice's voice sounds different, almost younger.

I look around, the fog and darkness making me dizzy. When I open my mouth, my throat feels better. I turn around and listen for footsteps. For if Seb is coming back.

"Can you hear me?" Alice asks.

I string the words together. "He did it. He's, he's—"

"What?" Alice's voice is unnaturally loud in my ears.

"He choked me." I say. "He choked me."

"Who? Where are you?"

"Outside," I whisper. "But he's not here."

Silence, and then her voice sounds urgent. "Can you go somewhere safe?"

I want to tell her to lower her voice, but then an overwhelming sadness washes over me. "I'm so glad I called you."

"Rachel, you need to go somewhere safe, okay? Can you do that?"

I shake my head, bring a hand to my throat. The initial shock has worn off. It only took a few seconds to happen, but it'll take a lifetime to forget.

"Is there a friend you can go to?" Alice asks again.

I picture Ruth with her mates, laughing at her pathetic ex-roommate. I picture Greg in the bar, talking about the chubby girl who thought he was her friend. I picture you and Eleanor shaking your heads at me.

"Rachel?"

I shake my head. "No."

"Can you go to a police station?" She's talking fast now.

"No," I say. "It's not like that."

"You said someone choked you."

I feel my heart racing and suddenly remember how drunk I am. How blurry the lines are. Suddenly, nothing from today feels real.

"I've had way too much to drink," I tell Alice. "I'm getting ahead of myself. I *feel* choked. You know what I mean?"

A few beats pass. She's probably picked up on my lie, but I hope she won't talk about it.

"Okay," she says slowly. "I don't know what's happening, but if you're hurt or scared, you must do something. Do something now."

Her voice is almost flustered. She doesn't sound like Alice at all right now.

"I'm sorry," I say. "I probably ruined your night."

"It's okay. Remember what we said?" Her voice slurs on the last word. "What we talked about. You need to be honest with yourself. Just honest. And *stop* saying sorry."

I can picture my note on the table in the bedroom. I wonder if Seb's found it already. I remember the plan I had. I need to get out of here.

"Don't you sometimes just want to run away?" I ask, trying to get to my feet. I use the wooden railing to pull myself up. "Just pack your bags and leave the ghosts behind?"

I don't expect her response. "All the time."

I try to calculate how long it'll take me to pack my bags. I need coffee to sober up. And lots of water. I also need a taxi to the airport. I wonder if I could ask Deb to take me.

"Maybe they never go away," I say, thinking of all the hurt of the last few years. All the people I've let down. All the people who've let me down.

"Maybe not," Alice says. "And maybe that's okay."

I smile at her words. Despite the clouds of mistakes, the road ahead looks a little clearer. If only the first few steps.

"Wait," Alice says, the word sounding like a slur again. "One more thing."

"Yes?"

"You'll be fine. Really. I don't know your life, but everything you've told me makes me believe you can do this. You've *got* this. You've had some shitty things happen to you, but you're getting through it."

I bring a hand to my mouth when I hear Alice swear. She's never done that before. But I'm not offended. In fact, maybe I like this Alice better. A more realistic version. I look out at the nothingness as she continues talking. "And if you ever need anything—anything at all—I'm here. Just let me know—"

There's a noise behind me.

Di-di-ding. Di-di-ding. It's a phone. I look down, and then back up into the fog.

The ringing isn't coming from my phone.

CHAPTER 66:

CAT

Present Day

Deborah's in the kitchen when I go back inside. The wine bottle is still on the countertop next to her, and she immediately sees the glass in my hand. Her eyes widen.

"Tough day," I say, tired of pretending.

She nods. Walking over to the fridge, she takes out a fresh bottle of red. "Want a refill?"

I look down at my empty glass. There's been enough guilt for one day. And if I have another glass, I know I'll regret it tomorrow. Plus, I need to be sober—or try to be—for what comes next.

I shake my head and walk over to the sink, pouring a glass of water. I take a sip and think of what my mother told me only minutes ago.

I can see how much this hurts you. I love you. Please come home.

It's like someone's hollowed me out and left me in the sun. I just feel empty. Incapable.

Neil will ask me what I remember from that night with Lisa, and I'll have to tell him the truth. I remain the prime suspect. And probably the culprit, too.

I'll need to tell him I confronted Sebastian. The one person who sits exactly with the same guilt as I do.

Everything works against me. Sebastian has an alibi. There were no bruises found on Lisa's neck. And when she spoke to me in her last moments,

I'd had too much to drink and couldn't remember everything.

But I'll tell Neil the truth.

And then I'll burn for it. For Lisa's life, for my acts of fraud on InCheck. Here or there or anywhere. It feels impossible.

"Do you want something to eat?"

I almost forgot Deborah's still here, looking at me oddly.

"I'm good," I say. "Thank you."

"Do you want to… talk about it?"

I look at her, her eyes confused. I shrug and nod, moving to the couch. She follows me and sits down as I lay back against the headrest.

I bring my hands to my temples. "It's a long story."

"I've got time," she says.

My eyes scan the house. It's just us. *Where's Neil?*

I look at her, this woman who's pretending to live a normal life, and wonder if we could share each other's pain.

"I've realised something," I say. "I thought I could just leave things behind in South Africa. But that was wrong. Because they just followed me here. To Gexta."

She leans back, her expression still perplexed. "What things?"

I shrug, feeling like I'm in therapy again. "We can be honest with each other, right?" I look directly at her and she stiffens slightly. "We know more about each other than we're telling."

She raises an eyebrow as if she's somehow not surprised. "What do you know?"

"A lot less than you know about me, I think."

My head is still leaning against the headrest, and there's a vague nausea in the pit of my stomach. Deborah sits forward. "Look love, I think you've had a bad night. Maybe you should—"

There's a sound. *Di-di-ding.* And then again. *Di-di-ding.*

Something clicks in my head. I've heard that sound somewhere before.

"Bollocks," Deborah says. "One second."

She gets up and darts to the island, pulling her handbag closer. Across the room I watch her, my brain racing at 100 miles an hour.

Di-di-ding. Di-di-ding.

Deborah pulls her phone from her handbag and jabs at it with her thumb, and the sound stops. But it's too late.

My mind is transported back to that night with Lisa.

CHAPTER 67:

LISA

Six Months Ago

The phone stops ringing just as I see her. "Deb? Is that you?"

There's a glow in her hand as she walks towards me. "Lisa?" She puts the phone in her pocket. "What are you doing out here?"

She takes a few moments to take in the scene, and her eyes widen. "What happened? What's going on?"

I want to hug her and tell her everything. Just cry with her. I breathe through the dizziness and smile. "I'm okay now."

"Come, let's go in," she says, taking my hand.

But I don't move. "I'm leaving."

"What?"

"I'm going back to the UK," I say. "Or maybe somewhere else. I haven't figured it out yet."

Her brow creases as she pulls her coat tighter around her. I notice she's wearing her slippers. "You're leaving?"

I nod. "I need to get out of here."

She looks baffled. "Why? Did something happen?"

"I just can't stay here anymore."

She's silent for a moment, and I can see she's confused. "I saw Seb walking back from the dock," she says. "From the window. He looked like he was storming off. I couldn't reach you on your phone and… I got worried. So I came to look for you."

She looks me up and down again. "Did you have a fight?"

I think of what Alice told me. How I should be honest with myself and own up to my life. I want to tell Deb the truth about what happened, but the last thing I want to do is talk about Seb. All I want is to move on.

"My phone's in the house," I tell her, pulling the scarf tighter around my neck, the memory of the last hour still making my skin crawl. Suddenly, a thought surfaces. "Where's Richard?" I ask.

Deb gives a small shrug. "His flight got delayed. But never mind that now."

I study her. Through the haze of alcohol and ibuprofen, I try to look into her soul, as if my pain could reach out to hers. Tell her that amidst all the darkness, there is a ray of sunshine. I don't know what lies ahead, but I do know that finally, I can trust myself again. Not with Eleanor's help, not with Seb's help, but mine alone. And if I can let another woman know that she has options too, then I'll do it.

I take a step forward. "You should leave too, Deb."

She frowns again. "What do you mean?"

"Richard's stealing money from you."

Until now, Deb has been shivering in the cold. Now, she's frozen to the spot. "What?"

I take a deep breath. "I should have told you sooner. I've been doing a bit of snooping about him. Ever since that day he came to the house—"

She holds up a hand, her voice suddenly panicky. "Wait. What? What are you saying?"

"Something seemed off," I continue. "I hated him for how he treated you. I wasn't looking for anything specific, but then I found his email open on the computer one day. And Deb, I'm really sorry for looking at it... but I found things that didn't add up."

She says nothing, her eyes boring into me. I can't tell if she's horrified or angry.

"I found a charity he's been donating to. For five years already. Then I asked you that one day if you both donate, and you said no. I found it strange that he would donate and not tell you. I figured he wasn't telling you. So I contacted the charity and they told me it no longer exists. It hasn't for years, Deb."

The words spill out of me in a heated rush. I need to rip the whole band aid off, no matter how hard it is. "It gets worse. I'm so sorry, but I then looked into your bank statements. The ones you print out and keep in the study. The money's been leaving your account each month. Five hundred pounds every time."

I pause, taking a breath. "He's been stealing from you. For years. I counted two years' worth of payments, but it could have been longer."

Then there's silence. The longer it expands between us, the uneasier I feel. I search Deb's eyes for a hint of something. Fear, distress, sadness. But she just looks shocked. Finally, she crosses her arms and frowns. "You invaded my privacy."

I look down, the shame running through me. "I know."

"You violated it," she says, her voice louder. "I thought I could trust you." My head shoots up. "You can."

We stare at each other. But I look away again. I feel so ashamed that I did this to her.

Deb scoffs and looks away. She stares out at the water for a while, then turns back. "So you say he's been stealing from me?"

I nod. "I think he's hiding assets. I think he wants to make it look like there's less money to split between the two of you when you divorce. The charity—it's just one thing I found. Who knows what else he's doing."

Deb seems to consider this, her eyes looking over my shoulder. "How do you know all this?"

"It happens in case law," I say. "It's been a while. But I remember reading about it at uni. Before the divorce, you need to declare your total savings and assets. When I spoke to the woman from the charity, she asked for proof..."

She puts up a hand. "Wait, what woman?"

"The woman I called," I say. "The one who said the charity didn't exist anymore. She said we can report the fraud. She says it happens all the time, actually."

Suddenly, Deb looks scared. "Did you give her our details?"

There's a flutter in my stomach. I keep telling myself I did this for a good reason, but I've meddled so much in Deb's life. I clear my throat. "Not yet."

"So what happens now?" she asks.

"We just need to send her proof. She can report the charity fraud." I feel the shame burning my cheeks. "I have screenshots to prove it."

Deb looks overwhelmed. She runs her hands through her hair. She paces the walkway and then moves to the railing.

"I'm so sorry Deb," I say. "But you can't let him win. He'll try to take everything from you. Everything you've worked for."

Her hands wrap around the railing, and she's quiet for what feels like a minute. Then, her head snaps back. "Have you shared the screenshots? With the woman?"

"No," I say. "I wanted to tell you everything first."

"Can you show them to me?"

I take the old phone from my pocket and start searching for the pictures.

"I thought you left your phone at home?" Deb asks.

"This is my old one," I say. I find the screenshots and turn the phone so she can see them. She takes my phone and zooms in on the pictures. I show her the fake email address I created and the messages I sent to Richard. And what he sent back to me.

"You went to a lot of trouble," she says after a while. "You must really hate him."

"I just wanted to protect you," I say. "You're better off without him."

She steps away from me and we stand apart for a few beats, and it feels like the air has suddenly become thicker. Deb meets my eyes, her face expressionless. "I know I'm better off."

Almost in slow motion, Deb's eyes grow narrower and colder. I watch her put my phone into her pocket. My stomach does a frantic somersault as the realisation kicks in. "You... you knew about it."

She stays motionless, her lips thin. Just when I think she won't say anything, the words come. They're low and deliberate.

"Richard isn't the only cunning one, you know."

For a moment, I struggle to understand what she's saying. But then I glance down at where my phone sits in her pocket. I blink. "It... it was you?"

She's still for what feels like an eternity. As if she's contemplating what to tell me.

"Yes," she says. "All of it."

I feel the nausea build as I realise she's proud of her admission.

I grip the wooden railing, everything suddenly shaky beneath my feet. "How? Why?"

She looks up at the dark sky, pulls her coat tighter again. "I just had to be smart about it."

"You faked a charity? Why?"

"I did what I needed to," she says curtly. She's never spoken to me like this before, and it stings.

"He always earned more than me. Call it a backup plan, if you will. A buffer. He's been splurging our money on his young mistresses for years. I knew at some point it would go badly for me. So I thought—why not cover myself? What's a little extra money on some kids in Africa? It would set me up well. Not for life, but at least for a few years. I had to convince him to donate to something, but since he never wanted kids and I did, it wasn't too difficult to play the victim card."

I'm stunned by her words. More than that, I'm stunned by how she's saying them. Completely calm, with no remorse.

"So the charity website? The fake emails every month?"

She shrugs. "A guy in Belarus I found online. He set it all up."

"And the donations?"

"All to an offshore account."

I stare at her, my body rigid. In what world was she capable of something like this? For weeks I've been watching her walk around her home in a drunken stupor. It's almost as if she wants to both love Richard and hurt him at the same time. She had me fooled.

I grip the railing tighter. Meet her eyes again. "Deb, you have to stop this."

"It's too late for that now," she says offhandedly.

"It's not," I say, shaking my head. "Even if your marriage is over, you want it to be on a clean slate. You don't need to do this to be okay. It will be so much better if you're just honest and move on."

I think of my own plan. How I intend to live my own truth from now on.

"Go away on a nice holiday," I cajole. "Like we talked about. Or go see your friends. You could even come with me. We could go away together."

She scoffs. "I don't have any friends."

Wow, I think. I thought we were friends.

"Okay, fine," I say. "But you don't need his money as a buffer. You'll be fine on your own. You just need—"

"What do you know about money?" she says, her voice high pitched and angry. "Sitting around all day pretending to be a writer, living off mummy and daddy's money. You haven't had to work for anything in your life. Don't talk to me about money."

I gape at her, the heat burning in my cheeks. I shouldn't have snooped, but everything I did was because I cared about her. I was just trying to do what was best for her. Just to find she doesn't care at all.

"Please give me back my phone," I say.

She takes my phone from her pocket and starts tapping at the screen.

"What are you doing?"

She doesn't look up. "Deleting the screenshots."

I want to run over and grab the phone from her, but the ground is too unstable beneath my feet. "It's my phone. You can't delete anything."

She keeps tapping at the screen, and I lurch towards her. I grab at the phone, but she easily blocks me.

"Stop it," I yell. "I won't let you do this."

A part of me feels betrayed. She lied to me and painted herself as the victim. She made me believe yet another lie when all I wanted for once was the truth. I'm so sick of people lying to me.

"Keep it," I say. I stumble to the railing again and lean on it for support. We're both breathing heavily, staring at each other. My phone is still in her hands, but I let it go. I don't need it anymore. All I want is to get away from here.

"You're going to regret this," I tell her, my words sticky. I start walking towards the street again.

"What are you doing?" she says, her voice suddenly nervous again.

"I'm leaving," I mutter.

She grabs my arm, and now I'm angry too. I just want to be away from all of this. "Let me go. Just leave me alone."

Her grip eases slightly. "Lisa. You can't just go. We need to talk about this."

I shake my arm loose, my eyes meeting hers. "I have nothing to say to you. You lied to me. You're committing a crime."

Her eyes are wide. But the words pour out of me like hot lava. "I don't care how bad things are. *Nothing* justifies what you're doing now. Lying to people who are only trying to help you. I thought we were friends."

I'm so angry. At her, at Seb and his lies. A part of me wants to not only escape all of it, but expose all of it. I want to shout their dirty secrets from the rooftops. All they've done is hurt me, and that hurt has turned into a red hot fury.

It's that same fury that makes me grab for my phone again. My body pushing against hers, and I feel her back push against the railing. I hear the phone fall onto the wooden planking of the dock. I turn to look for it, but we scuffle. Suddenly I'm the one against the railing, trying to push Deb away.

"Get off me," I try to shout, but her hands are covering my mouth. The anger runs up my throat and out of my mouth, the words muffled by her hands. "I hope they lock you up."

Silence. It can't be more than a few seconds. Her mouth opens with horror at what I just said, but I won't take it back. She deserved it.

Before I can stop her, her hands grab at me again, her eyes inky black with fear. I'm so angry I don't register what she's doing. She grips me tightly, then pushes me. Hard.

And then I'm falling.

CHAPTER 68:

CAT

Present Day

"Sorry," Deborah calls from the kitchen, silencing her phone.

I'm in a daze, fragments of reality spinning around in my head. The thunderbolt realisation feels like it's suffocating me, taunting me.

You've looked everywhere, except here. Right in front of you.

I think of Lisa's voice. Of the fear mixed with hope. Of Sebastian, out there in the night, the pain raw in his eyes. The puzzle pieces haven't been fitting because I've been missing a piece.

The sound of a phone ringing in the background.

Di-di-ding. Di-di-ding.

Deborah walks back to the couch. "So, where were we?"

She grabs for her wineglass and looks at me expectantly. I sit still, trying not to look shocked.

My mind churns through all our encounters while I've been here. She's always seemed wacky, but never threatening. And she's been through a lot, with her divorce from the real Richard and having to live alone in this house.

I sip my water, trying to buy time. Deborah raises an eyebrow and my stomach lurches. Can she tell something's wrong?

I heard that exact ringtone that night on the last call with Lisa. And that would mean Deborah was on the dock that night with her. But why would she lie about it?

What was Deborah's relationship with Lisa really like? And if she hurt Lisa that night, for whatever reason, why would she continue to insert herself into Neil's investigation? Surely if she was guilty of anything, she would have tried to get as far away from this place as possible.

All I have is that ringtone. If I have any hope of this going anywhere, I need to turn this lead into hard proof.

I need Neil.

I stand up, trying my best to hide the quaver in my voice. "Just going to the bathroom. Be right back."

Deborah stays seated. The hint of a smile tugs at the corners of her mouth. It unnerves me that she's saying nothing. It could be my paranoia talking, but it's as if she can sense my discomfort.

In the bathroom, I frantically type a text to Neil.

Where are you?

The message delivers with only one tick. I curse to myself. I can't call him from here. I walk to my room and close the door as quietly as possible, and I press the call button. When Neil answers, it sounds like he's in a car.

"Hey, where are you?" I ask, keeping my voice low.

"Why are you whispering?"

"Where have you been?"

"Bilbao."

"Bilbao?" I repeat. "What were you doing in Bilboa? Are—are you almost home?"

"Half an hour. Why?"

I know what I have to do. I need to buy time until he comes home. Then I can share my suspicions about Deborah with him. But my anxiety gets the better of me, and I think of all the horrible things that can happen in half an hour.

"I think I know."

"Know what?"

I step away from the door, whispering urgently into the phone. "I think I remember what happened that night."

He's quick to reply. "I found something too. You were right."

I hold my breath. "What?"

"Lisa had another phone. We found her old number, and we're trying to trace it now. It might take a while, but it's something."

There are so many things I want to ask him about this, but I can hear footsteps from downstairs.

"Okay, hurry," I say, and before Neil can get another word in, I end the call.

I scoot out of the bedroom and back into the bathroom, looking around to see where Deborah is.

I hear her footsteps coming up the stairs, and I close the bathroom door. I open the tap again, and my eye falls on an ancient comb in a porcelain container next to the basin. For a moment, I picture using it as a weapon.

I hear her shuffling around her bedroom, so I close the tap, flush the toilet, and head downstairs. I pick up the glass of water I left on the island and check the time on my phone. It's only been two minutes. There are twenty-eight more to go until Neil arrives, and it feels like an eternity.

It's not long before Deborah's back in the kitchen. She's put on a blue sweater.

We look at each other silently. But the tension in the air is palpable. We're both on our guard.

"Suddenly chilly, isn't it?" she says, clutching her phone to her chest. Her cheeks are flushed, and she looks nervous.

"Is something wrong?" I ask.

She shrugs. "There's been an... incident."

"An incident?"

She looks up. "A disturbance at the office. They think someone broke in."

"Oh." I shift my weight from one foot to the other. "That's not great."

"I should go and check it out," she says. "Just to be sure."

She's standing close to the kitchen island. "Mind passing me my keys?" she says.

I see the keys on my side of the counter. It's a set of four keys on a cheap London Bridge key ring. Then, as I reach for them, I see something.

As Deborah pulls her handbag towards her, I see an emerald green folder under her arm. The type of folder that carries documents. Why would she be carrying documents if she's going to check a burglary at her office? It all seems too rushed. Too planned. How could all of this have happened in the last five minutes while I was in the bathroom?

"Should I call Richard?" I ask. "To help you?"

She shakes her head. "No, it's fine." She looks up, gives me a tight smile. "Just tell him when he's back from Bilbao."

Deborah holds out her hand for her keys.

But I clutch them to my side, frozen. She frowns, but I keep still. It could be nothing, but it could be everything. When I speak, my words seem to vibrate between us.

"I didn't tell you he was in Bilbao."

CHAPTER 69:

LISA

Six Months Ago

Water.

All around me. Everywhere.

In my mouth. In my ears. My eyes. It's cold, *so* cold. I don't know which way is up. It's so dark.

I need air. I need to move. Left or right? Up or down? My knee hurts. My lungs hurt. Everything hurts. It feels as if there's water *in* my leg. It's everywhere.

The current feels strong. It's tossing me around like a ragdoll. Was it always this strong? I need to swim. I *can't* swim. But I *must* try.

Swim, Lisa. Swim.

I flail my arms and legs. Which way is land? I can't see anything. I need air. But there's just water.

I'm sinking. Down, down, down. Keep swimming, keep swimming. *Please*, keep trying. Don't give up. Don't. Give. Up.

The roaring in my head gets louder. It's in my eyes and in my ears. In my mouth. It's the water. It's roaring. It's black.

Bubbles in my nose. Bubbles in my eyes. My mouth makes the bubbles. My heart is beating, beating, beating. I can't hear it. Just feel it. Going so fast it's going slow. Slower than slow.

Water. Everywhere.

I'm a human waterfall. All I feel is bubbles. Bubbles in, bubbles out.

346

Bubbles in, bubbles out.

Hold me. I'm sinking. I'm slipping away. Slipping. Away.

The bubbles slow. I need air. But it doesn't matter. I need truth more.

But I am water. Only water.

CHAPTER 70:

CAT

Present Day

It's always the little details.

I didn't tell Deborah that Neil was in Bilbao. And he wouldn't have told her, either.

I'm reminded of what he said just yesterday. *We keep to ourselves.*

Deborah narrows her eyes at me. "Richard told me he was going to Bilbao. This morning." She stands, her hand still outstretched. "Now, can you pass me my keys?"

I retrace my footsteps. Where I went when I called Neil. Bathroom, bedroom, bathroom. She'd been downstairs. She couldn't have heard me.

Unless...

I think of the tiny eye, the secret camera watching me from the dresser in my room. Did I leave it covered? Neil said there was no camera in my room, but what if there was?

My question blurts out. "Have you been watching me?"

Deborah lets out a snort. Looks at me like I'm something she's just stepped in. "What?"

I eye the folder under her arm. My chin juts. I summon all the courage I have. "What's in there?"

Is it my imagination, or does a tiny bead of sweat form on her forehead? "Just some documents."

"For the office?" I say.

"Yes. Now, can you hand me my keys already?"

She takes a step forward, and I take one back. It shocks us both. How instinctively, how quickly we moved. We lock eyes. The air is charged.

"I know," I say, the heat blazing in my cheeks. "I know Richard's real name is Neil." I pause. "He told me about the investigation."

Deborah stares at me. Pursing her lips, she takes a deep breath. "Well, I can't imagine why he would do that."

"And," I continue, "When Neil told me the truth about why I was here—in town—I didn't think you'd go along with it. But you did."

She shrugs, looking more irritated than before. "He said it was better for the investigation."

"Right," I nod. "Well, I've discovered some things about Lisa since then. Things that the police investigators didn't know until now."

She says nothing, her lips a thin, unmoving line.

"She had a second phone," I say, holding her gaze. "Did you know that?"

Her face reddens. "No, I didn't."

"Well, she did," I say. "Neil told me. I was just talking to him on the phone. But maybe you already knew that."

Her nostrils flare, and her voice is shrill with indignation when she speaks again. "*How* would I know that?"

"I keep thinking about my last phone call with Lisa," I say. "She called me that night from the dock, you know."

Deborah's eyes flick to the keys in my hand again. Then she looks up, and glances at the knife rack in the centre of the island. It's quick, but I catch it.

"But something strange happened," I say. "Just before Lisa hung up, there was this sound in the background. Like a phone ringing."

I pause for a moment. I can swear I see a twitch in Deborah's eye.

I forge ahead. "It sounded just like your phone."

A few moments pass. "It's a bloody ringtone," she scoffs. "Anyone could have it."

"I've never heard it before," I say. "It's pretty unique."

"So, what..." she says, glaring at me. "You think *I* was there? With her?"

"You were."

349

"And you're basing that on what? A phone that you thought you heard ringing?" she sneers. "You're barking up the wrong tree, love."

My hands are shaking, but I will my voice to stay steady. "I think I know the truth about what happened to Lisa that night. And you do too."

"The truth? Well yes, actually, I do," she says. "Like you, I also know a bit about this investigation. And from what I've heard, you were drunk when you spoke to Lisa that night."

Deborah almost spits the words at me. "I bet you said something horrible to her. Something that was just enough to send her over the edge."

How did she know I was drunk that night? Did Neil tell her? My mind is racing, looking for angles, trying to find something I may have missed.

But Deborah's not done yet.

"And you're wrong. I was right here," she says, pointing her finger at the floor and stomping her foot in emphasis. "In this house."

I'm almost willing Neil to arrive. If only he could be here now. He could be the objective one. He could corroborate my story.

And then I grab for another straw.

"If you're not involved, then I'm sure you wouldn't mind the police searching the house. Right?"

Her lips twist in a parody of a smile. "And why would they do that?"

"The second phone," I say, standing straighter. "I told you. Lisa had a second phone. They're busy tracing it now. And you said you were friends. So she could have left the phone here."

Deborah's face turns white. It gives me the push I need to keep talking.

"Unless you know exactly where the phone is. Because you hid it."

Her eyes are wide and frantic. "Give me my keys. Now."

I put my hand behind my back defiantly. "No."

My brain registers her movements too late. In a split second, she lunges for the knife rack. There's a glint of metal in her hand as she hurls herself towards me. And then she's on top of me, and I can't breathe.

CHAPTER 71:

LISA

Six Months Ago

—

CHAPTER 72:

CAT

Present Day

It feels as though I've been punched in the stomach. Harder than anyone has ever punched me.

I crash to the kitchen floor. When I look up, Deborah has backed away from me. She's staring at me, her eyes wild. The knife falls from her hand, landing with a clank on the floor. It's crimson red.

It's blood.

I look down. My one hand is clutching my abdomen, and blood is pouring through my fingers. In my other hand, I'm still holding Deborah's keys.

"Oh my God," she screams. Her hands cover her mouth in horror.

Every inch of my body hurts. I slide myself up against the kitchen cabinet, keeping my eyes on Deborah. I drop her keys behind me, and press both my hands over my stomach to try and stop the bleeding.

"You stabbed me," I wheeze. "You... stabbed me."

"You didn't give me a choice," Deborah shouts, her hands in her hair. She looks almost unhinged.

I open my mouth, but a wave of pain hits me, and I groan.

Deborah's voice is frantic. "I ... I just... I just panicked, okay?"

I briefly close my eyes, wondering where Neil is. When I open them, Deborah is still rooted to the same spot.

"Is that what happened to Lisa?" I gasp. "You just panicked?"

"No," she says, her head shaking furiously, her eyes pleading. "I did what

I needed to." She jabs a finger at her own chest. "To protect myself."

I rest my head against the cabinet. "How?"

Deborah looks around, and I realise she's searching for her keys on the floor. Then her eyes meet mine again. "I was going through a divorce. And Lisa—she didn't like Richard at all. He was—*is*—a bastard."

I say nothing.

"He was leaving me. For someone else. There was *always* someone else. But this time, he was leaving. For good. He told me he didn't view me as a woman anymore. Can you imagine that?"

I shake my head tiredly.

"That really got me. I moved here for *him*, supported *his* career—gave him the best years of my life. Gave up my dreams. And then he just ups and leaves, taking everything with him. Do you get it?"

I don't. I'm only twenty-four. I stare at her, my hands covering the growing burn in my abdomen.

She waves her own question away, her face crumpled. "Of course you won't. You're young, like she was. I told Lisa the same thing. To trust *no one*. And then she thought she could come in and be the hero. But I don't need a hero. I don't need any more wildcards in my life."

I stretch my legs out in front of me. The blood is seeping into my jeans and pooling on the floor around me. I try to keep breathing. Neil should be close by now.

"She started sneaking around," Deborah continues. "In *my* house. I was a mess, so I didn't pay attention to what she was doing. But she was snooping. And sure enough, she found things she wasn't supposed to."

"What things?" I say.

Deborah looks at me. "A few years back, Richard wanted to keep our assets separate. To cover his lies. It was clear as day. He wanted to hide what he was doing on the side."

"You knew he'd leave?" I ask. I need her to keep talking, to pass the time. *Where the hell is Neil?*

She nods, staring into the distance. "I saw the signs. And we didn't have a prenup. So I had to make a plan. I paid someone to set up a fake charity, and guilted him into donating. He wasn't keen. But it was for kids in *Africa*. You know, the kids we didn't have. The kids that I had always wanted. So he donated. Whenever the invoices came, he just glanced over them."

I shake my head. The lengths some people will go to.

She almost seems proud. "It worked well. Richard kept screwing around. And I got a nice nest egg to protect myself."

I try to sit up straighter. "But Lisa found out."

Deborah's face darkens. "She found the emails from the charity. She tried to call them."

And there it is. "So you killed her."

She shakes her head. "It's not what you think. When I found her on the dock, she was drunk. Probably a bit high on something too, by the looks of her. She told me she'd found all this evidence. She thought it was Richard. She said she was going to report it. And then when I told her it was me, she didn't let it go."

Deborah is silent for a moment, staring that faraway stare.

"She snuck around *my* house, going through my stuff, and then she has the audacity to tell me I should stop what I'm doing? She had no right. She was going to put everything—*everything*—at risk. I had to stop her."

I catch my breath. "Stop her how?"

She's expressionless. "Push her. Off the edge. Push her away."

I can almost see it in my mind. Lisa falling backwards, her mouth open in shock. Her body hitting the water, struggling to keep afloat. Quickly sinking beneath the surface, flailing helplessly.

Deborah's voice is almost wistful now. "I didn't know what I was thinking. I just pushed her. But I knew she couldn't swim."

"And her phone?" I ask, my teeth gritted against the throbbing pain.

Deborah closes her eyes. "It was evidence. I had to destroy it. I smashed it and buried it in the garden."

I think of the ugly yellow rings on the grass outside. The pot plants that look so out of place. My eyes meet Deborah's.

"Don't look at me like that," she says defensively. "I know what you've done. Did you really think when Neil came to live here that I wouldn't install cameras around the house? I had to make sure I was in the loop on what he was up to. And you."

She takes a step towards me, and I instantly—painfully—bring my knees up and curl into a ball. She stops walking, her expression hurt. As if I've offended her for thinking she could ever hurt me. Go figure.

"What else was I supposed to do?" she says. "I thought this nightmare was finally over when the police finished their investigation. I was going to leave Gexta. And then Neil shows up. I had to get involved. For my own protection."

I twist my body, feeling a fresh gush of blood from the wound. Deborah keeps talking. "I know how you knew Lisa," she glares at me. "You're not exactly the hero either."

I shake my head, my voice a croak. "No, I'm not."

"I'm leaving," she says. "I heard you on the phone to Neil. I've got my passport and everything." She motions to the folder on the counter. "Just give me my keys and I'll go. I'll call an ambulance as soon as I leave."

I say nothing.

Deborah takes a breath. "If you don't, you'll bleed out."

I bite my lip, wondering what to do. "They're behind me—your keys. I dropped them after you—I can't get up. You need to come and get them."

Deborah frowns, her eyes drawn to my wound. "Fine, I'll lift you."

She walks towards me, hunching forward. I look at her knee. The one she hurt a few weeks back when she slipped and fell. Mustering all the strength I have left in my body, I kick her in the knee as hard as I can.

CHAPTER 73:

CAT

Present Day

Deborah screams and drops to the floor like a felled tree, her hands clutching at her stricken knee.

As she writhes on the floor, I reach behind me for her keys. I lurch drunkenly towards her, my father's words ringing like a siren in my head.

As hard as you can.

I stab wildly at her, the keys protruding from between my fingers. The first blow hits her on the chest. Then on her arms as she desperately tries to protect herself. But I keep stabbing.

I stab again at her chest. At her neck. At her face. At anything I can reach. Her neck again. Her shoulders. Her arms.

And then, finally, she's still.

I lie flat on my back next to her, my blood and hers mingling, my breath coming in ragged gasps, the pain overwhelming me. I drop the keys and moan.

From my pocket, I grab my phone. My fingers tap frantically, bloodily, at the screen. Trying to dial Neil's number.

"Cat. I'm five minutes away."

"Garden," I croak. My vision is blurry. But I need to tell him. I can't die here on this floor without telling him. "Look. Look in the garden. It's there."

"What?" he says. "What are you talking about? What's going on?"

356

But I can't talk anymore. I'm deathly cold. I try to keep my eyes open, hands on my belly. Keep breathing. In. Out. In. Out.

Finally, I hear Neil's car pull up outside. And then I close my eyes.

CHAPTER 74:

CAT

Present Day

"You scared the hell out of me."

I open my eyes and look up at the sound of Neil's voice. The hospital's fluorescent lights are blinding.

"Ditto," I whisper hoarsely.

Neil's sitting next to me on a chair that's somehow too small for his body. Despite his concerned frown, there's a hint of a smile playing around the corners of his mouth. "Can't trust you to follow the rules, can I?"

I don't remember Neil finding me in the kitchen that night. But now the memories come flooding back. Me and Deborah lying next to each other on the kitchen floor, the tiles glistening with crimson pools.

"What happens now?" I say.

"Your mum's on the way," Neil says. "She'll be here in a day or two. Something about a visa holdup"

I clear my throat. "I should call her."

My eyes flick to the door of my hospital door, searching for someone in uniform. The police, maybe. "What happens now?"

Neil runs a hand over his head. "When Deb gets out of hospital, she'll be arrested and questioned. The police are getting a search warrant for the house."

"To look in the garden?"

"Yes."

I look up at the ceiling.

"You really did a number on her," Neil says. "Didn't know you had it in you."

"So," I look at my fingers, remnants of blood still crusted under my nails. "Did you tell the police why you're in Gexta?"

He nods. "Had to. They were going to find the papers anyway. I told them I was doing a private investigation."

"Are you in trouble?"

"Doesn't look like it."

I purse my lips. "Good. And me?"

He looks at me almost apologetically.

I shrug. "It's okay. Someone was going to find out about InCheck at some point."

Thinking about it now, everything started going pear-shaped the moment I got that Instagram message.

I know you're a fraud, Alice.

Neil rubs at his chin. "I think the police are more worried about finding the phone right now. How did you get Deb to confess to that?"

My mind goes back to the scene in the kitchen. Deborah's keys digging into my palm. The bead of sweat on her forehead.

"She was going to leave town. She heard me—or listened in, I guess—when I talked to you on the phone, and she got scared. She had cameras all over the house."

For a moment, Neil looks surprised. "And then?"

"She told me there was a break-in at her office and she needed to go and check it out. But she had a folder with documents. Something just felt off. I had her keys, so she couldn't leave. From there, I just improvised."

"That's one hell of an act," he says.

I shift gingerly, trying not to move my abdomen too much. "It was worth a try. I'd just come back from..."

I hesitate for a moment. Then I continue. Neil will find out eventually.

"I'd just come back from talking to Sebastian. I confronted him. But you were right. He didn't kill Lisa."

Neil's face is expressionless.

"I had nothing else to go on," I say. "Then back at the house Deborah's phone rang, and suddenly I remembered everything. Right before Lisa hung up on me that night, I heard that ringtone in the background. Deb was there. As soon as I connected the dots, I called you."

Neil looks baffled.

"So you reckon we'll find Lisa's phone in the garden?" he asks.

I nod. "I think it's buried under a pot plant. It's probably broken, though."

"Doesn't matter. Finding it on Deb's property is enough to reopen the police investigation. And with your statement, they'll probably have enough to convict her. She'll probably confess as well."

"Why would she do that?"

"Well, she didn't put up a fight when the paramedics took her away," Neil says, sitting back in the tiny chair.

I almost feel a pang of sympathy for her. I think back to the night she hurt her knee. How terribly sad she seemed at the mistakes she had made. How desperate she was to cling to the only sense of control she felt she had.

But then I think of how she pushed Lisa off that dock, and any feelings of sympathy disappear like mist before the morning sun.

Neil stands up. "I feel like something sweet."

"Like what?" I ask.

"Ice cream. Want some?"

It's the best question I've heard in a long time. "Yes, please."

As he reaches the door, he turns back for a moment.

"Kid," he says. "Try to take it easy while I'm gone."

I smile. But I hold my breath for what may come next.

CHAPTER 75:

CAT

Present Day

In the end, it took six months.

For the stab wound to fully heal.

For me to enrol in university.

To find a therapist I finally trust.

And it's been worth every moment.

The campus is bustling with young, beautiful people bubbling with anticipation for the lives they dream of. They're collecting and connecting. When I'm with them, I look more like a teacher than a student.

"You'll have so much life experience to bring to the table," Sam had teased, after I'd come back home and told her everything.

It was hard to start a psychology degree. And I didn't exactly have the most brilliant academic record until now. Younger Cat hadn't exactly done older Cat any favours. But I took a couple of bridging courses, and here I am. For real this time.

The journey after the day that Neil and I shared an ice cream in the hospital was long and complicated. My mother had arrived a couple of days later from South Africa. We held hands, and we cried together for the first time in ages.

Because the stab wound was just a physical wound. The tip of the iceberg. The rest of the iceberg was my own issues and challenges. And I was tired of hiding and lying. I wanted to get it all out.

THE LAST TIME YOU CALLED

"How did you know Lisa had two phones?" a police investigator asked me while I was still in my hospital bed. "How were you so sure?"

"I wasn't," I said.

He nodded and said he'd be in touch. The interview felt cold and awkward.

A week later, I was released from hospital. Neil drove us to a hotel in Bilbao.

"Adiós, shithole," he said as we drove out of town.

The investigator called a few days later while my mother and I were eating breakfast with Neil at the hotel.

"We found it. The phone," he said. "And the sim card."

"And?" Neil asked. He had the investigator on speakerphone.

"We managed to put it back together—used the sim—and it's all there. The Gmail account. The InCheck profile. With Deborah's confession, it's all the evidence we need to wrap up the case. It also seems like her husband was laundering money," he added. "A completely separate case from this one."

"A real pair, those two," Neil said.

"And what about InCheck?" I asked.

Neil gave me a look of caution. We talked about this before. If you're not asked, don't tell, he said. But I just wanted it all to be over with.

"It's not in our jurisdiction. InCheck is set up in the United States. All I know is that there's a pending enquiry," said the investigator.

There was a flutter in my stomach. "What type of enquiry?"

"Fake accounts. One person holding more than one account. Seems you weren't the only one pulling that stunt. If you ask me, the company will take the fall for their lack of security," he said. He seemed almost disappointed that I was getting off so lightly.

Months later, InCheck filed for bankruptcy, suffocated under the weight of dozens of civil lawsuits.

"What about Lisa's family?" I asked Neil on one of our last days in Bilbao. "Are they going to take me to court?"

I'd been stalking Lisa's social media, looking for a sign of change.

Neil shook his head, eating a plate of eggs. "They got what they wanted. Deb is being charged with manslaughter."

But there was still one loose end. The Instagram message.

I know you're a fraud, Alice.

"Did you contact me anonymously on Instagram?" I asked Neil. "Before I came to Gexta?"

He looked at me blankly. "Nope."

If he didn't, then who did? Was it Deborah? Maybe I would never know.

"Relax. You're off the hook, kid," he reassured me.

I tried to believe it. But I could never entirely lose the nagging feeling that a storm would break over my head. That I would get the consequences of my actions.

But it didn't happen.

So instead, I went back home to South Africa.

"Be good," Neil said before we parted ways at the airport. He was going back to the UK—to his real life. I'd stared at him, afraid to say goodbye. To open the next chapter in my life. He hugged me, and all I could do was nod. A resounding *yes*.

It was a month later when I decided to try therapy again. My mother and I were sitting in the garden as David prepared the braai.

"Would you help me find one?" I asked her. "A therapist?"

My mother smiled, and our lips quivered together. "Of course."

It's a work in progress, my therapy. But the iceberg is slowly cracking into smaller bits, which are floating away on the currents of life. Leaving me with more space to breathe.

I leave campus at midday, and drive to the other side of town. My mother and therapist convinced me to put my father's inheritance to good use—my psychology degree—but it wasn't enough to sustain myself whilst I studied. Luckily, I had a friend who was all too happy to welcome me back to the world of work.

"It's going to be a busy year," Sam grinned when I asked her if I could come back to the academy. "I hope you're ready."

Somehow, the teaching gig feels less like a chore this time. Maybe it's the therapy, the studies, the newfound freedom of just being myself. Or a combination of all of the above.

When I pull into the parking lot of the academy, it's packed. I find a parking spot near the back, grab my bag from the passenger seat, and start walking to class.

I don't notice the woman until she's right in front of me.

She looks strangely familiar. As she gets closer, my heart starts pounding.

She takes a final step towards me, her eyes meeting mine. "Cat?"

"Yes," I say.

She lets out a relieved sigh, reaches out to shake my hand. "Hi, I'm—"

"Eleanor," I say. "You're Eleanor. You're Lisa's mom."

CHAPTER 76:

CAT

Present Day

"Is there somewhere we could go?" asked Eleanor. "Somewhere we can sit? Maybe grab a coffee?"

My inquisitive side was shouting 'YES'! But I breathed.

"I have a class right now," I said. "But I can meet you in an hour?"

I gave her directions to a coffee shop down the road and headed into the academy. I could barely concentrate through the class. My mind was racing with all the possibilities. Was she here to sue me? Rage at me? Ask for answers that I couldn't give?

By the time the class finished, I'd gone over every option I could think of, rehearsing what I'd say if she asked me. But as I sat across from her in the coffee shop, everything went out of the window.

"I hope you don't mind that I came here," she said. "It's been a difficult time."

I looked at the dark circles under her eyes. She was a long way from home, at every level.

"I wanted to meet you," she said, her gaze level. "To see the person Lisa spoke to. I wanted to thank you. Heaven knows you've been through a lot yourself."

I felt a twinge in my abdomen, and I put a hand over it. "There's no need."

"Please," she blurted out. "Without you, we would have never gotten justice for her. We would never have known the truth. Everyone would

365

THE LAST TIME YOU CALLED

still think that she… she…"

She trailed off. I thought of Lisa, and how she had been haunted by the obligations and duties that dominated every aspect of her life. And I realised that for this desperate, sad woman, manslaughter was more acceptable than suicide. Something she could live with.

"Your daughter was so loving," I said. "She cared a lot about her friends and family. It was the first thing I noticed about her."

Eleanor nodded and said nothing.

"But she had some issues she was dealing with," I said.

I felt an invisible barrier going up between us. Her desire to maintain the façade was strong. Before I could say more, she reached for her handbag. "Like I said, we wanted to thank you."

She took out a business card and slid it towards me. "This is our attorney," she said. "Let us know if you ever need any help. Financial support, whatever. As a token of our thanks."

She swallowed hard. "For clearing Lisa's name."

* * *

"She offered you money?" Sam asks, eyes wide. We're sitting in a bar near work having drinks.

I scoop guacamole onto a chip and pop it into my mouth. "Yup."

"Wow," Sam says. She leans forward conspiratorially, "Did you take it?"

I shake my head. "No."

"Cat, that could be a lot of money."

It's true. And it's money that I need. At my age, who doesn't? But I can't.

I don't tell Sam how angry I felt when she offered me the money. Even after Lisa was finally at peace, her mother was still rushing around trying to buy solutions to her problems. Like money fixed everything. Money hadn't been any help for Lisa. She hadn't wanted money. She'd wanted love and acceptance. Approval from the one person who would never give it to her.

But my anger quickly dissipated. I couldn't be angry at Eleanor for following the only path she knew. She only knew one way to solve problems. With money and power. And she couldn't understand why it never brought her closure.

There's still the matter of taking responsibility for my own part in the whole mess. My therapist says I take on too much. That I can't be responsible for other people's emotions. But it doesn't stop me from thinking of Fred and Susana. Do they feel cheated by Alice – by me?

I hope things will get better.

That Fred can shower without the knot in his chest.

That Susana can find true comfort in her daughter's smile.

That they both get to talk to someone wiser and more qualified.

"I would have taken the money," Sam says again, downing her drink. "Another?"

I look down at my empty virgin cocktail glass, and smile up at her. "Sure."

"Good, because I need to confess something."

We order another round.

"So, what do you need to tell me?" I ask, sitting back in the booth.

She takes a deep breath.

"So. Okay. A few months ago, I got drunk. I was upset that you didn't want to come and teach full time. Remember?"

I nod.

"I knew you wouldn't give up the app. And as long as you had that damn app in your life, you were obsessed. It was holding you back from going out and living your life. I was worried."

I'm silent. A little light goes on in the back of my head. I think I know what she's going to say.

She breathes deeply. "So, I created a fake Instagram account. I wanted to scare you, I guess. But only enough to make you think someone knew what you were doing. So you'd stop. But as soon as I sent the message, I felt so terrible. I deleted the profile, but I couldn't delete the message. I'm sorry."

We look at each other for a moment, her face red.

I reach across the table and take her hand. Her relief is palpable. "I'm really so sorry, Cat. I shouldn't have," she babbles.

"It's okay," I say. "It's okay. It's done. I'm okay. We're okay."

She smiles at me gratefully.

But inside, my brain is buzzing.

My friend Sam's got some real issues.

Maybe she should talk to someone.

Acknowledgements

For me, a book isn't fully read until I've read the acknowledgements. But I'll try to keep this brief.

This book is my second attempt at a novel. It's also my 'life lesson' book. It started with a nugget of an idea, and then tapped into every feeling, every memory and every loss I've ever had as it evolved into a fully-fledged novel.

It takes a village to write a novel, and my village is a pretty cool bunch.

To my critique partners, Janice Okoh and Alta Turner, thank you for helping me give this novel direction and shape. Six more years until we make it big!

To Lauren North and Lesley Kara, I cannot thank you enough for your mentorship and insights. I'm so lucky.

To the supremely talented Luísa Dias, thank you for capturing the essence of this novel so perfectly with your cover design. I love the purple!

To my editor, Peter van der Merwe, thank you. You're not only a content genius. You're my best friend.

To my amazing mama, thank you for your endless calls and voice notes about psychology, and what you can (and cannot) do.

To Jet and Roma, thank you for bearing with me through the initial drafts and cheering me on.

To Mr. and Mrs. Ambrose, thank you for being my champions through this publishing journey. Kinga, you're a force to be reckoned with. Luke, you're next!

Dad. I know you would have loved this book. Wherever you are, I know you're so very proud.

To my Bookstagrammers and Booktok buddies, thank you for all the love and support. My TBR pile is ever-growing, and that makes me very, very happy (and maybe a bit anxious!).

To Ruben, my soundboard, my rock, my biggest fan. I owe everything to you. I love you.

And finally, to you, my dear reader. Thank you for picking up this book. It means everything.

About the Author

Born and raised in South Africa, Carmi Heyman currently lives in The Netherlands with her husband and beloved British Shorthair cats. She's a self-confessed foodie, a voracious reader, and a serial expat who's lived across the Middle East and Europe. When she's not reading, writing or travelling, you'll probably find her in a coffee shop or a bookstore. She writes expat suspense and women's fiction. *The Last Time You Called* is her first novel. Find her on Instagram and TikTok @carmiheymanauthor

Printed in Great Britain
by Amazon